I0638166

Watershed

A novel about the
insidiousness of political corruption,
the dangers of social injustice, and the fragility
of democracy.

Gillian Long

Watershed

Copyright © 2015
GILLIAN LONG

All rights reserved.

This book is a work of fiction. While historical people, places
and events may be referenced, these are imagined through a
fictional lens. Any portion of the text thereof may not be
reproduced or used in any manner without the express written
permission of the author except for the use of brief quotations
in a book review.

Cover art and design by: John Russell, Qld. Australia.
Library of Congress Control Number: 2018675309

First Published, 2015
ISBN: 978-0-9942671-4-6
Millaa House Publishing
PO Box 89
Millaa Millaa
Queensland 4886

All things truly wicked start from innocence.
Ernest Hemingway

Prelude.

Blake Lincoln runs his palm across the day old shadow. This is his second month as an intern and he feels so ignorant he can't believe he warrants the title. Fake it 'til you make loops like a mantra. He sighs and pulls out a chair to sit at the computer interface, pressing his stethoscope flat against his chest as he lowers his frame.

The dank communal office is next to the geriatric ward. Scuffed beige walls flake paint in a line along the edges of a threadbare carpet. There's a sour smell of old trainers, and mould completing the atmosphere of casual neglect, of a place used by all, but owned by none.

It's nearly midnight. His shift ended six hours ago, and he's missed another date with Ava, but her wrath doesn't worry him as much as his patients' welfare. Anyway, his friend Rory offered to escort her to the fashion premier tonight so he might be off the hook. At least someone realises what's important even if his fiancée doesn't.

Blake looks at his watch. The time of death still registers. She was brought in by a good Samaritan, an attractive woman called Charlotte Miller who had found her lying in the street.

Most people were so inured to the social problems, they stepped over the prone bodies of the homeless, so the event in itself was unusual. But it was too late for the poor woman. She was just another statistic: one of many who arrive daily with symptoms of beriberi, pellagra, and scurvy: diseases rarely seen in Australia for the past hundred years. Adults raving with starvation-induced psychosis bring in kids with distended bellies. Usually a vitamin shot helps, but she was too far-gone.

He leans back, folding his arms as he stares at the screen, waiting for his patients' files to load. A flashing icon catches his attention and he touches the breaking news story to see how the election went. The film feed shows a hotel room full of cheering people. A spotlight falls on a handsome couple, cocooning them in its radiance.

Frustration, tinged with despair, rises in his throat with the realisation the government is returned. 'Bugger,' he mutters shaking his head as he increases the volume.

The Prime Minister's voice resonates. 'My friends in these difficult times, I am humbled by your faith in returning my government for a third term, and for saying yes to the referendum question. You will see; people will look back in time and proclaim this as Australia's watershed moment.'

'Bullshit!' Blake vehemence has no effect.

The Prime Minister continues smooth, and dark as crude oil. 'It would be foolish to lie to you. Liberty is not won through indolence and complacency, but through hard work. We have an uphill battle to fight. Every one of us must shoulder the burden. Only then can this country rise from the ashes. A phoenix reborn from the fires of destruction. It will not happen quickly, or easily, or without sacrifice, but my pledge is that it will happen. Patience and determination will be our watchword as we keep the faith. My government's plan will succeed.'

The Prime Minister pauses, gazing about the crowd, his face serious, his eyes solemn. Blake leans forward looking for signs of discomfort, but he can see none. The man looks sincere. Then his mouth twists and he holds up a hand. The crowd quieten. 'But, I must warn against doubters, for evil men will whisper sedition in your ear. We must stand united against them. In this country, there is no place for those not of one heart, and one mind, prepared to sacrifice for the betterment of all. We know there is simply one truth, one true cause, and one path to choose in the fight for liberty and justice.'

'Liberty and justice my arse,' Blake lowers the sound.

The picture fades and the news anchor says, 'That was Prime Minister Priestley. What a great man. It makes me proud to be an Aussie. Now I can announce in breaking news that already he has honoured his election promise. Food stamps will be available from your local council office from next week, but you will need your Oz cards to access them.'

Blake opens a new file to log the old woman's death. He doesn't know her name and writes, *Jane Doe, age approximately seventy years*. At least with food stamps, some of them might survive.

1.

Jarrod von Wilkins squints against the glare as he watches riot police filter into the street below. Overhead, the over-exposed sky domes in desiccated uniformity, but sunglasses diminish his view. He slides them back to the top of his head.

From his vantage point on the fourth floor of a vacant office, the Chairman of Homeland Security Enterprises has a view along both Roma and George Streets. As he waits, he anticipates the events about to unfold, and suppresses a shiver of trepidation. An unexpected sense of his own destiny prickles at his nape. It's what he must do, but he will be forever marked by this day, as history's dark instrument.

A sneeze takes him by surprise. His concentration was so intense he didn't notice the dust. It creates havoc with his sinuses. He pats his left breast, feeling for the antihistamine tablets his wife usually slips into his pocket before he leaves home, and pops one into his mouth.

In the street four floors below, heat rises in waves from the bitumen where mounted officers manoeuvre into place. They spearhead the gathering force, keeping a tight rein on burnished geldings. The animals, wired in anticipation, stamp and paw, tossing their heads with impatience.

Behind them, two armoured vehicles—BearCats—idle. Bolted-on water cannons make them look top-heavy and alien. A bus pulls up and scores more men disembark. They position themselves in phalanx formation and move forward. The tramp of their booted feet and the occasional jingle of a bridle are the only sounds above the purr of engines.

Once assembled, they wait and swelter with fixed eyed stares, their dark protective gear absorbing the western sun. The smell of horse manure, and diesel fumes, merges with the rising reek of gutters, and the stench of brimming café bins, to mingle with the sour aroma of their own sweat.

The police chief, a man with steel grey hair and determined jaw, cocks his head to listen as the mob advances toward the intersection. Its discordant volume grows as the mass of people approach. He looks at his watch then depresses his earpiece, receiving the signal; *it's time.*

Around the corner, a column of hundreds, perhaps a thousand people, straggles back along the length of George Street. The carnival brings traffic to a standstill. Costumed citizens' surge out from side streets to join the throng. They holler their grievances, waving banners that add to the forest of brandish captions.

A woman, draped as Justia, leads the procession. She wears a blindfold tied around her forehead, its lower edge obscuring her eyebrows. Occasionally she tilts her head to see where she walks, pushing the scarf out of her eyes. In one hand, she holds a set of scales, and in the other a banner. A canvass bag hangs over her shoulder, bumping against her hip as she strides ahead.

A child skips along at her side, sometimes clutching her skirt, sometimes dancing away to pirouette into the air. It's the girl's sixth birthday. After the protest, they will celebrate, but for now, she's happy to be here. It's a chance to show off her birthday gift of spangled fairy costume complete with wings and wand.

Jellybean drawings decorate her mother's banner with words saying, *End Conscription Now!* In tentative letters below, a postscript adds, *Please bring my daddy home.*

Her mother turns to walk backward, shouting to the following protestors. 'What do we want?'

The crowd responds, 'Rule of law.'

'When do we want it?'

'Now!'

'What do we want?' She says again.

'End the war!'

'When do we want it?'

'Now!'

'What do we want?'

'Priestly out.'

'When do we want it?'

'Now!'

Blake races to catch up with her, zigzagging from pavement to road, dodging the crowds, vaulting over obstacles, and sidestepping pedestrians.

Justia smiles as she sees him arrive. 'Hey Blake.'

She digs in her bag, pulling out a black legal gown and wig. He plonks the tie-wig on his dishevelled dark hair. It's back to front, but she says nothing. Protocol is irrelevant.

The wig slips sideways, and he grins trying to straighten it. 'How's Richard? Have you heard anything?'

She shakes her head. 'Not much, but he's okay, thank God.'

Blake jerks the legal gown over his white hospital coat. She points at the stethoscope and he pulls it off, stuffing it into his pocket.

'You're late,' she says.

'Sorry Allie, I got held up.'

'Not Allie, Justia.'

'Okay Justia,' he grins.

'Where's Ava?'

'She said she couldn't make it, some photo shoot she has on.'

'More like a cop out,' Allie says under her breath, but Blake doesn't hear.

The little girl bounces up waggling her wand. Two of her milk teeth are missing, and the gap shows as a dark hole. She laughs at Blake all dressed up in Grandpa's old wig and gown.

Blake touches her wings. 'Hey, happy birthday Sproglet.'

'I'm not a soglet, I'm a fairy.' Her forehead creases in a frown.

He gives her the thumbs up before turning to the mob and shouting, 'Marabou's a wanker.'

The crowd whoop at the use of Minister Marabaux's nickname, and someone sets up a new chant. 'Marabou's a wanker.'

They join in, echoing, 'Marabou's a wanker,' and surge forward.

Two of the other procession leaders carry a banner that says, *Blind Justice Demands the Rule of Law.* They are also dressed in legal wigs with black gowns that flap and cling to their legs. They jiggle their banner in greeting.

Blake waves, 'Bloody fine banner mate.'

As he turns to follow Justia, he notices a woman in a hotel doorway. It's the good Samaritan who brought the old woman into the hospital. He wants to speak to her, tell her he couldn't save the woman, but she's waving to someone down the road who waves back.

The crowd moves Blake along and he turns to find Allie. She is already twenty metres away, approaching the intersection to Roma Street, and he hurries to catch her.

Around the corner, the police commander raises his gloved hand in readiness. His men lower their goggles, fitting them snugly against gas masks. As his arm's long shadow travels in a dark band across the road, the officers' eyes remain fixed on his signal. Those mounted extend their batons, rising in their saddles thigh muscles taut, and slacken their grip on straining horses. The commander's hand falls. The animals surge, gathering momentum as the riders' human distinctiveness blurs into robotic singularity.

As the police charge, the advancing column turns the corner, plunging into the jaws of the trap. Truncheons slash their blows indiscriminate as flesh gives way to thwacking steel, and flailing hooves. The demonstrators scatter, terror replacing protest in an orchestrated cacophony of screams.

Allie abandons her scales and banner, crying out with fear as she runs to rescue her child. Hoisting the girl into her arms, she turns to flee, but a steel blow knocks her to the ground.

Blake battles through the panic to reach her, vaulting and dodging obstacles, ducking between horses, running to save the woman and child, cursing his momentary distraction. He bends to protect Allie and reaches out to draw Sproglet into safety. Something slams into him, and he falls to the ground. Blood seeps from a gash in his head, blossoming to stain his wig.

The child, crouching beside her dazed mother, stretches out to touch his head. She pulls her hand away, and stares at her fingers, sticky with his blood. Etched terror pulls her eyes wide, and she pants in fear. Her mouth opens in a silent scream as she sees the BearCats advance.

Metres away her fairy wand lies crushed on the road and a little further still, the fractured scales. Her mother groans and struggles to get to her feet. The girl tugs her arm to help, while foaming mouthed horses trample an arc around them, their eyes wild.

The rear of the chanting column falters as they concertina into the corner and see their leaders under attack. For a moment, they dither. Then some run into the fray while others hesitate at the brink. A few just melt away, taking alleys and side streets as they shed their costumes.

Charlotte Miller ducks back through the doorway against which, moments before, she had leaned watching the procession pass. Her friend, Evan Chandler, was in the crowd and she wished she could leave her post to join him.

She had waved, cheering-on the protesters, thinking it was like the old days. So excited was she by the cheerful mass of citizens rolling towards her along George Street, she didn't notice the police amassing around the corner.

The bar of the hotel where Charlotte works straddles the northeast corner where Roma and George Streets meet in Brisbane city. The hotel is a relatively new. Its sixty-eight storeys of wedge-shaped gleaming steel, marble and glass rises to an imposing tower that casts the street below into deep shadow.

Charlotte dashes across the empty cocktail bar to a frescoed window so she can see what's happening in Roma Street. The coloured glass makes it difficult to see out. As she presses her forehead against the pane, a jet of water from the armoured truck's cannon crashes against it. She leaps back in fright, then runs back to peer out the clear glass panes either side of the entrance door.

People run in all directions to escape the advancing BearCats. They turn into George Street, firing more water jets. The high pressure bowls the escapees over like leaves tossed along a storm-flooded gutter. Mesmerised, she flinches at each new attack.

Behind the BearCats, officers on foot march around the corner and halt. Those in the front row raise weapons to unleash a hail of rubber and pepper bullets. Only a few men aim their rounds to ricochet off the road. Projectiles slam into fleeing flesh, increasing the terror.

The sharp double crack of real bullets makes Charlotte jump. Simultaneously a plate glass window across the street shatters. Her head hits a hanging brass lamp. She rubs the spot, unconscious of the pain. The lamp above swings wildly and she ducks to avoid another collision.

Her breathing shallows as she peers through the window. Four shielded riot police break ranks to lob smoke bombs into the crowd. Seconds later, an opaque pink squall fills the street. A gust of wind shreds the rosy smoke spirals, snaking them towards Charlotte. Twenty metres away a toy wand glitters in a shard of light. Then it's gone, hidden by the pall.

Her friend Evan appears from the fog supporting an injured man. Blood runs down his face and soaks Evan's shirt. Another man runs to help. Between the two of them, they support a man, who Charlotte recognises as the doctor she spoke to at the hospital Emergency Ward the other night, when she took that poor woman in. His legs are no longer obeying his will. Charlotte jerks open the door and cries out for them to hurry.

Two mounted police break through the smoke, hunting the fleeing men. In practised unison, they cast a sticky riot net. It finds its mark and the three fugitives falter and thrash for freedom. Only Evan escapes.

Charlotte calls out again, opening the door wide, but he darts down an alley opposite the bar and disappears. The police let him go, concentrating on the other two.

Blake lies motionless with eyes shut next to his struggling companion. 'For Christ sake, keep still. The bastards will only hurt you.'

One of the officers dismounts. He walks towards the captives, reeling in the rope that tightens the net. With his booted toe, he prods Blake who doesn't respond. As he bends forward to cuff his wrists, Blake's hand shoots out through the net's diamond mesh, wrapping the stethoscope around the officer's throat. The police officer drops the ropes, scrabbling at the tube. His face turns blotchy as he sinks to his knees.

'Go,' Blake shouts at his comrade.

The man doesn't hesitate, struggling from the now loosened net. He escapes and runs down the alley after Evan.

The second officer slides from his horse and runs to his mate's aid. He pulls out a taser and fires. Blake's body contorts and twitches with the repeated zaps of high voltage electrical current. Disrupted brain signals spasm muscles, and Blake's hand flops and jerks on the ground.

Charlotte pushes the door closed unable to watch the carnage. Her eyes smart from the tear gas laced smoke. She rubs her tongue against the roof of her mouth, and bends over an under-counter sink to rinse her face, feeling the stinging itch in her nose. Memories of the last time she got a face full of gas crowd her mind.

That was when protesting was almost a weekly event, when they were still at university, before the economy crashed, before the new national security laws banning mass assembly. This time it's not so bad. She knows she only received a fraction of the gas she breathed in back then.

As she dries her face with a paper towel, an image of the tasered bloke, the doctor, in the net fills her mind. No one is safe. Not even a doctor. He's finished. He'll be conscripted for sure and dead before the year is out like all the rest. She wants to cry at the futility and unfairness.

Across the road in a fourth-floor office, Jarrod von Wilkins rubs his forehead, pleased with the result. He will wait until they mop-up. It wouldn't do to report success prematurely. Paddy wagons pull up and take off in orderly fashion, six prisoners per van. It's almost done. The commander will get his bonus as promised, as will the others around the country.

A bleep distracts him from the scene below and he presses the side of his watch to hear. The commander in Darwin reports, his disembodied voice rising from the e-cript light-CellTab sitting on the window ledge. The operation was a success nationally. Von Wilkins could have delegated command, but he was keen to make sure there were no mistakes.

The national community-policing contract is due for renewal soon, and he doesn't want to lose it. It's only one of the government contracts for Homeland Security his company has, but he's aiming for the big prize. One day perhaps they will contract out the old federation policing agencies too.

He's enjoyed himself. There's a certain ironic appeal in devising and organising a nationwide crackdown on a protest he planned. Its creating history and besides, he's never found violence disturbing. It's just a part of human nature, a way of sorting out the pecking order, the competitive nature of humanity. All animals do it and he's not the squeamish sort. In his mind, it's straightforward; you do the crime you wear the time, regardless of whom led you to temptation.

Jarrod von Wilkins is a man of medium height with a broad chest. Today he has on a brown shirt with a gold dragon motif. His wife gave it to him for his last birthday, telling him the dragon is good luck. It hangs untucked over pressed beige slacks. The grizzled stubble on his head and cheeks catches the shafting light. Its afternoon shadow shows his hair receding into the shape of a tonsure.

Usually he shaves his head. It's a vanity, but today he hasn't had time since flying back from Perth last night. He hasn't slept for forty-eight hours and his eyes feel gritty. Now he has a sinus headache, but it was important to ensure the preparations were perfect.

He's satisfied with the result and rubs his hand over his chin, feeling the day old growth, then looks at his CellTab on the window ledge. Next to the phone is a movie camera transmitting the film feed to Canberra, 950 kilometres away.

He touches his watch and says, 'are you receiving okay boss?'

Sir Arnold Marabaux, Minister for Homeland Security, sits in a darkened study crammed with his passion for electronic surveillance. He glances at his own watch and then leans forward to pick up a remote sensor from his desk. His fingers fumble with the small buttons until the film feeds coalesce into ghostly light pixels that form holographic images in the space before him.

He says. 'The footage is coming through now. You've done well.' After watching for a minute, he depresses the remote switch to cut off the Brisbane carnage and pushes another. A new image forms of a similar protest crackdown in Perth. As he pushes the button again, the picture changes from Perth to Sydney, to Adelaide, to Darwin, patching from city to city.

Every new image shows simultaneous insurrections around the country. Von Wilkins has excelled himself, he concedes. The final film feed is of Williams Street in Melbourne, outside the National Court. A gaunt, lined face comes into frame. It's the local commander in charge.

'Yeash?' The commander's tone is slurred.

The man is drunk again. Von Wilkins has to get rid of him, but Marabaux stifles his irritation. 'Was Jonathon Castile among them?'

The man rolls his eyes. Why else are they doing this? He has already told von Wilkins. He says, 'He's in custody.'

'Good.' Marabaux stabs the remote and the pixels vanish. He leans back in his chair, and places his hands on the desk before him, fingers drumming. His plans are taking shape. A small thrill of triumph runs through him but he suppresses it, knowing only he can make their strategy work, and he's proved it.

Bart Priestly may have the charisma but he has the brains. The others in Cabinet are all idiots, and not worth the time of day, but appearance is everything. If he hasn't learned that in his life, he's learned nothing. It's just a matter of time. It won't be long before they re-evaluate their candidate.

He speaks to a shadowy figure standing at ease near the door, 'Right, get the photos delivered and make sure she understands the consequences.'

The man nods. 'Capo,' he bows, and leaves, closing the study door softly behind him.

After a minute of contemplation, Marabaux straightens his dark suit jacket, tugging at the sleeves to cover the protruding shirt cuffs. He pats his silver blue silk tie ensuring it lies flat and neat on his white linen shirt. When he is satisfied with his appearance, he leans forward to press the e-cript phone button to transmit.

At Kirribilli House in Sydney, the Australian Prime Minister reclines on a mahogany-coloured Chesterfield. A petite young blonde woman stands in front of him holding out an etched crystal whisky glass. He takes the aged single malt from her smiling his thanks, and pats the sofa beside him. The phone rings and he depresses a receiver button in the sofa's arm. An image forms as he runs the back of his fingers up the woman's arm. 'Thank you sweetheart,' he says.

Jenna Martin, his Chief of Staff, smiles at him and turns to look at the image.

Marabaux waits until he has their attention and then says, 'it's done.'

'And Castile?' Jenna leans forward, the eagerness in her face a disturbing glimpse of vengeful fury.

'Arrested.' Marabaux ignores her, looking only at the PM. This is not about Castile's rejection of her ardour all those years ago, but about the threat, he poses to their plans. The woman needs reminding of her place, but she can wait.

'Any media?' She asks.

'No,' he snaps, irritated by her domination of the exchange. To cover his abruptness he adds, 'none licensed anyway.'

The Prime Minister understands the source of his friend's irritation. He also knows Jenna's obsession. People are so transparent. It makes his job easy, but God save him from a woman scorned. His thoughts remain concealed as he leans forward, his hand resting on Jenna's thigh. 'Well done Arnie. It flushed them out just as I predicted. I take it we have all the Blind Justice leaders?'

'We'll know soon enough but the back is broken I think,' Marabaux says, noting Bart has taken credit for his plan.

'What about the opposition?' Bart asks, but he's losing interest. Details bore him; leave the menial slog work to people like Marabaux who seem to thrive on it. It's why they are a great team. 'World beaters,' Marabaux once said referring to Bart's genius, coupled with his dedication to detail.

'The opposition leader will not be worrying about the arrest of a corrupt Chief Justice. Once the photos arrive, she'll be more worried about her party's survival. She will have to resign and Huge Valentine will replace her.' Marabaux remains watchful as he says, 'what about the replacement appointment for the Chief Justice position?'

'I haven't forgotten. As agreed, I will advise the Governor-General to make the appointment as soon as a decent interval has passed. Who have you in mind to take over the Solicitor General's role when Newel Bramly is appointed?'

'Stoker.'

Startled Jenna interjects, 'You're kidding aren't you?'

Bart pats her knee. 'Stoker will be fine. He's loyal, and he has the requisite qualifications.' He turns back to Marabaux. 'I imagine you have someone in mind to head up ASIO in his place.'

'Yes, I want to collapse all the intelligence agencies under Baz Mulholland. It will save money and duplication as well as break down the silo mentality they have developed. It will give us a more holistic view.'

Bart laughs. 'Ken Bowan will have a fit if you touch his military intelligence. What does he have to say, or haven't you told him yet?' He refers to the Minister for Defence.

'No not yet, but he'll come around. He understands the need for uniting the powers of the military and intelligence communities in these uncertain times. One doesn't know who has infiltrated the system.'

'Does he indeed?' Bart says it absently. 'I'm not even sure that I do.' He gazes thoughtfully at Jenna's shapely body leaning across his lap. Her finger hovers over the switch to terminate the connection, but Bart holds up a hand and she waits watching him. 'What about the foreign Minister, she'll hardly agree surely.'

'She already has, but she is more distracted by considering her retirement from politics at the next election.'

'Ha,' Bart smiles. 'I suppose you offered to take their intelligence sections off their hands and let them keep the Departmental money, like you did with the others, but if you think I will give you her portfolio as well...'

'No I don't want it.' Marabaux's expression doesn't change.

Bart is suddenly bored with his dour Minister, and the machinations of arranging his Cabinet. 'Just as well. You have enough on your plate. Well, I suppose you know what you are doing. So long as they are loyal.'

'They are all loyal...,' Marabaux says as Jenna's finger severs the connection. '... To me,' he finishes, but the Prime Minister has gone, and there is no one else in the room to hear him.

2.

Two and a half years later two men sit at a table in the bar on George Street, their forms silhouetted against the sunlit blue and red etched window. The bar is styled as a 1930s French café calling itself the Writer's Bar. The room has less than a dozen patrons, most sitting alone, nursing drinks, or concentrating on their CellTabs. No one writes.

Blake leans back in the chair, arms folded across his chest, his mouth a pressed line of white rimmed restraint. The story about Rory's sister Emmy, wangling her way out of paying a fine, fuels his anger.

He interrupts his friend. 'That gives me the shits.'

'Why?' Taken aback at Blake's vehemence, Rory leans back in his chair.

'Well it's always the little things isn't it? Corruption never begins full blown. It starts with the little things and before you know what's happening, you're choking on the shit. But that's complacency for you.'

Rory says, 'Fuck mate lighten up. It's just a speeding ticket.'
The

It's late afternoon, a quiet time before the evening rush. Standing behind the counter a barmaid gazes across the room to the clear narrow windows flanking the door. She takes her time drying glasses as she daydreams.

Rory glances down into his glass, swirling the remaining tawny liquid, before throwing it back. 'Want another beer?'

Blake checks his rage, 'Yeah thanks.' He runs his hand over the short dark bristles on his head, fighting for control. It's such a small thing. He loves Emmy, and doesn't know why he's reacting like this, but nothing is as it was. The dreams that kept him sane for the past two and a half years have disintegrated in the harsh light of home. He drains the dregs of his beer and stares into the empty glass, listening to Rory's self-assured tread crossing the room. Rory hasn't changed, and yet everything else has or perhaps it's just him.

Rory's leather-soles snap against the tiled floor as he walks to the bar. Usually, he likes the confident sound they make, but today he can't take his customary satisfaction from the rhythm. Frustration and worry consume him. There's something wrong with Blake but he can't figure out what. The bloke is his best friend and while he should be as familiar as the taste of beer, he seems odd: distant and opaque.

Rory doesn't know what to do about it. As he leans against the counter, the barmaid puts down her tea towel and walks towards him. She has a nice body, and it distracts him. Automatically his eyes follow her contours as he tries his practiced charm offensive, straightening to show off his height and broad shoulders.

'Two more thanks,' he holds up two fingers. She points to the brand, and he says, 'yeah the one on tap. You're new aren't you—got a name?' He smiles trying out the new smile he developed while shaving this morning. It feels weird, so he looks away and pulls out his wallet to pay. 'Can I buy you one?'

The barmaid barely notices his attempts at flirting and speaks in a bored tone that tells him men hit on her twenty times a day.

'Not so new: Charlotte: and no thanks, but a tip in the jar will do fine.' She nods, indicating an empty olive jar sitting on the bar.

The red woollen beret on her head wobbles as if it's alive. She looks up from the beer tap to catch him staring and her gaze slides away across the room to his companion.

Across the room, Blake slumps against the table, staring into an empty scum-lined beer glass. The afternoon sun, shining through the etched glass of a stylised portrait of a youthful Hemingway, casts him in brooding silhouette.

As she slides a beer across to Rory, she nods in his direction. 'What's wrong with your friend? He looks like an angry storm.'

Rory continues to watch her. 'Oh don't mind him, he always looks like that.' His gaze travels down her body to her waist pressed against the bar and back up to linger on her breasts.

The scrutiny annoys her, and she tries to distract him by pushing the second beer across the counter, slopping froth over the edge so it dribbles down the glass.

'He looks familiar,' she says.

'That's because you've seen him on the news.' Rory's gaze is captivated by the froth sliding down the glass.

'Really?' She casts another glance at the brooding figure, trying to see his shadowed features. 'Is he famous?'

'More like notorious. That's Blake Lincoln. The bloke who escaped Baghdad. News is full of him.'

Now she knows who he is, although she doesn't have time to watch the news on the multimedia screen in the bar corner, she's heard of him. Who hasn't? She certainly doesn't get a chance to see the news anywhere else. Who can afford the cost of streaming even if they have electricity? Typical rich boy she thinks glancing at Rory. He has no idea how the other half live.

Aloud she says, 'Course I've heard of him.' With a mild rebuke aimed at his ogling attention she says, 'he's gorgeous, introduce me.'

Rory grins, but doesn't take offence. 'Hey I'm the one tipping you.' He stuffs a fifty into her jar.

Caught off guard, her smile freezes. She's stunned at the size of the tip and wants to snatch it up before he changes his mind. He picks up the two glasses and walks back to the table. As soon as he turns away, she slides the note out of the jar, stuffing it into her pocket and returns to polishing glasses, astounded at her good fortune.

Rory puts the beers down and says, 'Barmaid wants to meet you, thinks you're gorgeous. Must be that face of yours that looks like a smacked arse.'

Blake ignores him and Rory sits down shrugging defeat at the barmaid, but she's not watching.

He turns back to Blake. 'Okay where were we?'

'You were telling me about Emmy's boyfriend.'

'That's right, Jeremy Marabaux.'

'You're kidding. The fucking Marabou.'

'Not the Minister dickhead, his son.'

'That's not much better. He's an environmental troll. The bastard got the Marabou to approve his development on the northern slope of Mt Coot-tha overriding all the environmental protections. Then he did that dodgy takeover of the pharmaceutical company we buy from.'

'How do you know that? I thought the business didn't interest you.' Rory's surprised. Blake never took an interest before his arrest and conscription.

'I've been catching up with all the Board minutes your Dad posts for me.'

'Jesus, does he still do that?' Rory says.

Blake nods.

Rory's mouth turns down, and he looks pensive. 'Jeremy's all right. Not a dour stick like his father. He can be quite charming on occasions. Anyway Emmy likes him.'

'How did he get Emmy off paying the fine?' Blake asks getting back to the story.

'He's also the president of Marabaux and Nathan.' Rory looks at his friend's blank face and says, 'it's a firm of lobbyists and he is a useful bloke if you are in trouble.'

'He's an evil prick.' Blake picks up his beer.

'Okay granted he's a bit of a dick, pompous, but he's harmless. And he did pull rank with the cops to get Emmy out of having to pay the fine. I say, good on him. Anyway, that's not why I dragged you out here. I don't want to talk about my sister or her boyfriend.'

'Why are you here?'

'Jesus that's nice. Why the fuck do you think?'

'Sorry. Thanks for the beer.'

'No problems. Mum wants to know when you are coming home.'

'I knew it.'

'Hey don't shoot the messenger.' Rory holds up his hands in surrender. 'She said to tell you to come for dinner and that we're having roast beef and Yorkshire pudding tonight.'

'Maybe another time.' Blake feels as if he's floating somewhere else, watching the conversation with his old friend from afar.

'Come on Blake, just dinner. They're itching to see you. Christ, they worried themselves sick over you.' Rory sees the stubborn set as Blake's mouth forms a thin line. 'Look I promised Mum I'd bring you home even if I have to drag you. You have obligations.'

'Not tonight, I have things to do and I'm not going near your place if Ava's there.' Blake frowns. It's an excuse. He doesn't care about Ava, but he can't bear the suburban banality of everyday life. Not just yet anyway, not until he's free to forget.

'Bloody hell, what's wrong with you? Sorry... Shit. Look I know you've been through the wringer, but cut us a bit of slack mate.' Rory drags his palm over his mouth, trying to understand Blake. 'You've been back weeks and you haven't seen anyone. Mum was upset when you didn't turn up for your homecoming party. So was Emmy, and you could at least try to straighten things out between you and Ava.'

'No, it's not happening.' Aware of his friend's frustration Blake feels too numb to do anything about it. The only feeling he has left is seething rage at the system. He couldn't give a damn about Ava.

'Well if you're not interested in wooing her back, you won't mind if I ask her out then.'

Blake covers his surprise. 'You'd be crazy. She cares more for herself than anyone else.'

Rory changes the subject. 'Will you tell me what happened in Baghdad?'

Blake shakes his head, 'another time.'

He wishes Rory would talk about something else, or just go. Blake wants to be alone, maybe to prowl the streets renewing his acquaintance with his home, or stay in his room and watch movies, or read as he's been doing for the last two weeks. He wants to understand what's going on, not make polite small talk, or dredge up the past couple of years, but he doesn't know where to start. His mind is blank, but it's not fair on Rory. He makes an effort to force the molten rage back to the solid core in his chest and takes a long drink of his beer.

'Why not now?' Rory wants to understand what's wrong. He knows it must have been bad, but he doesn't understand Blake anymore. He's like a different person. He looks the same except for the glowering. Rory gets that. He would be angry if what occurred to Blake happened to him. Who's he kidding? He would never have survived. It's not that, something else is missing.

Blake doesn't answer.

Rory tries another tack, trying to regain the camaraderie of their student years. 'Hey remember that last fight at Uni. The one where you annihilated that bloke; the one who claimed he had studied Karv Maga with the Israeli Special Forces.'

As soon as the words are out his mouth, he wishes he hadn't said them. That was where he took Ava for their first date. Where she met Blake. What a disaster that turned out to be.

Blake smiles briefly. 'Yeah he was good. I was lucky that time.'

'Bullshit. It wasn't luck, you were the best in the club.'

'No he was good. I was lucky. If we had a rematch he would have won.'

'Trouble was you partied too much otherwise you would have won the national championship, no problems.'

Blake shifts uncomfortably. 'It was a long time ago.'

Not so long ago Rory thinks, saying aloud before he checks his words. 'That's where you stole Ava from me.' The moment the words are out of his mouth he wants to stuff them back in. He tries to turn the remark into joshing. 'You're a bastard you know that?' Blake's weird behaviour is making him act crazy too.

Blake looks up surprised. 'What the fuck are you talking about? I never stole Ava from you.'

'Forget it.'

Blake shakes his head. 'Fuck mate, I didn't know. You should have said. Anyway, fat lot of good it did me.'

Again Rory says, 'forget it,' wishing he could keep his big mouth shut.

With an effort, Blake forces a quick grin. For a second Rory sees a flash of his old mate beneath the forbidding exterior, but as quickly as it came it's gone.

Blake knows he's being unfair, shutting Rory out, and makes an effort. He looks down at the table speaking in a low voice. 'See that bloke near the door, the one reading the paper.'

'The bloke with the beard?' Rory asks.

'Yeah.'

'What about him?'

'I think he's following me.'

'Shit—press?' Rory casts a surreptitious glance across the bar, but the bearded man looks up catching his eye and quickly shifts his gaze away.

'Maybe, I don't know.' Blake shrugs.

Rory takes a long slug of beer, searching his mind for something neutral to talk about, wishing they still had the easy friendship of their student years. He puts down his glass and leans forward, putting his elbows on the table and his chin on his fists. 'Okay let's talk about something else. What will you do now, finish your internship?'

'I'm not out yet, just on recovery leave. I still have five months left, but I'll do it in Canberra— some bullshit policy unit, but better than going back to that shit hole sand trap.'

'But after what you did... and your wounds.'

'Yeah—but they're not going to let me off the hook. You're a lawyer you should know that.'

'I guess, but it's not so much longer, and at least it's safe. So what will you do when it's over?'

'I don't know.' Blake's been asking himself that since he arrived home.

Rory tries to think of something more cheerful. 'Well you don't have to worry about earning a crust. Business is booming and Dad paid off your study debt. Just as well or you'd have a debt the size of a small kingdom's GDP.'

The volcanic rage surges in Blake again. 'It's this fucking Government. Who keeps voting them in? Inflation is out of control. The more they charge for degrees, the more professionals demand to cover the debt. They are ruining this country. I can't believe the change in the time I've been away. How come no one tries to stop them?' He stops embarrassed by his outburst, trying to contain the rising bile and runs his hand over his jaw. 'Sorry.'

'Jesus, you're a cheerful sod.' Rory sits back, lips pursed.

Blake straightens his back. 'I'm not very good company at the moment. It's a bit of an adjustment you know.' He drains his glass and puts it back on the table. 'Okay, let's go to dinner at your place. Your folks have been good to me.' Pushing his chair back, he stands up waiting for Rory to finish his beer.

As the two men walk across the room to the exit, the bearded man also gets up leaving his beer half-full on the table. He walks out leaving the door to swing back with a thump. It's as if he wants them to know he's on to them.

Blake stops and puts out his hand, not quite touching Rory's arm. Rory raises a querying eyebrow, but Blake says nothing, turning instead to go to the bar. He waits for the barmaid to put down her glass and attend to him.

'Another beer?' She asks.

His gaze lingers on her mouth as he wills his features to blandness. 'No thanks. I'm Blake and your name's Charlotte—right. What time do you get off tonight?'

'Eleven.'

'I'll see you then.' He scans her face, but she stares back at him not answering, her expression masked, and he turns away to re-join Rory.

'Jesus you jammy bugger! How do you do that?' Rory says as Blake walks back to him.

Blake ignores the comment saying, 'come on we have just enough time to catch the five-thirty ferry to Hawthorne.'

Outside the bar, a car screeches to a halt. Two men and a woman jump out. One of the men carries a camera and runs to intercept Blake, the camera held to his shoulder as he focuses on Blake's face. He runs backwards as he films. Blake swears and with his head down, strides along the street.

The woman runs after him, microphone in hand. 'Mr Lincoln, Mr Lincoln, what's it like to be home?' She trips on uneven paving and swears.

Peter Cassey watches his colleague chase after Blake, but stops to talk to Rory. 'Hey Rory Fuller, long time no see mate.'

'Pete what are you doing in these parts. I thought your stomping ground was Canberra now.'

'Just visiting the folks and got a call. I see you and Blake are still mates.'

'Give us a break; he's not ready to talk yet. But congratulations, I hear you are in line for a Walkley.'

The woman stops and Blake hurries down the street. She glances back to Peter. Should she run after Blake or go back and hear what Cassey and the other man are saying. Obviously, Lincoln's not going to talk to her.

The cameraman is still running backwards, camera focused on Blake's face. Too late, she sees the bench and shouts a warning. It catches the man behind the knees. He tips over backwards, cracking his head on the seat before rolling onto the ground. Blake strides on, ignoring the cameraman who lies on the pavement, his camera in the gutter.

The woman runs to help him up. 'Are you okay. Look your head's bleeding.'

'It's fine. How's my camera?' He bends to pick it up and his vision swims. 'Maybe I should get checked out, but I got good footage.'

They walk back towards the car.

The woman calls, 'hey Cassey we're losing him.'

Peter waves and turns back to Rory. 'Okay deal – we give you a break now, you promise when he talks, he talks to me.'

3.

As the day disappears beyond the smog-smudged western skyline, Blake and Rory walk towards the Fuller's home in silence. Twilight casts long shadows across the suburb, patterning the road and shrubbery either side with dark pools. The street lights flicker on, but they are ineffective against the sunset gloom.

On their left, tall narrow buildings set back in their manicured gardens, jostle for position, as they claim Brisbane's most exclusive street in its most desirable suburb. On their right, stately homes front the Brisbane River, their backs turned to the rear aspirants vying for street frontage. It's safe here. Security is high, paid for by the wealthy owners of the river front homes.

Yet Blake remains vigilant. He knows he puzzles Rory, but he doesn't have time for that now. With his senses on high alert, he scans the road ahead looking for cover, searching for the enemy, his skin prickling as he sees potential for ambushes everywhere. He tells himself this is Australia, and he's safe, but it changes nothing. Rory's chatter is a distraction, and he is glad he's stopped talking.

At the end of the street, they pass through a barrier lifted by a private security guard who greets Rory. 'Evening Mr Fuller.'

Rory nods, 'evening Neal.' He walks over to the guardhouse, and introduces Blake before they continue down the road to the house. When they arrive, he opens the garden gate, holding it so it doesn't slam as he turns to look down the street. 'I think you were right, the bloke was following you, but I can't see him now. Security probably stopped him.'

He and Blake walk up the path to the house. The imposing edifice rises above them to command a hundred metre stretch of the Brisbane River bank. It sits high above the water line on massive stone floodwalls. A metre below, a tennis court flanks the right of a lawned garden. Steep steps lead down to an ocean cruiser moored at a jetty. The tip of its radar mast is all that shows above the garden wall. Across the river, the sprawling city's skyscrapers rise in full view as their lights flicker on, combating the deepening gloom.

Rory's mother crosses the entrance hall as they open the front door. Her face lights up with pleasure. 'Oh Blake, you're home. Thank goodness. I thought you wouldn't come, but you have. I'm so glad darling. You were a naughty boy ignoring us.'

'Hello Mrs Fuller.'

'But mustn't worry about that now. You're here, that's all that matters.' She gazes up at him, her eyes swimming behind barely contained tears. To cover her emotion she says, 'I am so glad you're home,' and laughs self-consciously. 'Did I say that already? But honestly darling I can't tell you how worried we were.' She holds his hands out away from his body. 'You look well, a bit thin but nothing a good feed won't fix. You are well now, aren't you?' Her concern crinkles the skin around her eyes as she scans his face. Then ignoring his reticence she hugs him, her arms encircling his waist, her head resting on his chest.

Her fragrance brings back memories of his mother. They always wore the same perfume and the surge of nostalgia swamps him. Despite himself, his arms slide around her shoulders hugging her diminutive frame close to his chest

Her voice muffles against him. 'It's terrible what they did, but we won't talk about that anymore. It's not something you'll want to remember. Come,' she pulls away clutching his wrist. 'William will be so happy... and here he is.'

William Fuller walks into the hall lost in thought, the tip of his little finger exploring his ear.

'Look who's finally come home with Rory dear.'

He stops surprised. Then his hand falls to his side and his face lights up as he strides across the room, arms held out in greeting.

'Blake my boy welcome home. Thank God, you're back. We were so worried... Huh hum.' He clears his throat, covering his unaccustomed emotion. 'Your folks would be proud...' He tails off and then adds, 'if they were...,' but he can't finish the sentence. Instead, he grasps Blake's free hand with both of his. 'How's the shoulder?' His eyes search Blake's face, looking for signs of the past years. It's there, that indefinable etched gravity deep in a combat veteran's eyes.

'No talk of the war William.' Margery Fuller pats Blake's arm. 'We have exciting news. Two things in one day, it's almost too good to be true. Come through to the terrace. Dad was just getting the champagne.'

'What's going on?' Rory says.

'Your sister is getting married. Jeremy's popped the question.'

'No shit!'

'Language Rory.'

'Sorry Mum. What's the other thing?'

'What other thing?' Marjory looks mystified.

'You said two things in one day.'

'Blake coming home of course.' She turns to Blake. 'You will stay. You can have your old suite in the east wing with Rory. It's all made up for you.'

Blake says, 'Thanks Mrs Fuller, but I have a room. I already paid for the month, but it's good of you.'

Rory rolls his eyes and his mother frowns at him, saying to Blake, 'nonsense, it's the least I can do.'

She scans his face, making certain he's aware of his welcome. He nods, and satisfied, she turns to lead the way to the terrace.

Blake clamps down on rising suffocation as he follows Margery Fuller. Waves of familiarity remind him of her cheerful fussing and determined organisation. She hurries across the hall and along a corridor, her high heels making loud clickity-clacks on the parquet floor. Behind them, Mr Fuller closes the front door and heads to the cellar.

As they reach the sitting room, a young woman skips in through the open folding glass doors to greet them. She is no taller than her mother and pretty, with dark blonde hair. It swings lose around her shoulders.

Blake smiles with pleasure as she comes towards him. 'Lo Emmy.'

'I thought I heard your voice. It's so good you've come home at last although I'm cross it's taken you so long.' She grins hugging him. 'Geez you're thin. I can feel your ribs.' She looks up into his face, once as familiar as her brother's, but now his eyes are closed off and wary despite his smile. He looks sad she thinks grabbing hold of his arm.

'Hey,' she holds up her hand, wriggling her fingers to flash an engagement ring. 'Come and meet my fiancé. Can you believe it, me engaged. Tra-la!' She swings his hand in hers. 'Huh,' she inhales, and covers her mouth. 'Blake, Ava's here.'

Blake looks at Rory, who holds up his hands in defence. 'Hey, I didn't know or I would have told you.'

'He didn't know honest.' Emmy says corroborating her brother's denial. 'I called her when Jeremy proposed. She came over to celebrate, but I wouldn't have called her if I knew you were coming.'

Emmy looks stricken, and Blake smiles to show her it's all right. Her face clears, and she tucks her arm through his again. 'It'll be okay won't it? It was ages ago. You're over that now aren't you?' They walk outside to the sandstone-paved terrace surrounding a swimming pool.

Two people sit at an outdoor table, their backs to the house. As Blake and Emmy walk up, their heads move apart. The woman looks across the river, watching the current ripple, reflecting the city lights in wavy orange lines. Her face is bathed in the tepid glow from the pool's underwater lighting.

A tall dark haired man stands as they approach. His hand runs across his head, smoothing his gelled black hair as he waits for them to reach him. He rolls his neck as if his collar is irksome, and his tendons ridge as he stretches his square jaw.

Emmy stops and looks up into Blake's face. 'Blake, meet my fiancé, Jeremy Marabaux.' She says it with a proud smile. 'Jeremy darling, meet the famous Blake Lincoln.'

Blake unhooks his arm. 'Congratulations man,' he says trying to sound as if he means it. He takes in the expensive suit, the beads of sweat on Jeremy's top lip, his clean-shaven jaw, and the crust of dried saliva that clings to the corner of his mouth.

Jeremy wipes his lips with his forefinger and stretches his neck. He straightens his shoulders to look Blake in the eye, tugging his shirt cuffs to delay having to shake Blake's outstretched hand.

Blake notices the nervous tick and observes the deliberate delay. He recognises the power game and knows he can't trust this man. A shiver of revulsion runs through him, but he tries to disguise it as he shakes the limp, clammy hand. The man's eyes are like that of a dead fish.

A small sneer curls Jeremy's top lip. 'Ah yes, the Nation's hero.'

Ignoring the jibe, Blake turns to the woman sitting at the table. 'Hello Ava.'

Ava is an elegant woman; demure with long legs folded sideways, ankles crossed above narrow feet clad in shocking pink stilettos. Her pencil-straight skirt shows the outline of slender thighs beneath clinging cerise silk. She perches on the edge of her chair uncertain whether to rise or remain seated, and drops her heavily blackened eyelashes as she fidgets.

Her dark bobbed hair swings forward to obscure her expression. 'Hello Blake. How are you?'

He watches the silver shine of her hair, but she doesn't look at him. Instead, she laces her fingers on her lap until her knuckles show white, and her long vermillion nails dig into her skin.

Rory breaks the awkward silence. 'Okay where's that champagne you were boasting about then Mum? Hello Ava, still as lovely as ever I see. Hello Jeremy, congrats mate or maybe I should say commiserations.'

'Rory!' Emmy tries to slap her brother who dodges laughing. She turns in appeal to her mother. 'Mum?'

'Rory don't tease. Go and help your father bring out the champagne glasses.' Rory pulls a mock contrite face and goes back inside and Mrs Fuller takes a seat. 'Come and sit next to me Blake.'

Emmy plumps down in the seat between Ava and Jeremy. She leans across to clutch her fiancé's hand, dragging it into her lap possessively, afraid if she doesn't hang on, he might vanish.

Blake walks around the table to sit next to Mrs Fuller. For a minute, no one speaks. Blake watches a river ferry chugging towards the city. The scene brings back memories of his capture in Baghdad. The imagery fills his mind, with the brown swirling waters of the ferry wake reminding him of the Caliphate patrol boat on the Tigris River.

The rest of their patrol was dead, killed in an ambush by Caliphate Guards. Only he and Richard got away. They hid for two days down alleyways, in bushes, in ditches full of muddy water festering with leaked effluent from Baghdad's inadequate sewers.

When they reached the western bank of the Tigris River Blake hesitated, but Richard was sure they could swim across if they abandoned their body armour. If they could make it to the other side away from the Caliphate palace, they might get away entirely, dress as locals and make their way back to Basra. They waded through reeds at the edge of the water and swam diagonally across the current. It dragged them downstream.

Suddenly Blake's back in the past. His body is submerged in the muddy water, swimming low, mentally kicking himself for not waiting for dark, but they are too far gone to turn back.

Three quarters of the way across, he feels his muscles cramping, but forces himself to continue swimming. The sound of Richard's voice reaches him and he looks back. A patrol boat looms up river travelling slowly, hugging the western bank. Are they searching for them? It's gaining on them. Have the guards seen them?

In an instant, he makes a decision, and shouts at Richard, 'go!' Blake points to the eastern bank before turning and swimming over arm, towards the boat. Adrenalin surges and his muscles pump as a new energy drives him forward. He glances behind to make sure Richard swims to the eastern shore, and then thrashes on towards the boat, splashing water to capture their attention. If the Caliphate Guard sees him, maybe Richard can get away. At least one of them can make it.

Jeremy leans forward, his dark eyes glistening. 'The news said you killed at least twenty men with your bare hands. That's got to be bullshit! No one could do that. So what's the truth?'

There's a collective gasp from Marjory and Emmy.

Blake doesn't hear as blood roars in his ears. The boat's turning; on full throttle, it races past him to cross the river. He stops, treading water, his breath coming in shallow pants as he watches Richard climb ashore, sees him run up the bank.

The boat's machine gun opens fire, stopping Richard in his tracks. Bullet puncture zip marks from hip to shoulder. He lurches forward ploughing into the muddy bank and lies still.

'Bastards, fucking bastards!' Blake shouts, but his voice is whipped away unheard. He watches in horror, helpless to do anything as the boat pulls up to the bank and an officer jumps out. The man swaggers towards Richard's prone body, pistol in hand.

Richard moves, raising his arms in surrender. The Guard raises the pistol, pulling the trigger three times. Two rounds blow Richards face apart and the third enters his left breast. The guard takes two more steps towards him and empties his pistol into Richard's lifeless body. Blake can't watch anymore. His friend is dead.

He sinks beneath the water, unsure if the Guards have seen him, but uncaring his lungs bursting as he swims down river. He can't tell if the red mist in front of his eyes is the river pollution, Richard's blood, or his own rage. Perhaps he should let go and just sink to the bottom.

He couldn't save any of them. His whole patrol is gone. They were his responsibility and they are all dead. He doesn't deserve to live. The image of Richard's hands held in surrender etches deeper into his memory as he swims.

The boat throttles back as it reaches him, and glides up to bob on the river's ripples. It's over. None of them escaped despite his futile gesture. He really believed Richard would get away, but he failed him too. The mission failed before it began, and it's his fault. He'll die now and join his mates, of that he's certain, and he's relieved. Where his mates go he goes too.

As they haul him into the boat, grief, exhaustion, guilt and fear tip Blake over the edge and he mutters, 'But from my heart no tear nor sound, for I have gone past carin'.'

The Guard fix weapons on him as he recites Henry Lawson, blotting out their presence. The officer who killed Richard cocks his pistol and prods Blake. To his surprise, Blake frowns and then with his chin thrust out, he swears in fluent Arabic. 'Filthy stupid sons of sows—why did you have to kill him?'

Mrs Fuller shifts in her chair saying, 'where is William with that champagne?'

Jeremy doesn't let Blake's silence go unchallenged. 'I spoke to you Blake. You might have the courtesy to respond.'

Blake returns to the present and pushes the imagery from his mind. He glances at Jeremy, taking in the haughty disdain, the raised eyebrow, the withdrawn chin. Jeremy's black eyes remind him of the Guard who shot Richard.

He has an overwhelming urge to feel his hands around Jeremy's neck. To press his thumbs against the man's jugular and cut off his carotid artery, to see the life fade from his eyes.

He pushes his chair back, the noise loud against the sandstone and says, 'I would rather not talk about it, thanks.'

Exasperated Jeremy goes on the attack. 'I expect the press are sensationalising it, saying it's up there with the great POW escapes from World War II. Is that why you don't want to talk about it? You fear the truth is too ordinary.'

Emmy says, 'Jeremy, darling...'

Jeremy is angry at Blake's apparent arrogance and ignores her, baiting Blake and hoping for a reaction. 'So Blake is it guilt or modesty? Perhaps it's just that you think you're better that the rest of us, and you think you have the right to keep the truth from the Australian public?'

'Please Jeremy...' Emmy's brow wrinkles with worry.

Jeremy pats her hand, realising he's overstepped civility's boundaries and changes tack. 'Maybe you are just angling for the highest price. Now that is something I do understand and can arrange. It just so happens, I am on good terms with the Randolph's who have the contract for the national broadcaster, the Australian Media Consortium. If you would like me to act for you, I can get you a good price.'

Blake struggles to contain himself. His throat chokes, but Jeremy doesn't stop.

'My Dad tells me you are recommended for the VC, but it's doubtful they'll agree to a medal for a convict.'

Mrs Fuller and Emmy both gasp, and Ava looks at her hands. Jeremy is oblivious, and doesn't realise how close he is to death.

Blake has to get away and stands, 'excuse me Mrs Fuller. I'll just help Rory.'

Margery Fuller waits until he's inside before saying, 'it's probably best not to push the issue Jeremy. Wait until he feels like talking about it.'

'It must have been horrific.' Ava fiddles with her fingers. 'I feel so guilty that I sent that letter. He must have got it just before...'

'Before what... What happened?' Jeremy turns his gaze on Ava pretending not to know, glad of the distraction, his eyebrow raised and his mouth pursed.

'She dumped him.' Emmy is still angry with her friend and refuses to spare her feelings. 'Sent back the engagement ring in a letter...'

Mrs Fuller says, 'look, I think we should just change the subject all of you. The poor boy, it's no wonder he avoids everyone. We're like a mob of ghouls. No more talk about this. I forbid it.'

Inside Blake finds Rory placing champagne flutes on a tray. 'Look Rory I shouldn't have come. I'll just go okay. Please tell your Mum I'm sorry.'

'Fuck no. You can't go. What's up?'

'I can't deal with that wanker.' Blake stops speaking as Mr Fuller enters the room.

'Ah lad there you are. Take these out to the terrace will you. I'll get a bucket of ice.' William hands two bottles of Bollinger to Blake and walks out to the kitchen.

'Come on mate. What's he said? The bloke's a prize dick, but just ignore him. Buggered if I know what my sister sees in him.' He picks up the tray and walks towards the open doors. 'Come on, just a drink with the family, then we'll have dinner, and you can go back to your barmaid. Mum and Dad will be really hurt if you piss off now.'

'Okay but if I deck the bastard you'll be responsible.' Blake grins at Rory to hide his fury. Rory's right. He's being ungrateful.

Rory's relieved by the smile. 'Okay but seriously, it's natural for everyone to want to know. Just tell 'em whatever you like and they'll eat it up. At this moment, you can do no wrong in the eyes of the great Australian public. Come on; let's get this lot out to the pool.'

Later that evening William rolls up his shirtsleeves and stands at the head of the table to carve beef. It's a tradition he cares about, painstakingly arranging the dark rimmed pink slices on each plate as his wife hands them to him. The people around the table watch the ritual in silence, knowing he likes to concentrate on getting things just right. When he sits down, he shakes out his napkin with a snap, laying it carefully over his lap. 'So Jeremy when do you expect they'll lift the curfew?'

Jeremy looks at Mr Fuller in astonishment. 'I wouldn't know. My father doesn't consult me about these kinds of decisions.'

William banks his irritation at the man, but tries to keep his voice level. 'No I imagine he doesn't, but you can speculate like the rest of us, can't you?'

'I suppose I can. From what I understand there's a battalion of regulars up in the Cape now. They think they have caught most of the terrorists. Possibly after the danger has passed, they may lift curfew.'

'They should make sure no more arrive.' Rory says

'How will they do that?' Jeremy asks. 'Put a fence around the Cape?'

Emmy giggles and Jeremy frowns at her. Quickly she straightens her features and turns to Ava. 'Help yourself to a Yorkshire pudding Ava. You don't have one and Mum's are the best.'

'No thanks.' Ava says watching Emmy put another on her own plate. 'Do you think you should?'

Emmy blushes and looks down at her food. She knows she could do with losing a few kilos.

Rory wants to recapture the conversation. 'I know the Cape is vast and you can't patrol it on foot or cover the whole coast line, but we have to do something. It won't be long before they are in the cities. Then we are up shit-creek.'

'Rory watch your language.' Margery says.

Ava leans forward eagerly. 'They won't get far. I heard they use those new autonomous weapon system thingies—attack drones, or whatever they are called, and they are terrifyingly effective.' She passes the gravy boat to Jeremy. His frown makes her lapse into silence.

Blake is interested, but Mr Fuller interrupts. 'I think you heard that from Jonathon Castile dear, but the government denied it. It wouldn't be right. AWS attack drones don't discriminate, and what if they blasted a fishing boat from the water?'

'Who are you talking about?' Emmy says it distractedly. She missed the man's name while she tried to work out how many calories were on her plate.

'What?' Mr Fuller looks at his daughter as if surprised to see her there.

'Jonathon thingy.'

Rory looks incredulous. 'Jesus Emmy you studied journalism at Uni. You'd think you would know the name of the ex-Chief Justice.'

'I prefer my future wife does not involve herself with anything as squalid as journalism.' Jeremy says, but no one pays him any attention.

Emmy scowls at her brother. 'I didn't hear.'

Jeremy pats her hand. 'He's a criminal dear, in gaol now. The Prime Minister sacked him.'

'The Prime Minister can't sack a Chief Justice.' Blake says it quietly. 'The Chief Justice is an idea above politics, not merely flesh and blood. All they can do is gaol the man. It's up to the Governor-General to instate a new person.'

Emmy looks at Blake confused by what he's saying. 'Well how come he's in gaol then?'

Margery says, 'he was such a lovely looking man. It was such a shame.'

'He was a treacherous pervert Mrs Fuller.' Jeremy frowns.

Emmy says. 'Is he the one they wanted to charge with sodomy?'

Jeremy scowls at her and she retreats into silence.

William weighs into the conversation putting an end to it with authority. 'No dear, he was convicted on a corruption charge along with conspiracy as a cartel, to pervert the course of law and order. No one should be above the law, but we should change the subject. It's not one for the dinner table.'

'Quite so.' Jeremy smiles and places his hand on Emmy's under the table.

She says, 'I remember his trial...'

Blake catches a look of pain washing across Ava's face and wonders why she is so subdued. Is it because he's there? He knows that feeling although her dumping him saved his life, but now is not the time for confessions. He'll tell her later.

'The Navy will be on to it, won't they?' Rory wants to get back to the terrorist incursion. The invasion of Australia worries him.

'Yes I suppose the Navy patrols the coast, but I really don't know. I'm just speculating. These things are classified and we should be more careful discussing them outside the family.' Jeremy flashes a glance at Blake. 'You can never be sure who might be listening.'

Emmy says, 'Oh Jeremy, Blake's family so is Ava. Well, as good as anyway. We can trust them.'

'Ahem.' Jeremy neatly divides a slice of beef and folds it over in a parcel to stab with his fork.

Emmy watches him, her forehead furrowed as she wonders why he's so short with Blake. She wants so much for them to get on, but they're like rival dogs forced to cohabit.

William Fuller changes the subject. 'I hear they are going to let a new contract for private consulting rooms to support the public hospital system. Rory I need your firm to get on to the tender as soon as the documentation comes out. We can't have someone else taking business away from us, can we?'

They all laugh except Blake and Ava.

Jeremy says, 'I will be happy to act for you in this Mr Fuller, at no charge of course.'

He squeezes Emmy's hand, but she is still worrying about the people she loves not seeing eye to eye. She glances at Blake and then at Ava, who appears preoccupied rearranging her food on the plate, keeping her head lowered as if she's not paying attention.

Mr. Fuller says, 'Blake my boy, now you're home, do you want to be involved with the tender?'

Blake shakes his head. 'Thanks Mr Fuller. I don't think I can. I have to go to Canberra next week, but you don't really need me do you? I'm grateful you asked, but I have absolute faith in the way you're running things, if that's okay with you.'

Mr Fuller nods and Blake turns to Jeremy. 'Where are the terrorist coming from?'

William answers. 'They are FISLO. Isn't that right Jeremy?'

'Yes I understand that's correct. They are from the terrorist group Freedom for the Islamic State of the Levant and Orient.'

Jeremy's pedantry irritates Blake, but he controls his response. 'I get that bit, but are they from the east or are they Arabs—from which part of the world? Has Papua New Guinea succumbed?'

'I see,' Jeremy says. 'They are Arabs as far as I am aware although there may be others.'

'And PNG?' Blake asks.

Mr Fuller again answers for Jeremy. 'No they're still muddling along fine. They've asked us to run their hospitals you know. We are in negotiations now. The thing is they don't have enough money to pay, and their hospitals are so run down. I feel sorry for the blighters, but what can a person do. We are not a charity. I suggested they try to secure more aid funding from the U.S. or Europe to meet our costs, and then we'll consider it. The trouble is if we don't keep them over there, they will try to get into Australian hospitals. They have that nasty strain of TB among other diseases. It's a killer and none of the antibiotics work.' He turns to Jeremy, 'but I heard your company was working on a gene therapy. Is that right Jeremy?'

Jeremy looks uncomfortable and shifts in his chair, focussing on pushing broccoli onto his fork. 'It's a conversation for another place I think Mr Fuller. My stomach doesn't do well on a diet mixed with diseases.'

William, immediately contrite, says, 'my apologies Jeremy. Where were we?'

Blake says, 'it's a strange place to enter the country don't you think?'

'Not for the Papuans my boy, they're just a spit away.' Mr Fuller misunderstands.

'The terrorist incursion I mean,' Blake says.

'Look you lot, can we talk about something more cheerful?' Mrs Fuller leans across the table and lifts the platter. 'More beef anyone?'

Emmy takes it from her and says, 'I'd like to get an early start tomorrow Mummy. I have so much to organise for the wedding and Nadine says she's having a fashion show in London in June. If I want her to make my wedding dress I'll need to book her now.'

While Mrs Fuller and Emmy talk about preparations for the wedding, Blake broods on what he's heard. The terrorist incursion into the Cape makes little sense to him.

He knows FISLO wouldn't make such a tactical error and he can't see any strategic benefit to such an incursion into Australia unless it's payback for having troops over there. Even then, why choose such an inaccessible spot? Why not just fly in as tourists?

4.

Blake lounges against the outside wall near the exit door of the Writer's Bar. His watch says 23:00 hours. He hears the ping of the till, and knows it won't be long before she leaves. After weeks watching her each night, he is familiar with her ritual.

When he arrived home, the first thing he did was to go back to the place of his arrest. The memory is almost unreal now as if imagined. It's as if his life began and ended in the Middle East. The time before, as a student and then an intern, is hard to imagine, hard to remember. Blake wants to remember. He wants to blot out the Middle East with memories of the person he was.

He stood in the middle of George Street, dark with the silence of curfew, and gazed at the spot he was tasered, remembering. What happened to the blokes who tried to help him? He hopes they stayed out of trouble, but he's grateful to them.

He looks up at the hotel in front of him and a memory of a girl bubbles to the surface. Her long golden hair swings in the breeze as she jumps up and down, laughing, her tongue poking out the side of open lips as she waves to a man in the crowd, the same man who helped him.

The next day he went back and checked into the hotel. For the last two weeks, he's watched her. She hasn't noticed him, doesn't appear to remember although he knows she saw his capture. He remembers the horror on her face as she watched from the half-open doorway.

He wasn't going to speak to her, never anticipated this. It's as if something other than him took over this afternoon. It was an aberration and probably a mistake. She's a weakness he cannot afford, but still he's here.

His foot presses against the building's marble base while his eyes scan passing pedestrians. Will it be the same bloke tailing him? He hasn't seen anyone who looks like a possible candidate since the ferry earlier in the evening, but it doesn't mean no one is there. He manoeuvres a toothpick from one side of his mouth to the other, watching the sign across the street flicker its message, complacency costs lives.

The door opens, and he straightens, waiting for Charlotte to step out. She walks down the three steps and turns left, passing him with her head down as if she hasn't seen him standing there.

He takes out the toothpick and follows her. 'So where are you taking me?'

'I'm not taking you anywhere. You're following me and it's kind of creepy,' she says, her face turned away.

Her response amuses him. 'I told you I would be back at eleven.'

'Yeah you did, but if you recall I didn't say I would go out with you. You're an arrogant bastard aren't you?'

'My parents were married when I was conceived or at least I think they were. Okay where do you want to go then?'

He's grinning at her, but she still won't look at him. 'It's past eleven already. Curfew's at twelve. Where are you going to take me at this time of night?'

'My room's upstairs. We can go there,' he says following two steps behind her.

'Fuck off,' she says half turning her head to glance back at him.

He laughs. 'Okay, I'll just follow you then.'

'Did you really escape from a FISLO prison in Baghdad?'

'Maybe.'

'Tell me about it.'

'I'll tell you if you come up to my room.'

'No. Are you a cop?'

Taken aback he says, 'what? Of course not.'

'Well, why are you hanging around me then?'

'Why would a cop want to hang around you? Other than the obvious.'

'What's obvious?'

'You?'

'What?'

'You're hot.'

Charlotte wriggles her bum and in two strides he catches up to her, grabbing her waist to turn her around to face him, his hands clasped loosely in the small of her back. 'You're hot, but I'm not sure about the tea cosy on your head.'

She remains in the circle of his arms, leaning back slightly to look into his face. 'It's not a tea cosy.'

'Whatever. Come on, Charlotte let's go somewhere and get a drink and just talk okay?'

'What about curfew?'

'Fuck curfew. They do it so the lazy bastards don't have to work night shift.'

'You know that do you?' Her head tilts to the side as she scrutinises his features.

'Yeah I do actually.'

'How?'

He turns his face away to stare along the pavement. 'Can't sleep.'

'So you walk the streets?'

'Yes.'

'What about the cameras?'

'I avoid them. They're not on every street, just the main ones or outside banks and places likely to tempt desperate people.'

Charlotte tries to catch his eye. 'Can I trust you?'

'Maybe.' Now he looks at her.

'What do you mean maybe? Either you're trustworthy or you're not. You don't look trustworthy.' She teases.

'Okay.' His face is serious.

'Okay what?'

'You can trust me.' Blake looks across the top of her head.

'All right you can come with me, but I warn you, you'll be going to the dark side. If you don't want to, say now. You can't get away until curfew's lifted in the morning.'

'I'm in.'

'Sure?' She pulls away from his loose grasp.

'Yes, I said so didn't I? Where are you taking me?'

'A club.'

'Cool.'

'So long as it's not raided. If you get caught they'll send you back.'

'Better not get caught then.' Blake grins and slips his arm around her waist as they walk down the street. She doesn't pull away.

The pavement is crowded with people hurrying home before curfew. Most of them look at the ground as they scurry past, their shoulders hunched, and their eyes avoiding connection in a mind-your-own-business kind of way.

Across the road, the old stock exchange, briefly established before the crash, and now an employment mart, has a running ticker tape in orange lights telling people that idleness helps terrorists.

It's a nice night, warm with a clear sky. The bright city lights illuminate the skyscrapers, showing the void above as a dark ribbon between the buildings. Once the curfew begins, the streets will plunge into darkness.

Charlotte says, 'they reckon this is world war three. Do you think they are right?'

'No, that's bull shit. This bloody war's been going on for thirty years—longer. More like forty, on and off. We shouldn't be over there. Bloody pollies lie about everything Charlotte, and no one challenges them. It's got me beat how they get away with it.'

'You'd better watch what you say. That kind of talk can get you into trouble. We're at war and loose lips and all that.'

'Who's going to tell—you? Are you a spy lovely Charlotte?'

She ignores him. 'They reckon there's been another infiltration of terrorist in the far north, up at the tip of the Cape.'

'I heard.'

'They evacuated all non-essential people.'

'Really, when?'

'About four months ago. Around the time, they imposed curfew. They said it's for our safety. Do you think terrorists are still in the country?'

'No. It's all bullshit like the rest of their lies.'

'How would you know? You haven't been here.'

'Can we talk about something else?'

'Okay.'

They walk in silence and Blake looks around him wondering where they are going. They're heading to the old Industrial area on low ground. It floods when the river is high. At this time of night, there are few pedestrians and not much traffic.

Charlotte says, 'I worry. My parents are up there.'

'Where?'

'They farm in the mountains west of Cairns. Dairy and Beef so they are considered essential, but I'm not allowed to visit. They reckon anywhere beyond Townsville is too dangerous.'

'What do your folks say?'

'Don't know. I can't contact them.'

'Shit. That's not good.'

'Why? Do you know something soldier boy.'

'I'm not a soldier.'

'Huh. The news said you are Special Forces.'

'Just shows you how dumb they are. If I were Special Forces they wouldn't know about it.' Changing the subject, he says, 'how long have you been a barmaid?'

'I'm not a barmaid. Or I am but only so they don't conscript me.'

'So if you're not a barmaid what are you?'

'I'm a singer.'

'That's cool. What kind of singer?'

'Alternative usually, some jazz. Sometimes folk—protest stuff mostly. They play some of my songs on the Pirate stations. I started off training for opera but...'

'What made you change your mind?'

'Who can afford it?' She looks at him, seeing he doesn't understand. 'You know... after the stock market crash when they stopped student loans?'

'Yeah I was here then.'

'Well they also stopped Austudy. I had to get a job to live.'

'Okay. I remember, I was still at Uni, but I lived with my friend's parents.'

'Lucky you. Anyway that's why I work in the bar now, at least it's a job.'

'Why don't you sing for a living?'

'You're kidding right? Like it's that easy. I don't move in the right circles.' She shrugs. 'Anyway, I only have to stay off their radar for four more years and I'll be out of their reach, at least for conscription. What about you? How come you ended up there? Did you volunteer?'

'No one volunteers.'

'Yeah they do. The law says conscripts have to volunteer to be deployed overseas, and there are the regulars.'

'The second part of that's true, but the first is bullshit.'

Charlotte turns her head to look into his face in time to see a flash of something indefinable, but it's gone quicker than she can register what it was. 'So what about you?'

His face clears, 'same really.'

'What do you mean same? Were you studying classical music?'

'No.' He laughs. 'I did Bio Chemistry and then post grad medicine. I hadn't completed my internship when I got conscripted.'

'Why?'

'Lots of reasons I guess.'

'No I mean, why did you get conscripted?'

He glances at her. 'I got arrested at a protest rally a few years ago. They found a joint in the gown I borrowed. I got done for possession, and unlawful assembly, and for resisting arrest.'

'Shit the bastards.'

'Yeah.' He smiles at her.

'What will you do now?'

'I have a month off on recovery leave, and then they told me I have to report to Canberra.'

'But surely they'll let you off now, for what you did. You can go back and finish your internship?'

'I don't know. They said not yet, maybe later. I've got five months left of my sentence, but because of... well you know, they let me have time off for recovery. General Badencamp insisted so long as I don't get into any trouble.'

'Who?'

'General Badencamp. He heads up the NATO strategic command.'

'Will you tell me about it?'

Blake's silent for a minute before he says, 'maybe another time. When I know you better.'

'What will you do in Canberra?'

'Don't know something to do with translation. I think it's because I speak Arabic.'

'Did you learn it there when you were in prison?'

'No I learned it as a kid. We lived in Saudi and I went to school there.'

'How come you lived in Saudi? Is that where you are from?'

'No. I'm from here in Brisbane. My father was at the embassy in Riyadh.'

'Where are your folks now?'

He wishes she would lighten up on the interrogation, and casts his mind about to find something else to talk about, but nothing comes. What the hell—it's not a secret. 'They're dead. The embassy bombing.'

'Shit sorry, where were you?' Her forehead creases in sympathy.

'Here at uni.'

'Which one?'

'Q.U.T.'

'Me too. How...'

He interrupts. 'You ask a lot of questions for a little girl.'

'I'm not a little girl, but sorry I didn't mean to pry. Anyway we are here, so you're off the hook for the moment.'

'Where?'

'Down that alley, but we have to make sure no one's around before we go in. They're unlicensed.' She looks at him worriedly, her bottom lip caught in her teeth. 'You won't tell anyone, will you?'

He slips his arm around her shoulders pulling her close. 'No I won't tell lovely Charlotte.'

He looks over her head, scanning the shadowy road looking for his tail, but the man seems to have vanished. The smell of carbolic soap rises from her beret and he moves his head aside, concentrating on the street, seeing smashed streetlights and dark abandoned buildings. There's no sign of life. Aside from a few parked vehicles, the place appears deserted. Perhaps it was a coincidence, and he was never following Blake.

Charlotte pulls away from his embrace. 'Okay come on then,' she says taking his hand.

They cross the road and walk down the alley, turning into a crumbling arched opening in a wall. It opens into a weed-infested lot in front of a six-story structure. She points at the brown brick building that rises above them. 'There's a squat up there if you ever need a place to stay.'

A few jagged glass panes remain, but most windows gape darkly. A large peeling billboard on the side of the building says together we will prosper. As they turn the corner, he spots a partly obscured entrance. Weeds and bushes grow haphazardly in front of it, but Blake suspects it's by design.

'Be careful going down the stairs. It's dark so you can't see much, but if you keep to the left and keep your shoulder against the wall, you should be okay. Don't step on my heels,' she warns.

The concrete steps down to the club smell of stale urine, mould, and garbage. On the landing at the base is a heavy steel door with a low wattage blue globe. Its glow barely casts enough light to see anything beyond a closed grill. Charlotte rings a bell and the grill opens. She tiptoes, her fingers grasping the bars.

'Hey Tony it's me and I have a friend.'

'You're late Charlie, they're waiting for you. Who's your friend?'

'His name's Blake, and he's okay.'

A face comes closer to the grill. Blake can see a lot of facial hair and dark eyes examining him.

Tony says, 'he looks familiar. Has he been in here before?'

'Na, he's the bloke on the news who escaped from the FISLO gaol.'

'Shit, no kidding.'

'Are you going to open-up or will we stand outside chatting all night.' Charlotte grins.

'Okay hold on.'

The grill closes and Blake hears gears grinding. He thinks they take their security seriously, and why wouldn't they? If the cops found this place, they would shut it down. Anyone caught would be conscripted, those under thirty anyway.

Tony is a small wiry man of about forty with a long bushy beard and a shaved head. He scrutinises Blake before saying, 'good on yer mate. You're a bloody hero. What you did... well you know what you did... we are damn proud of you man.' He looks abashed by his outspoken emotion.

'Thanks.' Blake nods and follows Charlotte down a dim corridor to a large room packed with people. They sit around or stand in groups, men, and women familiar with each other, and more relaxed than Blake has seen anyone in public since he arrived home. The hum from their voices rises and falls with occasional punctuations of laughter.

The room's furnishings are sparse with upturned crates for seats, and a trestle table bar at one end of the room. Vapour from a hundred vaptubes rises in a mist that hangs in the air like a lowered ceiling, dotted with points of light glowing from the tube ends.

Across the room, four men wait on a raised wooden platform. Two of them tune guitars and another sits on an amp with a saxophone across his thighs. The band's drummer, sticks in one hand, slumps over his drums staring trance-like into the crowd. He sees Charlotte and straightens, rapping a tattoo on his drums.

She turns to Blake. 'I'm late. Can I leave you to sort out a place for yourself? You can get a beer over there.' She points to the bar. 'If we get raided, make for that doorway behind the stage.'

'Sure.'

She pushes through the crowd, disappearing into the mass until only her bobbing head, with its daft red knitted beret, is visible. The crowd falls silent as she pulls it off stuffing it into her bag and chucking both down next to the drummer. Hair the colour of Pilsner tumbles over her shoulders and down her back. She lifts the microphone from its stand and turns to the band, her foot keeping time with a slight tap. Then she turns to the audience and sings.

For the first time since Blake arrived home, perhaps for the first time in more than three years, he feels tension drain from his shoulders. His skull expands, clearing his head and loosening its steel casing. His chest fills with air, and he feels his spirit soar with her voice. The sound takes possession of the room, and his soul, soothing and healing until he wants to lie down, close his eyes, and lose himself in her.

He walks over to the bar to order a beer and leans against a wall to watch her across the dim vapour-hazed room. No one speaks. The only sounds above the music are the small sounds of a room with perhaps a hundred and fifty people breathing, vaping on nicotine or dope, and small clinking noises from the bar. They don't distract him. At the end of her song the crowd claps, stomps and whistles as she bows. He's mesmerised.

A voice to his right says, 'she's good isn't she?'

Blake turns his head seeing a man standing nearby. 'Yes.'

'I saw you come in with her. You look familiar, have we met?'

'No.' Blake says it automatically assuming the bloke is making small talk, but he appraises him more carefully.

'Okay, I'm Evan Chandler. Me and Charlie go way back.' He holds out his hand.

Blake takes in the emaciated frame, the brown hair curling over a fraying collar, the pasty skin and jeans rubbed thin with wear. As he moves closer to shake the man's hand, he glances down seeing the lace-less shoes, their stitching fraying at the seams. 'Blake.' He says and shakes Evan's hand scrutinising his features. 'Actually you do look familiar. Maybe we met somewhere?'

'Na. It's unlikely. I imagine we move in different circles.'

Blake does know him, but he can't think from where. It'll come to him. 'Can I get you a beer?'

'I'm right.' Evan looks away.

'Don't you drink?'

'Sure I do, but I can't return the favour.'

Blake shrugs and walks back to the bar, returning with two beers, and handing one to Evan. Then he leans back against the wall as Charlotte begins a new song. It's a jazz number this time.

'How do you know Charlie?' Evan asks.

'I don't really. I just met her in the bar where she works.'

'That's strange.'

Blake takes a slug of his beer wishing the bloke would stop chattering. He wants to listen to Charlotte sing, not make small talk.

'It's not like her to be so trusting.' Suspicion curls in Evan's mind.

Blake doesn't answer, watching Charlotte across the crowd. Evan stares at him for a moment then lifts the beer to take a long sucking pull. The biting-cold of bitter malt on his tongue makes him shudder.

From somewhere in Blake's memory an image bubbles up, and he turns to look at Evan again. 'I think I know where we've met before,' he says.

Evan lifts the bottle to his lips again, relishing the nectar filling his mouth and gurgling down into the hollow cavern of his stomach. Reluctantly he lowers the bottle, looking at its label and says, 'is that so?' He doesn't trust this bloke. He's too well dressed and his clothes look new and expensive.

'Yeah I think... no I'm sure. You're the bloke who tried to help me and my mate's wife and kid a few years back in that protest rally on George Street.'

'I don't think so. I would remember that.'

Blake turns fully. 'You are. I remember you now and I owe you.'

Evan does remember, but scans Blake's face before he replies. The man looks genuine. 'What happened to her and the kid?'

'She was fined and got community service.'

'She was lucky, others got worse,' Evan says.

'It was because of the kid, there was no one else to look after her if they locked Allie up with the rest of us. Her husband, Richard, was my climbing buddy at Uni, but he was conscripted a month before me and got taken out about a month before he was due for release.' Blake swallows his guilt and looks away.

'Jesus, poor bastard. What happened to her?'

Blake stares at the floor. 'Don't know. I heard a rumour that after he died, she took the gap, fled the country and went to New Zealand with her kid.'

Evan pushes away from the wall. He doesn't think it's safe to continue the discussion about the escape route to New Zealand with this bloke, even if Charlie does think he's okay. 'Thanks for the beer mate.'

'No problem.' Blake watches Evan pushing through the crowd to reach the door behind the stage. Then his gaze returns to rest on Charlotte, and he pushes memories of Richard back into the locked trunk in his mind.

After a few more songs, the band takes a break, and Charlotte looks for Blake. He straightens from slouching against the wall as she makes her way towards him.

He says, 'can I get you a drink?'

'Thanks a beer will be great.'

He returns handing her a beer and says, 'you're a good singer.'

'You think so? Thanks.' She smiles and flicks her hair over her shoulders. It swings down around her waist, and he reaches out to touch the ends. 'Who's Evan?'

'Did you meet him?' Her face tilts to look at him.

He feels his throat tighten. 'Yes he introduced himself.'

'Ev and I grew up together. His folks were on the farm next to ours, but the banks got it, so he came to Brisbane about ten years ago when he started Uni—before the crash. He can't find a job and he's terrified he'll be conscripted for having no work I.D., so most nights he's here. He's like you, a night animal roaming the streets. That's why I knew you were telling the truth. He also reckons no cops patrol after curfew.'

'I could be an undercover cop and know that.'

'You wouldn't admit it though, would you?'

'I might if I was trying to convince you.'

'Jesus, I didn't think of that. No, the news said you're a soldier. I know that. You're not a cop.'

He grins. 'A conscript not a soldier.'

'It's the same thing.'

He changes the subject. 'Why doesn't this place get a licence, so it's legal? It can't be that hard.'

'No, they don't want one. There are too many regulations. You have to close at eleven so people can get home before curfew. A lot of us don't finish work until then. Then you have to charge membership fees. Most of us can't afford that. The cops collect members' lists and do spot checks. Its better they don't know we exist, that way people like Evan can hang out here, and I get to sing when I finish work. No one tells us what to do, or who can be here, or what music to play.'

The drummer comes out from the door behind the stage and heads back to his drums. Charlotte takes another gulp of her beer. 'Here can you finish it? I'm back on.'

'So soon. What time do you wrap up here?'

'Why, sick of it already?'

'No. I could listen to you sing forever.' He smiles at her. 'I'd like to get to know you, talk that's all.'

'I'm done at two and then another band comes on, but we have to wait until curfew's over before we can go home. Usually I just sleep in the back.'

At two-fifteen, Charlotte leads Blake into the back room. Several people sit or lay on the patterned carpet covering a section of the concrete floor, some talking in low voices, some sleeping.

The place smells of dope, unwashed bodies, and mouldy carpet. Blake wrinkles his nose and puts his hand on her arm. 'Let's go back to your place, or mine.'

She swings around to face him. 'No way, I'm not risking it.'

'There's no risk. I'll look after you.'

She gazes at him, searching his eyes and a sense of destiny overcomes her. 'Okay, but if we are caught I won't ever speak to you again.'

Blake smiles at the absurdity of her statement. 'We won't get caught.'

Outside the moonless sky is brilliant with stars flickering in the velvet ribbon between the skyscrapers, their light casting the dark streets below in silvery glow.

'Where are we going, yours, or mine?' Blake asks sliding his arm around her shoulder.

She pulls away and stops. 'Blake I hardly know you. I'm going home. You can come with me, but that's all. We sleep—me in my bed you on the floor. Or you can see me home safe then

go home. Or I go back to the club, now before we go further.'
She pulls on the red beret, tucking her hair into it.

'Don't you have a couch?' He sees the doubt in her eyes, and
stops teasing. 'Okay yours it is, lead the way.'

'It's in Newstead.'

'Christ. No-man's-land.'

'It's not so bad. Its reputation is worse than the reality. Most
illegal stuff happens elsewhere like the club 'cause everyone
knows Newstead is the first place the cops look. Anyway, who
can afford anywhere else now. Anywhere that doesn't flood
every year costs too much.'

As they walk on in silence, his eyes scan the streets, flicking
up occasionally to the buildings above, checking the dark
windows of shops looking for shadows. The tense vigilance is
back, and he feels the strain. Before he was so used to it he
barely noticed, but her singing gave him a reprieve. Now it's a
necessary compulsion, but he needs to talk to her so she doesn't
think he's crazy.

He says the first thing that comes to mind. 'Why do you
wear that beret?'

'Why, don't you like it?' She puts her hand up to touch it.

'No.'

She sighs. 'I wear it to be invisible.'

He laughs distracted from his surveillance and turns to look
at her. 'The thing is cherry red. How does that make you
invisible?'

'People see the hat not the person. They judge me as just
another povo and don't look further.'

'That's good.' Blake turns back to resume his watchfulness.
Ahead, a man steps out of an alleyway, and he curses his
inattention. He puts his hand on Charlotte's arm pressing her
back to the wall of the building. Above her head, a large sign, its
L.E.D. solar paint peeling, says we h ve a plan for th fut re.

'Give us a dollar.' The man whines.

'Sure.' Blake puts his hand in his pocket as if to take out his
wallet. He takes his time all the while moving closer to the man.

Every sense is alert as he takes in the black gloves and sturdy boots, the lank hair caught behind in a rat's tail, the leather jacket, and watery eyes. If it were lighter, he would see the bloke's sclera, veined and red, his pupils huge. Now, two metres away he pulls out his wallet, tugging as if it's caught. He continues scanning the streets, waiting to see where the others might be.

The rat-tailed man fidgets. 'Hurry it up. I don't got all night,' he says glancing away from Blake.

Blake follows his gaze knowing Rats-tail's tension is more than drugs. It's anticipation. The sturdy beige boots, laced up the ankles, gives it away. They are army-issue desert boots. These are not just street thugs. They are deserters. His peripheral vision catches the shadows of two more men at the edge of the alley. Is this it? Are there only three? He's lucky.

A second man saunters out from his cover, walking towards him, grinning and cocky. He wears trendy jeans and an open necked shirt with the sleeves rolled up. In his gloved hand, he holds a knife, but he is too confident, turning it over with a flick of his wrist. That makes him careless. Blake turns sideways pushing his wallet back into his pocket.

The second man sees the action and yells, 'hey,' running towards him. Blake swings around, and his bent elbow hits the man full in the face. He follows with rapid, repeated hammer blows and hears the expected crack of cheekbone and crunch of nose cartilage. The knife clatters to the pavement. The man screams and falls on his knees next to it, clutching his face.

The third man charges. Blake has no time to deal with the knife as he moves to meet him. He lifts his leg and thrusts, driving his boot into the assailant's stomach. The man gasps, and Blake grabs his head jerking it down as he brings up his knee. The jarring crunch disorientates the man. Blake, steps aside and in careful delivery, drives his foot into his bent knee. The force snaps the joint back tearing ligaments. The attacker screams and collapses. As he falls, Blake's fist catches his temple. The man folds onto the concrete.

Rats-tail looks at his comrades then at Blake and backs away. Blake goes after him. He leaps into the air, and his foot connects with Rats-tail's solar plexus. The force drops him to the ground where he lies on his back gasping for air like a landed fish.

Blake's blood thumps in his ears as he surveys the scene. His mind flashes and he sees himself kneeling in the dirt behind the mud brick wall of a compound.

As he scans the street for life there's only silence, and the rubble of a road cleaved into smoking craters. Broken masonry is strewn among carelessly flung body parts; a severed leg with boot attached; a left arm still with its smart watch in place; and a bodiless head, one eye staring manically heavenward. Overturned vehicles blaze, and bits of charred and tattered flesh festoon the steel wreckage like a Dantesque barbeque. Dark patches soak into the ground—the bombing's blood-sacrifice to war.

The sulphurous smell of solid propellant, along with the ubiquitous stench of Baghdad sewers, mingles with the aroma of scorched flesh. Blake's gaze sweeps the road. Through the grooved sights of the purloined AK 47, he picks out a child. He crouches unscathed, but in shock, staring in glassy eyed terror.

Blake's fix moves away from the kid, scanning the rest of the road for movement. There is no other sign of life as he waits for the next round of shelling to cover him. When it starts, he signals to Jason further back along the wall with the others. Then he runs, bent and zigzagging through drizzling dust and oily black smoke. His lungs heave as his legs pump, running for the truck, waiting for the slam of tumbling brass and steel that will stop him.

He shakes his head to clear the images and focuses on the paved roads, the skyscrapers of glass and concrete, and the three injured assailants. The second man still kneels on the pavement his hands over his face, blood oozing out between his fingers. Muffled noises bubble through blood. The third man drags his damaged leg as he stoops to pick up the knife in his right hand.

He hobbles towards Charlotte, whose back is pressed to the wall, rigid with fear.

In six strides, Blake reaches him, and grabs his right wrist. The man struggles, but he's too slow. Blake forces his arm down and back while slamming his hand into the man's elbow. The man screams again and Blake hears the satisfying crack of breaking bones. The knife clatters to the pavement. In a coup de grâce he strikes the fork of the man's carotid artery, and the unconscious body sinks to the pavement.

Blake kicks the knife away. 'Don't touch it Charlotte.'

She stares at the unconscious man lying at her feet. Blake once more scans the street and glances back to the men. Satisfied they are alone, and the muggers are contained for the moment, he kicks the knife towards the road. It glints as he manoeuvres it into a drain, waiting for the clink as it falls onto the concrete channel.

He pulls Charlotte away and hurries her past the men on the ground. They're damaged, but they are not his problem. She is, and he wishes she hadn't seen it. He draws her close and feels her shivering along his flank.

After a minute, she pulls out of his clasp and walks ahead. He follows in silence, knowing she needs time. The fight made him feel good. The adrenalin still sings in his blood, but he wishes she hadn't seen it. It's shocked her, but he can't undo that now. He wonders how many deserters live in the city.

It's the first he's seen, but he knows they exist. No one else has boots like that except the army. Regular soldiers don't hang about the street after curfew, and conscripts are confined to barracks until they're deployed. These must be deserters because he doesn't believe the bullshit about terrorists infiltrating the cities. If she weren't with him, he would have got it out of them. Now he needs to get her home and make sure she's okay.

Charlotte turns into a dreary tenement and climbs dark stairs to the second floor. She doesn't look to see if he's following. A couple with a small boy held between them, stirs in a dark recess under the stairs. The boy sleeps, but the parents are alert at the sound in the darkness. As she passes they draw themselves in, afraid of being seen by either the police or criminals. She says something that Blake doesn't catch and opens her apartment door, leaving it ajar behind her.

Blake hovers, doubting his welcome, but follows her in as she lights a paraffin lantern. In its glow, he sees the flat is a bedsit, one small room with an alcove for a bathroom. To his right is a single mattress. Between him and the bed there's a square of unbound beige coloured rug, roughly two by one metres. A wooden bench under a narrow window holds a single gas burner for cooking along with a small battery powered radio. On the wall ahead is a rack with a few clothes. That seems to be the sum total of her living space.

She places the lantern on the bench and then stands staring at it. He walks up behind her and slides his arms around her waist. She stiffens.

'I'm sorry Charlotte,' he says resting his forehead on the top of her beret. 'I'm really sorry you saw that.'

She turns, her eyes fixed on the small hollow at the base of his throat, and with toneless voice she says, 'you almost killed them.'

A bone deep weariness overtakes him and he wants to lie down. 'No, I just hurt them, but if I hadn't stopped them they would have killed us.'

'Why? What for? Who are they?'

'Don't know but they're desperate and it's what they do. We might have something useful like money. Do you have tea?' It's a distraction. He doesn't want to talk about the attack. 'Can I make tea? It'll help you— the shock you know.'

'I'm afraid.'

He pulls her to him, and her voice muffles against his chest.

'I'm afraid of you Blake,' but she doesn't pull away.

He slides off her beret, chucking it to the bed as her hair tumbles out. His palms feel its smooth silkiness as he arranges it in long strands down her back, tucking it behind her ears, giving himself time to think. Then he grasps her shoulders, holding her away from him so he can see her eyes. 'I will never hurt you Charlotte.'

She lowers her lashes unable to look at him. He kisses her forehead and drops his hands, turning to search the kitchen for a kettle. She pushes past him, taking a pot from a cupboard below the bench, and goes to the alcove to get water. Then she lights the gas ring, and places the pot on to boil while she takes two mugs from the cupboard, and a small box. He realises the building has no electricity, and wishes he hadn't mentioned tea.

She hands him a mug and says, 'there's no milk or sugar, sorry.'

As they sit side by side on the mattress sipping the hot liquid, his whole body tingles in awareness of her. She turns her face to him and he takes her mug, putting it on the floor with his. Then he kisses her, exploring her soft lips, pressing them apart as his breathing becomes more urgent. Blood thrums in his temples and he lowers her head to the pillow, his lips not leaving hers.

She stiffens pushing him away. 'Do you have condoms?'

'Christ.' He sits up and puts his head in his hands, rubbing his temples, concentrating on getting his body back under control. 'No.'

'I don't want to get pregnant.'

He's surprised. He would have bet her wanting condoms was a disease prevention thing not birth control. 'Don't you use birth control?'

'No, I used to but I can't afford it, and now it's not so easy to get since they changed the law. Going to the doctors costs as much as I earn in a month. Can't afford the doctors and can't afford the prescription, even if I could find a doctor who would give me one, seeing I'm unmarried. Sorry I shouldn't have let you kiss me. I should have said up front.'

'I'll be careful.'

'No. It doesn't work. My friend's bloke said that, and she got pregnant. They made them get married. I don't want to be forced to marry you and live with you for the rest of my life. I hardly know you.'

'Okay, it doesn't matter.' Blake says lying.

She says, 'if you don't want to go home you can sleep next to me. The floor's a bit hard. I'd like you to hold me, but you have to be good okay? Just cuddle.'

He lies back next to her on the narrow mattress, his arm around her. She rests her head on his shoulder with her body fitted along his flank, her leg hooked through his.

Blake tries to distract himself, listening to her breathe, and wonders what screwed up law prevents her getting contraception and forces people to marry. He hadn't heard of that. It's another adjustment among the many of his homecoming.

As she drifts into sleep, he closes his eyes, trying not to imagine her warm soft flesh, wondering how he can get hold of condoms. Are they also only on prescription now? He'll ask Rory about it tomorrow. Rage flares at the state of his country. Since he met Charlotte outside the bar tonight his anger had been silent, but now it's back.

As the sun creeps over the windowsill, Charlotte wakes with a start. Blake thrashes on the narrow mattress shouting, but she can't make out what he says. His elbow connects with her shoulder and she scrambles away to kneel on the rug, holding her hurt shoulder, her heart thumping in fear.

It takes a minute for her to realise he's still sleeping. It's just a bad dream. She's seen this before in the backroom of the club, and now she does what she's seen others do, stretching out her hand to shake his shoulder. 'Blake, wake up.'

His hand snakes out and grabs her throat, choking off her scream as she scrabbles desperately at his fingers. He wakes and drops his hand, horrified at what he's done.

She coughs, rubbing her bruised throat, wary he'll do something else to hurt her.

For long minutes, he stares and then his eyes clear. 'Christ sorry Charlotte. Fuck, I am so sorry.'

'What is it Blake?' Her voice croaks and she coughs again.

'It's a dream. That's all. It's a dream. I am so sorry.' He sits on the mattress his head bowed.

Gillian Long

Sadness swamps her. It's like this for so many men returning from war. She puts her arms around his waist, resting her cheek on his back. 'Do you want to tell me?'

5.

Jeremy stomps down the hall, a towel around his waist, his feet leaving damp imprints in the deep pile carpet. Despite his irritation, he hurries still dripping from the shower. The e-cript is playing the National Anthem, the tune he selected for his father's ring tone. It fuels a sense of urgency he can't ignore. He clears his throat as he flicks the remote saying, 'hello Dad.'

His father's face fills the screen. 'You left a message.'

Arnold Marabaux sits behind a large desk. The unforgiving Canberra sunlight floods through the window, casting him in featureless silhouette. He is in his own study, but still he wears his dark suit jacket, white shirt, and silver blue tie. The sparse hair on his head appears to flee backwards, retreating from his skull in windblown white fuzz. With his shoulders permanently raised and hunched, he reminds Jeremy of the gutter press's nickname for him. Marabou, the undertaker stork.

Jeremy glances away from the screen to gaze out the penthouse window. The view shows a section of the Brisbane

River across which he can see the ferry terminal. Above the terminal is a large signboard.

The picture depicts central Australia with Ayres Rock in the background. Two stockmen stand in the foreground, hats in hand, as they gaze across the vast dry land. White words scrawled across the red earth say, your country needs you.

Jeremy watches a ferry pull up as he says, 'I asked her to marry me.'

'And?'

'She said yes, of course.'

'Good. Is that all?'

'Yes.'

'I'll tell your mother.'

'Dad, you might be interested.'

'What is it?'

'Lincoln was at the Fuller's last night. I must say, I don't know what all the fuss is.'

'Did he say anything of interest?'

'Not really. I found him rather rude. He looks more hooligan than hero to me, hadn't even bothered to shave before he arrived for dinner.'

His father's face doesn't change, but a small sigh of exasperation escapes. 'You don't know what you are dealing with Jeremy. Don't do anything foolish. The man is not someone to get off side. The whole country thinks he's a blasted hero and the American and British Governments are making noises about what they're calling his treatment. I'm warning you son, you're not playing Buraco with your mother here. He's a dangerous man. We need him onside, at least until all this heroic furore blows over and people forget.'

'Can't we just get rid of him? He'll prove a traitor like Castile, you mark my words...' But his words go unheeded as Sir Arnold Marabaux hangs up, leaving Jeremy in a rage at his father's imperiousness.

Angrily he throws himself down onto a black leather sofa, and flicks the remote to switch from phone to video setting, looking for the AMC morning news. Lincoln's face fills the screen, and in frustration, he turns it off, throwing the remote onto the black glass and chrome coffee table as he gets up to finish dressing.

In his bedroom, he stands in front of the mirror, spraying product on his hair. Then with two brushes, he simultaneously slicks it back from his face. The dark strands gleam in helmeted obedience as he places the brushes back on the table. His hands smooth his hair and he bends his knees to smile at his reflection. One day the old bastard will realise who has the real power. When that day comes, he will ask his son's forgiveness for doubting him, ever seeing him as incompetent.

Jeremy examines his features, first from one angle then from the other. He winks with approval at the image and decides he will get breakfast down town before he goes into the office, but first he'll make a detour to pick up his brief case. He left it behind in Fuller's study last night when he offered to give Ava a lift home.

Five minutes later Jeremy leaves the apartment and walks down the deserted corridor to the bank of lifts. He wasn't surprised by Ava's nervousness at Lincoln's arrival last night. After all, she dumped him for Jeremy even though their relationship is not one he wants known. It gives him satisfaction to think that she preferred him to Blake, but it's a secret pleasure. Their common blood ensures that.

At the time, Jeremy wanted her to keep up the engagement pretence. It was convenient for her to have a fiancé, and would stop any rumours. He never thought Lincoln would make it home alive. She wouldn't listen to reason and had to tell the bloke. The wasted emotions of guilt, he smirks. It's not something from which he suffers.

When he drove her home, the tantrum surprised him. Ava had shouted, 'I would never have introduced you to that simpering bitch if I knew you were going to ask her to marry you. You're a fucking bastard. You're using her like you use me.'

It's not as if he has a choice, but he's not going to admit that. It doesn't excuse her behaviour although she's probably premenstrual. She wouldn't let him in her bed and it might account for her temper.

God save him from crazy women. What did she expect—that he would marry her? Where's the profit in that alliance even if it was legal to marry one's half-sister. But he doesn't want to think about Ava and her bad temper right now.

Sometimes he wishes he had never found her. It took him years to piece together his father's secret past. It's his insurance against his father's control. He hasn't used it yet but when the time comes, he will.

Jeremy smiles. It's one thing hiding a past that would have the Australian establishment in shock, but if the world found out, it would also hurt Jeremy as much as his father. Circumstances would have to be just right to use the information.

Old man Siarlosa, his paternal grandfather, may be out of gaol and exiled back in Cosenza, but he wouldn't countenance divorce. Nor would he look kindly on Jeremy's parent's marriage. Not if he knew Arnie's first wife, Ava's mother, was still alive and living in an Australian private mental health clinic. Mental health is an interesting euphemism. Unless someone doped up to the eyebrows all the time can be called mentally healthy.

Two identities would be useful he supposes, one for use in Italy one for Australia. In Italy the name Siarlosa is revered, in Australia the name Marabaux instils fear. But his Dad's secret is safe, and it will stay like that until the moment of Jeremy's choosing. One day it will come in handy.

In the meantime, Jeremy wouldn't be keen to become a bastard if Hester and Arnie's marriage was annulled by Rome, even if he could manage to keep the bigamy under wraps from the law. That and he hasn't yet finished enjoying Ava.

Sometimes he fantasises about telling her, revealing their real relationship. He imagines the look on her face when she realises what they have is incest in its purest form. There is a certain deliciousness in the taste of forbidden fruit. But Ava can't know, not until he's ready to tell her.

Today he has better things to worry him, like the meeting with the chairman of Homeland Security Enterprises about the community-policing contract. Something about the Northern quadrant being cut that he wants Jeremy to discuss with his father. It'll bring in a tidy profit and Jeremy's partial to money, especially when it takes little effort to make.

He likes Jarrod von Wilkins. The man does what he's told. They understand each other, unlike Zac Randolph or his old man Sir Miriam. Why is it, media moguls always think they run things? Still, he'll give Zac a ring and see if he can tone down the hype on Blake a little. He's sick of it. Surely, the public are too by now. It's been going on for weeks. The more the bloke avoids them, the more they seem to feed on his story.

They should never have allowed Lincoln leave. If they had kept him confined to barracks, and suppressed the story in the first place, the press would have no oxygen. He blames the Americans and the British, thinking they can interfere in his country's domestic politics.

Jeremy sets the Fuller's address in the sat nav., and the four by four drives up the ramp towards the underground car park exit. It stops under a large sign that says cast light into the shadows of evil: a vote for Priestly is a vote for Australia. The road is clear as the vehicle pulls out into the street. At least with fuel rationing the congestion is not as bad now.

Petrol, even when it's available, is so expensive few can afford it, but it keeps the fuel cartels in business and that pays the bills, which suits Jeremy fine. As far as he is concerned, most people don't have enough collective brain cells to drive, let alone vote. There is definitely something to be said for a two or even three-tiered society.

The old European class system had something back in the day. It's just a pity they became all holier than thou about it. No wonder his grandfather left the old country to make a new life in Australia. Europe has gone to the pack. Now the old bastard is back where he started, albeit with a bit more dosh in his back pocket. There's a lesson there, don't get caught before you know you are holding all the cards. Jeremy smirks. He's a master at that.

Half an hour later, he pulls up outside the Fuller's mansion. Closing his car door softly, he walks around to the side gate. Blake and Rory are standing inside the open front door. He doesn't want to talk to them, and he certainly doesn't want Lincoln ruining his day. He wonders if he can sneak in unnoticed, retrieve his briefcase, and leave. With his back against the corner of the porch, out of view of the front door, he eavesdrops on Blake and Rory's conversation.

What Jeremy hears causes him to risk a look around the corner, just as Blake pulls off his shirt and hands it to Rory. He waits as they move off together towards the East wing. Then he runs on the balls of his feet through the entrance hall and branches off down a corridor towards the study, to retrieve his briefcase. He leaves before Rory and Blake return.

No one sees him as he retreats across the lawn and opens the gate, and no one notices his car as it pulls out into the road. He heads downtown smiling in triumph. What he overheard is gold.

6.

While Jeremy drives towards the Fuller's house, Rory stands on the terrace looking out across the river. He thinks of his father's quote from a forgotten American politician. Is he really confusing the unparalleled with the implausible? He blows across the surface of his coffee to cool it before taking a sip.

The heat rises as the sun climbs in the sky and he glances at his watch, eight am and 36 degrees. It'll be another scorcher. They seem to go on for weeks lately and it's already April, but there's still no sign of rain. What happened to the supposed cooling of the sun that was to bring on a mini ice age?

Perhaps the warming doomsayers weren't trying to undermine the economy after all. Blake would say that, but the jury is still out in Rory's opinion. Anyway, even if they are right, it's too late now to do anything. At least with the drought, the river won't flood this year. If you look hard enough, you can always find the positives.

The garden gate slams and he smiles. Only Blake forgets to hold the bloody thing, so it closes slowly. There's an hour and a half before he needs to be at his office, so he and Blake can eat breakfast together. It'll be good to sit and chat. Blake might loosen up when the others aren't there.

He calls through to the kitchen. 'Mrs. Clarke can you rustle up some breakfast, bacon and eggs, beans, mushrooms the works, sausages too. Blake's here. We'll be on the terrace. Oh, and more coffee and maybe juice, but only if it's freshly squeezed.'

'Yes Mr Fuller.' Mrs. Clarke rolls her eyes as she returns to the fridge where she has just put away the breakfast things.

Rory walks to the front door, opening it as Blake lifts his hand to ring the bell. 'Ah the wanderer returns. How did your date go with the barmaid? I have Clarkie organising breakfast for us. Come out to the terrace. Do you want coffee or tea? Good grief is that blood?' His finger jabs at Blake's shirt.

'Coffee'd be great thanks.' Blake walks past Rory into the house. 'Where is everyone?'

'Out—busy with their lives. Dad's gone to sort out a crisis at the warehouse and Mum's taken Em shopping.'

'What about you?'

'I have an hour and a half before I need to be at the office. That's enough time to eat and for you to tell me all about it.'

'About what?'

'Whatever I can wring out of you, like why you have blood on your shirt.'

Blake looks down, pulling out his shirt to look at the spray of blood dotted across the right of his midriff. 'It's nothing. Can you lend me a clean one?'

'Sure and if you give that to me I'll chuck it in the wash.'

Blake pulls off the shirt, and Rory scans his friend's lean muscled body, taking in the puckered angry round scars at the base of his right shoulder.

'Is that where they got you?'

'Yep.'

'The news said the bullets didn't hit anything vital.'

'Na went straight through and out the other side.'

'Shit, you're lucky to be alive. What does it feel like to be shot?'

'Like shit. Where's that shirt?'

'Okay. Sorry... It's in my suite. Come.'

After changing into one of Rory's shirts, the two men go out to the terrace and sit at the outdoor table. Rory leans forward to pour juice from the condensation-beaded jug. 'So, two visits in two days. Can't keep away from your old mate hey, or have you just come to gloat?'

'Gloat?'

'Yeah another conquest on your never ending list.'

Blake takes a long drink of juice and places his glass back on the table. 'What the fuck are you talking about?'

'The barmaid, did you bed her?'

'No, and it's none of your business, except I need a favour.'

'So that's why you're here.'

Blake looks at Rory. 'You know you're my best mate. It's not you I've been avoiding. It's hard to deal with people at the moment, okay. I can't handle it. Last night was fine. Your Mum and Dad are... well they are always good to me. No one gave me the third degree, except that wanker Em's marrying. Christ, I don't know what's got into her.'

'He's listed as Australia's most eligible bachelor.'

'Yeah, but I thought she had more taste.'

'He's all right; a bit pompous is all, but he'll look after her. What's the favour?'

'I need condoms.'

Rory looks taken aback and then laughs. 'Christ is that all. I thought you were going to ask me to get you out of going to Canberra, and while I will do anything for you, you know I can't do that.'

Blake shakes his head. 'It'll be all right going to Canberra, maybe even interesting. I don't mind.'

'I'll try to get some today. How much longer are you here? Will a carton do?' He laughs at his joke. 'So the barmaid's a goer then. She doesn't have a friend does she?'

Blake shakes his head. He doesn't want to talk about Charlotte. She's not just shag, but he doesn't know what she is yet either. 'Can you get her birth control?'

'You want condoms and birth control. That's a bit over the top isn't it?' He sees Blake's mouth set in a hard line and says, 'okay, okay. What type?'

'I don't know, I'll ask. Who thought a law like this was a good idea? How did it get through Parliament? What is wrong with Australia that they keep voting these bastards in?'

'Come on mate. You can't speak like that, there's a war on.'

'There's been a war on for years, so what. What happened to free speech? Have they banned that too?'

'Geez Blake, it's just unpatriotic. The country's fighting for survival and has to do anything it can to stay afloat. We can't afford the freedoms we had in more innocent times. There are potential insurgents everywhere, trained and battle hardened from fighting on the side of the terrorists. You of all people should know that. If you keep shooting your mouth off, you'll get into serious bother. Hold on, here's our breakfast. Thank you Mrs. Clarke. Just leave the trolley next to the table, we'll help ourselves.'

The men remain silent until Mrs. Clarke leaves, and then busy themselves with their breakfast. Rory separates his food on the plate and stabs a mushroom.

Blake says, 'I don't recognise this country anymore. What the fuck happened?'

Rory looks thoughtful. Then with the mushroom on his fork, he jabs a piece of bacon on the tines, dipping the duo into the yolk of a fried egg. He lifts the lot into his mouth and masticates his food as he gazes out at the river. When he's finished chewing, he puts his knife and fork on his plate.

'It was bad, don't you remember?' He looks at Blake's face. 'No perhaps you were inside then, but I think it was before you were shipped out. It was after they tightened the new work laws to boost productivity for the war effort. Jesus, women were getting pregnant just to get the maternity payment, and avoid work. All of a sudden, we had a baby boom. Then the second crash happened, and the jobs dried up completely. The maternity payment was the first thing to go, a good thing in my book.' He takes another mouthful of food and chews, musing before saying, 'anyway, no one had any money least of all the Government. They said that having three layers of administration cost Australia a hundred billion.'

'Bullshit. Jesus Rory I can't believe you buy this crap.'

Rory ignores him saying, 'it was bad Blake. You were lucky you weren't here. People were starving. At the time, the Government promised free food stamps and medical care.'

Blake says, 'I was here then. I saw them, but it doesn't account for draconian laws.'

Rory shakes his head, unaware of the irony of him thinking Blake's deployment was better than being in the country. 'It got worse. You couldn't go out in the street without being mobbed for a job. Everyone agreed the States were wasteful, a luxury we couldn't afford.'

Blake feels his anger brimming over and fights for control. 'The bastards offered free food stamps as a bribe. It was a ploy to get people to vote for them, along with a yes vote for the referendum so they could rewrite the Constitution. Most of the hundred million States spent went on services, stuff they have contracted out now, like the police.'

Rory says, 'they haven't contracted everything.'

'You tell me what's left then.'

'They didn't contract out the Military or the National Homeland Security Police, or the Intelligence Services, or the Treasury.' He pauses. 'There was talk of the NHS Police being merged with community policing, but it hasn't happened yet.'

Blake frowns. 'Marabou will never let his secret police be outsourced, no matter what the speculation is. Anyway, none of those services was ever State run. I can't think of anything the States ran that they left intact. Schools, universities, licensing, prisons, child safety, aged care, the courts, energy, communications, all contracted.'

'And the hospitals,' Rory says dryly.

'I'm aware of that… and the hospitals… But that was the stuff on which the States spent the hundred billion. It wasn't waste. They could have saved billions from ending the war in the Middle East. Instead, people blindly let them do what they like, so long as it doesn't concern them. It's bullshit the way people will turn a blind eye to what makes them uncomfortable.'

Rory raises his eyebrow. 'Mister holier than thou, and from where do you think your money comes? Anyway, I'm not here to argue the toss. You asked and I'm just telling you how it all came about. What I was saying is that the abortion rate went up exponentially after the crash. Most people couldn't afford babies, and as usual the povos had nothing else to do but make them.'

'The fucking crash wouldn't have happened if we'd bothered to read the writing on the wall. You can't abolish taxes and give carte blanch to businesses to do what they want without blow back. If we don't redistribute wealth, it is locked up in the bank accounts of the elite, or goes off shore. That's a recipe for economic disaster. We sold our birth right to multinationals in exchange for cheap shonky shit we didn't need and very soon couldn't afford.'

Sighing Rory says, 'if you are going to keep interrupting I won't bother.'

'Okay sorry, go on.'

'Well, where was I? Oh, yes… When the churches and right to life groups lobbied to ban abortion. The Government didn't cave because they thought that mothers would abandon their babies. It's hard enough getting foster parents for abused kids, without adding to the burden. Anyway, it's usually the wrong kind of people having kids when they can't afford them. Australia has more than we like of those.'

Blake interrupts. 'No. Its bullshit. They want to ban abortion to grow markets. They need more people to buy their rubbish…'

Rory rolls his eyes but carries on as if Blake hasn't spoken. 'So, in the end the Government had an insurmountable problem. There was no money and no easy way to solve a growing crisis, let alone the internal conflict it caused the country. You remember when it started; people marched protesting the changes every week. You were one of them. Everything from unlawful assembly to mandatory sentencing and conscription. Fat lot of good it did you.'

Blake shakes his head. 'I never heard about the contraception and forced marriage laws.'

'Yeah.' Rory glances at Blake's frown and decides to skip the wise cracks. 'I'm getting there. The final straw happened when they proposed laws against abortion. You remember there were eight killed in that demo.'

'I don't think I was here then.'

'No, maybe not. Anyway, what else could the government do? Eventually they dumped the right to life laws in exchange for changes to the Marriage Act. It cuts down on undesirables breeding and amended all the other forms of perversion that bleeding hearts over the years had brought into law.'

'Jesus. It's archaic. Why didn't the people march on that one also?'

'Don't know... but by that time, they had cracked down hard against unlawful assembly via the national security laws. There was a big media blitz against unpatriotic behaviour. They said it encouraged terrorism. Also, I guess it was a confusing policy, and with everything else happening, it slipped under the radar. The trouble was there was this crazily fractured Senate full of conspiracy theorists, and people who could barely read and write, let alone understand legislation. One of the journos back in the day called Australia the Tin-Foil Hat Republic.' Rory smiles at Blake. 'I thought that was pretty funny.'

Blake shakes his head. 'No it's not funny, it's seriously wrong.'

'Jesus.' Rory wipes his mouth on a napkin. 'What happened to your sense of humour? Keep your shirt on, sorry my shirt. You asked. I'm just saying how it happened.' He pauses collecting his thoughts. 'Anyway there were a lot of rumours. Then... well it was too late, the law passed. Remember, they had a majority in both houses—still have amazingly enough. So you can't complain. Its democracy, something you are always banging on about. It wasn't all bad though. You have to admit the Marriage Act was an elegant solution, and practical. We get to choose who breeds, and if you have no money, you can't breed—simple. Problem solved and let me tell you we were being swamped by people who didn't want to live like Australians. Yet they were breeding like crazy. The place was overrun with refugees, and their sprogs.'

Blake can't believe what he's hearing. 'I bang on about democracy for good reason. Once we give up its principles, even a few of them, we are on a slippery slope. We will never wind it back, but never mind that. The law is just wrong, and worse if a woman is pregnant she's forced into marriage.'

'So is the man. It makes a bloke careful you know. Anyway, if she puts it out there what can she expect? If he's good enough to fuck he's good enough to marry right.'

'What about you Rory, do you abstain?'

'Christ no, but I'm careful and that's the point isn't it? I use condoms and for men it's different—more physical than for a woman.'

'I don't think that's right.' Blake's bewildered by his friend's views. He's sure Rory wasn't always like this.

Rory puts a large chunk of sausage in his mouth, and chews thoughtfully. 'Not that I have much success. Unlike you, they are not banging on my door to get in. That's why I want to get married.' He pauses wondering if he should say what's on his mind. To hell with the consequences. Blake will just have to live with it. 'And I'd quite like to marry Ava if that's not going to put your nose out of joint. She's the right sort and will suit me well as a wife.'

Blake looks at his untouched food and takes a sip of coffee before lifting his fork, giving himself time to think. Does he care? He's surprised Rory likes Ava, although why not, she's an attractive woman. He searches for an emotional reaction, but there isn't one. 'I have no feelings on the subject one way or another. I'm well and truly over her so if you want her, go for it, but I'm warning you the woman is shallow.' He shakes his head. It's none of his business. 'The real question is does she want you? Have you asked her yet?'

'No.' Rory grins. 'I thought I should get the all clear from you first. I didn't want to encroach on your turf.'

'She's not my turf as you so gallantly put it. Nor has she ever been my turf. Ava's her own woman, so you'd better seek her consent before planning wedding bells.'

'You know although you don't see me as such, I am quite a catch; perhaps not as influential or good-looking as Jeremy, but I have more money, and given my uncle-in-law is now the Governor-General my influence is growing. She'd be mad to refuse. Hell, marry me and she'll have a title one day.'

Blake grins. 'You're a tosser you know that. You're as bad as Jeremy.'

'Careful. I might resemble that remark. Na, no one's as much of a tosser as Jeremy. Eat. Your breakfast is getting cold. I have to head off soon. You can stay here or I can give you a lift into town. I'm taking the car so we can stop at the warehouse on the way, and see if Dad's got some condoms damaged in shipment,' he says making speech marks in the air, 'that haven't been registered yet.'

8.

The Watch House has no windows. Its electric lights flicker, dazzling Blake as he enters handcuffed, and guided by the charge officer. Silently, he complies knowing the drill. It's a different Watch House, but the same procedure as when he was first arrested. He struggles to contain the rage building from its bed of fear because he knows it's pointless protesting.

Silently, he recites Richard Lovelace as he once did in Baghdad to conquer his claustrophobic panic. Stone walls do not a prison make, nor iron bars a cage. They take his watch, phone, wallet, keys, belt, and shoes before pushing him into one of the glass booths called fishbowls at the back of the room. There are six men in this one, but they look away as he enters.

A rank odour rises in a miasma of stale sweat, sour grog breath, and unwashed feet, but it's better than the prison he was first thrown into in Baghdad. That was a room with no windows, too low for him to stand upright, and too short to stretch out. It was a concrete box in a compound of similar concrete boxes. At the time, he didn't know there were other men in each box.

The horror still gives him nightmares as he relives the pitch-blackness. His shallow breath told him the stench that rose from the sticky floor, was old blood, shit, and vomit, and it was cold, winter cold. He jerks his head to one side taking deep breaths, forestalling the flashback. With herculean mental effort, he contains rising panic as he stands inside the fishbowl.

There is no bench space left, so Blake leans against the glass. An officer bangs on the wall and tells him to get off. He squats to his haunches going within to explore his mind and block out the present, but his skin prickles with hyper-vigilance, anticipating a lunge from one of the prisoners.

Thirty minutes later, the charge officer opens the fishbowl, jerking his head for Blake to follow. He stands up assuming Rory has arrived and follows the officer down a corridor to an interview room.

Rory remains silent until the man leaves, locking them in together, and then he says, 'Christ Blake, a woman was murdered. They say you did it. Tell me you didn't do it, please mate.'

The anguish in Rory's eyes shows Blake how worried he is, but why would anyone think he murdered some woman. 'Who is she?'

'They're still trying to find out.'

'They don't know who she is, and yet they think I killed her. Doesn't that sound a little strange to you?' He shakes his head, his hands clasped on the table in front of him, his knuckles showing white. He is worried, but he thinks Rory's panicking. 'Where did the murder take place and when?'

Rory runs his hands through his hair. 'Sorry man you're right, it's screwy. They said they found the body near your hotel. Apparently, she died in the early hours of yesterday morning, the night after you had dinner at home. They found her blood on your shirt.'

Blake's shocked by the accusation. It's unreal—just another horrendous screw-up.

'Just say you didn't do it, please.' Rory says.

'No.' He shakes his head and puts it in his hands. 'I didn't kill her. I wasn't even near my hotel in the early hours of yesterday morning.'

'Where were you?'

'Never mind.'

'Come on, Blake.' Rory watches his friend who leans forward on the upright interview room chair, elbows on the table and his forehead resting on clasped hands, as he stares at the floor between his knees. 'Okay if you didn't kill her why was her blood on your shirt?'

Blake raises his head. 'Bullshit. It wasn't her blood.'

'Whose blood was it then Blake?'

'I don't know. A deserter.'

'What?'

'He attacked us with a couple of his cronies and I broke his nose. He had a knife.'

'Where? If we can verify this...' Rory looks excited. 'When did you break his nose?'

'The night I came for dinner, or early the next morning anyway.'

'What time.'

'About quarter to three.'

'I thought you said it was morning.'

'Yeah.'

'You broke curfew. Shit.'

'Yep, I'm done for no matter what.'

'No, no don't say that.'

'You said he attacked us. Was the barmaid with you?'

'Yes and stop calling her the barmaid. Her name's Charlotte, but you can't bring her into it.'

Rory looks pensive. 'Why would they say it was the woman's blood on your shirt if it was someone else's—a deserter? How do you know he was a deserter?'

'I know them, or their sort.'

'Okay. Let me think.' Rory stares at the door. He can't quite believe it, but he has to focus. Blake's screwed unless he can figure something out. He wants to believe him, but he can't get the blood match on the shirt out of his head. Forensics like that don't lie. What was Blake doing at that time in the morning? It fits, but where's the motive. It makes little sense for Blake to kill her, but all he has to do is ask the barmaid. 'Let me talk to the barmaid.'

'No. Rory you can't talk to her. I don't want her dragged into this. You know once they start asking questions, they'll implicate her, and she'll end up in shit for breaking curfew. I don't want to do that to her.'

'I'll just talk, nothing more, until we find out what they've got on you or why they think you've done it. I just need to talk...' Rory trails off wondering if the dead woman could be the barmaid. 'Blake, um... the dead woman... It's not... it couldn't be the barmaid could it?'

'What? No, she's fine. I left her at ten-thirty this morning.' It penetrates Blake's mind with sudden clarity. Rory doesn't believe him. Christ, even his best friend thinks he did it.

Rory says, 'okay let's back track. I need to get this right. You went straight from home to the bar after dinner, and then where did you go?'

'Shit Rory, you're talking to me. You know I wouldn't kill... you know I wouldn't lie about something like that.'

'Okay sorry. Look, I called a colleague. He's a barrister.'

'No, I want you to do it Rory. I don't trust anyone else.'

'Blake I am a corporate lawyer. You need a criminal lawyer and a barrister. We'll get a QC to get you out as quickly as possible.'

'You have to get the shirt Rory. The blood on the shirt will prove I didn't do it or at least I can prove it's not her blood.'

'I can't Blake—its evidence.'

'So what—they can just say it's her blood and I can't defend myself against that claim?'

'Okay. I get your point. I'll see what I can do. You said the bloke who attacked you had a knife. Where is it now?'

'It's down a drain, but you don't want to touch it. It'll kill you.'

'What?'

'It's something they learned over there. They coat the weapons with poison, so anyone without protection dies. It's a pretty horrible death, but that's classified. You can't talk about it okay.'

'Christ.' Rory rubs his hand over his mouth.

'Yeah it's pretty ruthless. There are no rules anymore, it's just kill or be killed. Rory...' Blake scans his friend's face before speaking again. 'Rory, I just want you to know mate, the reason I haven't told you what happened over there is because I don't know the words, I haven't sorted them out in my head. There are so many lies, I don't know what to believe or trust. It's not something to be proud of. It's brutal and you don't want to know. It's not something anyone wants to know.'

'But you saved all those people.' Rory sees Blake's mouth press into a line as he shakes his head. 'Whatever man. Look I have to go. I'll be back as soon as I've sorted out a few things.' He stands up, 'they're opposing bail. You'll have to stay in the lock-up until I can get you before a magistrate.'

Rory leaves Blake in the Watch House and goes out to his car. For a moment, he sits in contemplation wanting to believe Blake. Then he takes out his CellTab to make a phone call to his office.

'Rochelle can you ring Lachlan Bowery and tell him I have work for him. Make a time for me to speak with him. Then apply for an independent forensic test for the blood on Blake Lincoln's shirt. The police have taken it as evidence.'

After he hangs up, he touches the screen on the dash that shows a map of the city. The car starts and pulls out into the traffic. Rochelle's a good junior and will get the job done. While the car drives, he scans the legislation regarding independent forensics. Ten minutes later the car eases into an empty parking space outside the bar.

It's three-thirty, and he's not sure if she'll be at work. He feels guilty ignoring Blake's ban, but he has to be sure. Anyone coming back from that war... well they are not the same. Look at the suicide rate, and the number of them in prisons around the country and Blake's changed.

He's not the same person he was at Uni. There is something cold and hard about him, a kind of ruthlessness. He doesn't seem to care about things, not like he did, and that worries Rory.

As he walks into the dim bar, his eyes take a moment to adjust after the harsh afternoon sunlight. There are five patrons, an elderly couple, two men in their thirties both engrossed in their CellTabs, and a solitary man in his sixties who reads a paperback.

The barmaid dries glasses behind the bar, gazing towards the etched window. As he walks in, she puts the cloth and glass on the counter. She's prettier than he remembers, lucky old Blake, trust him to get all the good-looking ones.

'Hi, I don't know if you remember me...'

'Yes you're Blake's friend. I thought he would be in today. Has something happened?' Her eyes are round and her hands pluck the hem of her tee shirt.

He's not sure what to say. Can he tell her that Blake's in gaol? He looks around the room. 'Is there somewhere we can talk in private?'

'No. I can't leave the bar, but no one's listening. Where is he, what's happened?' Charlotte feels panic rising and takes a breath, but her chest is tight.

'Look, he's been arrested.'

'Huh.' She sucks in a breath, staring at him. 'What for?' The three men flash into her mind, but surely not.

'Murder.'

It's true. One must have died. She holds her breath, wary now of saying anything. She thinks this man is Blake's friend. But what if he isn't.

'I just need to know if you were with him.'

'When?'

'The night before last.'

'Who are you?'

'I'm his friend and his lawyer.'

'Okay,' she lets her breath go.

The man reading comes up to the bar for service. Charlotte says to Rory. 'You'll have to order something so we can talk.'

'Okay.'

'What will you have?'

'A beer. The one on tap.'

She pulls the beer, takes his money, and serves the man waiting. When she's finished, she picks up the cloth, and begins drying glasses again, standing side-on to him looking towards the fresco-etched window. 'Okay, I'm listening.'

'I just need to know if you were with him.'

'What time?'

'Christ. Either you were with him or you weren't. I'm not trying to trick you. I won't dob you in or anything. I just need to establish his alibi.'

'Do you think he killed the man?'

'What man?'

'The man you said was murdered.'

'I didn't say any man was murdered.'

She bites her lip putting down the glass and picking up another one. Panic tugs at the edge of her mind. She's not thinking straight. Why did she listen to him? If she hadn't breached curfew none of this would have happened. Now she's in deep shit. If she says she was with him, she's admitting a crime. She'll lose her job, and they'll conscript her. Tears sting her eyes and her throat chokes. If she doesn't say anything then Blake has no witness to say the man attacked them first. He was just defending her. They'll arrest her for breaking curfew as well as being a party to leaving the man there to die. She doesn't know what to do.

Rory watches her, puzzled by her distress. Either she was with Blake or she wasn't. What's the problem?

In a low voice she says, 'he was protecting me.'

'What?'

Resigned she turns to face him. 'He was protecting me. The man had a knife.'

Rory breathes a sigh of relief. Blake's story is true. 'Okay thanks.'

'What will happen now?'

'What do you mean?' He drinks his beer and looks around the bar as someone opens the door to the street. It's the elderly couple leaving.

Charlotte puts down her tea towel and goes to clean their table. When she returns she says, 'where is he, can I see him?'

'No. He's in the Watch House. They won't allow visitors. Sorry I've forgotten your name.'

'Charlotte.'

'Oh yeah. I appreciate you being honest with me, but I need to know one more thing.'

Her eyes slide sideways as she bites her lip.

'I know it's a bit indelicate, but was he with you all night?' Tears well, glistening on the rims of her lower lids, and he feels guilty again like he's somehow breaching his friends trust, but he has to be sure. 'What time did he leave you?'

'I don't know, maybe seven.'

Rory lets out a sigh of relief. Blake arrived at the Fuller's about eight so he must have gone straight from Charlotte to the house. 'Thanks Charlotte.'

'What will happen to him? Will I be arrested also?'

'What? Why would you be arrested?'

'Because I was with him when it happened.'

'When what happened?'

'When he killed the man.'

'What man?' It dawns on Rory. 'Did he kill the man with the knife, Charlotte?'

'You said he did.'

'No I didn't. Did he kill him Charlotte?'

'I don't know. There was a lot of blood. I think the man's nose was broken.'

Rory laughs and at once pulls himself together. 'I don't think a broken nose would kill him,' he says relieved that Blake is telling the truth. 'This has nothing to do with that Charlotte.

A woman was murdered, and he's accused of killing her, but if he was with you all night, it can't be him. Don't worry about the other. I'll try to find out, but if they are deserters, they won't dare tell the police. It's the murdered woman that's the problem.'

'What will happen to me if you tell them I was with him?'

'I'm not going to tell anyone anything just yet Charlotte.' He realises how that sounds and says, 'I am just doing some preliminary investigations that's all. Don't worry okay?'

'But if you say I was his alibi they'll let him go, won't they?'

'Yes, probably.'

'So why won't you say anything?'

Rory sighs, 'because I shouldn't be here. He told me I wasn't to implicate you, but I had to know he didn't do it. Screw it. Sorry.'

'Why doesn't he want to implicate me?'

'What? I don't know.' Rory finishes his beer and gets up to go.

'Please. Please tell me.'

'Ah, it's probably some kind of misplaced gallantry. The bloke's a romantic fool.'

'Please wait. If I tell the police he was with me, what will happen to me?'

'You'll be charged with breaching curfew and so will he. Don't do it Charlotte. I can get him off this charge because it's obvious he didn't do it, but I can't get him off breach of curfew. If you tell them that's what he was doing, they'll send him back.'

Later that night, when Charlotte's finished singing, she goes into the back room of the club and finds a corner of carpet on which to sleep. Evan comes into the room and sits next to her.

'Where is lover boy?'

'Who?'

'Come on, Charlie it's me you're talking to. Two nights in a row, you're all over him, then he's gone. Did he get what he wanted and dump you?'

'No, and it's not like that. Don't be horrible Evan. He's in gaol.'

'Jesus, you're kidding. What happened?'

'Oh Ev, they said he killed someone, but he didn't he was with me. I feel awful. If I tell them, he'll be charged with breaking curfew. If I say nothing, he's charged with murder. I don't know what to do.'

Evan sits next to her, silent for a while and then he says, 'who is he Charlie? I mean what do you know about him?' She takes a breath, but he interrupts. 'Yeah, yeah I know he's some kind of hero who saved a whole lot of people, but other than that what do you know about him?'

'He's kind.'

'Bullshit, he's just trying to get into your knickers. Men are always kind when there's that in the offing. What do you really know about him?'

'He was a trainee doctor, an intern before he was arrested and his parents were Embassy types. He grew up in Saudi and speaks Arabic.'

'That's it.'

'Yep pretty well.'

'Where does he live?'

She shrugs, 'a room in the hotel where I work.'

'Shit, he must have money.'

'Yeah. I don't know, but I think his friend's rich.'

'His friend?'

'Yes. He's a lawyer, and he told me Blake's in prison.'

'What's the lawyer's name? I'll see what I can find out.'

'Thanks Ev. His name's Rory Fuller, but be careful, don't get into trouble over it.'

'You know me Charlie... the phantom.' He grins and winces.

'What is it Ev are you in pain?'

'It's nothing, just toothache.'

'Do you have anything?'

'Yeah, I know a bloke. It'll be okay. I'll go there tonight, but I need dollars. Do you have Charlie?'

Charlotte pulls out her purse. 'I only have a hundred. Will it do?'

'Can you spare it?'

'Yes,' she says lying, wondering where she'll find her rent money.

'Thanks I owe you big time.' He hugs her and gets up to leave.

The next morning Evan's back, shaking Charlotte's shoulder to wake her. The room she's in is windowless, dark, and dank with the breath of fifty plus sleeping people. The smell of unwashed bodies and old shoes greets Charlotte as she opens her eyes.

Feeble light from the passageway illuminates the array of humped forms around her. People huddle, curled up with others or alone, some stretched out on the carpet, some in sleeping bags. Charlotte creeps out, following Evan, trying not to wake them.

Outside the predawn light casts ghostly shadows into the stairwell. There are still fifteen minutes before curfew lifts and Charlotte can walk home, so they sit on the steps. Evan's cheek is swollen and red. She lays her palm on his face feeling the heat from his skin. 'It looks painful. Did they pull it?'

'Yeah bloody butchers, but it had an abscess, so better that than blood poisoning I guess. I found out heaps about your bloke Charlie.'

'How?'

'There's a way into the library... never mind. I looked it up on line.'

'Shit Evan you must be careful. You'll get caught.'

'Na. I spend a lot of time in the library.' He grins and grimaces, wiping the blood that drools from the corner of his mouth with his thumb. 'It's the safest place don't ya know, pigs don't read.'

Charlotte casts a worried look up the stairs as if she expects someone to be listening. 'Okay what did you find?'

'Get this; your man's a bloody billionaire.'

'What... no. He's a conscript.'

'I'm not sure he is. I couldn't find any record of his arrest, but maybe it's suppressed because he's a rich boy. Anyway, his parents died in the bomb blast in the Saudi Embassy a few years back. They left him shares. He's the majority shareholder in the Australian Medical Conglomerate, the one that manages all the hospitals in the country. The Chairman of the Board and next largest shareholder is a bloke called William Fuller, and he has a son who is a corporate lawyer, Rory Fuller. He owns the third largest block of shares.'

'Rory, that's his friend, the one who told me Blake's in gaol.'

'Yeah but get this. There's a girl also, Emilie Fuller, and she's engaged to Jeremy Marabaux. You know who that is, don't you?'

'Shit—who doesn't? Christ, I had no idea. I'm not sure if I'm in deeper trouble now or not. He seems so nice. I was sure I could trust him and you know me, I can smell bullshit from a thousand paces.'

'There's more.'

'What?'

'He was engaged to Ava Murchison, the model.'

All Charlotte's energy seems to drain from her as she remembers photos of the glamorous model.

Evan sees her wilt and hurries to change the subject. 'He's a martial arts expert too, like he won all these championships at some fight club. I can't remember its name. So, maybe he did kill the woman.'

That explains a lot, Charlotte thinks.

'They found the body yesterday, close to your hotel. You never know Charlie....'

'Hang on a sec,' she says. 'Are you sure it was yesterday?'

'Yeah.' That's what the paper said.

'Not the day before?'

'No I don't think so. A street cleaner found her yesterday morning.'

Charlotte grabs his arm. 'What time did she die?'

'I don't know. Do I look like a pathologist?'

Charlotte smiles at him. 'No, but you look a bit like a pathologist's specimen. How can I get hold of Rory?'

'He lives on the river at Hawthorne, and he has an office in the city.'

The cathedral clock strikes six, and Charlotte gets up to go. 'Thanks Ev, I hope your mouth is better soon.' She kisses the top of his head and stuffs her hair into her beret. 'Do you want to come back to my place? It's still early and the cops are not usually around asking for I.Ds. just yet. I might have some eggs left.'

'Na can't eat with my mouth like this, but thanks.' He watches Charlotte run up the stairs and duck through the crumbling arch before getting up and going back to the club.

7.

Charlotte lets herself into the empty bar. She feels exhilarated and there is an aria playing in her head. She can't get the smile off her face, but tries to suppress it in case she jinxes her luck. What happens if he doesn't come back? He said he would, but what happens if he doesn't? She can't let herself fall for him; it would be too much to bear. Why is she thinking about him? She has work to do. The idea they are somehow connected and she is no longer alone, is all an illusion.

'Charlotte, before you open the bar I want to speak with you.' Malcolm Patterson, beverage manager for the hotel, stands at the door behind the bar. One of his narrow shoulders presses against the doorjamb. He's been there five minutes waiting for her, his irritation building as he anticipated her lateness. He glances impatiently at his watch, but it's one minute to eleven. She's cutting it fine.

'Yes Mr Patterson.'

'Come through to my office.'

Charlotte follows. He waits until she closes the door before walking back to his desk. Picking up a letter opener, he flips it over repeatedly with a practiced flick of the fingers of one hand. It reminds Charlotte of the assailant flicking his knife and she shudders. The desk is clear except for a remote propped in its ornate holder.

Charlotte stands in front of him, hands linked behind her back waiting for him to speak. He leans back in his chair, letting his gaze linger as it travels the length of her body. She shifts, uncomfortable with his scrutiny, and folds her arms across her waist.

His free hand rests on the desk, the one with the missing fingers he lost when a beer barrel exploded. She focuses on it knowing it makes him self-conscious. Moving the mutilated hand under his desk he says, 'why do you wear that God awful hat Charlotte. Is there something wrong with your head?'

'No Mr Patterson. It's a beret in keeping with the French theme you know.'

'Get a smaller one then. Something chic, not knitted, and not red. Get a proper black felt beret.'

She tries another tack. 'It keeps my head warm in the air-conditioning.'

'That's nonsense. Take it off. I forbid you to wear it while you are working. You look like a bad joke. How will the clientele see you?'

'I'd really rather not, please.'

'You'll either take it off, or I can find someone who will work without a hat.'

Reluctantly Charlotte pulls it off, and the man sucks his breath, hissing through closed teeth. Christ, she's beautiful. How is it he didn't notice how attractive she is? He leans back in his chair with lips pursed, examining her. 'That's better. Doesn't it feel better?' He laughs and shifts his weight in his chair.

'Please Mr Patterson. Please let me wear it.' She knows what happens when men see her behind the bar without her hat. It doesn't happen in the club. The men there still seem to hang on to some level of respect, but in the bar, it's like a sign saying here I am, proposition me. The beret puts them off, although it didn't put Blake off. She wonders why.

'Enough. You will not wear it. You can tie your hair back so it doesn't fall into drinks, but no hat.'

'Yes Mr Patterson.' Charlotte turns to leave, her shoulders sagging. She felt so good this morning. The man has sullied her mood, making her feel dirty. Even the violence in Blake doesn't make her feel bad like this man does.

Once he awoke from his nightmare, they lay talking until dawn. He told her a little of the dream, but mostly he said things to make her laugh, brushing over the horrors. She wants to know what he went through, but she didn't press him. He'll tell her when he's ready.

He's kind and thoughtful too, and he didn't even complain when his arm cramped from her lying on it. She was so scared last night, but she knows he won't hurt her, not intentionally, although she still can't get over the way he laid into those men. Within minutes, it was finished. It wasn't the violence so much as his unruffled efficiency in despatching them. She supposes he learned that in the Army.

'Charlotte I haven't finished with you.'

She looks back. 'Yes, sorry Mr Patterson.'

'I wanted to speak to you because management have decided you'll share your tips. I want them handed in each shift. They'll be divided and added to your pay.'

'Oh no, please Mr Patterson.'

'The decision's made. You have the best tips because you have the cocktail bar and a more upmarket clientele who can afford it. You either share your tips or work in one of the public bars.'

Charlotte feels defeated. 'I'll share my tips.'

'Good girl.'

He watches her leave, his hand smoothing over his groin. He wants Charlotte, but he can't let his wife find out. She's been looking for proof of adultery to get a divorce for ages and he doesn't want to lose his livelihood. If it leaked out, he'd lose his job, and the fat cow will get everything; his house, his money, the kids, and he'd have to marry the girl. He can't afford for that to happen. He'll just have to be careful.

In the bar, Charlotte plaits her hair in a tight braid, finding a length of string to tie it. At least she'll see Blake. He said he was going to see a friend, and then he'll call in at lunchtime. She's late opening the doors, but steps out into the hard sunlit street, hoping he'll be there. There's no one waiting, and her shoulders wilt in anticipation of a slow day.

At midday the bar fills up with its usual lunchtime crowd of office workers looking for a pint and a bar meal. June Riley comes in to take the meal orders. Charlotte is busy pulling pints and pouring wine when Blake walks through the door. He sits on a stool at the end of the bar near the till. She smiles and returns her attention to her job. June takes his lunch order, and when she's finished Charlotte walks over as if to take his drink order.

'I like the no hat effect,' he says as she pushes her hip against the bar opposite him.

Her face clouds over, but she says nothing about Patterson. 'Do you want a beer?'

'Yeah.' He searches her face. 'Are you all right?'

She rearranges her features, trying to look cheerful. 'Yes fine, a bit tired is all, but then I'm always tired. I don't get enough sleep, but it's my choice.' She smiles. 'I'll be a bit busy until this mob move out, around two probably.'

'That's okay, I'll eat and go. Can I see you tonight?'

'Okay. When?'

'Eleven?'

'Yes.'

'Good.' He pays and watches her move to the till.

Goose bumps run along her arms and she wants to abandon caution, but instead she turns to attend to the next customer. Half an hour later, he leaves. The afternoon drags as she cleans the bar, washing glasses, and clearing the cluttered tables. Even though she didn't talk to him, it was enough knowing he was there. Now she will have to get through the hectic evening before she sees him again. Perhaps he'll come in for dinner.

An ambulance siren sounds in the street outside, and she wonders about the men last night. How would they get medical treatment, and how would they explain their injuries. They could hardly admit they broke curfew. Perhaps they could claim a car accident, but they would have to wait for morning.

Eventually the clock on the wall shows ten-thirty. A day has never seemed so long. Blake didn't come in for dinner, but in half an hour she'll see him. Hurriedly she cleans the place, praying the couple in the corner don't stay long. She'll scream if they make her late.

They take the hint as she retrieves their empty glasses and leave their change on the table. As they step out the exit she scoops up the money, and for a moment contemplates putting it in her pocket.

The door behind the bar opens and Patterson enters. She wipes the table and walks back to the bar. 'It was a quiet day today Mr Patterson.' She places the dirty glasses on the sink, and the tip money in the jar.

He moves towards the counter, his arm brushing against her breast as he leans in. She moves out of his way, surprised. He's never come on to her before, and she assumes it's an accident.

Patterson clutches the jar to his chest and says, 'not many tips today. Are you stashing some in your pockets?'

'No Mr Patterson, I swear that's all of it. Honestly.'

He swaps the jar to the hand with the missing fingers, and says, 'come here.' With the flat of his whole palm, he pats her right hip pocket. Then his hand slides up and across her waist to her left breast pocket. The door opens and Patterson drops his arm, irritated by the intrusion. It's the same bloke as he saw Charlotte leaving with last night.

'We're closed.' His voice is curt as he glares at Blake.

Charlotte's face tells Blake all he needs to know, and rage rushes up making his eyes glitter, but his voice remains even, 'you ready Charlotte?'

'Yes. I'll just lock up. Is there anything else Mr Patterson?' Charlotte is close to tears, but keeps her lashes lowered.

Patterson snaps, 'the bar doesn't close for another five minutes. You won't finish until then. You...,' he looks at Blake. 'You need to wait outside while she's locking up.'

'Sure.' Blake keeps his gaze level, but doesn't move, taking in every detail of the man, his missing fingers, his paunch, his skinny thighs and shiny forehead, his veined nose slippery with greasy sweat.

Patterson drops his gaze and walks out clutching the tip jar.

When he's gone Blake says, 'are you all right, did he hurt you?'

'He was looking for hidden tips.' She looks around as if expecting to see him spying. 'I'll tell you later.'

He nods and walks to the door. 'I'll be here waiting. Yell if you need me.'

Ten minutes later, they walk down the street. Charlotte has on her red beret and it wobbles as she hurries to keep up with Blake's stride. She's breathless as she explains what happened with her boss. Eventually she gives up and drops back. 'Blake I can't keep up with you.'

He turns, looking surprised. 'Sorry.' He walks back to her and takes her hand.

'Don't be sorry, just walk slower.'

'Okay. I was just.... I wanted to kill the fucker when I walked in. Ah, sorry Charlotte.'

'Stop saying you're sorry. I wanted to kill him too, but I can't afford to lose my job.' She grins, 'but it's okay now and I'm not going to let him ruin my life. Forget the arsehole. Let's just have fun.'

In the early hours of the next morning, they walk home through the curfew silent streets. They're going to his place above the bar. Its further from the club, but they won't have to walk through Newstead at night. It's safer, and anyway he has a double bed and electricity. She's scared, but also thrilled, feeling indecisive and weak with desire.

His room is a standard hotel room with an en suite, but she wonders how he can afford it. Conscripts aren't paid much. In fact, she heard they get less than she does. Even if he had saved his money for the past three years, he couldn't afford this for long. One night here is probably as much as she earns in a fortnight.

He's tender as he takes off her beret, smoothing the long strands of hair. Then he pulls up the edge of her tee shirt, sliding it up to uncover her breasts. She steps back, taking over to drag it over her head. He pulls her back, holding her tightly until she raises her face to his, kissing him, and wrapping her arms around his neck. Then he lifts her and walks to the bed, his mouth still on hers.

She lies still as he pulls off her skirt, wrinkling it over her thighs and down her legs. Then he stands gazing at her for a moment before draping her skirt over the back of the chair. She sits up and unbuckles his belt. He helps her, pulling off his clothes. She wriggles out of her knickers trying to kiss him as he kneels next to her, and then his hands are in her hair, his mouth on hers, burning into her, until she arches her back.

He stops and leans over to take something from his bedside drawer. His eyes hold her gaze as his mouth twitches into a smile. It's a small square package he rips with his teeth, grinning at her surprise.

'Where did you get them?'

'A friend. He can get you birth control too. But we can talk later. Come here. Christ, you're gorgeous Charlotte.'

The next morning Charlotte wakes with the sun streaming through the window. She lies still, disoriented by the strangeness of the room, memories of last night flooding her consciousness. Blake's lying on his stomach, head to one side facing her, eyes closed. At least he didn't have nightmares again, or not any that were obvious.

She rolls over to face him tracing the ragged scars that radiate across his shoulder blade in two angry Y shaped broken lines. The scars are still livid and much worse than the two round entry holes in the crease between his chest and shoulder. He opens his eyes staring at her, unmoving.

'I have to go. I need to shower and change into clean clothes for work.'

'Not yet. Shower here and I'll take you home.' He pulls her to him burying his face in her neck as her hair falls across them in a curtain. 'Christ you're delicious Charlotte.'

'You said already.'

He laughs and kisses her.

It's ten o'clock before she's dressed and ready to go home. 'You don't need to come with me Blake. I can go by myself.'

'I'll come. Just to make sure everything is all right, but I can't stay long because I have to report in.'

'Oh.' She's intrigued.

'I have to report daily, so they can make sure I keep my end of the bargain.' He smiles at her. 'I'm a dangerous criminal you know.'

A frown flits across her face.

'Sorry.' He grins. 'Just kidding.'

'You're still saying sorry.'

'Yeah, bad habit, but I don't want you to think you can't trust me. Not even kidding.'

'I do trust you.' She walks into his arms then pulls back laughing.

He smiles ruefully at her. 'Come on, if we stay here I won't be able to resist you. Let's get you home. See you tonight at eleven?'

She nods.

'Hey, give me the name of the pills you used to take.'

An hour later, Blake arrives at the police station, a neo colonial building with steps leading to wide front doors. It's covered with pigeon droppings and looks in need of a good scrub. A billboard high on the side of the building says 'from darkness into light, we will triumph.'

He walks up the steps and through the doors into a vaulted entrance. Three community police officers, a woman and two men, sit indolently behind a barred counter. The expressions on their faces tell Blake they are bored. Empty benches run along one wall. A lone homeless man stands with his emaciated dog, waiting for someone to attend to him.

Blake waits at the counter for one of the officers to notice him. The bloke who usually signs his report isn't there, and he doesn't recognise the two men or the woman. He hands over his I.D. to the officer behind the desk who glances at it, then at Blake.

The look bothers Blake, but he doesn't know why, except it's not the usual procedure. 'Where's Constable Boshof?'

The officer's eyes narrow. 'Wait here.'

Blake's surprised. Usually he signs a paper and leaves. He's never been asked to wait. Sweat trickles down his back, and it's not just because of the heat. Something's wrong. His muscles tense as adrenalin pumps through his system.

This is not Baghdad. It's Australia. They won't do anything bad to him. He has to get a grip and stop seeing everything as a threat to his life, but anger rises at his helplessness.

While he stands at the counter waiting, he stares at the poster on the wall behind the charge desk. It's of a blue sky with puffball white clouds above a tranquil rolling green meadow. White writing says, 'their best weapon is our complacency,' but he doesn't see it.

Instead, he's thinking he doesn't want to go back. He wants to spend the rest of his life lying between Charlotte's warm silky thighs. Anger never helps, and it stops him thinking clearly. He needs to keep sharp. Breathe man, breathe, don't let them panic you, but he knows that feeling, and it's never good. He fumbles with his CellTab.

'Rory.'

'Yes Blake? What is it? You sound like you're down a tunnel.'

'I'm in the police station. They've made me wait. Something's going on and I have a bad feeling.'

'Christ. The cops were here this morning asking about you. They took your shirt. Have you done something? No, wait don't tell me. Where are you? I'll be down as soon as I can.'

9.

His long fingers delicately remove the wrapping as he feels the familiar thrill tingling through his body. Her open eyes stare up at him like glassy marbles. In one eye is a speck of something, mucus maybe. It offends him and he looks for a tissue to wipe it away.

Up river in the Penthouse apartment Jeremy sleeps, lying on his back in the middle of an emperor-sized bed. The room is dark with heavy chocolate brown drapes edged with a gold fleur-de-lis motif. The sound of the National Anthem playing merges with his dream. It's a critical part as he takes the last layer of gold tissue paper off the girl, and the anthem annoys him. It doesn't fit, and he doesn't know who plays it.

He turns over trying to ignore it, but it persists as the dream retreats, and he can't recapture the fantasy. His eyelids flicker, and Jeremy realises the sound is not part of the dream. It's his father calling.

Hurriedly he gets out of bed, his mouth gummed from sleep, his eyes scratchy, and his brain still struggling to transition to wakefulness. By the time he gets to the sitting room, he is awake.

It's only just gone five a.m. What the blazes does the old man want at this time of the morning?

Why his father can't call on the CellTab is anyone's guess, except he is paranoid over interception, insisting the e-cript is a safer means of communicating. He flicks the remote to answer the persistent tone. His father's a dupe; Jeremy knows that a determined eves-dropper wouldn't have a problem hacking an e-cript either. He's had it done himself.

The image shows his father standing at his desk, still in his dressing gown. His opaque hunched form blocks the light, but he's not sitting behind the desk, and he's not dressed in his suit. That makes Jeremy uneasy.

Arnie Marabaux's voice is calm as he says. 'I've just learned that Lincoln's been arrested. This is not something you've cooked up I hope.'

Jeremy is not fooled by the even tone. 'I thought...' but he doesn't get to finish saying what he thought as his father's fury unleashes.

'Christ, you're a bigger fool than I realised. Get him out. Get him out this morning, and no press. If you cock this up any further I'll...' Arnold Marabaux reaches across his desk and severs the connection, but before he does, Jeremy swears he can hear the old man's snarl.

Screw him. He stalks back to his bedroom where he climbs into bed and closes his eyes, but he can't recapture sleep, dreams, or the images he was so enjoying. His father's fury has unnerved him. He didn't get a chance to explain. Surely, he must be able to see how fortuitous Lincoln's arrest is.

How is he going to get him out now he's been charged? The police are one thing, but the courts and the press are less predictable. He'll handle Jarrod von Wilkins no problem, but what will he have to trade to keep Zac Randolph quiet? It's too late now.

Fuck his father. Jeremy wouldn't put it past the old bastard to do something to hurt, physically or financially, in fact, in any way a person can hurt or ruin another person, and Jeremy's known plenty of those.

He gets up and opens his bedside drawer, pulling out a small gold-plated box and glass vial. Flipping open the lid, he taps out a small amount of the greyish-blue powder onto a mirror lining the inside of the box, and cuts a line of the new designer meth-salts. Then he picks up the gold plated tube and snorts up each nostril. With a rush, the anxiety dissipates as strength flows through him. He can handle his father and the Randolph's.

He picks up his CellTab. Jarrod answers and Jeremy says, 'morning sunshine did I wake you?'

'Um morning Jeremy.' Jarrod clears his throat and swings his legs out of bed. Hang on a tick while I get to another room. He looks over to his wife, but she's still asleep. Only the top of her head shows darkly against the white sheets. Closing the door behind him he says, 'okay, Christ where's the fire? Do you know what time it is?'

'It's nearly six. Surely, you're not still in bed on this fine morning with all those criminals running amok on our streets.' Jeremy feels the power. If only he wasn't surrounded by incompetents and imbeciles, his father would have more respect for him.

Jarrod ignores him. The bloke sounds cooked already but all he says is, 'what can I do for you Jeremy?' He walks into the kitchen and flicks on the kettle to boil. He's up now so he may as well make tea.

'Give me something on Zac, or his old man Muriel Randolph, or one of the family, even one of their staff. I need it within the hour.'

'I'm not sure...'

'No buts Jarrod. I thought you wanted the Homeland Security contract?' Jeremy smirks. The bloke's an idiot, making his ambitions so obvious by calling his company Homeland Security Enterprises. Another moron, he's drowning in them. 'Just make sure I get it by seven, if you want to keep up your current lifestyle. And by the way, get Lincoln out pronto.'

'Lincoln? Christ, it's not that easy Jeremy... there are processes to go through.'

'You can't keep an innocent man in gaol.'

'No, but you said...'

'Yes but the blood on the shirt won't match, so get him out. There's no evidence to hold him. Get him out now.' Jeremy chucks his CellTab onto the bed and heads for the shower feeling good. All they need is direction. Clear concise instruction. All this rubbish about a collaborative approach to problem solving, is just crap.

Jarrod hangs up the phone, and leans on the kitchen bench, his head hanging between his shoulder blades as he waits for the kettle to boil. Jeremy is a menace, but he's in so deep he doesn't know how to extract himself. Fuck, he wishes he had never entered into this arrangement. Sure, it's given him and his wife plenty, but is it worth it? Daily there are new orders. Appalling things that don't sit well with Jarrod's conscience, but he has no choice.

The steam whistles from the spout of the kettle, and Jarrod stands erect, flicking the switch, and pouring boiling water into the pot. He'll have tea first before waking anyone else to issue the orders. He needs to think about what to say. At least this order errs on the side of justice, unlike locking up the bloke for murder. They all know how the poor woman bought it, and why. The fucking man is a psychopath. As Marie said, she would have died anyway with all the drugs in her system so he shouldn't worry about it, but it niggles.

As he sets the tray down next to the bed, she stirs and rolls over, looking at him. There are sleep granules clinging to the corner of her eyes; brown doe eyes smudged with remnant waterproof mascara. She sits up and stretches her arms, their sinewy strength reaching fists to the ceiling. Her shoulder length hair falls in a fuzzy black cloud.

She is still beautiful despite fifteen years of marriage although maybe she's a bit too thin now. He preferred her with a few curves, but she won't have an ounce of spare fat on her body, fanatically training in the home gym every day to maintain her looks.

She was a security guard for a mining company when he met her. He was celebrating his promotion to Chief Superintendent when she walked into the bar with one of his mates. She was recovering from a bad marriage, and his wife had died in a car accident five years previously.

He never thought he would find someone else to replace his wife, but when he met Marie, he took one look and had no qualms about muscling in on his mate's date. He chased her for months before she agreed to go out with him. Now after fifteen years of marriage, and him pushing fifty-eight, she ten years younger, he is still smitten.

He leans over to kiss her and she rubs her palm over his head. 'You need a shave darling, either that or grow it out properly.'

'I'll shave after breakfast. I can't grow it out; it looks ridiculous like a monk's tonsure. You wouldn't love me if I looked like a monk with a bald head would you.'

'Huh I love you now don't I?'

Jarrod laughs. 'Yeah but I look bad-assed now, not like a monk.'

'You keep telling yourself that honey.'

'Tea?' He smiles holding out a cup and saucer, the delicate porcelain one with roses. He can't understand why women are so fussy about what they drink their tea from, but she insists that it taste different out of thin porcelain, and won't drink it if it's in a heavy china mug. Tea is tea to him regardless of its container.

She leans against the headboard and takes the cup, sipping delicately as he pours himself a mug.

'Who was on the phone?'

'You know.'

'What does he want now?'

'He wants dirt on the Randolph's and the release of Lincoln.'

'But he just...'

'Yeah I know honey. Don't let's go there. Let's have tea in peace and then I'll do something.'

'We should get out Jarrod.'

'Hm, not sure how I can.' He stirs his tea.

She frowns, her forehead creasing into vertical lines between her eyebrows. 'The man's a lunatic. It's getting out of control. If we are not careful we'll go down the gurgler with him.'

'Yeah but who's going to send him down. His father's tentacles are everywhere, and we're in it with him, right up to the noose line around our necks, and he knows it.'

10.

'You're free to go Mr Lincoln.' The police officer is standing at the fishbowl door. 'Just sign for your stuff at the counter.'

'Sorry I don't understand. Where's my lawyer?'

'Can't help you there. All I know is that the charges have been dropped and you're free to go. Most people we have in here don't hang around to argue that point.'

He grins and Blake gets up, confused by this sudden turn of events. At the counter, he signs for his shoes, and belt along with his phone, wallet, and watch. The police officer opens the Watch House door for him to leave. The sunlight blinds him after two days in the windowless cell.

Taking out his CellTab, Blake waits for it to charge in the light, but as he looks up a taxi passes and he hails it. It pulls up beneath a billboard saying, save your country, report suspicious activity. On the way to his hotel, he rings Rory, arranging to meet him after he's showered and changed. He's relieved he's out, but no wiser and that makes him cautious.

In the office an hour later, Rory explains. 'Once we made the request for the independent blood test they became much more cooperative. Then the barmaid turned up here at the office saying she spent the night in your room, and she was willing to testify. She's a brave girl.'

He stops, seeing Blake's mouth tighten. 'Don't look like that. I made sure her name stayed out of it. Jeremy was really good. I must say, I'm warming to the bloke. Anyway, I told him that the evidence showed it was clearly not you, but the whole thing would take forever to sort out through the proper legal system. I asked if he could help expedite the process. I explained that the blood forensics would show it wasn't the woman's blood, and a girl will swear you were with her all night. He asked her name, but I refused to say okay, explaining it was not a woman you were intent upon marrying. He thought that was pretty amusing. Anyway, like you said, I kept her out of it, but she threatened that she was going to come to the station if I didn't tell the police she was with you. Jeremy said to leave it with him and hey presto here you are. Sorry, I just got off the phone to him less than an hour ago. I didn't think it would happen so quickly or I would have come down to the station to pick you up. I told you he's a useful bloke to have around.'

'How much did it cost?'

'Come on Blake, it's only money.'

'No it's not Rory.'

'Jesus, lighten up mate. You're free. What about, thanks Rory for all your help so I didn't have to languish in that skunk hole.'

'Yeah sorry, thanks.' Blake runs his hands through his hair feeling the tightness in his shoulders. 'I appreciate you looking out for me. What did the media report? I've had nightmares about the Military Police knocking on my door claiming I breached parole and have to go back.' He grins at Rory.

'That's another thing for which you have Jeremy to thank, and he didn't charge a cent. He rang old man Randolph, and they didn't publish anything except that some woman was murdered.'

Blake looks puzzled. 'If it wasn't in the news how did Charlotte find out?'

Rory looks awkward. 'I told her.'

'You didn't trust me did you? You actually thought I could do something like that.' Blake looks bleakly at his friend.

'I'm sorry. Shit I had to be sure you know. I didn't believe it, but I had to be sure.'

'Forget it. Are there any other leads about who she is?'

'Don't know, but I don't think so.'

'Okay. Thanks for getting me out. I owe you man.' Blake stands up to leave.

'Come to the house for dinner tonight. Screw it Blake come back and stay with us in your old room. Why do you have to stay in that dodgy hotel?'

'It's not dodgy. It's convenient, centrally located and there's life all around. I missed that over the past few years. And Rory, I don't have to worry about anyone's feelings, or be forced to answer questions. I just need this break. Soon I'll be in Canberra and back in barracks. I need this time to sort out my head. It's a big change—Baghdad, prison and here. There's no transition. One minute you're in the army trying like hell not to be killed, the next you're a civilian and expected to behave as if nothing's happened, nothing's changed. It's bewildering and I need time to sort out who I am now. They take everything from you including your sense of self. I left Australia an intern, and now I don't know who I am. It's nothing to do with you and your family.'

Rory has a peculiar look on his face. 'Okay. Thanks. That helps.'

'I'm going to see Charlotte. I'll see you later.'

Blake waits outside until she unlocks the door to the bar. He's the only patron waiting, and he wants to see her alone. She leaves the door and walks back to the bar unaware he's watching her. As she swings behind the counter she sees him standing at the entrance, and her hand flies up to her mouth. For a moment, she remains frozen, then she skips around the counter.

His throat chokes, overwhelmed with emotion as he pulls her to him, kissing her until she relaxes in his arms. She thinks bugger Patterson. Let him fire her—the dirty bastard. The outside door opens, and he lets her go, but keeps his gaze locked on hers. She straightens her shirt and walks back to the bar.

A man enters, looking from her to Blake as he walks up to the bar for a beer. Charlotte serves him, a secret smile playing across her mouth as she tries to look serious, but the aria is playing again.

Blake leans on the bar admiring her quick graceful movements, watching her skirt hem swinging around at mid-thigh. She serves the man and walks to the till to exchange a note for change. The man drops it into her tip jar.

His gaze runs down her body, admiring her as he takes a sip of his beer, then he says, 'do you come here often?'

Blake's eyes narrow, 'Jesus! You put up with this shit,' he says to Charlotte.

The man flashes a worried look at Blake, and picks up his beer, turning to hurry away to a table on the far side of the room. He doesn't want trouble and the man at the bar looks dangerous. Pulling his CellTab out, he pretends to be engrossed.

Charlotte ignores his comment saying, 'when did you get out?'

'This morning.' Blake drags his gaze away from the man and looks at Charlotte. 'I understand I have you to thank for saving me.'

His intensity makes her feel weak, and she slides her hand across the counter to his. He takes it in both his hands. She watches his fingers as they play with hers. 'Blake, you didn't tell me about your fiancée.'

He frowns. 'Ex fiancée. Who told you, Rory?'

'She's silent.'

'He's got a big mouth. It was ages ago Charlotte. She dumped me more than two years ago.'

'Do you still love her?'

'No.' He looks into her eyes. 'I don't think I ever did. Look can we get out of here?'

'I can't Blake. I'll get sacked.'

'I'll look after you Charlotte.'

'No thanks.'

His smile is wry. 'I can get you a decent job.'

'What in your company?'

'Yeah. How do you know?'

'Evan looked it up. I'll tell my boss I'm sick and ask him for half an hour after the lunch crowd goes. I'll come up to your room. But if you want to do something for me...'

'Name it.'

'Can you get Evan a job and work I.D.'

'What can he do?'

'He can run a farm.'

'Shit.' He runs his hand through his hair.

She looks at him feeling the stubborn thrust of her chin. Trying to soften the challenge, she says, 'but it's a favour, not payment. I'll come to your room anyway because I want to.'

'Okay, I'll see what I can do.'

'If I'm not there by three you know my boss won't let me go. It's not because I don't want to.'

He squeezes her hand and smiles, 'okay.'

Pulling away from him, she holds out her hand.

Confused, he looks at it. 'What?'

'The beer.'

'Of course.' He stands up and pulls out his wallet, chucking a hundred dollar note on the counter. 'I've got to go Charlotte. See you at three maybe.'

'You haven't drunk your beer.'

'No. I don't want it. I just wanted to see you.'

'Wait your change.'

'Put it in the tip jar.'

'No Blake. No... Please.'

'What?'

'I don't want your money Blake. It's like you're buying me. I don't want that. I want what we have, but not your money.'

Three hours later, after the lunchtime rush and the last patrons have left, Charlotte clears the tables, putting the glasses and plates in the dishwasher, wondering how she can convince

Mr Patterson she needs time off work. He doesn't care if his employees are sick.

She remembers when Stella in the public bar tried to get time off because she had stomach pain and wanted to go to the hospital. The bastard wouldn't let her go and her appendix burst. She nearly died, and she's still paying off the ambulance debt.

The bar is empty when Charlotte picks up the internal phone. 'Mr. Patterson I have a medical problem, and I need half an hour please.' She doesn't wait for his approval, grabbing her bag and slipping out the bar to make her way through the corridors and upstairs into the main part of the hotel.

Blake's door is open when she arrives, and she closes it quickly, walking along the short passage to the bedroom. He's lying on the bed flicking through channels. The news is on, and she pauses to watch, as a graph presents evidence of decreasing crime rates around the country.

The film snaps to Marabaux at a press conference. He's talking about performance-based police services, and how since the contract was let, the crime rate has trended steadily downwards.

'Ha! Everyone knows that's bullshit,' she says.

Blake flicks off the remote and gets off the bed. 'You made it. I was afraid you wouldn't.'

She buries her face in his chest, inhaling the smell of him, clean with the perfume of expensive soap or after-shave. 'You smell delicious I want to eat you?'

Taken aback he looks at her laughing face, and a thrill tingles through him. He wishes he were free to protect her properly.

'I don't have much time Blake. I said I would be back in half an hour.'

He drops his arms. 'Christ, I hate this.' Walking over to the window, he looks out to the street.

'What Blake, you're scaring me again.'

'I hate that you have to do this. That the bastard who employs you can treat you like... like... And this scurrying about as if we are committing some kind of crime.'

'We are.'

'What?'

'We are committing a crime.' She walks up and stands behind him at the window. 'Like it or not, this is it. If you and I want to do this, we are committing a crime.'

11.

Blake's promise hangs over him, clouding his concentration as Rory bangs on about the weather, but he's not listening. Instead, he wonders how he can do it. How does a person get another person an Oz card?

It's one thing giving the bloke a job. Jesus that's the least he can do, and it's not hard. All Blake has to say is Evan's working for him as anything—pick a title, so long as it's registered in the national database, but the I.D. is a completely different problem. Maybe it'll be easier if he gives him a job managing a farm. They treat people in charge of businesses or with money differently.

'Rory,' he says interrupting him, 'how hard is it to buy a farm?'

'You want to buy a farm?' Rory loses his train of thought, taken aback by the nature of the interruption.

'Yes.'

'What for? Have you lost it entirely?'

'No. I think it would be nice to live on a farm somewhere out in the country when I get out. I can be a country doctor.'

'Bullshit. What do you know about farming? Farming is a mugs game. Haven't you heard there's a fucking drought on?' He looks at Blake's face. 'You haven't heard a word I've been saying for the past twenty minutes, have you?'

Blake puts his head in his hands rubbing his temples. 'You're right, I know nothing about farming.' He stares out across the river to the city.

'What's this about?'

'I promised to get someone a job, but all he's ever done is farmed and he needs a work I.D. I have no idea how to go about doing something like that.' Blake looks up at Rory, his brow furrowed.

'Who?'

'Does it matter?'

'Yes if you really think you have to buy a farm it matters. It's that barmaid, isn't it? It's her that's got you acting like a lovesick puppy.'

'That's harsh mate.'

'True but.'

'Na, it's her friend. He's out of work and hasn't got I.D.'

'Geez how is it he hasn't been conscripted?'

'It's just a matter of time. I promised. What can I do?'

'Okay. The job part is easy, but the work I.D. might be a bit more difficult seeing as he has none. It means there's no history. No history means he's been living outside the system. Being outside the system means outside the law. Outside...'

'Yeah yeah, outside the law means conscription.'

Rory pulls his chin back offended. 'You come to me with every lame duck bleeding heart problem and expect me to solve it for you...'

'Ah sorry man... It's doing my head in. How did the system get so bent out of shape?'

'Look Blake it's a good system. Some people fall through the cracks, but that happens with all systems. We're fighting a war on terror and we can't afford complacency or we'll be overrun. We have to keep track of our population, otherwise we won't spot the infiltrators. The old tax file system didn't work because people never carried it around with them. To have work identification attached to the tax file number was the only option. World trade has collapsed because of bloody terrorism. We have the worst drought in history. There are terrorist incursions in the north. The country's in debt to its eyeballs. People need to make this country more productive so we don't sink into oblivion. Radicalism is escalating. What would you have us do? Go back to the puerile socialist days of last century. That's what caused the problems and sent the country broke. Now we have to fix it. If you've got nothing to hide you have nothing to fear from the I.D. laws.'

'Surely, you're not blaming terrorists for the drought. In any case, I don't believe complacency caused our problem with terrorism Rory. I know these people. We marginalised and treated them with disdain—brutality even. For decades, the West screwed them over for our own gains, oil mostly. It's no wonder they have become what they are. That kind of perpetual violence and oppression breeds radicalism. War brutalises families, and violence corrupts kids' normal development. Some of them are bound to grow up spoiling to do harm in retaliation. You can't suppress people or destroy cultures and not get blow back.'

'You're trying to tell me we are responsible for FISLO atrocities! You've lost it mate.' Rory's not going to accept that, and his face reddens.

Blake runs his hand through his hair. 'No, that's not what I am saying, but you can't subject people to horrors, and not expect a few psychopaths with warped world views to rise from the ashes to extract revenge. The aftermath of the First World War spawned Hitler, a man on a mission to wrest power back for his country after the repressive consequences of the Versailles Treaty. I'm not saying it's right, but it is a consequence of war. And in the Middle East, who armed them and taught them to fight in the first place? We're the architects of our own disasters, and what we are doing now, is perpetuating it.'

He sees Rory's indignation mounting and tries to move into less controversial territory. 'As for world trade, well most of that is just greed, the need to increase profits for some, at the expense of others.'

Rory blows air through pursed lips. 'Now you sound like a bloody radical. Anyway, you can talk. You're one of the wealthiest men in Australia and you're complaining.'

'No, I'm not complaining, but I would give it all for a fairer, more just society.' Blake looks thoughtful, wondering if it is something he can work towards after his sentence is completed, but Rory's not finished yet.

'Ha! I'll remind you of that one day.'

'Okay, but what about this bloke, Evan Chandler? You said the job part is easy.'

'Yes, Dad can arrange a job in the Warehouse if you want that. Lugging hay about on a farm and lugging boxes in a warehouse can't be too dissimilar.'

Blake bites back the angry retort burning his throat. He doesn't want to argue with Rory anymore. At least it's a job. 'What about I.D?'

'The I.D. card is the stumbling-block.' Rory stops and looks sideways at Blake. 'I can get Jeremy's firm to straighten it out, but you get all sulky when I ask Jeremy for anything.'

'I hate being beholden to the bloke.' A muscle in Blake's jaw jumps as he struggles with the dilemma. 'The whole system is corrupt when you have to have money so you can buy access to circumvent the law. Otherwise you're just a poor sucker destined to have a rifle placed in your hand and told to go kill your fellow man.'

'Beggars can't be choosers,' Rory says with feigned nonchalance.

Blake hesitates before he says, 'okay, ask Jeremy to get the bloke a card. How long will it take?'

'I'll ask him. You must be his best customer at the moment... and Blake, I'm sending you a bill. These favours are mounting.'

Rory picks up his CellTab to ring Jeremy, and Blake gets up and walks across the terrace. The sprawling city covers the opposite bank. Its endless acres of concrete and bitumen disappear off into the distance. Maybe he should buy a farm. At least then, he won't have to deal with this Machiavellian shit every day.

When Rory hangs up Blake says, 'mate I still want to buy a farm. The idea appeals you know.'

Three days later Blake takes the steps up to the Writer's Bar in one stride and puts his palms on the glass, to show Charlotte he's waiting for her. She smiles and ducks her head so Mr Patterson doesn't see. He's checking the levels of alcohol in the bottles, waiting for her to finish cashing-up the till. Under his arm, he clutches her tip jar.

'The till's balanced Mr Patterson.'

'Hm.' He turns his attention to her, walking closer and putting out his hand to dust an imaginary speck from her shoulder. The hand brushes her breast. 'Are you well now?' His watery eyes glisten in the low bar light.

Charlotte wilts in defeat then she straightens. 'No Mr Patterson. The doctor thinks I've picked up some sort of infection and it's getting worse.' She wants to laugh as he jerks his arm away from her.

'See you don't miss any more work because of it.'

He picks up the till and leaves. Charlotte contains her laughter as she watches him go. As soon as the door shuts, she grabs her bag and runs to the exit, pulling the door to lock behind her.

They walk along the street towards the club with Blake wishing they could go to his hotel room first, but he can wait. Listening to her sing is almost as good as holding her naked on his bed, but he wants to carry on doing it. It's doing his head in that he only has a couple of days left before he goes to Canberra, and he wonders how he can take her with him.

Once inside the club she heads for the stage. He goes to the bar and leans propped against the wall with a beer as he scans the room for Evan. It's ten minutes before Evan walks into the club and drifts over towards Blake. 'Hey mate.'

'Beer?'

'Yeah thanks. I don't feel so bad sponging off you, now I know how rich you are.'

Blake laughs. 'Still a conscript though, but keep your voice down. I'll be thrown out of the place.'

Evan takes the beer and leans against the wall next to Blake to watch Charlotte. 'What's it like Blake? What's it really like? You hear horror stories man, but the media portray it all so heroically. I reckon they're going to get me one of these days, and I just don't think I'll survive?'

'You don't want to go there Evan. Forget it. Here,' he takes the work I.D. card from his jacket pocket. 'Do you know where the Company's medical warehouse is?'

Evan stares at the I.D. his brow furrowed and mistrusting. 'How did you get this?'

'Don't ask questions. I'm not proud of it, but it is legit. You won't get sprung. Just take it and report at seven tomorrow morning to Harry Billcotts at the back entrance to the warehouse. There's a job. It's not much, but it'll keep you safe for the moment.'

For a while, the two men concentrate on Charlotte singing and then Evan says. 'Thanks you've saved my life.'

'I'm just sorry we live in such a fucked-up system that it's necessary.' He shrugs turning back to watch Charlotte, pretending he doesn't see the tears welling in Evan's eyes.

Charlotte's voice swells, filling his soul with its sweetness as yearning hollows out his chest. When he's free, he'll take her away to somewhere that doesn't have these oppressive laws. Maybe to England where they'll drink beer overlooking the Cam.

When he was a kid, they went there on holiday. It's a good memory, safe and secure in the shield of his parents love. They sat in a garden outside a pub. His father, James Lincoln, brought out lemonade for him and white wine for his mother. He tipped a small amount of his beer into Blake's lemonade and winked, his blue eyes reflecting his amusement. In a father son conspiracy, he angled his broad shoulders to screen the illicit action from Helena, who pretended not to notice. Blake remembered he hadn't liked the bitterness of the shandy and wished his father hadn't ruined his lemonade. But it made him feel important and grown up.

They sat watching the punts gliding on gleaming green waters, trying to avoid collision with the water birds; swans, geese and ducks he thought, but wasn't sure of his memory because he was only about ten at the time. He remembers begging his Dad to take him out on the river.

In the punt, his mother sat reclining in the flat-bottomed boat, her long tanned legs stretched out, and her hand holding onto a broad brimmed sun hat. Blake's Dad showed him how to propel the punt across the water, telling him to push against the riverbed. It was harder than it looked, and in the end, his father did most of the work while Blake scowled at the other men on the river ogling his mother.

Blake imagines him working the pole with Charlotte sitting holding on to her sun hat. It'll be a proper one, not that daft red beret. Men will ogle her too, but he won't mind because she's beautiful like his mother was, although as fair as his mother was golden.

Then when dusk falls he'll take her back to their hotel, and no one will ask for their marriage licence. They'll go upstairs and he'll caress her silken skin, pressing her soft lips with his, until it's time for dinner.

At dinner, they'll sit at a white linen covered table next to a real fireplace, and order more wine and food, and talk of each other and the things they've seen. They won't even think of conscription or work I.Ds, or paying for access to politicians. Instead, they will sit secluded in their own bubble of light.

When dinner is over, they'll walk by the river until they're tired, and go back to the room where he'll make love to her all over again, safe in their big bed, listening to distant noises of foxes barking and owls screeching as they hunt for prey in the dark night. The smell of damp lawns outside the window will drift in, mingling with the earthy smell of the river and the cool night air.

Or maybe they'll go to the Kenyan Highlands and stay in a hotel among the treetops, where they went when he was fourteen before a new strain of Ebola swept through the continent in 2019. The exotic place enthralled him as he sat with his parents in the bar overlooking a clearing in the forest.

He and Charlotte will sit in that same bar and drink chilled white wine and eat dried chilli shrimps. They'll marvel at the elephants, hogging the salt lick, keeping the other animals at bay until they finish and rumble away.

At night while she sleeps next to him, he'll lie awake listening to her breathing. Outside the safety of their room, they'll hear the groaning whoop and chuckle of hyenas, only to be silenced by a lion's cough. The cough will escalate to a grunting roar that will reverberate through the high-veldt air, and he'll hold Charlotte tight, so she's not afraid.

In the morning, they'll awake to sunlight filtering through mountain mist. After breakfast, they'll take their leftover toast and toss small pieces to greedy crested cranes. Then he'll take her to the Rift Valley lakes. They'll watch vast plains of moving pink brush strokes, stretching from horizon to horizon, as flamingos feed in the shallow acidic water.

But what he'd like most would be to trek through the swooping Carnarvon Gorge, or to explore the cathedral forests of Tasmania. Perhaps he could teach her to climb in the sun-drenched Blue Mountains, or maybe they could visit her parents on their farm in the highlands of North Queensland Province, where he's never been. So long as he can go to the mountains.

It was all he dreamed of in Baghdad. Cool damp mountains with their early morning mist, mingling with smoke from a campfire, the crisp air crackling with vitality, along with bacon sizzling in a battered frying pan. They'll find water in crystal streams, so cold it freezes your hands as you scoop the pure water into your mouth.

If only they could picnic high in the mountains, and watch Wedgetail eagles glide and swoop, riding the updraughts. They will gaze lazily across valleys, to the forested peaks poking out of clouds and imagine the mountains rolling away in the distance.

But they can't. They can't go anywhere in this country together. He's not free and she can't leave her job. What a fucked-up world. Anger rises in him again at the sense of helplessness he feels against the system. The surge of rage almost overwhelms him as it erupts through the sublime calm brought on by her singing.

Charlotte song ends and the audience applauds, whistling and stamping their approval. It gives Blake a moment to regain control. He watches her bow and turn to her fellow musicians holding out her hand in credit.

Evan speaks, and he moves closer to hear above the noise. 'Sorry I didn't catch that.'

'How well do you know Jeremy Marabaux?'

Blake tenses. How could Evan have guessed that's where he got the I.D? Maybe it's common knowledge that Jeremy is the go to man. He decides honesty is the best defence.

'I know him. Not well but he's engaged to a good friend.'

'Your mate Rory's sister.'

'Yes. You are well informed.'

'It's no secret Blake if you have access to the internet. You're the who's who of the establishment.'

Blake says nothing and Evan asks the question that has been puzzling him for a while. 'How come there's no public record of your arrest and conscription?'

That surprises Blake. 'Isn't there?'

'Nope.'

'I don't know.' Blake shakes his head. 'Maybe they don't publish these things.'

'They do for other convicted conscripts.' Evan is sceptical, but Blake doesn't seem to be hiding anything. The man looks genuinely perplexed.

'Really,' Blake runs his hand through his hair. 'I don't know.'

Evan isn't giving up until he finds the man's Achilles heel. He can't believe anyone as wealthy as Blake could be convicted and conscripted. The establishment protect their own. 'Maybe someone paid to suppress it.'

'Not me. You know Evan I wasn't that well off when I was arrested. My friend's father made most of my money in the last few years. My parents gave me an allowance until... anyway—then I got a student loan. When they died, I took out a bigger loan. It was so big it scared me shitless and I figured I could never pay it back, but what the hell, things change. When I was arrested, I was living on an intern's salary. The business was beginning to make real money, but I didn't know much about it then. My father's friend and business partner runs all that side of things, and he does a good job. So I got rich, and I did nothing. It's a bit sad really.'

Evan watches Blake's expression carefully in the dim light. 'Yeah I saw. Your business interests are everywhere.'

Blake grins, 'I'll take your word for it Evan. I haven't exactly been here to keep track of it. It's not really anything that interests me. My parents and the Fullers set up the Company, and we got equal shares. When my parents died, I got their shares as well as mine. That's as far as I know. Are you into this kind of stuff?'

'Yes. I was doing a PhD in economics when the country imploded.'

'I didn't know. I thought you were a farmer.'

Evan laughs. 'The last time I saw a farm I was about fifteen and the banks evicted us. That's why I wanted to do economics to understand it.'

'What about your folks Evan, are they still here?'

'No.'

'Okay.'

They lapse into silence. Blake is aware that like him, Evan doesn't like questions. They all have something to hide.

'Look Blake, Charlotte trusts you and you've been good to me. I feel I owe you mate, but I need to know what you think about Jeremy Marabaux.'

Blake frowns wondering what he can say and plays it safe. 'I hardly know the bloke, why?'

Evan wonders if he's sealing his fate, but his instincts tell him Charlotte's right and the man's okay. 'The model—Ava Murchison, she was your ex right?'

Blake feels his muscles tense again as if he's in fight mode. He forces himself to relax, but a deep sense of foreboding crowds his mind as he scans Evan's face for clues to what he's after. Eventually he says, 'that's right.'

Evan shifts, glancing around to make sure no one is listening. Charlotte is singing a folk song and people stand in front of her swaying with the rhythm. 'Marabaux was at her place the other night. There was a row about you.' He watches Blake's face.

Blake wasn't expecting that. 'How do you know?'

Evan shrugs, 'a couple of blokes I know overheard them.'

Charlotte finishes singing and places her microphone back on the stand, smiling at the audience. They are still clapping as she makes her way through the crowd. They reach out to touch her as she passes. She smiles and grasps their hands, fingers touching as she acknowledges their thanks.

She is the light in their lives Blake thinks, his eyes following her, and mine he realises, startled by the intensity of his feelings. He turns to Evan who smiles as he watches her come towards them. Blake makes up his mind. Evan could be in danger. He should know.

'Evan.' Blake grabs his arm. 'That work I.D... Marabaux got it for me. Be careful.' He drops Evan's arm and turns to greet Charlotte. 'Your voice is a wonder.' He smiles at her and rests his hand in the small of her back. 'I'll get you a beer.'

As Blake waits for the beers, he watches Evan and Charlotte, wondering if he has brought disaster into all their lives. Somehow, he's managed to get into Marabaux's debt very quickly, and he can't help the nagging feeling that it's not merely coincidence.

12.

In the early hours of the morning, Blake lies awake with his hands behind his head afraid to close his eyes. The curtains are pulled back from the window and lights from the street below chase across the glass panes, casting the room in light and dark shadows.

The image of arms held in surrender is still vivid in his mind. Did he make a mistake sending Richard across the river by himself? Is his mate's death his fault? If they were together in the water, maybe he would still be alive.

He rolls onto his side to watch Charlotte sleep. Not even her eyelids flicker. The rhythmic rise and fall of her breast is all the evidence of life. How can she sleep so soundly when their lives are about to be torn apart?

There's a repetitive refrain in his head. One more day, one more night, is there no way of stopping time? To suppress the surge of anger he controls his breathing. They own him body and soul and until he's free, he can do nothing.

Evan's account of the argument between Marabaux and Ava pops into his head. That bothers him. He doesn't trust Jeremy, but he didn't think he would do anything to harm Emmy. What was he doing with Ava and why were they arguing about him? The niggling certainty of something amiss lurks at the edge of his mind. Perhaps he's becoming paranoid. Jeremy hasn't solicited one thing from Blake, but the slide into his debt seems so fast and easy.

Charlotte snuggles under the covers as he gets up and walks to the window. The grey dawn light creeps in, lightening the room. He stares out, waiting for sunrise. There is so little time before he goes to Canberra.

Across the road, a billboard flashes orange, yellow, and green lights, your country needs you. He barely notices. He'd marry her if he could get a licence, but he knows until he's free he can't without their permission. If they were married, she wouldn't have to work for anyone, let alone the arsewipe in the bar, but he can't marry her, and can't protect her.

An hour later, he climbs back into bed and holds her.

She stirs. 'Blake, what time is it?'

'It's early Charlotte, but I need to ask you something.'

She stretches, her fingers woven together as she pushes her hands above her head. What? Her eyes widen and fully awake now, she struggles to sit up, the covers falling from her, revealing her nakedness.

'Charlotte I have so little time before I go. I can't bear to leave you here alone.'

'I'm not alone and five months is not so very long, but I will miss you.' She smiles at him cheerfully, but her eyes scan his face with wary caution.

Now he's faced with explaining his fear, it seems foolish. She's waiting for him to speak and suddenly he doesn't know what to say. How can he tell her he has a feeling of impending doom, but has no idea what it might be?

'Charlotte let me get you another job so you don't have to work for the bastard in the bar anymore. You can work for Mr Fuller. That way you can get time off to visit me in Canberra.'

'Can't I visit you anyway?'

'What reason can you give for the travel permit, and how will you get off work? If you work for Mr Fuller, you can accompany him. He has reason to go to Canberra because his sister is there, and he has business interests...and I can ask him...'

'I don't know. Bloody hell Blake you can't spring things on me this early in the morning.'

She's looking at him strangely, but he can't read what she's thinking. Christ, he's screwed this up. He should have waited until later, but he doesn't have time. 'Charlotte listen, there's something funny going on.'

'Yes there is—you waking me so early with crazy schemes.' She sees his worried face and stops. 'What is it Blake?'

'I'm not sure yet. It's a more feeling than fact, but too many things don't add up. The weird thing is how the police knew about my shirt. It got splattered with blood the night before the murder, but they took it from the Fuller's house, like they knew it was there.'

A cold shiver runs across her shoulders and she asks guardedly, 'why did they suspect you in the first place?'

'I don't know Charlotte, but I'm indebted to my eyebrows to Marabaux. First, he gets me off the murder charge, then the media doesn't report my arrest, and there's the I.D. for Evan. He's offered to get me a payment for my story. I also found out, I have no record of a drug charge, or any other charges for that matter. It's all a bit weird, like I'm being set up for something.'

'And you think getting me a job with your firm will keep me safe? It sounds like just knowing you, is dangerous.' She laughs with relief as her scepticism softens. 'It could all be coincidental and not some conspiracy. After all the bloke's a sleaze who takes money for favours, because he has access through his father. Everyone knows that. He's really just doing his job.'

'You could be right. I don't know anymore. Sorry I haven't slept and things are getting on top of me.' He stops as her hand runs along his thigh. Why is he worrying so much? She's right; it's probably just a coincidence. 'Come here you lovely woman.

You can't sit naked on the bed and expect me to ignore you, but I still want you to change jobs.'

'Why do you care Blake?' She waits for him to answer, holding her breath.

'What do you mean? Of course I care.' He sits back on his haunches, and scans her face.

He knows what she wants him to say, but can he? Is this love? Isn't it too soon to say its love? Is it lust? How can he be so concerned about her if it isn't love? Christ, he's ready to marry her. It must be love. How does a person know something like that? When he became engaged to Ava, it was easy. She arranged everything. All he had to do was go along with her instructions. Now he stares at Charlotte, knowing she's waiting for his reply.

'Because I think I might be in love,' he says.

Her face relaxes, and she reaches for him, 'thank God.'

He pulls back. 'That's not the response I expected.'

'No, but for a moment I thought you wanted to protect me like I am some useless bit of fluff. But if you love me that's different, and I might even accept your job, but when you get back from Canberra okay. By then you'll be sure, not just think you might be in love.'

'What about you Charlotte?'

'Me?'

'Yes.' He averts his eyes and stares out the window.

She smiles at his nervousness. 'I was sure when you told me at the bar you were coming back to see me at eleven that first night remember.'

She watches his eyes flick back to focus on her, and she wishes she could know what he's thinking, but his eyes are shadowed in the early light.

Later that same day, she is so busy at work she hasn't a moment to herself. When June comes in to serve lunches Charlotte asks her to mind the bar for a few minutes, but when she returns, June isn't there. Instead, Patterson stands arms folded in fury. Customers are lined up at the bar waiting to place their orders, but he ignores them watching the door behind the bar as she enters.

Where the fuck is June, Charlotte wonders as she rushes to the counter saying, 'sorry who's next?'

Paterson's hand lands heavily on her shoulder. His fingers dig into her flesh making her wince as she turns to look at him. His head jerks, 'my office.'

'But the customers...' She glances worriedly at the crowd two deep along the bar.

He doesn't look at them. 'You've kept them waiting this long. They can wait a little longer.'

He propels her through the door into the corridor and stops. She faces him, her eyes challenging. Indignation makes her bold. It's okay for him to take her away from the customers to yell at her, but it's not okay for her to go to the toilet. Her lips press into a thin white ridged line as she watches his face change hue.

His voice cracks with rage as he says, 'I've a mind to sack you without notice. Do you think this hotel is a charity that it can employ you to swan about while the customers wait?'

'I went to the ladies.' Charlotte tries to maintain evenness in her voice. 'I asked June to cover for me.'

'Liar you have been with that, that... that convict again. I'm calling the police. You have the morals of an alley cat.'

'No please Mr Patterson, I was in the ladies.' Charlotte is beginning to worry. She's never seen Patterson in such a fury.

Patterson lifts his hand, and she flinches. She can't believe he intends to hit her, but just at that moment, June comes traipsing along the hall and Mr Patterson's hand drops to his side. He turns away saying under his breath, 'you're on a short leash missy, one more slip up, one more visit to that criminal's room and you're gone. You'll pay for this—one day's pay docked.'

'What the fuck were you thinking?' She spits at June as soon as Patterson has gone.

'Sorry I didn't think he'd mind. I only went to get another lunch order pad from the office.' Her round freckled face folds in on itself as her eyes become pink with tears.

'How could you leave the bar unattended? My pay is being docked again and I don't have enough to pay my rent as it is. Why couldn't you just wait for one more minute? Ah shit!' Charlotte throws up her hands as tears roll down June's cheeks. She feels guilty for taking it out on June, but Jesus she was only gone a couple of minutes.

The day doesn't get better. The bar is busy all afternoon because of a conference in one of the function rooms upstairs. It seems to Charlotte that it's an excuse to get together and drink. The conference goers are all men and Charlotte is convinced they think it's their God given right to hit on her. If she goes to clear a table, someone gropes her, and by the time Blake comes in at six o'clock, she's ready to scream.

As she slides a beer across the counter to him he says, 'can you get off early tonight?'

'No I don't think so Blake. You know what he's like. Why?'

'I want to take you to dinner at the Fullers'. They want to meet you?' He smiles.

'What did you tell them?' Dread at the thought of meeting his grand friends clutches her stomach.

'I said I wanted to introduce my girl. They can look after you while I'm gone.' His face becomes serious as he pleads. 'Please Charlotte let me tell your boss to go screw himself. Both Mr Fuller and Rory have said you can work in their offices. Maybe they can get you an audition with the Australian Media Consortium, or the National Opera.'

Nervousness and the strain of the day snaps something in Charlotte's mind. Men are all the same, they think they own you and can push you around just to suit themselves. 'No, and I'm really pissed off with you for not asking me. Stop trying to run my life. Just because you have money, you think you can order the rest of us around...' She stops. 'Screw it. I've got work to do.'

'Charlotte.'

'Just go Blake, I'm too busy. I can't do this...' She shakes her head and goes to serve another customer.

Bewildered by her outburst he gets up off his bar stool and fishes in his pocket for change. There is none, so he slaps a hundred dollar note on the counter and walks out. A man with a beard gets up from a dark corner of the bar and follows him. Blake strides down the road confused and angry, and his hurt turns inwards.

Of course, what a fool he's been. It was too good to last. There's a peculiar ache in his chest and he feels as if he can't breathe properly. He walks faster. Her rejection and the fear of losing her collide in a potent force. What did he expect? Never tell a girl you love her, they immediately shit all over you. He knows that's not fair, but it hurts.

It hurts more than Ava dumping him did. His mind flashes back, and he's there again under the hot desert sky. They had just returned from patrol, and he was cleaning his weapon when one of the blokes said there was a letter for him. He knew it would be from Ava and his spirits soared, but first he would finish cleaning his rifle and maintaining his kit. It was a discipline that kept him alive.

While he worked he savoured the anticipation, knowing once he had everything in order he would be able to sit in solitude and devour her words. It was a moment of relief in the relentless grind of the war's stalemate. Her letters were always entertaining, full of malicious gossip and cutting wit, cruel but funny. The longing he had for home just about swamped him with its ferocity, and Ava represented home.

After six months in the Middle East, he was one of the few remaining men from his intake still alive; a seasoned hand. They wanted him to train the new intake, and he agreed. Maybe he could keep some of them alive. In the beginning, he hadn't known enough to keep his mates safe, but he did now and he wouldn't make the same mistakes again. Their contorted blind-eyed faces flare in his mind.

The training he'd received when he arrived was haphazard. Maybe he could do better although the poisoned weapons weren't something anyone expected. He'd train this new lot to think for themselves, to be wary of everything like he was. Stand back and assess before rushing into anything.

It kept him alive... so far anyway, although he was never sure if it was worth it. Sometimes he was so tired he almost envied the dead, at least they were out of this living nightmare. Then he would try to shake off the lethargy, knowing that thinking like that was a one-way ticket to hell. Just do the job and don't think, don't feel, just focus on accomplishing the mission.

Now he's back in Australia he had almost forgotten that lesson. Charlotte made him believe things might be different. For weeks, he tried to hold off when he saw her, only watching from afar, but it didn't last. He shouldn't have spoken to her. He knew it was a mistake from the beginning, but he'd almost convinced himself it would be okay; that it was fate.

It was like he told the new grunts over there, they needed to learn quickly or die. When he first arrived, no one had time to train, but he surprised himself at how good he had become at this game of killing others while he survived. It was a win lose game of high stakes, and he was winning.

Even in that last offensive, in the push through Kuwait to Basra, he knew the key was to focus, not panic no matter what they threw at you, and keep your wits. Not everyone was as lucky though, but there was no time to stop and think about it. You had a task to do, and you just concentrated on completing it to the best of your ability, without distractions, without idle imaginings. He had long since learned emotions weakened your resolve. Bury them deep until he's back in civilised, safe, and democratic Australia.

Well now, it seems he still needs to keep them buried, even in Australia. He's got soft. Over there he steeled his nerve and learned not to worry about dying. Going out on patrol was like playing roulette, every corner you went around could be the one with the bullet or incendiary device that got you, but Blake was developing a sixth sense for danger. It's a pity he let it slide now he's back, but he won't make that mistake again.

When he was there, he convinced himself you only die once, so it doesn't matter when you die. You won't know about it anyway, so there's no point in worrying. That's like a living death and he didn't want to live like that. If he had to be there, he would live every moment, and if he had to die there, he would do that too, but he wouldn't know anything about it. He would be dead and only Ava would mourn him. Once he saw her letter, he realised none of it mattered anymore.

They had retaken Kuwait, and the area that had once been the southern tip of Iraq. They were feeling confident, with bets doing the rounds among the men about whether the brass would split the country along tribal lines or revert to the pre Caliphate boarders.

For the NATO and Allied coalition there were six key targets, Mecca, Medina, Jerusalem, Damascus, Cairo, and for the American, Australian and New Zealand contingent, Kuwait then Baghdad the seat of Caliphate power. They had to take Baghdad not only militarily, but also for the propaganda advantage.

FISLO still controlled Baghdad and everything north including the area they called al-Sham, which included the countries that were once Lebanon, Syria, Jordan and Israel. Their affiliates also held countries from Nigeria to the Philippines, but Blake knew little about those operations.

The Americans ruled out carpet-bombing Baghdad, until there was more information on where they held the prisoners. There were dozens of them and one was rumoured to be the American President's son, but Blake thought that was probably bullshit. It was just that no one wanted a repeat of the media blitz featuring rows of dead and mutilated women and children, like when they finally took the rubble that was Basra.

He found a secluded place behind a supply container, and sitting on an upturned crate, he slit open the letter. That's when the ring fell out. He was numb after that. Didn't even read it just stuffed it in his pocket, but he was still holding the ring so he dropped that in too. Then he walked back to the mess, burying his hurt deep and continued as if nothing had changed.

Ava was another life, and he'd deal with that life once he finished dealing with this one. When his Sergeant told them that the Major wanted volunteers, he put up his hand before he knew what he was volunteering for, but he didn't care.

It was funny, instead of having to deal with how he felt about Ava and her dumping him, he found by the time he let himself address the problem he no longer cared. He had a lot of time to think after his capture, but he was lucky. He was the only one of the five men who was.

It was because he spoke Arabic and knew the Sunni manners and Islamic beliefs that he managed to stay alive. That and his medical training which they found useful. But he doesn't know if it was worth it. Maybe if he had died, one of the others might have survived—a life for a life.

He reaches the ferry terminal before he hears her voice calling him. She's running down the road, her beret in hand and her hair loose from its string and streaming out behind her.

His eyes narrow as she runs up panting. He's still angry. She bends over coughing, trying to recover her breath. He waits, hard and unrelenting, the memory of Baghdad still large in his mind.

'Blake,' she coughs again. 'Blake,' her eyes stream making her nose run. 'I'm so sorry. I was a bitch. I had such a bad day with work and Patterson...'

He tries to push aside the wedged stone in his chest and forces a smile, forgiving her with his words even though his mind doesn't yet follow.

'Have you changed your mind—are you coming to dinner?'

'May as well, if you'll have me,' she says wiping her eyes and nose with the sleeve of her shoulder. 'I haven't run that far ever, or so quickly. You walk so fast I thought I would never catch you. I was yelling, and carrying on like a lunatic, thinking you were ignoring me on purpose.'

Her heart begins to pound at its regular rate. She looks up into his eyes seeing something cold and hard, where before she saw tenderness, and she's frightened. 'Please Blake; I'm sorry for being such a bitch. It's just so sudden you know. I need time to adjust.'

His numbness thaws a little. 'It's okay,' he says wondering if it is. 'How did you get away from work?'

'I just phoned him and told him I had to go off for the evening and left. I didn't wait for his response so I am going to cop it tomorrow, but I'll worry about that then. Now I just want to do what you want.'

'He says come on we'll miss the ferry.'

'Blake...' She is overcome with nervousness.

He turns back to her. 'Yes.'

'Am I all right to go to dinner with your friends in this?' She indicates the plain black skirt, tee shirt, and sneakers she wears every day to the bar.

'They won't care what you're wearing. It's not important Charlotte.'

She doesn't believe that for a minute, but follows him trying to smooth her hair and straighten her clothing. She can put up with their sneers and condescension so long as she has Blake.

13.

Honour, duty, integrity, discipline, self-sacrifice, and his men, these are the things that get Captain Henry out of bed every morning, but he doesn't know how to categorise this.

'What the blazes am I to do with you? You're a bloody conscript aren't you? Why have they assigned you to me?' He looks up from his desk, his eyes looking over the rimless glasses as if he's expecting an answer.

Blake stands to attention, his eyes fixed on the mustard coloured panelling behind the man's head. The office smells of wax polish and paraffin. The room is an office in the Royal Military College, Duntroon, Canberra.

Henry shakes his head and looks at the file in front of him. 'Well at least it says here you are a doctor.'

Blake says, 'intern sir,' and regrets saying it the moment the words leave his mouth. In his experience, you don't contradict officers, not without consequences, but Captain Henry doesn't react the way Blake expects.

'What do you mean? It says here you are fully qualified. You even have a registration number.'

Blake looks the Captain in the eye and says, 'I didn't finish my internship sir.'

Henry shakes his head. He can only deal with one dilemma at a time. 'This is official, and if they say you're fully qualified, I'll take their word for it, but I've never before seen a conscript assigned to this Corp. I'm not really sure what to do with you. A conscript doesn't have a rank, so where am I going to put you. You're a doctor so you should be an officer. What are you doing here Lincoln?'

Blake remains silent.

An exasperated sigh escapes from Captain Henry. 'I asked you a question Conscript.'

'Sorry sir. I am here because I am a convicted conscript.'

'Are you being deliberately stupid?' Captain Henry's neck flushes an angry pink. The skin looks puckered and shiny like it's been grafted after a burn.

'No sir, sorry sir.'

Henry leans back in his chair and pulls out his drawer. He takes out a small square of cloth and takes off his glasses, polishing each of the lenses as he scrutinises Blake. 'What was your crime?'

'Ah, sorry sir. Unlawful assembly and dope,' he says leaving out resisting arrest.

'Pushing?'

'No sir, possession.'

'How much.'

'One joint sir.'

'And they gave you three years?'

'Yes sir, and I took part in a protest march and um... resisted arrest.'

Henry raises his eyebrows, 'must have been your unlucky day. Any previous?'

'No sir. Sir...'

'What is it Conscript?'

'I understood I was to report to Strategic Services for translation duties.'

'Hm.' He replaces his glasses, adjusting them to sit halfway down his nose, and picks up a paper. 'These orders came in this morning and it says nothing about Strategic Services. You will bunk in with Lieutenant Brady. He won't be happy, but too bad. I have nowhere else to put you. You report for duty at 08:00 hours tomorrow. For the rest of the day you can find your way around.' Henry gets up, 'Corporal Hollish, get in here.'

A diminutive soldier with blonde hair braided tightly against her skull, walks into the Captain's office. 'Sir,' she says.

'Take Conscript Lincoln and show him what's what will you. I've put him in with Lieutenant Brady.'

'Conscript sir?'

'Yes, you heard me Hollish.'

'Yes sir.'

Blake turns to follow Hollish, but the Captain calls him back.

'Conscript...'

'Yes sir.'

'Well done on the Baghdad episode.'

'Yes sir.'

'While you're with us you might give consideration to joining up with the regulars. If you're as good a doctor as you are a hero, we'll be glad to have you. Think about it.'

Dismissed, Blake walks out following Hollish. She speaks to someone in the outside office and turns to Blake. 'Ready Conscript?'

'Yes Corporal.'

'Do you have a bag?'

'Yes Corporal.'

'Well go and get it. it's not going to walk by itself.'

As Blake moves across the room to retrieve his bag from where he left it, she turns to the other soldier sitting at the desk. 'A bloody conscript, can you believe it?'

Blake follows her out the building. A blast of forty-six degree heat hits him as they descend the polished steps of the building to cross the parade ground.

'Where are you from Conscript?' she asks.

'Brisbane.'

'Is it as hot there?'

'Not at the moment Corp.'

'It's fucking April already. The weather should have cooled off a bit by now, don't you think?'

'Yes Corp.'

'What did the Captain mean about you being a hero? Is it something I would know?'

Blake shrugs. 'It's nothing.'

'Must be something,' she stares at him her mouth pursed in a rose pink pucker. Then it comes to her. 'You're that bloke on the news aren't you? I didn't recognise you straight off. You look different in real life, taller maybe. Good on you. You did us proud.'

Blake doesn't know how to answer and shifts uncomfortably, the heat making his uniform stick to his back. 'Thanks and you're right it's much hotter here than in Brisbane,' he says trying to change the subject.

'You'll want to get used to it pretty damn quickly.' She turns and walks away and he follows. 'Your day begins at 06:00 hours. At 06:30, we run for five kays. Then back, shower and breakfast at 07:30 hours. We used to do it the other way around, but it's too hot to run any later so they do it before breakfast now. I hope you don't suffer low blood sugar. If you do, you can take a snack from the mess. They hand out energy bars for those that can't run on an empty stomach. You will report for prayers at 08:00 and work begins at 08:30.'

'Prayers Corporal?'

'Yeah a new fucking order came in a while ago. Here are your quarters. Yours is the second door on the left.' She pivots on her heel and leaves him.

Blake knocks cautiously and opens the door. Across a common room, a swarthy-skinned soldier sits at a small desk looking out the window, his room door open. He looks surprised at the intrusion, his brown eyes fringed with curled black lashes giving him a startled doe-eyed look.

'Who the fuck are you?' His eyebrows join in a single dark smudge across his brow as he stares at the conscript greens.

'Conscript Lincoln sir. Captain Henry said to bunk in here.'

'Screw that. A bloody conscript. Was that Hollish-Delish-Delightful?'

'Yes sir.'

'You sure she said this block?'

'Yes sir.'

'Christ,' he drags his palm down the plane of his cheek as he stares at Lincoln.

'Hang on, don't I know you?'

'I don't think so.'

'You look bloody familiar. Are you sure I don't know you.'

'Yes sir.'

'Okay well there's a vacant room. Stay out of my way and keep quiet. I'm studying.'

Blake takes his bag to the room. As he opens the door, stale emptiness wafts out, along with dancing dust beams that blink in the light from the window. The room is narrow, and built-in with a bed, wardrobe, and desk. Its functional rather than comforting. The narrow window looks out over the road to a playing field. He glances out as he places his few possessions in the locker.

Brady leans his shoulder against his open door. 'You don't own much do you?'

'I like to travel light sir.'

'If we must live in the same quarters you can drop the formalities. Cut out the sir bit while were in here. Outside it's a different matter. So tell me what you're doing here.'

'I don't know sir... sorry.'

'What do you mean you don't know?'

'I don't know why I'm here.'

'I get that, but how can you not know? They don't usually assign conscripts to this Corp.'

'I can speculate.'

'That will do.'

'I'm a doctor,' Blake says. It feels strange even though his FISLO guards called him Doctor, and it saved his life. This is real. They are not going to strip him of his degree after all. They will let him remain a doctor after all, despite his criminal conviction and conscription. A strange sensation creeps into his chest. 'I guess that's why they sent me here for the rest of my sentence.'

'Well, well, you're ahead of me then. If you weren't a conscript, they'd make you an officer. How long did you get?'

'Three years, so long as I signed to fight.'

'Christ. That's a good chunk. So you're here for three years.'

'No I've done most of it. I have five months left.'

'So three years. What would it have been if you didn't sign on to fight?'

'Three, plus the mandatory seven for drugs.'

'Shit. You're lucky to get out alive. I hear many don't.' Brady waits for Blake to speak, but he says nothing, folding a tee shirt, the last item, and placing it neatly in his locker. 'You're a communicative sod aren't you?'

Still Blake says nothing.

It dawns on Brady who Blake is. 'Ah... Now I see it. I thought you looked familiar. You're that bloke who saved those prisoners in Baghdad; Yanks weren't they?'

'Brits and Australians too.'

'Jesus! That was some feat. Ready to talk about it?'

'No.'

'Okay. Anything I should know about you. PTSD or whatever. You're not going to go crazy in your sleep and try to cut my throat or something?'

Blake smiles. 'No.'

'So you might be useful if you're a doctor. I'm studying to get through the Graduate Australian Medical Admission Test. I have a degree in medical science, but I'm sick of rookies who know less than I do about medicine. Yeah people like you I imagine. But never mind that now. Want a drink? We can go to the mess for a beer. Do you play pool?' He laughs, 'this is wild. A fucking conscript in the officers' mess—maybe they won't let you in. Come on, let's give it a go shall we, the rules were written before the invention of you blokes. I fucking love it.'

'Permission to ask a question sir.'

'Fuck Conscript, just ask.'

'Corporal Hollish says we have prayers at 08.00 hours...'

'Yeah that God bothering pollie, who thinks he's in charge of the ADF, has a bee in his bonnet about this being a Christian country, and us leading by example. Now we all have to go to prayers daily, if you can believe it. No exceptions or you're on a charge. Three strikes and you get a dishonourable discharge. Fucking lunacy, but who can explain politics.'

'What about people who have a different, or no religion?'

'No place for that kind here Conscript.' His voice changes, its tone sonorous, taking the piss out of someone who Blake assumes is the politician.

The next morning Blake runs ahead of the others. The sun rises above the grey green hills rolling away into the distance and already he feels the heat rising. It's nothing to the heat he's experienced, first growing up in Saudi then fighting in the Free Islamic State. The dry air is familiar, but it's not quite so dusty and the ubiquitous smell of overfull sewers and goats is missing. He turns left at the lake.

Despite the heat or because of it maybe, the leaves on the trees are turning red and orange and yellow. He's awed by the colours of autumn. You don't get that in Brisbane. The whole palette rests against a backdrop of grey-green eucalypt, and distant mountains washed blue in the morning light.

The neat orderliness astonishes him. This is the capital, the seat of power and yet it looks so ordinary. The wide tree-lined boulevards are empty of vehicles or other pedestrians.

As he runs, he smiles at the commotion he caused in the mess. People were flummoxed over a conscript in their midst until the Major said he was a doctor. That seemed to settle it. There is no rank for conscripts. You either are a conscript or not and usually considered not much better than a waste of good rations. Good cannon fodder for the real Army. Blake doesn't know how he got so lucky getting this gig, but he's not going to argue.

He'll do his remaining few months and be out of there. Things are working out fine. As soon as the thought has formed, he worries he's tempting fate, and he tries to clear his mind, focussing on his breathing instead. He'll write to Charlotte and tell her about the autumn colours as soon as he has time. She promised to write back, but he wonders if she will.

When he left Brisbane a couple of days ago, she went with him to the station. As they stood waiting for the Bullet train to Canberra, she had tears in her eyes. He wiped them away with his thumb. Then he put his arm around her shoulders, feeling the warm softness of her down his flank.

The green fatigues, with the white conscript band, labelled him a criminal. It caused a few turned heads. What was this conscript doing on the platform without a guard? He ignored them, focussing on Charlotte, trying to imprint her face on his memory so he could conjure it across the months ahead.

He wanted to ask her if she'd wait for him, but didn't. It wasn't fair to ask that of her, but he hoped she would. He was wary of her thinking he was trying to run her life, and didn't mention staying with the Fuller's, or suggest she work for the company again.

When they arrived for dinner the night before he left, Mrs Fuller insisted on champagne because she said it was a celebration. Emmy linked arms with Charlotte and laughed saying, 'it's just because Mum wants an excuse to get out the Bollinger. She's an addict, but we humour her.'

Blake was grateful for the way they welcomed her, but why wouldn't they? They're the nearest thing he has to family. He took Em aside after dinner and asked her to take care of Charlotte if she could, and then he asked her to postpone her wedding.

'Bloody hell Blake, you don't ask for much do you?'

'Please Em; I really want to be there. Aren't you going to ask me to be your flower girl or something?' He smiled at her, covering his unease about her marrying Jeremy.

Emmy said, 'Jeremy won't be happy. He doesn't think long engagements work.'

Blake wanted to say screw him, but instead said, 'I'm sure he'll understand Em. After all, I'm almost like a brother aren't I? You'd wait for a brother.'

'All right, but you better get out quickly.' She looked up at him and smiled. 'Don't do something stupid like tell an officer to go screw himself and get your time extended.'

14.

Captain Henry sits at his desk pulling his bottom lip, thinking this task goes against everything he believes. A shaft of sunlight angles through his office window, highlighting dust specs suspended in the air, before falling on the desk to spotlight a pile of mail. There is no honour in doing this, and he's had enough. But an order is an order.

He picks up the top letter and gazes absently out the window as he slides in the letter-knife to rip it open without looking at the envelope. It's his job to intercept and vet Conscript Lincoln's in-coming and out-going mail. He wasn't happy, and told the Military Police he's a soldier, not a bloody gaoler, but he had little choice.

He tries not to enjoy it, especially not the letters from lovely Charlotte who sent that photo. If she was trying to get attention, she succeeded. He couldn't help scrutinise that one, the lucky bastard.

He likes Lincoln. The man's a good soldier and a fine doctor. Since he joined the unit, he's done well. He knows more about battle injuries than most doctors Henry's met, despite not completing his internship, and he's generous with sharing what he knows. In Henry's view, he has a good attitude for a conscript. It's his job to entice the man to sign on, but even so, he wouldn't mind having him in the unit as a regular.

Now as he reads the communication in his hand his heart races. He re-scans the letter and stares out the window. This is big, and he isn't sure how to handle it. He shuffles through the pile of mail looking for the other letter he saw that was addressed to Lincoln. He better read that one too before he decides what to do.

'Jesus!' He sits back and takes off his reading glasses, staring blankly at the two letters open on his desk. What the fuck does he do with this? He's never heard of anything like it. He knows a little about Lincoln, but this is unbelievable.

The bloke is tight-lipped about Baghdad. It's Henry's job to find out as much as he can, but all Brady's winkled out of him are small, unconnected bits of information. So far, he's pieced together that the Caliphate Guard killed Lincoln's entire squad in an ambush. He escaped, but they captured him later swimming across the Tigress.

The thing he doesn't know, what the Brigadier wants to know, is if he was radicalised by the bastards. But given the content of these letters, it's more likely there will be an alien invasion of earth by Martian bacteria.

To Henry, Blake's sacrifice to help his fellow inmates escape makes him beyond suspicion, but orders are orders so he's done what he could to establish the man's bonefides, and kept him away from sensitive information in the meantime. As far as Henry is concerned, the whole thing is a beat up. Just more shiny-seated bureaucrats afraid of their own shadows.

Counting what he knows about Blake's time in the Middle East, he itemises each fact. The bloke spent two years locked in a prison in Baghdad. There were concessions to move the prisoners to cells in the barracks, from some horrifying punishment blocks in the compound. The others say Blake wangled those concessions, but no one knows how. Their food improved, and they were provided medicines; again no one knows how or why, but they put it down to Lincoln's influence.

It wasn't just because Lincoln spoke fluent Arabic and knew the Sunni customs. Captain Henry knows Lincoln pretended to be a Muslim, which is what some people say helped the other prisoners, but Henry doesn't buy that.

The question the boss wants answered is, was it all bluff? No one believes that just being a Muslim would be enough to get the Caliphate guard on side, not an enemy combatant, not with those murdering thugs.

He read the official report of Lincoln's escape so he knows that after Lincoln and his fellow prisoners arrived safely back in Basra the first time, Lincoln ignored his own exhaustion to treat the surviving wounded enemy they had brought back in the truck. In gratitude for Lincoln saving his life, one of the Caliphate soldiers told Blake about other infidel prisoners. He drew a map of their location. It would be surprising if they were still alive given they were right under the last American bombing raid.

Blake insisted on returning to Baghdad to get them out. Two of his fellow escapees, Australian Special Forces soldiers, volunteered to help. Together they went back into the hellhole, with the Americans re-running their earlier bombardment of the oil refinery, to provide cover and keep the enemy occupied.

They got the British platoon out, but Blake was wounded. Henry knows that much because they all know it. It was in the report recommending the VC for gallantry, but it's all based on other people's accounts, because no one seems able to get Blake to speak about it.

The only new bit of information Brady has extracted for Henry, is that Lincoln bribed a guard to smuggle medicines and food for his fellow prisoners. The bribe was a two-carat diamond ring. An engagement ring for Christ's sake! That's the least believable bit of the whole bloody shemozzle. Who runs around a battlefield with a two-carat diamond in their pocket?

He looks at the letters on his desk. The bloke deserves the medals, but it shouldn't take foreigners to do it. It makes him sad that the recommendation for the Australian VC went nowhere. He pushes his chair back, standing to make the call to the Major. Once connected he straightens his shoulders saying, 'sir, I need to speak with you as a matter of urgency.'

Major Cadell listens and tells him to go to the Brigadier's office. Henry stuffs the letters into a folder, and leaves, calling out to Hollish as the door shuts behind him. He crosses the parade ground and walks along pathways to a building the other side of the campus.

His heart beats a tattoo to match his stride like a water bird high stepping across lily pads. He's not sure what the Brigadier will do. How often do you have a bloke in your command who receives one of these, let alone two? Lincoln deserves the commendations, but he isn't sure how the Brigadier will take it. A bloody conscript! Still bravery comes from all sorts of unexpected places.

The Brigadier takes the letters and Henry stands at ease watching his face. He takes far too long reading the content. It's a ruse, and Henry knows he is playing for time. The old man doesn't know what to do. He watches the spiky eyebrows draw together over a bulbous nose that might once have been viewed as patrician before red wine and brandy changed its contours.

Eventually the Brigadier says, 'you did right bringing these to my attention. I'll take it from here.' He raps the end of his pen against the edge of the desk, his only sign of agitation.

Henry waits, knowing he's overstepping the mark, but also knowing that by law these letters belonged to Lincoln, or they need to be returned to sender. They can't just swipe the sodding things. He won't be anyone's fall guy for that if it comes out later, not with the NATO command involved.

'Permission to speak sir.'

'Yes, get on with it Henry.'

'The letters are by rights Lincoln's sir. They should be delivered to him...'

'He's a bloody conscript. He has no rights.' The Brigadier throws the pen onto the desk glaring at Henry, his face flushing.

Henry takes a breath and braves the backlash. 'Yes sir... in that case the letters should be returned to sender and marked as inappropriate mail for a conscript to receive.'

'Are you bloody mad? The foreign press will have a field day.'

Major Cadell leans across the desk and says something under his breath.

The Brigadier frowns. 'Yes, I suppose so,' he says. 'Right, I'll just get copies and you can have these back tomorrow.' He turns to the Major. 'Can we get a suppression order over the press in the U.K. and the States?'

The Major shakes his head and turns to Henry. 'You can get along now Captain.'

As Henry closes the door, he hears the Brigadier saying, 'maybe the PM can ring her and talk sense into her, leader to leader you know.'

That afternoon the orders come, and Captain Henry knows why although he makes no comment. This Lincoln bloke is proving to be a bit of a thorn in the proverbial. It will mean he won't get the notice of his awards for at least a few more weeks. Time enough perhaps to get a reconsideration of Lincoln's merit.

It means Henry will miss his daughter's tenth birthday. His wife will be furious. Perhaps he can send a section and stay back himself. He'll speak to the Major. After all, it's Lincoln they want out the way not him.

If only the bloke would relent and sign on as a regular. Then they'd be glad to let him have the awards. It would mean his unit would have a British Military Order of Merit recipient awarded by the King himself, and the Medal of Honour from Madam President.

Still no award from the Australian Government though, interesting despite the recommendation. Henry wonders if the Conscript really is a terrorist spy as they suspect. He can't see it, but what would a lowly soldier like him know. How could they believe such a thing, when they too would have read the dispatch from the Commander in charge of the Australian Forces in Basra, the one who put forward Lincoln's name for the Australian Victoria Cross?

For crying out loud, he's a mere Captain in charge of training medical personnel to behave like soldiers, not a spook. Why don't they give the job to the Australian Intelligence Services? What does he know about conscripts anyway? He's never even met one until now. Usually they go straight from basic training in the Kimberly, to deployment through Darwin and overseas. He has never heard of one being assigned in Canberra, but then he's never heard of one of this lot winning medals for gallantry.

Ah well, a trip to Cape York will do them good. At least he won't have to read Lincoln's mail for a while, and July is a relatively dry month up there. If you have to go, it's better in winter than in the heat or the wet. The worst thing they will face, from what he has heard, is the mind numbing boredom.

'Hollish,' he calls, 'get in here.'

15.

The overhead lights cast shadows along the stark ribcage of the plane's fuselage. Time has lost its meaning as the engine drone fills Blake's universe with its soporific monotone. He has lost all sense of where they are, or how long they have been travelling. A glance at his companions tells him they are in the same state, slumped into indolence as the hours drag.

Blake accepts the feeling of never knowing where he's going, its purpose, or its reason. He focuses on the here and now, on controlling his mind, his body and his immediate surroundings. Usually he likes flying, but it's not much of an event when he can't see out the plane, and he doesn't like long periods of inactivity. The flight to the Cape has been uneventful, but he looks forward to landing.

He stretches his back, stiff with stillness as the drone changes pitch and the plane banks to line up the runway of their destination. Weipa is command HQ for Operation Sovereign Shield now, but it wasn't always. Once it was a mining town and the scars of mining are still visible as the Boeing P-8A comes into land at Scherger RAAF Base at Mission River.

Captain Henry and Lieutenant Brady sit either side of an attractive nursing officer, tendrils of dark hair making their corkscrewed escape from her tight bun. Two medics, a dentist, a chaplain, and a psychologist sit opposite him. Their mission is to carry out complete health checks on all the troops stationed here.

Weipa is where they send the wounded and injured, both physical and psychological. They'll have their work cut out, so Captain Henry said. Brady told him they'd be driving big distances and camping for most of the time although it doesn't turn out like that. For now, he's looking forward to it. He's never seen the Cape.

Once on the ground the Officers move towards a small demountable leaving Brady, Blake and the two medics to unload. A dusty transport truck drives up to the plane and two soldiers climb out. They salute Brady who stands in the wing's shade directing the unloading, his forehead glistening.

'Did you bring mail, Lieutenant?' It's one of the men from the truck, his sandy eyelashes blinking against the bright light. Behind him, another dark haired man hovers, looking eagre and Blake figures, the sandy haired bloke is probably asking on his mate's behalf.

Brady nods to Blake, and he holds up the mail sack. The dark haired soldier looks agitated. His square jaw is clenched with suppressed tension.

Blake feels sorry for the bloke. He guesses he's waiting for news of family, but soon forgets him as he turns his attention to lugging supplies and bags from the aircraft to the truck. When the transfer is complete, he stops to take in the landscape.

The northern wilderness stretches away either side of the runway. It's mostly Stringybark woodland, underscored by tussock grass. Although it's mid-winter, the weather is hot and dry. The washed out sky stretches endlessly across a vast red land, only broken by scrub and orange mounds of dirt.

The dark haired soldier walks up and stands next to Blake. 'Old Bauxite mounds,' he says, pointing with his chin. 'They used to mine it here in huge quantities until they quarantined the whole place. You'll get a better view on the way to the head shed.'

Blake looks around, surprised that the bloke is talking to him. Conscripts are usually ignored. He takes in the dark eyes, smooth brown skin, and strong jaw. 'You've been here long?'

'You could say all my life.' The soldier laughs self-consciously. 'This stretch has been six months but.'

'What did you mean, all your life?' Blake hasn't missed the bitterness.

With his chin pointing and a quick pursing of his lips, the man indicates to the southwest. 'My home is about twenty-two clicks that way or was until they made this area restricted. Napranum,' he says proudly. 'We'll pass it on the way to the garrison.'

A Bushmaster arrives to collect the medical staff, and the soldier walks away.

Blake watches him go. For the first time, he thinks about the people who were displaced from this region and wonders at the real purpose.

Brady interrupts, saying, 'Conscript you ride with the supplies.'

Blake watches the troop carrier as it backs up to turn. Then he climbs into the back of the supply truck. The two soldiers get in the front and take off after the troop carrier. Blake holds on to the tailgate as the camouflaged canvass rattles it's resistance to the wind.

The landscape either side of the road is eucalypt woodland but in the distance he sees what he thinks is a lake before realising these are old tailing dams. He's glad he's here. It beats the boredom of Canberra.

The truck pulls over and stops. Blake waits surprised. They seem to be in the middle of nowhere. The dark soldier comes around to the back. 'Mate I can't wait. Can you look in the mailbag for a letter?'

Blake knows he shouldn't do it, but he looks into the bloke's eyes, glistening with worry and gets up to grab the bag. 'What's your name?'

'Wilson.'

He flicks through bundles of mail but finds nothing until the third lot. There's a white manila envelope with scrawled writing. 'Yes it's here, but if we get caught we're in shit?'

'Thanks, it's okay. You can put it back. I'll get it through the normal channels. I just had to know.' There's relief in his eyes as he turns away to the passenger side of the truck.

Blake shrugs. It's weird, but he says nothing, closing the bag and replacing it. The truck lurches onto the road and he grabs one of the steel struts to make his way back to the tailgate.

An hour later, he joins the others in the barracks common room waiting for Captain Henry to come in from his briefing with the Operations CO.

'He's agreed to the health checks and vaccinations,' Henry says, 'but they have their own health personnel who look after the troops on the Cape. They are visiting a base about 100 kays north of here at the mouth of the Wenlock River. Bad news I am afraid, we are confined to the garrison until further notice, sorry no trips up the Cape. It's restricted... apparently dangerous so we can't even join the team at the Wenlock. It sounds like you'll be busy Jackson,' he turns to the psychologist. 'This is where all the bloke's diagnosed with PTSD are sent; ever since that legal ruling in '21 that the ADF are responsible for them.'

'Keeps them off the street,' Nursing Officer Blackwell says, 'but seriously sir, what's dangerous. I heard, all that was up there were crocodiles.'

Blake watches the crew. They're an egalitarian bunch when they're alone together. None of them treats him like a conscript although he doesn't know the chaplain, but he seems a good enough sort and the rest are all right.

Blackwell says, 'I have whisky sir. Is it okay?'

'Anyone else?' Sheepish glances tell the Captain, they've all had the same thought. 'Right pool the grog. We can set up a bar over in the corner. There is not much doing here; we may as well enjoy ourselves. Lincoln go scout around and see what you can find. You can set up the clinic for the morning and then put up notices of the health checks around the place. There's a computer and printer in the office along the hall. No one pays any attention to conscripts, do they?'

'Not sure sir. Do they have conscripts here?'

'Hm, Chaplain do you want to go with him. Blackwell your men might want to see the clinic.'

The chaplain shakes his head. 'I have an appointment...' his voice trails away.

Blake sees the exchange of looks between Blackwell and her two medics. They all want a drink and to relax. 'I'll be right sir, I don't need help. I'll be back within a couple of hours.'

By the time he gets back, the sun has set. Captain Henry is telling them about his daughter's birthday party that he's missing. Brady and Blackwell are sitting closer than Blake thinks is regulation. The chaplain is not back from his appointment. The dentist, a woman called Trindy Macintosh, is standing by the window trying to get her CellTab to work, and the psychologist is not in the room.

Blake walks over to the dentist and says, 'there's no signal here. There are signs all over the place saying mobiles, particularly e-cript cells, are prohibited...sorry.'

'Jesus, you're kidding. How am I supposed to ring home? I promised.'

'You can use the phone in the office down the hall. That seems to work.' Blake says noticing her agitation.

Henry looks up, his brow furrowing. 'You didn't use it Lincoln?'

'No sir, I just tested it to see if there was a dial tone.'

'Good man. Trindy, the phones will be monitored. Keep it clean okay.'

'Yes sir,' she grins at him and walks out.

Henry sighs, 'newlyweds.' The others laugh and Henry says, 'you deserve a drink Lincoln. Here.'

Henry passes over a slug of neat whisky and Blake takes a cautious sip. He's a beer man, but it's not too bad. The clean smoky liquid burns down his throat leaving a warm glow in his belly. He takes his drink and sits down in an armchair, a little apart from the makeshift bar. As he watches the officers' joke and chat, he realises he might have to sleep somewhere else tonight. It's unlikely he'll be bunking in with the Lieutenant. It looks like he might have other plans.

A rush of nostalgia washes through Blake as unexpectedly an image of Charlotte fills his mind. She's singing a slow lament of lovers lost to each other through cruel fate. Her hands reach out yearning and her eyes search across the dim foggy club. Christ, he runs his hand over the short bristles on his head. He misses her.

For the next few days, Blake sticks to his role as conscript, running errands, cleaning up after the medics and dentist, completing details in the health care cards of the soldiers, running his eyes down each to see any patterns before handing them to the medic. There's an understanding between them that he has far more experience with medicine than they do, even though he is a conscript, and they rely on his advice. To Blake it's a surreal experience, but nothing like the bizarre nightmare of Baghdad.

At night, he sleeps on the floor in the office and pretends not to know what the Lieutenant is doing with Blackwell in his bed. As he lies on his back, hands joined under his head, he thinks about Charlotte. He wants to marry her and it's not just to keep her safe as she accused him. Missing her is a physical ache. Restlessly he tosses and turns wishing he could sleep.

He gets up, deciding to go for a walk. There aren't any restrictions within the camp, or none of which he's aware. The night is clear without a moon and there's a southerly wind blowing. The air is briny with the swampy smell of mangroves. The place is quiet as he walks across the parade ground.

Earlier, they passed the river mouth on the way into the garrison from Scherger, but that was a few kilometres to the south. The coast should be to the west. It smells close. A shadowy form runs across the road ahead and disappears into a grove of trees, a dingo out hunting.

Two blocks on there's a fence and a guardhouse. With a sigh, he turns back. A dark figure leans against the outside wall of one of the long barrack buildings. Blake can see the glowing coal end of a cigarette as it arcs upwards, lighting Wilson's face.

'Where do you think you're going mate?'

Blake steps closer, 'just a walk. I was hoping to see the sea. Did you get your letter okay?'

'Yup. Thanks. I know you could have been in a bit of bother if you got caught, but like I said hey, I just wanted to know if it was there.'

Blake stands next to the soldier. 'Was the news okay?'

'Yeah. My girl got into a bit of trouble. She was worried, but it was all right, she was found not guilty so no conscription, thank Christ.'

'I get it. If they found her guilty there would have been no letter, right?'

'That's right. I've been waiting for weeks to find out. It was killing me. Sorry I guess you understand.'

'Yep, but sometimes it's worse for those left behind. They don't know what's going on. The imagination can conjure worse things than are actually happening.'

'You're right. My imagination has been doing overtime. Why are you still in Oz, not over there?'

'I was, but my time's just about done so these are my last few weeks.'

'Is it really as bad as they say?'

'What for conscripts or regulars?'

'Both.'

'It's pretty bad. Are you going?'

'I don't know. I'm in Signals so I might be sent across to Combat Systems. It's pretty boring here but. Not much going on and I think that's the way I like it.'

'What about the insurgents?'

'Mate the only living humans moving about freely out there, are a few of my relatives who refused to move when the evacuation order came.' He grins, his teeth white in the dark night.

'That's interesting man. Are we looking for them as well?'

'Na, we pretty much ignore them. I don't think we're actually related. Mostly they are from Mapoon. It's the second time the Government's tried to move them on. Last time it was so they could open a Bauxite mine, now its insurgents. They're pretty pissed off and are determined to get their homeland back, but shit man, the life of a hunter-gatherer existence can't be much fun. Anyhow, they refuse to follow white man's laws. I don't blame them, but there aren't many left now. A lot more protested at the beginning, but it's hard out there. Why would anyone do it if you didn't have to, and when the incentive is a furnished house and car in one of the cities of your choosing, one house per family; Mum, Dad and up to six kids. We never had it so good. When I grew up, there were thirty-two people living in our house and we were the lucky ones. The only thing the army is worried about is insurgents.'

'I'm surprised insurgents would choose this place to enter Australia. It's a hell of a hike to get anywhere, hot and dangerous geographically, not to mention difficult. They would be better heading to the Western Province from Indonesia, or better yet fly in on a holiday visa.'

'They're coming in from New Guinea. They follow the coastline to get here. If they fly in, they can't bring weapons. That's what we are told anyway, but I'm yet to see any of them. Do you want a smoke?'

'No thanks. Is there any place I can get to the sea around here?'

'Na off limits, all of it except for the brass. They have houses, married quarters along the road you turned back from, but the blokes from engineering say they're going to have to move soon. The coastal erosion is bad, and the shoreline is sinking. If there's a cyclone, they'll all be gonners. They are working out what to do about it now. Either, seawalls or move all the houses.

It's a big job. I have a cousin in engineers and he says they're worried the sea is rising rapidly, and the whole garrison might have to be moved.'

'Shit, no kidding?'

The two men stand in silence for a minute until the soldier says, 'I'm Rodney Wilson by the way. Roddy to me mates.'

Blake shakes his hand, 'Blake Lincoln.'

'Hey you're that bloke on the news. I thought you looked familiar.'

Blake looks away.

Roddy notices the look and says, 'I never thought much about conscripts until they charged my girl. It's pretty bad stuff though. What was your charge?'

'Protesting and possession for dope. What about your girl?'

'Shit man they said she spat at a copper. There were no witnesses, just his word against hers.'

'Jesus, I thought I was hard done by, but not all those convicted and conscripted are forced into signing for deployment overseas. Depends on the sentence and depends on their skills. They don't send everyone. It also depends on your family connections. Anyway, girls with kids or influential family don't go because it gets the attention of the media. The public don't like it. They have to portray the conscript as a threat to a safe society to sway public sympathy.'

'How long did you get?'

'Three years.'

'Bugger. How much dope?'

'A joint.'

'Christ. She was lucky she wasn't done. I've heard not many survive.'

'Yeah.'

'But you did...'

'Yes. I was lucky.'

'What do you need over there... to be lucky I mean.'

'You have to stay alert all the time. Never let your guard down.'

'Okay.'

'All war's like that isn't it. Also, I speak the language so I understand what people are saying behind our backs.'

'No kidding, you speak Arabic. How did you learn that?'

'I grew up in Saudi before it joined the Free Islamic State,' Blake says. 'Look I'll head back. I'm glad your girl's okay. Take care.'

'Yeah see you. Hey if you need to get a message out, home or anything, I'm your man.'

Blake walks back to the barracks wondering how they came to this. That they can sentence people and potentially force them to sign on to cross the sea and fight a ruthless and bloody war for spitting at a copper. The place has gone mad. Is Australia really in danger from terrorist extremist invading and taking the country? He can't see it. It makes little sense, but he seems to be the only one who thinks like that.

He knows FISLO believe in a world dominated by Islam. They want a global Caliphate with Sharia Law. But democratic countries are not easy targets, and it's easier to focus on places where inequality is entrenched, fomenting unrest with people who have nothing to lose. Then FISLO agents step in to bring order to a duped, but grateful nation.

In Blake's opinion, seizing the Western World for the Caliphate is impossible. Mohamed Abdullah Al-Jishi, his guard in Baghdad, told him they weren't particularly interested in places like Australia. There were bigger objectives like Pakistan, the next on their list.

Abdullah said, 'how would you like it if foreigners invaded your country?'

Blake chose his words with caution. 'The west claims they are here to bring back democracy. They say the people who governed before the Caliph, asked them for help. Sharia Law allows democracy and in their view, the Caliph invaded a democratic country.'

Abdullah laughed. 'You are naïve doctor Australian. The idea of democracy is an opiate to allow business to do what it wants, while its people feed the market, believing this makes them happy. It leads to corruption and decadence. Even so, western armies are not here for such lofty ideals as democracy. They come for oil. Twenty years ago the fight for such control brought renewed tension. CIA backed Sunni insurgents, operated through the Saudis to gain access to the pipeline, but if they had succeeded, the Russians and their Iranian Shia allies would have missed out. Russia couldn't tolerate that, and once more simmering differences escalated until they found themselves on opposite sides. And thus, we flourished. So, just like the first war, we have what we have because of western interference. If there were no oil, no one would care about this part of the world. The West change their allegiances depending on business needs, not ideology, or concern for humanity. Big business runs the so called democracies for whom your armies fight.'

Blake felt indignation rising but controlled it, moderating his voice. He was careful to appear as a student, remembering he was a good Muslim forced to fight against his will. Half of that was at least true. 'I've heard that before, but democracy is about people having the right to choose and control the kind of country they live in.'

'Again you are wrong. Look to your trade deals where business has more rights than your so called representative governments. Ever since the first flow of oil in this region, the West has been fighting wars to get at it. It's about profit—even the first war.'

'I don't think that's right. The First World War began in Serbia.'

'Ha, you do not know your own history. Let me explain to you how it was. After they found oil in this land of our fathers, Britain wanted it for their Empire and as they had a stranglehold on shipping, they controlled the export of oil. The Germans were jealous and wanted to get their hands on oil to challenge British market supremacy. They needed to bypass British domination of the Suez Canal, and link up with their holdings in Africa. So they began building a railway line across the Ottoman Empire.'

Blake interrupted. 'But the First World War began when a Yugoslav assassinated Arch Duke Ferdinand, every school kid learns that.'

Abdullah pursed his mouth and blew. A great gob of spit landed in the dust. 'That's because every school child learns a lie. Oil started the First World War and all those in this region since. The assassination of the Arch Duke was the last spark to ignite a slow burning ember.'

The European and Russian powers all had their own vested interests. They were spoiling for a fight for years before war was declared. But none of it would have amounted to much if in the first place, Germany hadn't wanted to knock the British off their economic throne. The Arch Duke's assassination was merely the end of a chain of reactions.

'The Infidels are fools who cannot learn from their past. Britain was caught up in the mess because of arrogant greed as well as a treaty with Russia that her politicians didn't understand. Still today, they have not learned. Look at Australia, a British vassal State—you have treaties that even your politicians do not understand the full extent of their consequences.'

Blake fell silent, digesting the information. He really didn't know much about who did what in the First World War. 'Okay supposing you are right about the First World War, it certainly wasn't oil that caused the Second World War. That was about Hitler's land grab to extend the country boundaries for his people.'

'Your schooling was poor, Tabib, even so you are a doctor.' He shakes his head. 'There are two points of view. One is that there was never two world wars, only one. The second war was just an extension of the first. Germany capitulated while they regrouped to deal with problems at home. Their trouble came when the Russian Tsar was killed. Germany's own communists took courage and agitated against capitalist markets. Trouble at home is what forced Germany to give in to armistice, and also why the war never ended in 1918. There was just a ceasefire until Hitler cranked Germany back into action. The first and second wars were the same conflict with a cease-fire in between. Western infidels set in train actions for political expediency, careless of the consequences.'

Abdullah paused and looked at Blake, his glance crafty and amused. 'You must realise that, for every war fought, opportunities are created for those with courage to seize them. Hitler was such a man.'

He paused again and then continued musing as if Blake was no longer there. 'War makes multinationals very rich. It is in their interests wars are fought. Consider the cost of one bomb and who profits. Even now with this war who really benefits?'

He turned on Blake demanding, 'who wins? Do you think that we could defend our land and our faith if we had no arms?' He made a crude gesture. 'Pah! Of course not. We do not manufacture armaments. So, from where do they come? I will tell you. They come from the American, Russian, and Chinese owned multinationals who make them. At the same time, these same companies sell to the west. Without war, they have no profit. So who really wins in war Doctor? It is never the people.'

Blake had been shocked and remain silent. He understood what Abdullah said, and no longer knew what might be true.' 'But why would Westerners want the Caliphate's oil. They are moving more and more to alternatives. Soon there will be no need for oil. Besides they have oil shale.'

Abdullah sneered. 'Extracting oil shale is polluting water aquifers and damaging the geological structures of western countries causing many earthquakes. The West needs our oil but they should buy it, not try to steal it.'

Now Blake was on firm ground. 'The Caliphate doesn't sell oil to infidels,' he challenged.

'Ha so you say, but you are wrong again. Even your country buys oil from our black markets.'

'Why? Why do we need oil when we have alternatives?'

'What you don't seem to know Tabib Australi is that the West needs our oil because if they move to alternative technologies, they will have to fight the Chinese and North Koreans. Better to fight Arabs than Chinese.'

'Why would they have to fight the Chinese? They are trading partners.'

'Once yes, Australia had what they wanted but their foolish governments chose short term profit goals through trade agreements in favour of protectionism for wealthy investors. Now they are at the mercy of international business interests. They further cemented their downfall by grovelling to Britain and America. Britain is the mother of capitalist markets. America is her independent son, but Australia is the daughter who remained at home. How do you say it, tied to the apron.'

'Apron strings,' Blake says without thinking.

Abdullah nods. 'Now the West must rely on the Chinese for Rare Earths, and so the equation changes. Australia sold its resources and now the Chinese have taken all the minerals, ore, and freehold land. Greedy westerners have nothing left to trade. Already more than a decade ago, the Chinese raised the price of Rare Earths almost two thousand percent and had the infidel over-a-barrel. He laughs, his bad teeth showing beneath the cracked and lined lips of his mouth. You get it, over a barrel—oil barrel.'

Blake nods acknowledging Abdullah's joke 'How do you know all this?'

Abdullah said, 'when I was a young man my father sent me to America to study western economics at Harvard University. It was the early days of our movement, but my father and the others who began the dream of re-establishing out Caliphate planned for the long term. Forty years ago, he sent me away and told me to learn all I could, to bring back western knowledge. One must learn about the enemy before one can defeat them.'

Blake fought to contain the bitter words burning his tongue. It wouldn't do, to point out the atrocities inflicted by the Free Islamic State. How many of their own people had they killed let alone the genocide and horrible slaughter of Shia, Pesmerga, Amhara, and anyone else who didn't share their beliefs, or toe their hard line. Besides he needed to keep up the illusion he was one of them so he asked, 'what Rare Earths?'

'The Rare Earths you need for new technologies, stuff like neodymium, praseodymium and europium. The Chinese control 97% of them. So how many lives lost doctor, and for what? Multinationals profit as the West corrupts the earth, and the poor suffer.'

16.

'They've picked up another boat, Corp. The Navy reckon they'll drop them off at the Mapoon landing at 12:00 tomorrow.' Signalman Roddy Wilson stands at the door, holding out a communiqué.

Corporal Nick Perry swings around in his swivel chair, rolling away from the desk. He stares at Wilson. 'You're kidding. They fucking don't stop. What's wrong with these people? Where the fuck are we going to put them? All the ICs are full.'

Out of Roddy's line of sight, a woman says, 'at least these are live bodies. Better than pulling more putrid corpses out the sea or finding them festering on the beach.'

Roddy recognises the provincial Queenslander drawl of Ellen Biloela, the terrifying Sergeant who is every man on base's fantasy, and probably many of the women too, but no one dares voice it.

Perry takes the offered comms from Roddy, scans it, and passes it over to Biloela. 'They need someone to translate and our bloke is on field leave.'

'What about the other bloke?' Biloela says.

'What other bloke? He's the only Arabic speaker we have left.'

'Didn't we have three?'

'Yeah but two left, dishonourably discharged for refusing Christian prayers, we're waiting for replacements.'

'You'd think the bloody Navy would have someone on board who can speak the language. Christ, they practically live with the bastards. Ask around, maybe someone can understand a little. There must be Arabic speakers somewhere. They were everywhere a few months ago.'

'We could use someone from the ICs who speaks English.'

'You can't trust them. Where was this one picked up?'

'Near Derby in WA. They nearly made it this time.'

'Corporal.' Roddy says

Perry looks back to the doorway. 'Are you still here Sig?'

'Yes Corporal.'

'Well, what do you want?'

'There's a bloke who speaks Arabic.'

'Who?'

'He's the conscript with the medical team at the hospital barracks.'

'A conscript. Jesus that's as bad as getting someone from the ICs. What do you think Sarge?'

'Might be, but beggars can't be choosers. I'll talk to the boss.'

'Okay. Bugger off Sig. I'll let you know when we have a response.'

'Yes Corporal.' Roddy turns and heads back down the corridor towards the signals room.

Two hours later Captain Henry sends Lieutenant Brady to find Blake. The clinic has a line of soldiers waiting for vaccinations against the new strain of Middle East Respiratory Syndrome. He waits until Blake is finished with the soldier in front of him and says, 'Captain wants to see you Lincoln. I've asked Nursing Officer Blackwell to send in one of her medics.' He looks at the line. 'You won't have to wait too long.'

The queue of waiting soldiers groan.

Blake pulls off his plastic gloves and follows Brady to the Captain's office wondering what he wants, but he knows better than to ask the Lieutenant.

Henry finishes writing something on a pad and looks up at Blake standing in front of his desk. 'You speak Arabic I understand.'

'Yes sir.'

'How well?'

'Fluent sir.'

'Good, can you read it?'

'Yes sir.'

'Good man. They need you up at the Wenlock River. You'll take off from Scherger at 06:00 tomorrow.'

The next morning the sandy haired soldier who drove the truck when Blake first arrived at the garrison pulls up outside the barracks. He'll drive Blake to Scherger Base. The sun is a thin line of light on the horizon, but the day is already warm as Blake swings into the passenger seat of the G wagon.

It's late July but there's a smell of spring in the air. The morning breeze heralds a day that will build quickly to thirty plus degrees, but without the stultifying humidity of summer.

The driver takes off before Blake's feet leave the ground. He falls into his seat, hurriedly grabbing the seat belt as he watches the asphalt rushing past the opening that serves as the vehicle's doorway. They screech to a stop to let two Hawkei armoured vehicles lumber by, then turn left, heading for the road to Scherger Base before the soldier speaks.

'Roddy says you're all right for a conscript. I'm Newel, Danny Newel, Transport Corps at your service. I hear you're off to Wenlock. Can you do me a favour?'

Surprised and wary Blake says, 'what's the favour?'

'Take a message up to my brother.'

'What message?' Blake scrutinises the bloke taking in his sandy lashes and light blue eyes, his freckles and blond hair.

'Tell him happy birthday.' Danny grins at him. 'We're twins.'

'Okay, happy birthday to you too then. I'll tell him if I see him.'

'Yep you'll see him all right. He'll be the one who picks you up from the airstrip.'

'What's his name?'

'David.'

'Does your mail get mixed up a lot?'

'Yeah all the time. How did you know?'

'Just a lucky guess,' Blake says dryly looking out at the passing woodland.

They drive south, and ahead the road curves to the east. On their left, raised banks covered with trees block his view. On the right, flat woodlands, interspersed with grassy banks, stir in a breeze laden with the smell of mangroves and salt.

Danny points. 'The Embley River mouth. Good fishing. If you've got time when you come back, me an' Roddy will take you. Just got to watch out for the Salties, but.'

At Scherger, Blake hardly has time to get himself out of the vehicle before Danny shoots off again, wheels squealing on the concrete apron.

A pilot officer walks over shaking his head. 'Fucking maniac. He'll roll the thing one of these days. You must be Lincoln. I'm MacDowell and I'll be flying you up to Wenlock.' He scrutinises Blake. 'Never met a conscript before. You look almost human.' He grins, his tanned face crinkling in lines that radiate from his light, almost turquoise coloured eyes. 'I hear you're a doctor. Can't say I understand the whole conscript thing, but I heard what you did in Baghdad. Bloody good show mate. They should give you a medal. Conscript or not, you're true blue. Come on, let's get airborne and you can tell a poor bored border jockey what's happening in the real war.'

They take off in a four-prop plane, and when they reach altitude and level out MacDowell turns to Blake. 'So tell me what you're doing here. They don't usually let conscripts in these parts, or anyone else for that matter. There's a high level of security clearance required to get into the Cape. You must be someone special.'

Blake doesn't know what to answer, so he says, 'thanks for the flight. It's amazing to see the place from the air.'

MacDowell says, 'yeah. It's not much of a trip, a roo-hop and we are there, but it's a good view and the best way to get supplies to the blokes up north.' He jerks his thumb at the back of the plane. 'This old girl doesn't move very fast, but she's a good old work horse. I'll drop you off in Wenlock, and move on to Jardine River, down to Lakefield, then come back for you. You should be finished by then. I guess it won't take long to find out where the sods are from.'

Blake scans the pilots face and risks a question. 'I'm not sure of the details really, how long or who I'm translating for...'

'My bet is that they are more Harzara Shias. Although it beggars belief, any of them are left over there. I reckon the whole population are over here by now. The bastards don't get it that we don't want them.' He laughs. 'That last escape livened things up a bit though. We had visions of a war between tribes. It took us a while to round them all up and get them back into the ICs. Trouble is they had help from the local Aborigines, otherwise, I reckon they would be gonners by now. I mean they're desert people aren't they. What do they know about this kind of bush? You said you're translating. Do you speak Arabic?'

'Yes.' Blake tries to work out what MacDowell meant by saying they escaped, and what are ICs. He says nothing, knowing he doesn't have the security clearance MacDowell assumes he has.

'Bit of a chatter box aren't you.'

Blake says, 'I'm a bit in awe of all this.' He nods towards the vast expanse of the Embley River catchment. Ahead in the distance, he can see line upon line of barrack shaped buildings and says, 'is that Wenlock?'

'Na that's the Turkmen Internment Camp.'

Ah, Blake thinks, ICs.

Mac Dowell says, 'the Wenlock Garrison is a little north west, nearer the coast. The bloody sea is rising so fast here they are trying to build further inland away from the salt flats and river mouths, on higher ground. They'll have to move Wenlock soon before it sinks into the sea as well.'

Blake can see the coastline ahead now and another river catchment he assumes is the Wenlock River. 'How is it that some people call it Mapoon?'

'That's its old name from when it was an Aboriginal settlement. Hardly anyone calls it that now except the Aborigines. They are still not happy at being moved although why they would want to live way up here is beyond me. All the sandbanks have disappeared, and the tidal action is undermining the old houses. The bloody waves on high tide wash through front doors, and there's not a decent club for miles, let alone any available women.' MacDowell grins at Blake again before fitting his microphone back over his mouth and speaking to someone about landing.

Blake stares out the window trying to digest all MacDowell has said. None of it makes sense. As they taxi along the dirt airstrip, he sees a G wagon arrive followed by two trucks, churning up dust in their wake.

'Your ride I guess,' MacDowell says jerking his thumb at the wagon, 'and the supply trucks. They will unload, but you can head off to the garrison to do what you have to do. You'll likely get a surprise at your driver.' He laughs.

Blake wonders what he's talking about and then remembers his driver's twin. 'Do they look that much alike?'

'Sure do. We have fun with new comers usually. They can't figure out how Danny got here so fast. Pity he told you.'

'Apparently it's their birthday.'

'Ah ha, and you bear birthday greetings.'

'That's right.'

'Okay, have a good one. I'll be back at 16:00 to pick you up. Home in time for a coldie.'

Half an hour later Blake is at the Wenlock Garrison administration block. He follows Able Seaman Murray along a corridor. Murray stops to unlock a door, and stands back so

Blake can enter, then he follows Blake into the room and locks the door behind them.

The room is about four metres by three with a grilled window overlooking the ocean, and Blake looks at the water longingly. A man stands silhouetted in front of the window. Next to him are a table and three chairs. The man moves behind the table and Blake sees his face.

He's old and afraid and looks half-starved Blake thinks saying, 'salam alaykum.'

'Wa alaykum as-salam.' The man glances at the Able Seaman.

'Are you well?' Blake speaks in Arabic and the man responds in the same language.

'I am well, but I speak better English than Arabic,' he says surprising Blake.

'We will speak Arabic.' Blake says not wanting to speak English.

The man nods.

'Where are you from?'

'From a refugee camp near Karachi but my father was from Khorasan before the war, and before that my grandfather was born in Hazarajat.'

'You speak Phasi?'

'Yes and Urdu.'

'Why didn't you say you spoke English?'

He shrugs, 'no one asked.'

Murray pushes a stylus and tablet across to Blake. 'You will need to ask these questions and tick the answers here, he says pointing at the buttons on the screen. If he says something that's not in the check boxes you can use the stylus to write on this new tab.'

'Sure,' Blake motions for the man to sit, and takes a seat opposite, with Murray on his left. He picks up the tablet and runs his gaze down the questions. 'Is everyone on the boat Hazara?'

Murray interrupts. 'No chit chat Conscript, just the questions.'

Blake ignores him and says to the man, 'it is better we continue to speak Arabic.' The man nods. 'My name is Blake Lincoln what is your name?'

The man replies, 'Safdar Sarkhosh.'

'Do you know why I am here?'

'No.'

'Do you know where you are?'

'Australia.'

'Okay good. I have to ask these questions on this list for immigration. If you want to tell me something different from the direct answers, you can tell me in Arabic. I don't speak Pharsi or Urdu and this man,' he indicates Murray, 'doesn't speak Arabic so he won't understand.'

The man nods looking puzzled, but philosophical, and Blake runs down the questions. He realises they are designed to elicit certain answers, each one phrased as a statement to which the responder is required to answer yes or no. Either way, he knows he won't get the truth and rephrases them to open ended questions. It doesn't last long because as soon as the old man answers in any length, the Able Seaman interrupts.

'Tell him to answer the question; we don't want him spinning a story here.'

Blake doesn't know what to make of it. He reverts back to the original questions, but he has enough information to know that the man is one of a boatload of refugees fleeing from the Sunni religious group Lashkar-e-Jhangviled led by Akram Ishaque, the grandson of one of the group's founders. Lashkar-e-Jhangviled are close affiliates of FISLO, and they claim the Caliphate will soon govern Pakistan.

'Okay that's enough,' Murray says, his mouth pursed in suspicion. He holds out his hand and Blake gives him the tablet and stylus. Murray's finger runs down the lists of answers looking for gaps, and then satisfied he says, 'right, that will do. I'll arrange for you to get lunch and a ride back to the airstrip.'

After lunch, Danny's twin drops Blake off at the hanger. The place is deserted but David says MacDowell is ten minutes away and takes off in a flurry of dust and gravel.

Blake ruminates as he waits alone in an iron shed. The building squats in the stifling heat with only the shrill of cicadas and buzz of flies for company. The omnipresent smell of mangroves permeates the still air. While he waits for MacDowell, he goes over what the old man told him, scarcely believing anything he's heard.

Half an hour later, they take off, and when he levels out MacDowell asks, 'so was I right? Was it a boatload of Hazara?'

'Yes.'

'Damn I'm good. I won another bet.' He grins at Blake's puzzled face. 'We have a bet going in the mess over the new IC, and who it will end up housing. I have fifty bucks on Haraza.'

Blake says nonchalantly, 'I haven't been into one of the ICs have you?'

'No mate. Us flyboys don't walk around on the ground much, not outside of Scherger, but I know people who have. The ICs are not so bad, and the people, once they get over the initial shock of being locked up, soon organise things, or their women do. They have elections for council, begin their market gardens and small businesses, and act just like they would in their own homes. The children attend school and learn English and Christianity. Not sure how that goes down, but most of the time they are quiet and get on with their lives. It's better than where they've come from anyway. The weekly supply drops always have western books and movies, and they can't seem to get enough of those. By the time this war is finished they'll be good little westerners I'd say.'

When Blake arrives back at the Weipa Garrison he wants to ask more, but is afraid he'll arouse suspicion. Instead, he stores this new bit of information along with the rest, building on what he already knows.

The next morning Captain Henry summons him to his office. Blake stands to attention in front of Henry's desk, watching the man read a text. Henry's brow creases in perplexed concentration, and he takes a handkerchief from his pocket to wipe his neck and his top lip, then he looks up at Blake. 'Read that Lincoln. Tell me you aren't withholding information.'

Blake glances at the text and stops, shocked. 'No sir, that can't be right. They were refugees, Haraza from a camp in Pakistan.'

'Not according to this. It looks like a full-blown incursion was thwarted. Jesus they found chemical weapons, and other armaments on the boat. They are all FISLO insurgents.'

'No sir, I am sure that is not right.'

'Face it Lincoln, the bloke fooled you. Not surprising really. Apparently, you are not the Arabic speaker you made out. The Able Seaman who was with you, told his leading Seaman you were struggling to understand the bloke or communicate with him.'

Someone is lying and Blake doesn't think it's Captain Henry, and it's not Safdar Sarkhosh. He leaves Captain Henry's office with a deep sense of foreboding. It's the same feeling he had when they gave him the story about the poisoned weapons that murdered his squad. Until he finds out what is going on he'll keep what he knows to himself.

17.

The Australian Prime Minister, Sir Bartholomew Priestly walks across to the drinks trolley and pours himself another scotch. He turns to look at his wife who sits in a wicker chair with a rug covering her knees.

She flicks through a magazine. A gin and tonic sits on a small glass topped table next to her. It's hardly touched. He raises his eyebrow in question. She shakes her head, and he takes his drink to the veranda edge, gazing across the harbour to the Opera House, blindingly bright in the winter sun.

The butler interrupts his reverie announcing a guest. Priestly turns around to see his Minister for Homeland Security walking through the shadowy interior of the house towards the French doors leading out to the veranda.

'Arnie, good of you to come all this way. My dear, you remember Sir Arnold Marabaux.'

'Of course dear, one doesn't forget people one has known for so long.' Her America accent rings with irritation at his absurdly trite comments. It's as if he addresses a stranger and not his wife.

Bart strides across to the French doors to shake Marabaux's hand. 'Come on over, what can I pour you to drink?' He gestures towards the trolley. 'You're a scotch man aren't you? Glorious day isn't it?'

Marabaux takes the drink. He dislikes scotch, but it's pointless telling Bart, the man never listens. Instead, he speaks to Lady Priestly saying in a monotone the words he knows she expects him to say. 'You're looking radiant Elspeth.'

'Flattery my dear Arnie. I'm far too old to fall for it.' She lifts her hand, palm flat, to push up her auburn curls to better frame her pale cheeks, while her red lips curl in coquettish satisfaction. 'How is your lovely wife Hester? You should have brought her for a visit, but I suppose you left her freezing in Canberra, you naughty man.'

'It's not much warmer here Elspeth.'

'Nonsense, the sun's shining isn't it? Although living in this old mausoleum, one wouldn't know it.'

Priestly sighs. It's her same old beef about quaint colonial Australia. She can't understand why they can't knock over Kirribilli House and build something more modern. He once said it would be like knocking over the White House, but she scoffed at that.

Now he says, 'Elspeth darling, will you excuse us while we talk business.'

'I was hoping to hear the latest gossip. I must admit I miss the social life in Canberra. In Sydney people are much too busy making money...' She sees the look in his eyes and adds hastily, 'but if you must.' She removes the magazine from her lap as if to rise.

The Prime Minister flaps his hand making a lowering motion and says, 'no my dear you stay here. We'll go into the study. I'll call Jenna. We'll need her brain.' He's referring to his Chief of Staff who has an apartment close by for the PM's convenience. 'Bring your drink Arnie.'

Bart has furnished his private study in Kirribilli House with mahogany matching chesterfield sofas and armchairs, rich red cedar furnishings sourced from the rainforest timbers of the North Queensland province, and a large antique Persian wool and silk carpet. He lowers his six feet two inch frame onto a sofa and gestures for Marabaux to sit. Marabaux puts his drink on an occasional table and chooses a wing backed chair where he sits immobile, but watchful, his hands resting on the arms.

A young man in navel uniform pokes his head around the door. 'Can I get you anything sir?'

'Ha Cyril, call Jenna will you and bring a bucket of ice, then make sure we are not disturbed.'

Bart adjusts his tie and stretches out his legs, ankles crossed. He glances at Marabaux and notes the whisky glass untouched on the table. An image of their early days at Sydney University flashes in his mind. It was the end of last century, the boom years of Australia. Arnie, a proud supporter of temperance, accused Bart of alcoholism. Bart was angry, justifiably so in his view, and retorted he only drank to cope with moronic and ungrateful friends.

Arnie apologised, but that was Arnie, loyal as a dog and as dumb. As Bart ages, he finds better ways of venting his spleen. Rather than outbursts of anger, he delights in tormenting the man. 'How have you been then Arnie, how is your gout.'

'I don't have gout Bart, that's Renfrey.'

'Is it, my goodness?' Bart is surprised his taunt has an element of truth. 'How can I have a Minister for Sport and Entertainment with gout? Well, what ailments do you have then? And more to the point how are they?'

Marabaux checks his mental list of bodily functions and finds to his surprise that everything is in order. 'No ailments thank you.'

'Come on Arnie, I can't sit in silence while we wait, at least try to make small talk won't you.' He flashes his charming smile at Marabaux, his teeth white and perfectly even in his handsome face.

'I'd rather discuss the details of the matter at hand if that's all right. I am worried.'

'Yes, yes, we'll get to it but I want Jenna here to hear it.'

'I can fill her in later, but I need to know what we will do. The situation is getting out of control.'

'You're a panic merchant, you know that Arnie, but you brought it on yourself. I told you to let the bloke have a medal. It'll keep everyone happy and why should we worry about him getting a shiny gong.'

'It gives him credibility.'

'You worry too much—top up?' Bart picks up his empty glass and stands waiting for Arnie's reply.

'No thank you.' Marabaux face remains bland, disguising his disapproval as Bart walks to a glass fronted cabinet.

Priestly picks up a decanter and seeing it's empty, replaces it before taking out a new bottle of aged single malt whisky. He pours a generous slug into his glass. 'The bloke's been fine since he returned, hasn't he? Hasn't set a foot wrong. I'm not even sure he knows anything. I mean, have we any evidence he has suspicions, or is it just you being obsessive. Has he spoken to the press? What is it that worries you particularly?'

'I'm not as convinced as you Bart, but there's more bad news.'

'Oh good lord, what now. I thought you were handling it. You sent him to Weipa Garrison so the bloody CIA wouldn't speak to him.' The PM walks back to the sofa. 'Someone ought to stop the Yanks from sending these people over here. I don't think it's very good manners spying on ones allies, particularly using our own resources at Pine Gap. That's just rude, not to mention their interference in our sovereignty.'

'We do it,' Marabaux says dryly.

'But that's different. We use our own resources, and we really can't trust the Americans.' Bart stops; there are things to which even Arnie shouldn't be privy. 'Never mind. What's the bad news?'

'It appears Lincoln has met one of the refugees.'

'What? Imbeciles, how did that happen?'

'Mm.' Marabaux covers his triumph by taking a sip of scotch, and shudders. He hastily puts the glass back on the table, and waits for Bart to lose control.

'Can't I leave you to do anything without cocking it up?' Bart's anger flares, and he struggles to suppress it, knowing there's too much at stake. All he wants is to punish someone, and he'd like that someone to be Arnie. To see that smug mug pulped—anything to shock the self-satisfied look from that cold-fish face.

'What's cocked-up?' Jenna Martin stands poised at the door, one hip thrust provocatively forward, her hand resting on it as she balances on black patent stilettos. Cyril hovers behind her, ice bucket in hand. Like a zookeeper afraid the jungle cat may turn on him any moment, he waits his eyes wary. She ignores him as her gaze sweeps the room.

'Jenna darling.' Bart forces down his rage, basting his voice with charm as he hurries over to take her in his arms. His kiss lingers and Marabaux looks away. 'Whisky my love?'

'Yes please Bart. Hello Arnie how are you?' Jenna walks into the room and Cyril hurriedly places the ice on a table and leaves, closing the door behind him. She stops a metre away from Marabaux, surveying him with pursed lips and folded arms, one foot tapping the thick pile carpet.

Reluctantly he struggles to his feet. 'Hello Jenna. I'm well, long drive and a bit tired but otherwise fine. How are you?'

She doesn't answer but turns to take her drink, her fingers lingering in the PM's for a moment longer than necessary. 'So what's going on?'

Bart turns to Marabaux. 'Well explain your cock-up Arnie.'

'Not mine Bart... ahem... Well, it appears there were no translators up in the Cape, and a new boatload arrived. Lincoln speaks Arabic, so the CO decided there couldn't be any harm in him doing the translating. He thought it was Captain Henry we didn't want leaving the Garrison. The good thing is, we know what Lincoln heard because he asked set questions and wrote down the answers.'

'Were there women and kids on board?'

'Yes.'

'Did Lincoln see them?'

'No I don't think so. He spoke with one man, their leader who claimed to be a Persian asylum seeker, according to Lincoln's translation.'

'We can tell him we've done background checks, and the man is lying. We can say the boat was full of weapons... chemical weapons perhaps.'

'Yes, I've taken care of that.' Marabaux says looking at his feet.

Jenna sips her whisky, watching Marabaux, wondering if she can use this debacle to gain the upper hand. Bart runs his palm up her arm saying, 'what's that pretty head scheming up now my dear?'

'I'm wondering if it's worth getting this bloke on our side instead of trying to keep him in the dark. That strategy doesn't seem to be working. Perhaps it's time for different tactics.'

'Are you mad?' Marabaux's neck flushes.

Jenna's exultant, but turns to Bart with a hurt look on her face.

'Hang on old chap; you can't talk to Jenna like that.'

'It's all right Bart,' she leans forward as if in persuasion. 'Arnie just figure. He already knows too much, but he's said nothing about Baghdad so who knows, maybe he will keep quiet.' She counts on her fingers. 'One, the bloke knows about the poisoned weapons. Two, we think he knows about the unofficial prisoner exchanges. Three, he saw his own mates die from the poison. Own goals happen, surely he knows that. Four, he hasn't squealed to the press yet. We can play on his patriotism. I agree we may need assurances, but...'

Bart interrupts. 'I thought we convinced him that the poison was the enemy's trick.'

Marabaux says, 'we did, and he bought it, I'm certain, but I don't yet know what his game is, except he's not interested in blabbing to the media. My son offered to get him a good deal with Randolph's outfit and he refused.'

'Good oh.' Bart slaps his knees. He's bored now. All this alarm is ruining his day and making him uncomfortable. 'Then we have nothing to worry about. Arnie, you're an old woman you know that old chap.'

Marabaux covers his irritation. Bart must worry or he'll lose the game to the witch. 'What about the wheat exchange. You know the agreement we had with the coalition not to do the exchanges for oil. If they find out... and now what about the Internment Camps? Its international law we are playing with, not just Australian law,' Marabaux says.

'There's no need for melodrama Arnie.' Jenna takes a sip of her drink to cover her dislike of the man. Arnie's a pain in the backside with his fussing, and she knows he would do his best to rid the PM of her, if he dared.

Bart swallows his whisky. Jenna's right and Arnie is overly pessimistic. 'I thought we had sorted this out. We told Lincoln the Sunni's were lying. The Brits and Yanks will keep out of it. They owe us, for sending Lincoln to get their prisoners out when they failed. They have no idea of the real situation and think his conscript status is an undercover disguise.' He looks at Jenna and arranges his face into fondness. 'That leak to the media about him being Special Forces was artfully done my dear.'

'Don't forget I also expunged his record.'

'Yes, you did.' Bart smiles at her, then seeing her whisky glass empty, he gets up to pour her another.

'And the refugees?' Marabaux struggles to mask his fury.

'We'll tell him they're lying,' Bart says from over at the cabinet. Perhaps we should actually declare war rather than calling it peace keeping. No one complained when we lock up German nationals in WW2. War allows all sorts of emergency powers.

'There are consequences to declarations of war and the NATO Coalition won't have it. What if buttering up Lincoln doesn't work?'

'Stop panicking Arnie. The bloke's human isn't he. You'll find his Achilles.' Bart hands Jenna her drink.

'Thanks darling.' She smiles, and turns to Marabaux to see if he understands, she is more important than he is. 'We need a proper strategy, not this piecemeal approach you're playing with Arnie.'

Bart sits down and Jenna leans against him. He says, 'all right we've tried it your way Arnie, and it's not working, now we should hear Jenna out. Darling what do you suggest?'

She rests her hand on his thigh. 'I said before, we need to get him on side. He's one of the richest people in Australia and how did he get there? Government contracts. He has a lot to lose by alienating his government. Let's treat him like one of us. Lay on your famous charm Bart. Woo him and find out how much he knows, then try to get him to see how his silence will be repaid, how much you value him doing his patriotic duty. Maybe even offer more contracts that kind of thing, perhaps hint at the possibility of a title, appeal to his vanity with a bit of pomp and ceremony.'

'Yes.' Bart is enthusiastic. 'We'll give him the VC, first before the Yanks and Poms get their oar in, as if it was our idea in the first place. They haven't managed to give him their honours yet have they Arnie?'

Arnie shakes his head. 'No, that's why we sent him up to the Cape, to keep him out of the way for a while.'

'That didn't work very well did it Arnie?' Jenna flashes a triumphant smile at him then looks at Bart, but he's not paying attention.

Instead, he says, 'Good. I'll get Elspeth to arrange a private function here for him.'

'No not here, do it at Government House, after the award— more pageantry,' Jenna says, knowing Bart's weakness.

'Hang on, what if he doesn't buy it.' Marabaux knows he risks Bart's wrath. He pleads, 'let's think this through. Don't give him more ammunition against us. What happens if he won't be bought and won't be silenced?' Marabaux drains his whisky in agitated distraction, gagging at the sourness.

Jenna and Bart laugh. Bart says, 'the days of saints in our society disappeared a thousand years ago, but if he is such an anachronism, we'll set up assurances. We can have the ceremony over before anyone has time for questions. The last thing we want is the wrong people demanding an invitation. Do it before the Yanks get their act together.'

'Didn't you tell me your son had started on an insurance portfolio Arnie?' Jenna's eyebrow arches.

'Yes but it's not much. I don't think Lincoln is the type.'

'You'll have to push harder, innovate. Get with the programme Arnie. Where are his weaknesses?'

Arnie battles a blinding rush of rage that this upstart can speak to him like this, but it will keep. Right now, he's in no position to challenge the witch, but he knows Bart. It won't be long before he tires of the woman. In the mildest voice he can muster he says, 'I had a bloke tailing him when he was on leave, and reports came in about a girl he met in Brisbane. From their letters they appear keen.'

Bart says, 'did Captain Henry persuade him to join the regulars? That would save so many problems.'

Marabaux shakes his head, but Jenna interrupts. 'What do we have on the girl?'

'I'll look into it.' Arnie rises from his seat wanting to end the conversation and leave. If he remains in the room with this woman much longer, he won't be able to control his words.

18.

Sir Arthur Scott, the Australian Governor-General says, 'pass the marmalade dear.' He is approaching his sixty-ninth year, and his thinning grey hair catches the sunlight that bathes their sheltered balcony corner, warming the late July air. He sits with his wife eating breakfast, gazing across the dew-damp lawns to Lake Burley Griffin.

Miranda, Sir Arthur Scott's wife of thirty-three years, leans forward and pushes a white porcelain bowl across the glass topped table with the knuckle of her little finger. Held between her thumb and forefinger is half a slice of dry toast. 'You might want to ring for Picardy. You've barely left more than a scraping.' She lifts the toast to her lips and then lowers it without taking a bite. 'It's too cold to sit out here Arthur. We should have breakfast inside until it warms up a little.'

'My dear girl, this isn't cold. Really it's not, and the sunlight is brilliant don't you think?' He lifts his face to the feeble warmth. 'It's good for you, get vitamin D into your old bones. We should soak up as much as we can.'

The man's impossible. She pulls her cardigan tighter with her free hand, and changes the subject. 'What did the PM want?'

'He wants me to confer the Victoria Cross on the young man who escaped imprisonment in Baghdad, then have a little soiree here afterwards.'

'Is he going to relent and give the Lincoln fellow an award?'

'Mm it looks like it.'

'I am glad. He deserves it you know. William's last letter said he will be released soon and they hope he will go home. Really I am not happy about the way he's been treated.'

'Who your brother or the young man?'

'Don't be obtuse Arthur. You know very well I don't mean William.'

'My dear the law is the law, and he did commit a drug offence.'

'Yes but it was such a little thing. It's not like he is the only Uni student to do such a thing.'

'I never did.'

'No, but you are a paragon,' she says dryly.

'No my dear it won't wash. If we are to have rule of law I have no problem with it being upheld regardless. Just because your brother was friendly with his parents does not mean he shouldn't be treated as anyone else is treated. He did the crime he should do the time. Although, I admit I'm impressed at the way he has conducted himself.'

'It shouldn't surprise you surely. He comes from good stock and it's not just my brother who knew his parents. I did too.' She glances at him slyly adding, 'you know I had a crush on his father before I married you?' She knows it annoys him.

'Yes, so you like to remind me although if you had married him my dear, look where you'd be.'

'That's terrible Arthur. What happened to them was awful. It could well have sent the boy off the rails, losing his parents like that.' She gazes thoughtfully across to the lake, watching small waves lap at the edge of the garden.

Her husband makes a sound in his throat. 'That's what Bart thinks happened, why the boy took to drugs.'

'Don't be so naïve Arthur. One little joint is not taking to drugs. I know you and Bart go back a long way, but I really have my reservations about the man. He's too smooth by half and doesn't give a hoot about anyone, but himself and his own power.' She replaces the uneaten piece of toast on her side plate and dusts the crumbs from her fingers.

'Miranda, don't start that again. Look, I have a job to do and I will do it to the best of my ability, but getting involved with politics is not my job.'

'But the law... You were Chief Justice once. Surely, you have a view on the laws they are introducing. Besides, you should have stood up for Jonathon Castile. I know the accusations against him weren't true.'

Arthur covers his irritation by taking a sip of coffee but it's gone cold. 'The man only has himself to blame.' He replaces his cup in the saucer. 'He didn't do himself any favours refusing the title in such a public and humiliating manner. The trouble was he was too politically ideological for words. How on earth can one uphold the laws of the land in such a partisan way, especially after you have got everyone offside by spurning the trappings of office?'

'You mean the title he rejected. It's ludicrous to penalise a man because he rejects an honour. He was just acting according to his beliefs. After all it's no secret he has always advocated for an Australian republic.'

'Let's not start that row again please. You know Chief Justice Bramly has provided a definitive review of the Constitution prior and post the changes. It is clear the Governor-General has always been Australia's head of State under Constitutional, not crown authority. We already have total independence from Britain despite the King retaining the status as King of Australia. It's preposterous to think a republic will provide any further independence. No my dear, it wasn't republicanism Castile wanted. He had anarchy on his mind.' Sir Arthur pauses and thinks bitterly, and my wife, but he keeps it to himself. Instead, he says, 'Castile called the government's legislative process criminal. He overstepped the mark. Really, he has no one to blame but himself if people turned away from him. He was always a loose cannon.'

Miranda stifles her irritation. She doesn't want another row, but she thinks her husband should do something. 'What about the corruption charges Arthur. You know they were not true.'

'I know no such thing my dear. The man is morally bankrupt. Bart was furious when his predecessor put him in the Chief Justice's job after I retired. He was convinced it was petty spite, knowing they would lose the election. In my opinion that government didn't make many good decisions and in opposition they are still battling an image issue. It'll take more than a change in leadership for people to forget.'

'Yes.' It's the one point of agreement Miranda finds she has with her husband. 'This new fellow who has taken the party leadership seems to be of a different calibre. He may be able to resurrect their fortunes.'

'Who Ballintine?' Arthur makes a noise of disapproval in his throat.

'Valentine dear.'

'What?'

'His name is Hugh Valentine.'

'Really I could have sworn it was Ballintine. Do you know, I'm really beginning to worry about my memory.'

'That's not your memory Arthur, it's your prejudice. You can never remember the names of people whom you think are your social inferiors.'

'Miranda that's unkind, and unjust.'

'But true darling. You think because he was an electrician before getting into politics he is somehow not as clever as you.'

Hurt by the truth of her barb he retreats scowling. She looks away, staring into the distance. She wears her silvery blonde hair in a chignon revealing a regal profile scarcely marked by her fifty-six years. Her graceful neck is looped about with natural pearls and she fiddles with them as a surge of nostalgia threatens to swamp her.

It was ten years ago, but she hasn't forgotten the thrill, the stuttering foolish girlish coquette she became when Jonathon Castile looked at her. She keeps it contained now as she has always done.

Her emotional control harkens right back to the unrequited love she had for William's friend. At twenty-five, she pined for him, but he was oblivious to her devotion, and married the Italian girl Helena Macri, Blake's mother. In a fit of despondent grief, she believed her life over and agreed to marry Arthur, who had been wooing her for some years.

The trouble with marrying someone whom you do not love, is the endless unrequited passion you must endure throughout your life, especially when an alternative presents itself. The money and position never makes up for it even though you believed it would. She chose her gilded perch and now she must be content to stay chained to it.

19.

'Guys I've got to sleep okay. I have work in the morning.' Charlotte gets up from her perch on the edge of the stage and tucks an empty beer bottle under the lip of the platform. The club hums with low voices under a cloud of vapour. She waves her hand in front of her face. 'They should fix the extractor fans in this joint.'

Flynn, the drummer, pushes his blonde fringe out of his eyes. 'You'll miss the new band, and they're good.' His hair flops back again. 'Not as good as us, but good. Ex-military, but nobody's perfect.' He grins at Charlotte and taps out a tattoo with his drumsticks on the stage floor she just vacated.

Charlotte picks up her bag. 'Yeah, Jay's mate Sol said he heard them before, but I'm too tired.'

Jay turns his turbaned head from unplugging his guitar. 'What's that?'

Flynn says. 'We're talking about you Jay.'

'Okay.' Jay turns away and continues packing away his gear.

Flynn shakes his head. 'Man you can say anything to Jay and he accepts it. To have so much cool. I admire it you know

Charlie? It's his religion.' He grins at Jay and turns back to Charlotte. 'So back to where we were.'

'Flynn, I'm going to get some shut eye. You can stay and watch the band. I'll hear them from the back anyway.'

'I can come and keep you company if you like Charlie.' Tyler the base player leans over and lays his chin on Charlotte's shoulder.

'Bugger off Tyler. Go tune your base or something.'

'So cruel, you know I love you.'

'Give it up Tyler. You know the rules. We make music that's all. Now I'm going. See you tomorrow night.'

'Hey how's your man Charlie?' Atif places his saxophone in its case. 'He should be out soon. When he gets back, you should introduce him.'

Tyler jerks his hips in a crude gesture. 'Yeah Atif wants to steal him away from you Charlie. He's been mooning over the bloke since you first brought him in here.'

'Fuck off Ty. Not everyone's like you,' Atif says.

She leans in to hug Atif. 'Maybe I will. In fact, just try to stop me. It's only two more weeks, three days and ten hours and I can't wait.'

He gives her a squeeze and removes his arm to snap the case shut. 'We can probably take the night off for that. What do you reckon fellows? Give little Charlie the night off...'

Her smile falters. 'He might have lost interest. I haven't heard from him for a while so maybe he's gone off me.'

Flynn laughs, his drum stick twirling through his fingers. 'You're kidding, right? Incarcerated all this time and not interested. The man would need rocks for bollocks. It'll be all that's on his mind Charlie, don't worry about that.'

Tyler interjects, 'hey Charlie, men are simple creatures and all he'll be thinking of is your delicious...'

'Don't say it Ty.' Atif's face is stern. 'Go on to kip Charlie. We'll see you tomorrow night.'

Charlotte stuffs her hair back inside her beret as she walks towards the back room. It's almost deserted tonight with most club patrons staying up to hear the new band, and she's glad.

She'll get a decent spot by the wall where no one is likely to trip over her in the night. She sits on the floor as someone else comes in through the door.

'Hey Evan, where have you been? I've missed you.'

Evan throws himself down next to Charlotte and takes out a small packet of weed. 'I'm a worker bee now Charlie. I can't keep the same hours I did before. Must get my beauty sleep.'

'And yet here you are.'

'Yeah I came to see the new band. Tomorrow's Sunday so I don't have to get up early, day off.'

'Lucky you. I wish I got a day off. How is the job?'

'It's hard you know. I'm not strong like the other blokes and they get the shits with me for being so slow, but otherwise it's okay. The boss said they are going to move me to a desk job, which will suit me fine. I've just about had this packhorse malarkey, but they're a decent outfit, unlike your mob. You should have let Blake set you up.' He rolls the joint into a thin white tube. 'Want some?'

Charlotte shakes her head. 'Maybe I will take up the job offer, if it's still on the table when he gets back. Where are you living?'

'Still the same.'

'What, nowhere?'

'It's always somewhere.' He leans forward to light the joint. The paper flares as the flame from the match catches. He blows the flame out so the end glows and takes a long toke. Then he leans his head against the wall and closes his eyes, sighing as stress rolls away. 'I had to give an address at work so I gave them yours. I hope that's okay Charlie but I couldn't say I was living on the streets could I?'

'No, but Ev if there's a tax audit match they'll say we are living together, and then we're in deep shit.'

'Yeah I know, but it's only for a while longer. Next pay I'll have the money for a deposit. Then I can rent somewhere. The trouble is I don't have a history, so it's hard to get anyone to look at me as a potential tenant. I didn't know what else to do. I might be able to get a place in a share house. Flynn said a bloke at his place is leaving this weekend, and he said he'd try to get me the spot, so I don't think it'll be long anyway.'

'Do you want to crash at my place? It's not like I'm there nights or not often anyway.'

'Na I'll be right. If the worst comes to it, I can always say I forgot to change my address, but if I'm caught living there, it'll be worse. Have you heard from Blake?'

'I got a letter a few weeks ago, nothing since, but he'll be home in a few weeks—yay, can't wait. He's not allowed to say much, but he sounds fine—doctoring instead of fighting.'

Even in the dim room, Evan can see her face light up, and wishes she felt like that about him, but he's glad for her. Blake's a good bloke, even if he is one of them. It's not his fault he belongs to the wrong crowd.

'How are your folks Evan? Have you heard from them?'

'Yeah they made it. They're okay. They want me to go over and join them.'

'Will you?'

'Shit I don't know Charlie. If I went, I'd be deserting. If we don't fight the bastards, we'll never get our country back. Anyway, the New Zealand Government is caving into the pressure. People are sick of Aussie refugees, and the Australian Government is putting heavy pressure on them to send them back. There's talk of them not taking anymore. Now contractors patrol the ditch because the navy refused to fire on their own. The contractors are brutal. If they see a boat, they shoot now and ask questions later. We've lost two boats recently, and no one seems to know what happened to the people on them. We assume they're drowned, but I don't know. Anyway where are we gonna find more boats, no one can contribute any more. There's just no money.'

Charlotte looks around worriedly. 'Be careful Ev.'

He opens his eyes, rolling his head sideways to look at her. 'You know Charlie if we can get Blake to join us.'

'No. I'm not going to ask him. Don't ask me to Evan.'

Evan sighs and closes his eyes again. 'Okay. How are your folks? Have you heard anything?'

'Yeah I got a letter last week from Mum. Things seem okay, but her letter was censored with black lines through heaps of it, so I don't know. She says everything is good. They are restricted on where they can go, but the army guards the region so Mum reckons they're safe. The army also sweep the roads for IEDs just in case. Mum says they have been warned to keep travel to a minimum, and have to get permits for everything, but otherwise life goes on pretty much the same.' She yawns. 'Evan, I should get some sleep. Are you staying here tonight?'

'No I'm going to check out the new band, and then I'm going to the library to research.'

'Research what?'

'You know the usual. What crap the government's up to now and what they'll hit next. It's more grist for The Dissident,' he says naming an underground newspaper. 'I've just about cracked into their system. Once I score that, I will have cart blanche to the files. Then the bastards will have something to worry them. All we need is proof of what they are doing and a bit of publicity, and people will have to protest. We have until next year to change voter's minds and we have to do it. The longer they are left to their own devices, the more entrenched the system becomes, the less power we'll have.'

Charlotte frowns. 'Evan you must be careful. No one's game to protest any more. The crackdowns last time picked up nearly two thousand and conscripted them.'

'Yeah we didn't do that very well. We need the oldies, beyond conscription age, and those in power; otherwise, it's portrayed as a youth rebellion, a bunch of drugged up, unwashed drongos who don't want to work. It's their method, smear your reputation until every decent human on the planet believes you deserve what's coming. Never mind innocence. All in the name of their particular brand of bogeyman called national security. I don't get it. They sucker everyone in with their bullshit propaganda.'

Charlotte yawns she's heard Evan on his soapbox so often.

Evan looks at Charlotte's sleep weary face. 'That's why the Dissident is so necessary. We need to educate people.' He hesitates. 'That's why we need Blake Charlie, people trust him. He has street cred. People will believe him.' He sees the expression on her face. 'Yeah, yeah I know.' He holds up his hands. 'Okay, I'll let you get some shut eye. I might see you in the morning. Maybe we can have breakfast together, I'm buying.' He grins as he gets to his feet. 'Fuck, it feels good to say that.'

'Okay, night Ev.' Charlotte pushes her back against the wall, her bag under her head and watches Evan leave. She's glad he has a job and is out of danger. Yawning again, she scrunches her fists under her chin and closes her eyes.

Two hours later, she wakes to a loud rhythmic thump reverberating through the club. It takes her a minute to realise the noise is coming from the steel front door. It sounds like a battering ram. She grabs her bag and stumbles to her feet. Others in the room are also waking.

'What's going on?' The voice is a sleepy whine.

Charlotte dodges and scrambles over waking bodies to get to the back corridor that leads to the fire exit. The corridor is already crowded as she squeezes into the mass of bodies. It's become a bottleneck and Charlotte is pushed and jostled. She trips and grabs hold of the person in front of her. He curses and pushes her away. She feels panic rising—she must remain upright.

A voice shouts, 'back up, we need room to unlock the doors.'

Whoever thought locking the fire escape was a good idea? Charlotte pushes between people to wedge herself against the wall.

'They have gas!' It's a woman's cry from further along the corridor, and Charlotte feels the familiar prickling sensation in her nose. Then her eyes begin to smart. She pulls up the neck of her tee shirt to cover her face, but it does little to help. Why doesn't the crowd move? She feels her throat constrict, and fights to control rising panic. She coughs and her nose runs. Her eyes sting and weep.

Everyone is coughing and rubbing their eyes. A woman screams. It's a long banshee wail of terror. Another voice joins her. A man tells them to shut up and take shallow breaths. Screaming will make the gas effects worse.

The crowd stirs and pushes forward, crushing Charlotte against the wall. She pushes back, and cranes to see above heads in the dim light. The rhythmic thumping in the background continues like a pulse to the growing panic.

Fear tears at her resolve. The doors grate open. Fresh air floods the gas-filled corridor. The crowd surges, its middle giving way as people push into weak spots. Those ahead flee into the streets.

Charlotte follows, her hand steadying her against the wall as she struggles to see where she's going. If she can only maintain her balance until she's out in the fresh air, she will be all right, but she can barely open her burning eyes. Then the cool night air caresses her face. Her entire focus is on staying upright, moving with the momentum of the crowd.

Don't fall, keep calm, don't fall, she repeats in her head as she pushes forward. There's another scream, and she stops. The icy grip of dread shoots ice through her stomach as she sees the flashing lights ahead. Colours bounce around the neighbouring building walls and race across the shadowy road. They have stumbled into a trap.

After all, the steel doors held, but they tricked them out of the club by the noise and the tear gas. They knew all along where they would exit. This is where they lined-up the paddy wagons. Like a fish trap, all they have to do is scoop them up as they fall out the building, blinded.

She staggers down a side alley, still hugging the walls. A police officer seizes her arm, twisting it backwards. She cries out and doubles over. The beret slides off her head. She tries to grab it with her free hand. The man kicks it aside, and ignoring her pleas, marches her to the nearest wagon.

Through scalded eyes, she can see six dark shapes squashed into the back of the van. They cough and rub faces lit by flashing blue and red techno strobes. Tear gas is the least of their worries.

20.

William Fuller retreats into his imagination as he stands within his family circle, an oasis in the eddying crowds of the reception rooms of Government House. 'Hubris blinds those who dabble,' he rolls the words silently around his mouth, 'it belies reason unto man's own destruction.' Is this what Zeus saw when he cast his people into Hades?

He rocks imperceptibly on the balls of his feet, hands clutched behind his back, watching the crowd of civil dignitaries. Politicians, military officers, journalists, business tycoons, and show-business celebrities, preen in the glittering Stateroom. He knows these people well, nods at their greetings, but avoids talking with them. He's here for Blake or he wouldn't be here at all.

'Pardon dear,' Margery says.

He turns to look at her. Did he give voice to his thoughts? 'Nothing dear, I am talking to myself.' He smiles to reassure her.

Margery feels self-conscious and oddly left out, but has given up asking him to introduce her to people. Earlier when they arrived at the reception he said, 'you don't want to know them Margie. Most of them aren't very nice.'

Lady Scott joined them saying, 'don't worry dear I'll introduce you.' Then she smiled at her brother. 'It's always difficult introducing someone when you can't remember their names, isn't it William darling?'

True to her word, she took Margery's arm and led her around the room, introducing her to small groups of people. They made the right noises, but soon lost interest once they discovered she was just Mrs Fuller, a nobody from Brisbane. After hovering at the edge of animated groups who ignored her, she realised why William said what he did, and begged off Miranda's effortless networking to go back and stand next to her husband.

Now Margery watches the guests as they squeeze through the bottleneck at the double doors and spill onto the terrace. Outside garden torches gain strength with the dying sun. The guests, freed from their obligation to pay homage to the gallant, can search for that which will satisfy their own conceit among kindred spirits. She tugs at her skirt, feeling gauche and middle class among such glamour.

Rory stands the other side of William. He too feels out of his depth and is grateful when Uncle Arthur and Aunt Miranda join them. Miranda takes Rory's arm, seeing his discomfort and says under her breath, 'doesn't all this pomp give you the shits?'

Stunned and unsure if he heard her properly, he looks into her green eyes full of mischief. As soon as Arthur arrives people approach their family, first greeting the Governor-General, Lady Scott, and then William, murmuring congratulations, and observing how William, 'must be so very proud,' as if he had something to do with shaping Blake's acts of gallantry. They ignore Rory and Margery, and none of them stays for long. Rory suspects they know his father's opinion of them.

Earlier when they arrived at the ceremony they were introduced to so many people, he can't remember who's who. Now he sees Blake and the other two medal recipients walking towards him. He envies Blake's apparent self-assurance and grabs his arm to pull him to the side, leaving the two soldiers standing a few metres away.

'Jesus, mate is there somewhere we can get a beer and some quiet time.'

Blake flashes a surprised look at him. 'I don't think I can. Have to play the part you know. I would have thought this would be right up your alley mate, but hey, it's not like I have a choice. Situation normal I guess.' He checks the bitterness in his voice. 'Even this,' he sweeps his hand down his dress uniform. 'Ever seen a conscript dressed like this before,' he jokes. 'Although, I must admit I prefer this kind of order to some of the others I have been given, and the champagne's good.' His eyes search Rory's face. 'It's a pity Charlotte couldn't come with you, but I guess I'll see her tomorrow anyway.'

A high-ranking army officer with crew-cut hair, greying at the temples, interrupts them. His level grey eyes observe Blake as he congratulates him and shakes his hand. 'You've done us proud soldier.'

Blake covers his surprise at being called soldier by the General. 'Um, thank you sir. May I introduce you to the Fullers? You will know the Governor-General...'

'How are you Arthur?' The General says before turning to nod at William. 'Bill,' is all he says.

'You know Mr Fuller,' Blake turns to include Margery and Rory. 'And this is Mrs Margery Fuller and Rory Fuller.'

General Rothwell, Chief of the Australian Defence Forces, turns on his famous charm as he smiles at her. 'How do you do Mrs Fuller or may I call you Margery?' He takes her hand and holds it in both of his for a moment while his cool eyes linger admiringly on her cleavage.

To Rory's amazement, his mother blushes and snatches her hand away. The General smiles and turns to Rory. 'Nice to meet you Rory. Bill keeps his family well hidden; frightened we'll entice you to the dark side. I hear you're a budding lawyer. The army needs the occasional lawman so if you have a hankering for the good life, commissioned of course, let me know. You might persuade your friend here to do his patriotic duty at the same time.'

Rory looks baffled, but shakes the General's hand muttering, 'how do you do sir.'

Rothwell turns back to Mr Fuller. 'So Bill, you old dog, how have you been keeping?' He glances back at Margery. 'Always did get the pretty ones.'

Irritated at being called Bill, William replies without thought. 'That was Lincoln you're thinking of, not me.' As soon as the words leave his mouth, he realises how they sound and hastily covers his faux pas. 'With one exception of course,' he adds glancing at his wife.

A subaltern approaches the group and says something to the General who turns to Mrs Fuller. 'Ah my regrets lovely Margery, my Minister the Admiral, has summoned.' There's imperceptible mockery in his tone as he says the Admiral. He takes her hand again, and this time raises it to his lips. 'Until later perhaps.'

Margery blushes and looks at her husband, but he's already retreating into the more interesting recesses of his own mind.

Rothwell nods at Rory and takes Blake's arm, 'think hard before you decide to leave us Blake. Your father and I were good mates, and we'll look after you. He would be proud of you. We are all proud of you son.'

Blake says, 'thank you sir.' Rothwell waits for more. Blake feels pressured. 'I'll think about it.'

'Good man,' Rothwell turns to walk away and winks at Margery as he goes.

She gazes after him, surprised at his height. There is something about the man that makes him appear larger than life in news stories. Even now, his presence seems to dominate the room, but in person, he's so much shorter than William.

'What was that all about?' Rory says to Blake.

'They're trying to get me to sign on as a regular, promised me the rank of Captain.' Blake looks grim. 'Fools, nothing will stop me from getting out tomorrow. I'm heading straight to

Brisbane to see Charlotte. I wish you had time to arrange for her to have been here.'

Rory's face pales and his eyes slide away from Blake's gaze.

'What's up?' Blake asks worried.

'Ah nothing, it's just a bit tedious standing around. That stuff they said about you at the Awards. Is it all true?'

Blake laughs. 'Well a version of it, but if it's any consolation I'm not enjoying this whole thing either.' He gestures to the two soldiers waiting nearby and introduces Rory.

Rory doesn't understand the medal structure, but he knows Jason and Noah are the Special Forces soldiers who went back with Blake to free the British prisoners. That much at least was read out at the ceremony.

Rory is in awe of the three men. He hardly recognises Blake in his uniform and beside him, feels diminished. 'Do you reckon there's somewhere we can get a beer?'

Noah says, 'Yeah mate, I saw some behind the bar. Let's go persuade them, beer is more our style.'

He walks towards the bar and Rory follows. As he leaves, he hears Blake saying, 'so how are you tracking Jason?'

Jason waits until they leave. 'I'm okay. Still not sleeping though.'

'Did they give you something for it? What about counselling?'

'Yeah, but Jesus man, I'm kicking myself for saying anything to the Doc. The moment I told them, I was given a choice—the Cape, or medical discharge. What can I do. It's all I know. I thought I'd be in until I retire.'

Blake nods. 'You have family?'

'Yeah my wife Belinda and two kids. Sam's six and his sister Lizzy is eight, going on eighteen. My wife and my Mom want me to leave, but I don't know. Dad won't give an opinion. My brother reckons I should stay. He says a stint in the Cape will be short term anyway until I'm better. Pete's a foreword scout and a gun tracker, but the dickhead joined up against my better advice.'

He smiles and pulls out his wallet, showing a photo of the little family group, a small boy clutches a dog around its neck. 'That's my boy with his dog, Rupe. My folks have a property in the Kimberly. Dad runs trawlers out of Broome, and Belinda and the kids are staying there until I get home. Dad's building us a house, and he says he'll teach me the fishing business if I leave, but shit... I don't know.'

He falls silent as they look at the photo then he says, 'they couldn't get down here in time; but I'll see them in a few days. What about you Blake, do you have a family?'

Blake shakes his head. 'No... Or I have a girl... I hope. Her name's Charlotte and I'll see her tomorrow.' He grins.

Jason falls silent and then glances at Blake. 'Do you have the problem?'

Blake's face becomes sombre. 'Tell me who doesn't and I'll tell you a man who hasn't seen much combat, or has no conscience. The odds shorten the more you're exposed. But my problem is more like an inability to adjust rather than full blown PTSD.'

Jason nods. 'It's like I have a contagious disease you know. People won't look at me when they find out, or they go quiet, like I'm ill or something.'

'Yeah. It's not heroic enough for the bastards is it?' Blake looks grim. 'It's bullshit; people just don't know how to talk about it. But hey, screw what people think.'

'The worst things are the memories, I'm not proud you know... some of the things we did...'

Blake nods.

'And there's the jumpiness. It's embarrassing climbing out of a ditch on the side of the road. My wife's like you. She says it's okay and who cares about people pointing, but it's humiliating.'

Blake smiles, 'yeah for me it was a constant rage. And the nightmares. For ages, I was scared shitless to go to sleep, but it's better than it was. There are good drugs to help so long as you keep working through it.'

'How did you get rid of the nightmares?'

'Well I haven't really, not yet, but I've been writing everything down and it's made it easier.'

A relaxed and poised Jeremy walks up with Emmy on his arm, interrupting their conversation. 'What have you been writing down?'

Blake ignores him and kisses Emmy, then introduces her to Jason.

Emmy's eyes sparkle with reflections of the room lights, her excitement barely contained. Rory and Noah return and Rory hands a beer to Blake and one to Jason.

Blake turns to Jason and says quietly, 'if you need to talk more, call me okay. Don't put it off.'

Rory watches his little sister chattering to Jeremy and looks over to his mother. She tugs at her skirt trying to reduce the static. His father looks stoic, almost as if he's disappeared into solving a knotty problem, as he does. Rory is sure he is no longer listening to Uncle Arthur.

The American ambassador walks towards them. 'Blake, I'd like to introduce you to someone. Would you mind Arthur, ladies, gentlemen, I'll only borrow him for a minute.'

Blake straightens his face, and hands his beer to Rory, wondering what now. He follows the ambassador across the room to a woman standing alone near the window. She is Silvia Marais, voted as one of the most beautiful women in the world, highly connected and very wealthy.

'Ms Marais may I introduce you to Blake Lincoln. Blake, the lovely Silvia Marais. She has been badgering me since the award ceremony to introduce you.' His eyes crinkle at the corners to show his smile although his mouth barely moves.

Silvia says, 'hi there Blake honey, it's good to meet you.' Her accent drawls with a deep southern inflection. 'I heard so much about you from my brother. You know he wanted to be here, but it's hard to get an invitation to these things.'

Blake takes in the woman's creamy complexion, heart shaped face, her white blonde hair, and her tiny waist below a deep cleavage. She is smaller than she looks in the movies or the posters, but just as beautiful.

'Of course you're Liam's sister. Sorry I didn't realise you were here... How is he?'

'Alive and well thanks to you. Congratulations Blake. You don't mind if I call you that, do you? Liam talks so much about you I feel as if I know you. He asked me to give you his best.'

She takes his arm turning away from the ambassador as if he is merely a servant doing her bidding. Blake glances at him to see his reaction, but he's already turning away, his duty done.

'I had to gate-crash this party. Lucky I was in the country for my movie premier or none of us would have made it here. I don't know why the hurry. I would almost suspect they didn't want foreigners hanging around. Are you all right Blake? Is there anything we can do for you? My Aunt wants to help.'

'Thanks Ms Marais, but really I'm fine. I will be a free man tomorrow, back to civvy street.' Blake tries to deflect Silvia's intense concern away from him to another subject. 'But tell me how Liam's doing. Has he left the military or will he be going back?'

'He won't be going anywhere darlin'. He wasn't supposed to go over there as it was, but boys will be boys. My family asked me to extend an invitation as soon as you are available. They want you over Stateside Blake. Will you consider it?'

'Ah I don't think I can Ms Marais, but thanks anyway.'

'Silvia darlin'. Only people I don't care about call me Ms Marais, but tell me why you won't consider coming on over for a visit?' She looks a little confronted by Blake's refusal 'It's only an iddy biddy visit, and we'll look after you. Liam made me promise.'

'It's not that I don't want to Silvia, but your country doesn't allow drug convicts to visit I'm afraid.'

'That's a load of old... well never mind that now. We can deal with that later. I must admit I don't really understand it, although Michael tried to explain,' she says looking over her shoulder at the Ambassador. 'My folks want to meet you and thank you in person. Liam says if it wasn't for you they would all be dead.'

He shakes his head. 'I didn't do much really...'

'Look honey, Liam told us how you kept them alive for two years and then how you got them out. It wasn't nothing, so don't shake your head. You are a brave man and deserve the highest honours.' She leans in close. 'My aunt, the President, wants you in Washington. Liam would have come over to Australia, but this little shindig they've put on for you was done a little suddenly.' She straightens and says, 'geez I don't get any of this. How can you be Special Forces and a convict, but Uncle Earnest will sort out any visa issues, don't you worry. And I guess you'll be coming over for the award, won't you?'

Blake looks confused. 'I'm not Special Forces... I'm sorry Silvia... but...' He trails off and glances around to see if anyone is watching.

She looks at him askance. 'You do know that you're getting the Medal of Honor? They did tell you, didn't they?'

Blake doesn't know what to say. 'I just got back this morning. They said to put on this uniform and they brought me here. It's not even my uniform.' His voice rasps and he clears his throat. 'Sorry, I'm a little out of touch, and to tell the truth, I really have no idea what's going on.'

Silvia's brow furrows as she purses her lips, but before she can say more Arnie Marabaux stalks over to them.

'Ah there you are Blake. The PM wants a word. So sorry my dear, but you won't mind if I drag him away for a moment.' Marabaux takes Blake's arm and walks him away. The pressure of his fingers above Blake's elbow leaves his intension imprinted through the uniform jacket.

Blake throws an apologetic look over his shoulder as he submits to Marabaux's lead. They walk through the house to a door with Private stamped on a brass plate fixed to the door. Marabaux knocks, waits a moment, and then ushers Blake into the room. As he leaves, he shuts the door behind him.

The Prime Minister steps forward. 'Blake my dear fellow, what can I get you to drink?' He gestures at a woman standing behind him. 'You haven't met my Chief of Staff have you? Jenna Martin may I introduce Blake Lincoln. Blake, this is Ms Jenna Martin.'

Blake takes the woman's outstretched hand, noticing her composed scrutiny. Her hand is dry and cool in his warm palm. 'Good to meet you Ms Martin.' Then he looks back at the Prime Minister who holds up an expensive bottle of single malt.

'Can I tempt you Blake. It's the best, or would you prefer something else? Beer maybe.'

'Ah that's fine sir, thank you.'

The Prime Minister pours three glasses with hefty slugs of whisky and hands one to Blake. He carries the other two glasses over to a coffee table. 'Where will you sit Jenna? Good. Blake you sit here.' He indicates a chair opposite Jenna. Then he waits until they sit and lowers his frame into the chair, arranging his trousers carefully so they don't crease. He leans forward to retrieve his glass, throwing back its contents. The entire two centimetres of golden liquid disappears.

Blake takes a more cautious sip, noting the smoothness of the whisky. It's not like the stuff they had in the makeshift mess at Weipa. He waits, his gaze fixed on the glass. Ever since he boarded the plane yesterday, he hasn't known what would happen next. It's like that old TV show where you walk into a room and people say, thank God your here. They know who you are, and why you're there, but no one's told you.

Perhaps it's what Alice felt like in Wonderland. Marabaux is definitely the March Hare, and he suspects Jenna is the red queen. He's not sure about the Prime Minister although he seems as self-absorbed as the Mock Turtle, but he's not stupid. Perhaps he's the Cheshire cat, perpetually displaying his immaculate teeth.

Blake waits for clues from which to take his lead. It's not as if he's unfamiliar with the pomp and ceremony or even the powerful dignitaries, given his upbringing in the Australian Embassy in Saudi. It doesn't bamboozle him, unlike poor old

Rory, but he doesn't really know why he's here. To say he was surprised when the Governor-General pinned the VC to his chest was an understatement. Now he's decided its best he goes with the flow, cautious and alert, but just doing what people tell him to do. That way he might survive another day.

'How are you feeling?' Jenna asks as she looks at him over the rim of her glass.

'I'm fine thank you.' He responds with gravity in his voice.

'You must be wondering what it's all about.'

'Yes I am a bit.'

Jenna turns to Bart. 'We need to be honest with him Prime Minister. There's no point trying to brush over things,' she says articulating their prearranged words. 'He's an intelligent man who will see through any fabrication.'

Bart nods looking at Blake, but not speaking.

Jenna sits forward on her chair. 'Look Mr Lincoln, or do you mind if I call you Blake, it's so much less formal don't you think?'

Blake nods.

'And you must call me Jenna of course.' She flutters her lashes at him. 'But we have to come clean with each other. I'll be blunt if I may. You have caused this government several headaches, refusing to conform to stereotype.'

Her smile is intended to soften her words, but to Blake it's carnivorous, her eyelash fluttering, a parody of allure. He places his glass on the table, suddenly fearful he might crush the delicate crystal.

'As I was saying, it's unusual isn't it? Well, the circumstances... and having reviewed your case it does seem a little harsh in retrospect, but you were among the first, soon after the law came into being, and perhaps the judiciary was a little cavalier.' Her mouth puckers into something resembling a duckbill. 'I'm not sure I believe in such esoteric stuff you know, but sometimes I do wonder if these things are fated.' She pauses as if waiting for a response.

Blake doesn't understand. He gives an almost imperceptible shake of his head and leans forward to pick up his glass, taking a sip to cover his confusion, hoping she will say something that makes more sense.

Her eyebrow rises in disbelief at his silence. She tries a blunt approach, her voice sharpening. 'If you weren't over there the brave Anzacs you saved, as well as those of our allies, would now be dead, so perhaps it was fate.' She pauses, but he says nothing, concentrating on his glass. Her voice is edged with exasperation. 'Even so, there's nothing we can do about the past. The government can't interfere with decisions made by the judiciary, but now your sentence is completed, well it's different isn't it. You've paid your dues and more. The medal is the least we can do to show our appreciation. What we want to know is what else can we do?'

She angles her face down biting her lip, coyly glancing out from under her eyelashes. Is she flirting with him? It's shocking and somehow inappropriate. He looks at the Prime Minister who says nothing, still watching with an encouraging grin.

Blake looks down at his glass clutched tightly between his two hands. The whole thing is surreal. They are waiting. He would like to ask so many questions about things that just don't add up, but he's lost his trust of the establishment. He glances at Jenna and knows he's right. She's waiting for an opportunity to strike.

The expectant silence is uncomfortable, and he says, 'I just want to go home. I appreciate your candour, really I do, but I don't need anything else. I just want to go home and get on with my life. I am grateful for this honour, but what I did wasn't heroism you know. I just wanted to escape, and so did the others. All we wanted was to get away, and we were lucky...'

'Blake, keep the modesty for the cameras.' Jenna's impatience runs furrows in her brow. 'We know what you did, but...'

'But never mind that now.' Bart leans forward speaking as if he is intervening before Jenna says anything more. 'What are your plans Blake?'

'Um I don't know sir. I've been thinking of a holiday, camping somewhere in the mountains. Maybe doing some climbing. I feel a little disoriented with all the changes so I need a bit of time you know, just to sort out a few things.'

Bart slaps his thigh, 'exactly what I told Madam President didn't I Jenna?'

The sudden movement and loud slap startles Blake, and his whisky sloshes in the glass. Hurriedly he places it on the table.

Bart continues, 'she was very insistent, but I said you would just want to get on with your life, move on.'

'Yes,' Jenna says, 'you said, let the poor boy get on with his life.' There's sarcasm in her voice, and Blake feels a chill run across his shoulders.

Priestly beams at Blake, 'but I am sorry to say she wouldn't have it, so here we are. There is one last tedious duty we need to perform. I thought you'd want time to yourself so at least I managed to persuade her that we could keep things low key, rather than you flying off to Washington. I didn't want it to conflict with our Australian celebrations, or detract from our fellow countrymen's desire to honour your achievement. It's why I've arranged this private ceremony.'

Blake remains silent, confused, and unable to untangle the meaning behind what either of them is saying. He picks up his glass to take another sip of whisky, but Priestly stands. Blake puts down his glass, and rises as the Prime Minister walks over to the other side of the room. He presses something recessed in the wall. A section slides open revealing another chamber.

'Come Blake let's get duty done, so you can go home. But before we see the others...' He sees the confusion on Blake's face and laughs. 'You haven't any idea of what I'm blathering on about have you?'

Blake says, 'no sorry sir.'

Bart looks surprised. 'What, no one's said anything to you? Extraordinary! How remiss. I will have to have a word. While you were in the Cape these honours came for you.'

He opens the first box showing an eight-pointed cross of red and blue enamel surmounted by the imperial crown with crossed swords in its centre. 'This medal is the King's gift. It's not used much nowadays, but you are following in a very distinguished line of recipients.'

Blake shakes his head, stunned and confused.

Priestly says, 'the British wanted you to have something to show their appreciation. It's tricky with our own medal system overlapping theirs, but the King can award this personally. Those boys you saved were from Prince George's own Regiment so it was important to him. You have the Australian VC, now you will wear the King's medal.' He opens the other box, larger than the first, and a bronze star glints in the light.

Blake wants to touch it, but remains at attention, his face expressionless, waiting for the Prime Minister to tell him what to do.

'Both Governments wanted you over in their countries, but I figured you'd be over all the ceremony and would probably need a break. As we were already planning this award ceremony, the Governor-General as the King's representative will preside along with the American Ambassador.'

Priestly pushes another wall button and the opening slides closed, leaving Jenna still seated in the other room. Then he walks across to a door and opens it. He beckons for Blake to follow, and they walk through to another room where numerous people wait, including the Defence Minister Admiral Bowan, General Rothwell, Marabaux, and the Fullers.

A minute later Sir Arthur and Lady Scott arrive. Blake scans the room, seeing the American Ambassador and a frowning Silvia Marais. Jeremy stands with the Fuller's and Emmy. He doesn't know any of the others although he recognises some faces from the news, like Chief Justice Bramly, and the head of Intelligence Services, Baz Mulholland.

A photographer sets up in front of a small dais. A minute later, a bizarre ceremony ensues where Sir Arthur Scott pins the Order of Merit to Blake's chest on behalf of the crown. The American Ambassador gives a speech on behalf of his grateful nation and steps forward. In a similar ceremony, he hangs a ribbon with the Medal of Honor around Blake's neck.

The photographer herds them together and arranges their pose. Blake is convinced he must be part of a crazy dream and will wake up soon. Finally, it's over.

The Prime Minister says to the people waiting to congratulate Blake for the second time that day, 'sorry folks, I have a little business to attend to with Blake so I must drag him away from you.' He leads Blake back along the corridor to the room they were in earlier. As he opens the door he says, 'thank God that's done. I'm sure you are over the formalities. I know I am. Before you go my dear chap, how about a small top up?'

Stunned Blake walks through the door and looks down at the medals, then back at the Prime Minister. It's as if he couldn't get Blake out the room fast enough and now... 'Sir I'm not sure what it's about.'

Priestly chuckles pushing the door closed. 'Come and sit down again and I'll try to explain.'

Blake follows him back to where Jenna still sits sipping her drink. Bart pours another two centimetres of whisky into his glass. He holds the bottle up to Blake who shakes his head. He still has most of the previous pour.

Priestly sits and leans his head against the back of the chair. 'It's just people wanting to show their gratitude. You're a hero and everyone wants a slice of you. That's the responsibility of being in the public eye. One has duties and commitments. Although I can understand your confusion and we,' he looks at Jenna, 'just wanted to make it as painless as possible for you. You are one of us Blake, and we care about you. Your father was a great friend. We knew each other from our school days you know. I knew your mother too, beautiful woman. It was a dreadful thing, dreadful. But I feel a connection between us and I know your parents would want, no they would expect me to look out for you.' He pauses, and then looking Blake in the eye says, 'I appreciate you will have dreadful memories that you will probably just prefer to forget. I do understand. I was over there in 03/4, when this conflict really kicked off, although unrest was simmering since the 90s.'

Blake looks with renewed interest at the Prime Minister. 'I didn't know sir.'

'That's why we thought we would get you through it with the least pain possible. So many dead, so many memories, so much regret.' He shakes his head, his face sorrowful as his hand comes up pushing his fingers across his mouth. 'It's dreadful, but at least you're alive, and after all that's what matters, isn't it. You're alive even though so many are dead, but you're ready to make a new life, right. We just want you to be happy now Blake and forget the memories. We look after our own, and we want to make sure your new life can begin as soon as possible. We can bury history. We can't make it go away, but we can do small things to compensate.' Then Bart has an inspiration. 'I am arranging a pardon. It'll take time to organise, but the paperwork will be through in a few weeks I imagine.'

He waves his hand as if dismissing Blake's gratitude, but Blake feels a strange foreboding and keeps quiet. Priestly looks at Jenna again before saying, 'now is there anything else I can do for you, anything worrying you, anything you feel you need to get off your chest?' He pauses for Blake to speak.

Blake struggles with the clash of questions demanding answers, but he dare not voice them here. To cover his indecision he takes another sip of whisky while he tries to figure out the angles behind the overt generosity.

Priestly feels his anger rising at Blake's silence and struggles to maintain his smile as he waits. There's an edge to his voice as he says, 'do you have any complaints you want to lodge about your treatment, or even advice on how we can do things better over there? I'd be interested to hear your views. You know in this office one doesn't always hear the truth of things. The Public Servant has a tendency to white-wash the unpalatable, and it would be good to get the facts from the horse's mouth, so to speak.'

Blake's mind spins. Is the man sincere? He looks sincere, but Jenna is still watching him like a cat watching prey. There's something not right about any of this, but he doesn't know what. The intuition that served him so well in the Middle East has him on high alert, and he feels those same shadows in the back of his mind. He's being set up for something. He shakes his head. 'Sorry sir. I think I need time to absorb all this. But thank you, I really appreciate everything you've done. All I want is to go home.'

'Ah there's someone waiting for you?'

'Yes sir. Or I hope so.'

Priestly throws back his scotch and stands up again. 'Well we won't keep you.' He says it as though Blake has already left. He's bored with the charade.

Blake puts the unfinished whisky on the table and stands.

The Prime Minister shakes his hand, 'anything you need help with, or want to ask about, anything at all that crops up, contact Jenna here, or Marabaux. I understand you and my Minister will be attending a special wedding soon—almost family. I hope I get an invitation. If we can help or answer your questions in any way, well... you'll come to us first won't you my boy? It's not just a matter of national security you know, but in here we're all on the same team, family so to speak.' He beams at Blake.

'Thank you sir and Ms Martin,' he nods his thanks to her, but her face remains bland and watchful.

Priestly says, 'Remember, come to us first my boy and once again congratulations. But Blake the press will be all over you. Don't give them the oxygen and they'll go away sooner.'

Marabaux is outside the door. 'There's a car waiting for you Blake. It'll take you back to Barracks, and you will be formally released tomorrow morning. I have explained to the Fuller's that you are still under Military command and won't be free until the papers are all in order. They understand and Rory will pick you up outside the Barracks tomorrow. Now you'll want to avoid the press.'

When Blake arrives at the Barracks, Lieutenant Brady takes him straight to the mess. As they enter, there's a rousing cheer, and a beer is thrust into his hand. To Blake's consternation, Captain Henry salutes him before clapping his arm around his shoulder and saying, 'you'll have to join up Conscript. No one who has all those gongs on his chest can possibly think of becoming a civilian.'

Blake realises how beguiling staying on might be with such camaraderie and acceptance. No matter whom you are, the feeling of belongingness and certainty in what you are doing creates a sense of security, even in the face of an enemy trying to kill you.

Even though he is a conscript, the army takes care of everything. All he has to do is follow orders. Someone else pays his bills and cooks his food and determines what he does and when. So long as he obeys and does his job, life is easy. Even faced with a lethal enemy, you are in it together with your mates who stick by you.

A strange surge of impending loss overwhelms him at the thought of leaving tomorrow. He never wanted to be here in the first place, but now he struggles to imagine his life outside the military. He has no idea what he will do or where he will live. No, that's not true. He'll go straight to the bar to see Charlotte and after that, well it's a dim blur, but he'll figure it out.

While the revelry storms about him, Blake stands at the bar watching the others, and tries to see his future. He supposes he'll find a place to live and begin work at a hospital, probably where he was before, but he isn't sure of anything any longer. He will persuade Charlotte to give up her job in the pub and do something legitimate with her singing. She shouldn't hide her voice in the shadows.

It's a vague plan, but he hangs on to it. The thought of getting out and keeping busy worries him, and yet he has a career, money, and Charlotte. How much more difficult would it be for those who don't have his advantages. Being a doctor and having money gives him privileges of which other conscripts might only dream. He can understand how Captain Henry's offer would seem to others, but he is resolute.

Earlier when he said, 'no thanks sir,' he felt a twinge of guilt when he saw how Captain Henry's face fell in disappointment.

Henry had patted his shoulder saying, 'well if you change your mind, you know where we are.'

It makes him feel ungrateful, but he needs time to sort out his head. It's like he tried to explain to Rory earlier. 'One minute you are part of something, your whole identity wrapped up in it, and then you are out. With nothing, no identity, no belonging, no idea where you're going or what you should do.'

Now everyone wants to buy him a beer, and Blake sways on his feet. The whole idea of being a hero baffles him. Why everyone makes such a fuss, he doesn't know. What he did was purely for survival, nothing heroic. It's not as if he deliberately risked his life to save theirs, not like real heroes.

The other officers take turns to examine the Medal of Honor around his neck. There is something awesome about the Yanks bestowing it on an Aussie, particularly a convict. It's because of Liam although at the time he didn't know who Liam Marais was. He certainly didn't know he was a Lieutenant Colonel in the American armed forces or the President's nephew.

After they escaped, he found out Liam's rank. He was staff officer to General Badencamp. While they were in the prison, he knew they were captured when a sandstorm brought down the American's chopper. It was amazing any of them got out of the helicopter alive.

At the time of Blake's capture, the Americans were already prisoners. Liam was in a bad way, but others were worse. Liam worked tirelessly to keep his men alive, but until Blake managed to bribe a guard with Ava's ring to divert drugs to the prisoners, two had already died from their injuries from the crash. For the rest it was not wounds they suffered, but terrible conditions, winter cold, and starvation.

Then Blake saved the life of the prison commandant's son when he took out the boy's appendix. That was when things began to turn around, and he was able to bargain for small concessions.

Soon he was treating many of the enemy's injured and sick. He understood from one of their medics that since sanctions against the Caliphate began years before, and the over-officious clerics had reduced the Universities to rubble, there was no real training left for new doctors. Many of the existing doctors were old or poorly trained, and there were no doctors to spare for the prison camp.

Then a year later three New Zealanders were brought in from another prison. Blake bargained for their lives, saying if they died, he would refuse to help anyone. The commandant tried threats, saying that if Blake refused to help their sick and wounded it meant he was not a Muslim and he would be beheaded.

Thanks to Abdulla's tutoring Blake recited the Koran at him, calling his bluff. By the time Noel and Jason were captured Blake had a well-established, but uneasy pact with the Commandant.

Now the whole hero thing makes him feel like a bit of a con. Sure, he kept them alive, but it was in exchange for keeping the enemy alive. That was the deal with the commandant—a life for a life. If anyone of his men died, a prisoner must also die. It focused Blake's mind.

Anyone of them would have done the same if they knew the medicine Blake knew. If they knew the language and customs as he did. They would have made deals, built sympathy, saved wounded enemy soldiers and their families, built trust, pretended to be converted, and if they had a two-carat diamond engagement ring to sell, well... anyone of them could have done what Blake did. He was just lucky.

His only motivation was to survive and get out of there. Getting the others out turned out to be less terrifying than going by himself. He was so busy planning and organising and making sure everything worked that he didn't have time to think about himself.

The escape was easier than his earlier attempt after the ambush. Then he and Richard crawled through mud for two full days, expecting a bullet in the head any minute. Only Richard got the bullet, and he lived. It's something he hasn't yet learned to live with, him alive and Richard dead. He still dreams about it.

When he escaped the gaol compound, the mission was almost a year in planning, and he had the guard's sympathy, the one he bribed with Ava's ring. He had too much to think about to worry about being shot.

Going back afterwards for the British Platoon wasn't planned, but neither did he think much about it, just acted. When the bullets slammed into him, the force knocked him sideways, but with his back wedged against the truck he managed to stay upright, firing at the place where he thought his assailant was.

Then undercover of the American bombardment he hauled himself into the truck, backing it up to where Jason and Noah were with the others. He barely noticed the pain in his back and thought he could deal with the injury. He was sure he'd killed the man who shot him because there was no more gunfire, just the maelstrom of bombs falling.

'So long as the Yanks get their coordinates right.' He remembers saying repeatedly in his head. 'Please don't let them fall on us.'

He drove the truck east across the Tigress for the second time in seventy-two hours, making his way from the targeted oil refineries, heading for the back roads that would take them to Basra. Later he could have killed them all when he passed out, but Jason grabbed the wheel. He learned later that while Noah hauled him out, Jason took over driving.

Blake was unconscious as they drove the last leg into Basra so he didn't think of himself as much of a hero. If it hadn't been for Jason and Noah, none of them would have made it out the second time, all because of his foolhardiness.

Today, the ceremony, the medals, the Prime Minister, and that strange woman Jenna left him wondering. The celebration in the mess was more genuine, and it made him feel good, but the PM's words still worry him. That shit about memories, responsibility, and duty. It is almost as if the man is trying to make sure he goes away with survivor guilt. He's not going down that path or he'll end up shooting himself like so many others. They are trying to manipulate him, but he can't figure out why.

The beers line up on the bar. He's drunk too much, and feels sick at the thought of drinking anymore. Blake looks around and slips out the mess heading unsteadily for his bed. He doesn't notice the man melting into the shadows as he arrives, nor does he notice that someone's rifled through his things.

21.

The next morning Rory parks outside the barracks. To pass the time he scans messages on his Cell, then checks the news headlines and weather. They forecast storms. He glances up at the sky and sees Blake approaching, his clothes dishevelled his face haggard.

'Jesus mate what happened to you?'

Blake shakes his head and groans as he puts his bag in the car. 'Don't ask.'

Rory laughs, jerking his thumb at the backseat. 'I bought you some clothes. I didn't know if you had anything else to wear besides your conscript greens.'

Blake flops into the front seat and straps on his seat belt. 'Thanks, these are rank after five months at the bottom of my pack. I should have washed them.'

'What about the uniform? Sick of it?'

'You can't take your greens with you. Government property you know. As if you'd want to—knobheads. Can we find somewhere to change before we go to the airport? I don't want to go back in there.' He nods towards the barracks. 'What time's the flight?'

Despite his hangover, Blake feels buoyant. It's a matter of hours and he'll see Charlotte. When he got back from the Cape, he half expected a letter, but there was nothing. Disappointment made him wonder if she had moved on. But he can't think like that, not unless he knows for sure. It's all he's dreamed about for months.

Rory does a three-point turn, 'I have bookings on the midday flight so we have time to kill. Hey, when we get to Brisbane, you will come home won't you mate? Mum issued instructions.'

'Thanks, but just until I find a place. I have a lot of catching up to do and I need to get on with it.'

'Will you finish your internship?'

'No, best part is I don't have to. I just need a place in the hospital, but I guess that won't be difficult will it?'

Rory laughs as he turns onto Morshead Drive. 'In case you're interested my aunt suggested we stay over until tomorrow with her and Uncle Arthur.'

'No!'

'That's what I said to her, but with a bit more finesse, like no thank you Aunt Miranda.'

'Ah shit—sorry. Mate I just need to see Charlotte. How is she?'

Rory glances at the gathering storm clouds to the west. 'I don't know. I haven't seen her.'

'What? Why? I asked you to keep a look out for her.'

'Hell Blake I tried, but she's not there any longer. She didn't come near us after you left. I figured she didn't want to know. I mean she has my phone number, and she knows where we are, but hell what was I supposed to do—leg-rope her? I called into the bar a couple of times. She seemed fine, but she was always busy so we didn't talk much. I knew she wrote to you. Then when we heard about your award, I sent Bryan to get her.'

'Who?'

Rory sucks his teeth. 'Tch... he's an articled clerk at the firm, but he came back and said she wasn't there. I went to the bar that evening, but still nothing. When I asked, no one seemed to know what I was talking about. The next day we flew to Canberra.'

'Fuck.' Blake feels the old anger rising at his helplessness. Maybe she's not interested, but she could tell him to his face.

'I figured you would know from her letters. If she needed me, she knows my number, so... well she's a big girl Blake. What was I supposed to do? I couldn't force her to keep in contact could I? Didn't she write to you?'

'Yes she sent a couple of letters, but I haven't heard anything for the past month. I thought it was because we were in the Ca... Oh forget it.'

'Where?'

'Nowhere, I shouldn't have said anything. It's classified and I could go straight back inside.'

'Okay but seriously she'll be all right. I just didn't know her phone number or where she lives.'

'Did you ask Evan?'

'Who?'

'Evan–you know the bloke Jeremy got the work I.D. for. You gave him a job in the warehouse.'

'Shit I don't know who he is. I don't even know what he looks like and I certainly couldn't remember his name. Do you expect me to go around the hospitals and warehouses yelling for someone with illegal I.D?'

'What do you mean illegal? I thought it was legit.'

'Yeah it's the genuine article, but still done underhand.'

'Okay. But I have to find her. Is there an earlier flight?'

'No, they're all booked. We can get a charter, but hell it's only two hours.' Rory pulls into the forecourt of a hotel and looks for a parking spot. 'I stayed here last night. They'll give us a room for you to change.'

'I'll only be a sec. Are you coming? You can wait in the bar; maybe order a beer. I could do with the hair of the dog.' Blake gets out of the car and grabs the shopping bag from the back seat, trying to control his unease about Charlotte. When he gets to Brisbane, he'll find Evan. He'll know where Charlotte is.

They walk towards the hotel entrance and Rory glances at the sky, 'I don't like the look of that cloud. It has the greenish tinge of a hailstorm. I hope it holds off.'

In the gents, Blake hauls out a pair of jeans and shirt from the shopping bag and rips off the labels. The clothes are a bit baggy, but they'll do. He stuffs his old clothes into a bin and goes in search of Rory. As he walks into the bar, there's a clap of thunder that rattles glasses.

Rory jumps at the noise, then grins at Blake in his new clothes. 'Fit all right then?'

'Yeah thanks. Shit, I hope this doesn't delay the flight. Thanks for the beer.'

Rory glances at his watch. 'Drink up, we should get a move on before the storm hits.'

As they drive to the airport the wind picks up, buffeting the car. Fat raindrops pelt the windscreen. By the time they pull into the car rental agency, the rain has crystallised to hail.

Blake and Rory stand at the entrance of the hire car office watching its vengeful fury. Ice bounces off a sign saying keep Australia safe: report suspicious activity. It piles in drifts, filling gutters, and cracking unprotected windscreens, denting cars unfortunate enough to be out in it. Blake shivers.

'Should have bought a jumper as well, but who the hell was to know this was coming.' Rory says. 'I just hope it doesn't last long.'

But it does, delaying the flight by two hours. It's nearly six o'clock by the time they land in Brisbane. Blake wants to go straight to the pub, but Rory says, 'she's not there mate.'

'Okay, Newstead then. We'll go to her place.'

When they arrive at her building, Blake leaps out before the car stops. He takes the stairs two at a time, ignoring the homeless people squashed into every available nook. Rory follows and waits at the base of the stairwell, looking around him in dismay. He didn't know anybody lived like this. The building should be condemned.

Blake hammers on the door, but no one answers. He turns to a man sitting at the top of the stairs. 'Have you seen Charlotte, the woman who lives here?'

The old bloke averts his face and mutters to himself. Blake feels rage rising, wanting to grab the man around the throat and force him to talk. Instead, he runs back downstairs.

'Give us a hundred,' he says to Rory.

When he returns the man's gone. Helplessly he stands wondering what to do next and then he sees someone slip through the doorway of the fire escape. He's not sure if it's the same person, but gives chase catching him as he rounds the bend of the stairs. Blake forces him against a wall.

'I asked you if you know where Charlotte is. Here.' He holds up the hundred.

A choking miasma seeps from the man's ragged clothing as he cowers in fear. Blake's eyes water as guilt at his brutality surges, but he doesn't let go his grip. 'Look she's a friend that's all. I don't want to bring trouble I just need to find her. Okay?'

'You a cop?'

'No. I'm her friend.'

'She's not here.'

'Where is she?'

'Haven't seen her.'

'Since when?'

'Maybe a couple of weeks, maybe more, I don't know.'

'Do you know anyone else who can tell me?'

The old man shakes his head, his eyes fixed on the hundred. Blake thrusts the note at him. 'If you see her, tell her Blake's home. Got it?'

The man clutches the hundred-dollar note nodding his head and then scuttles away down the fire escape and out a landing door.

Blake goes back to find Rory. 'We need to go to the warehouse.'

Rory worries. Blake's acting crazy, but shit how was he to know she was in trouble. This should be a day for celebrations not this crazy drive all over Brisbane. 'She'll be fine. She probably just got another job and moved.'

Secretly he thinks, no sane person would choose to live in that building. Or maybe she didn't want Blake finding her. Maybe she found someone else, but Rory knows better than to suggest that. Instead, he glances at Blake and says, 'are you sure you know what you're doing?'

Blake remains grim faced and silent, and Rory sighs as he punches the address into the map. The car noses out into the afternoon traffic. Half an hour later, they pull into the warehouse parking area. Once more Blake is out the car and running to the entrance before the car stops.

A man in blue overalls pushing a loaded trolley, directs Blake to an office beside a loading bay. Blake pushes the door open.

'Are you Harry Billcotts?'

'Hey you can't just barge in here...' The man stands, his broad olive skinned face indignant at this invasion of his space. Then his face clears, 'ah sorry, Mr Lincoln isn't it? I recognised you from the news. Harry is off shift. I'm Nicko Tadros, night supervisor. Harry will be back at seven.'

'Yeah sorry. Look Nicko I'm in a hurry. I'm looking for Evan Chandler. He started work here about five months ago.'

Nicko shakes his head. 'I don't recall the name. One minute I'll check the files.'

Blake paces, until Nicko says, 'looks like he was transferred.' Blake stops waiting for the man to get to the point. 'Yes. We sent him to head office. Apparently, he has a Masters in Economics and almost a PhD.' Nicko laughs. 'The boss thought it seemed dumb to have him lugging boxes in a warehouse given he was pretty useless at it.'

Blake, jittery with frustration, says, 'so where is he?'

'It says here he was transferred to accounts.'

'Okay good. Where's that?'

'It's over at the head office Mr Lincoln, but it'll be closed now. They knock off at five over there.'

'Shit.'

Nicko's worried. 'Is there something else I can help you with?'

Rory walks in and with relief Nicko says, 'Ah Mr Fuller, good evening sir.'

Blake doesn't give Rory a chance to answer. Grabbing his arm he says, 'we have to go back into town. Evan's moved to head office.' He turns back to Nicko. 'Do you have his home address?'

'No Mr Lincoln. That will be in his HR file over at head office.'

'Okay thanks. Come on, Rory.'

Rory rolls his eyes. 'Thanks Nicko.' He closes the office door as he follows Blake back to the car. 'What do you expect to find at head office Blake? It will be closed. We can go home and ask Dad for the keys, but what are you looking for? This bloke won't still be there.'

'Can we get his address?'

'Well I imagine the HR files are on line, but we'll have to ask Dad, he may not have the password. I can't imagine he has much use for that sort of detail. Can't it wait until morning?'

'Shit no, I'm going out of my mind here.'

Rory can see his agitation. 'Why, what do you think happened to her?'

Blake's voice is bleak, 'She might be locked-up.'

'Shit why? She probably just moved. She's hardly the criminal type.' He glances at Blake. 'You know something don't you?'

'Yes.'

'What? Why would they arrest her?'

'She sings at an underground club.'

'Christ.'

'Yep.' Blake stares out the window. A new storm front rolls relentlessly towards the coast blocking out the setting sun and darkening the horizon.

On the way home, they stop at the Writers Bar. Rory lets Blake out and goes to find a parking. Blake waits at the counter for the woman serving to attend to him. She's about thirty, dark haired and would once have been pretty, but now she is thin and looks worn out.

Blake turns as Rory joins him. 'Is this the same woman you saw before?'

'No. It was a bloke.'

The barmaid chews gum as she slops towards them. She leans against the counter. 'What'll it be?'

'I just want some information,' Blake says.

'You have to buy a drink.'

'Okay, two beers thanks, the one on tap.'

While she pulls the beer, Blake says, 'what's your name?'

'Stella.'

'Okay Stella, can you tell me what happened to the last woman who worked here? The one with the red beret.'

'Who's asking?'

'I'm a friend that's all.'

'You a cop?'

'No, I'm a friend. She and I, well I took her out a couple of times you know and...'

Stella laughs showing blackened teeth. 'Now I know you're lying. Anybody works this bar never gets to go out on a date. Its twelve hours, seven days a week—unless you took her for breakfast.'

Blake smiles. 'Okay, saying we dated is a bit of an exaggeration, but still... I would like to catch up with her again.'

'Well she's not here so you are looking in the wrong place.' She holds her hand out for the money.

Rory pulls out his wallet, holding up fifty dollars. 'There's another fifty if you know where we can find her.'

'Look I don't know anything okay. All I know is that she didn't turn up to work one day and we've been taking it in turns to run this bar. No one wants to take it on regular like because of the shit hours, so we all do a stint. I don't know where Charlotte is, but if you see her tell her to get her ass back in here. We're sick of covering for her.'

'When was she last here?'

'How the fuck do you think I would know that. I hardly know her okay.'

'Please Stella.' Blake looks apologetically at Rory, 'give her another fifty.'

She takes the money, examining Blake's face as she stuffs the money into her bra. 'You're that bloke in the news who got all those hero medals aren't you? I saw on the screen,' she nods to the corner of the room.

'Yes.'

'Bloody good show mate. I hope you killed lots of the bastards. Fucking terrorists scum, coming here thinking they can take away our bleeding country.' She stops, sizing him up before she speaks again. 'Okay, far as I know, Charlotte chucked in the job about two or three weeks ago, but that's all I know. As I said, I hardly knew her.'

22.

Margery Fuller walks down the corridor towards the laundry, a bundle of clothes in her arms. She hums an old tune from her childhood, trying to remember the rest of the words. If you could read my mind love, what a tale my thoughts could tell.

Her daughter crosses the entrance hall to the front door and Margery calls, 'going out dear?'

'Yes Mum. I have a Pilates class.'

'Don't be late then Emmy. You must be home by six tonight for Blake's homecoming. Rory rang to say the flight would be late, but they should be here by six or six thirty at the latest. We'll have a nice dinner—just the family.'

'What about Jeremy?'

'No I think we should let Jeremy have a night off dear.'

'He's almost family,' Emmy's affronted.

'I don't think so dear. Last time he and Blake didn't seem to hit it off very well. It won't hurt to let the man have a night off, without you clinging to him.'

'Mum that's horrible.'

'Well... oh all right, sorry. I'm in a tizzy trying to get Blake's room ready.'

Emmy sniffs mollified, but she's relieved. Perhaps she and Jeremy have been in each other's pockets too much lately. 'What about Ava? Or will Blake bring that girl he was keen on before he left.'

'Oh no darling, that's finished. She seems to have moved away. Rory went to see her, but she has left her job and gone off somewhere.'

'Should I invite Ava then? Maybe they will decide to get back together. I do wish Ava hadn't dumped him. It would be so good if they were married. We could do things together, couple things. Now Ava's always mooning about because I'm engaged and she's not. She says it's because she's lost her friend, but I think she's jealous.' Emmy grins. 'I'm sure she'll want to see Blake again. Last time she didn't get the chance to speak to him.'

'I'm not sure. I don't want Blake to feel uncomfortable. You know how he is. I don't want him bolting off to stay in a sleazy hotel again.'

'Okay, well I'll ask her if she thinks it's a good idea. I'll be back in an hour. Shall I pick up anything on the way home?'

'No dear, it's all set.'

Emmy walks out the house, flicking through her cell to call Jeremy. Margery continues on to the laundry singing, 'just like an old time movie, 'bout a ghost from a wishing well.' She dumps the clothes in the basket and turns back to the kitchen to supervise the preparations.

They had roast beef last time especially for Blake, but this time it's her choice, and she's decided on a seafood buffet on the terrace. The night is balmy for August so it will be perfect. They can eat prawns with their fingers without her worrying juice will drop on the carpet.

A few hours later Margery looks at her watch. It's nearly seven-thirty, and she frets that Blake won't come at all. William, Emmy, and Ava, sit around the outdoor table sipping drinks in silence. She glances at her husband, irritated by his passivity. He stares out across the river as if he hasn't a worry in the world.

'William, where can they have got to? Surely, the flight is not this late.'

He turns to her, surprise furrowing lines between his eyes. 'My dear, I have no idea, but they will turn up eventually. Probably celebrating.'

There's a faint sound of garage doors grating and she sighs. 'Open the champagne William.'

A few minutes later Rory and Blake come through the house. As they step onto the terrace, Marjory leaps up from her chair and skips to meet them. 'Darlings, I thought you were lost. You're so late Rory. Welcome home Blake.' She kisses him and tucks her arm through his, walking with him across the terrace. 'We have champagne. Will you have a glass or would you rather beer?'

Blake smiles. 'Champagne will be fine Mrs Fuller, but I need a quick word with Mr Fuller, if you will excuse us a moment.'

'Business already—can't it wait dear?'

Blake sees her disappointment and squeezes her hand. 'It'll only take a minute.'

'I'll sort it,' Rory says. 'You go and sit with the women and have a drink. I'll talk to Dad.'

'Thanks.' Blake nods gratefully at Rory.

'What's all this mystery?' William Fuller says pouring champagne and handing Blake a glass. 'Welcome home son.'

'Thanks Mr Fuller. Hello Em.'

Emmy jumps up and throws her arms around Blake. 'Welcome home Blake. Come and sit next to me.'

'Where's Jeremy?'

'He's not coming tonight. It's just a special dinner for you.'

Relieved Blake turns and says, 'hello Ava.'

'Hey Blake.' She smiles at him.

Her friendly greeting is a surprise. Last time she barely spoke to him.

Rory and Mr Fuller withdraw into the house. Twenty minutes later, they are back and Rory hands him a sticky note. Blake takes it wondering how he can break the news to Margery that he has to go out again. As he reads, his heart sinks. It's Charlotte's address, and he knows he won't find Evan there.

Rory notices. 'What is it?'

Blake shrugs not wanting to discuss it. All he says is, 'I'll see him in the morning,' and watches relief cross Rory's face as he plans his next move.

When they are all asleep, he'll go to the club. Perhaps Charlotte is living in the squat above, or if not, someone may know where she is. He might even come across Evan. The difficulty is crossing the river after curfew. All bridges are patrolled even if the streets aren't.

The others stare at him, and he rubs his head feeling the short bristle under his palms, searching for something to break the silence. Rory does it for him. 'He's in a stew about Charlotte. She's vanished.'

'How sad.' Margery frowns. The girl might have let the poor man down gently. 'Blake darling you didn't know her that well, did you?'

Emmy's says,. 'Well you can do better Blake.' She doesn't understand it. Blake's so nice and he's handsome in that brooding way of his. He's a bit intense for her taste, but lots of girls like him. Yet he can't seem to keep a girlfriend. First Ava dumps him, now Charlotte. People are so fickle. 'She doesn't deserve you.' If the woman were here, she'd give her a piece of her mind. 'But don't worry, now you're out you'll be the catch of the year. You're so famous and good-looking, and now Jeremy's taken, you can be the most eligible bachelor in the country. All the girls will want you, won't they Ava?' She looks triumphant as if to say, see what you lost.

'Hey what about me?' Rory says, 'I'm a pretty good catch too.' He looks hopefully at Ava.

Later that evening Blake offers to see Ava home. It's his solution to how he'll cross the bridge before curfew.

Rory casts a dark look at him, and says, 'I'll drive her.'

Emmy and Mrs Fuller are at once conspiratorial and drag Rory away, leaving Blake wishing they wouldn't see things that aren't there. All he wants is to be able to get across the river before curfew so he can get to the club. He'll worry about not getting home again later.

In the car, Ava is quiet, but Blake is too preoccupied with worrying about Charlotte to notice. They drive in silence over the bridge. At the other side, he pulls up at the police roadblock.

'Good evening sir.' The police officer bends at Blake's open window scanning Ava and then Blake. 'Where are you heading?'

'New Farm.'

'Ah that's not far. You will be in doors by twelve?'

'Yes.'

'Licence and car ownership disc please?'

'The car's not mine,' Blake says stretching in his seat to pull his wallet from his pocket.

'Do you have permission to drive it?'

'Yes. It belongs to my friend Rory Fuller.' He hands over his driver's licence and reaches across Ava to unhook a small plastic disc from the inside of the glove compartment.

The officer scans the bio imprint. 'You will barely have time to get home to this address. Are you going home?' He leers through the window at Ava.

'I'll stay at a hotel.'

'Have you consumed alcohol or medication today?'

'Yes, I've had two glasses of champagne.'

'Look at me please sir.'

Blake fixes his eyes on a hand held machine and flinches at the small flash as the officer takes a reading.

'You'll need to hurry to get off the streets. Have a good night.'

Blake eases the car into the road, feeling the sweat trickling down his sides as he breathes a sigh of relief.

Ava says, 'you won't have time to get back before midnight.'

'I'll be all right.'

'If you want to, you can stay at my place. It's no problem, and I have a spare room.'

Blake glances at her. Yes, that will work. He can stay until she goes to sleep and then let himself out. It's not that far to the club from there, and if he runs the distance, he can make it while Charlotte's still on stage. 'Thanks that will be great. If you're sure it's no problem?'

Fifteen minutes later, they pull up at a security barrier at the end of the road leading to Ava's apartment. After clearing security, Blake pulls up behind another car, a four by four, at the entrance to a grand apartment building.

'You've done well for yourself Ava.' He glances across and smiles at her, catching the look of panic flashing across her face.

'I'm sorry Blake. I forgot. You can't stay, I....' She opens the door and fumbles with her bag, dropping it on the ground and snatching it up again. 'There's a hotel at the end of the road. You can just make it if you hurry. I'm really sorry.' She slams the door, and almost trips in her haste.

Blake calls after her. 'Hey wait up. I'll see you safe inside.' But she's gone, and mystified Blake watches her run up the pathway, wondering what made her change her mind so suddenly.

A doorman opens the foyer door and speaks to her. Blake lowers the window, but the voices are too low to hear. Ava looks frightened. The club can wait a few minutes. He takes out his phone and presses a number. Rory answers.

'Hey mate I'm not going to make it back before curfew. We got held up at a road block.'

'Bullshit! You're staying with Ava aren't you?'

'No Rory. Look, I've just dropped her off and I have to get to a hotel. She said there's one at the end of the road, but I'll have to hurry.'

'Promise me.'

'What? For Christ sakes. I said I'm not interested. If you are, you have to tell her. Look we'll talk tomorrow. I have to go okay. See you in the morning.'

Blake watches the building and sees a small window light up on the third floor, and guesses it's the rear of Ava's apartment.

Around the side of the building, a cyclone fence tops a flood-mitigation embankment. Once over the fence he edges along the narrow lip of the embankment, holding onto the diamond mesh until he reaches the corner of the building. Ava's apartment faces the river three stories above.

Below, the river slaps and gurgles as Blake finds hand and foot holds in the rock walls. He makes for the lower floor balcony, five metres away. It's in darkness as are those above, and he hopes they stay that way. It would be difficult explaining to Ava why he is trying to break into her apartment.

He reaches the third floor and grasps the rail to hoist himself over the balcony railing. As he does, he hears a muffled cry. Adrenalin shoots through his body. Throwing away caution, he pulls himself onto her balcony. It's dark. Curtained glass doors block the escaping light, and he creeps across to peer through a chink.

In the lamp-lit sitting room beyond, Ava huddles on the sofa, her legs drawn up, and her hand holding one side of her face. Jeremy towers above her, his hand raised as she cringes. Blake scrabbles for the door latch, but before he can do more Ava stands and wraps her arms about Jeremy's neck.

Jeremy's arms slide around her and unzip her dress. She lets it fall to the floor and steps out of it. Her slender, almost emaciated body, is naked in the dim light as she twirls around, preening for Jeremy. Then she takes his hand and leads him through a doorway at the back of the room.

Blake flops on an outdoor chair at a loss. How, why? He knew Jeremy couldn't be trusted, but he never thought Ava would do something like this to her best friend. What's he supposed to do with this information?

He'll have to tell Emmy. Rory can't hold a candle for this woman. She's treacherous. Thank Christ she broke it off, or he might be dealing with this betrayal right now. But why did Jeremy ask Emmy to marry him if he's carrying on with Ava? What's the point?

Blake wavers for about twenty minutes, unable to make up his mind about what to do when a noise alerts him. Ava's hand clutches the curtain, and Blake vaults over the edge of the balcony, hanging by his fingers, his feet scrabbling for traction.

She throws the curtains open and slides back a glass panel, flooding the balcony with light. A lighter flares and Blake smells cigarette smoke. Then he hears Jeremy.

'Christ Ava put some clothes on, or turnoff the light. Do you want every telescopic lens in every building across the river trained on you? If you do that's fine, but I don't want to be seen here.'

'Sorry.' The light goes off as Blake's foot touches the lower floor balcony rail.

'Do you want a snort?'

'Yes darling, leave me some. I'll just finish my cigarette.'

Blake scrambles back across the rock wall and over the fence, dropping down onto the road. As he walks back to the car, a man steps out from the bushes, his voice a nasal whine.

'Hey man, this is our patch. You can't move in here.'

So much for neighbourhood security Blake thinks, but says in a friendly tone. 'Mate it's all yours, I was just visiting.' A memory flares of Evan saying he knew people who overheard Ava and Jeremy arguing outside Ava's apartment, and he says, 'maybe you can help me. I'm looking for someone. You might know him. He's a friend of mine.'

The man looks at him suspiciously and glances over his shoulder as another man comes up silently behind Blake. 'Who is it?'

Blake relaxes his muscles. He doesn't think these people are violent. They are scavengers not hunters. 'Evan Chandler. He told me he knows you blokes. It's really important that I find him.'

'How do we know you're not a cop.' The first man sniffs. 'You're too well dressed to be one of us.'

'Have you ever seen a cop on the streets after curfew? I haven't.' He grins. 'Look, do you know where Evan is or not? Thing is my girls disappeared and I'm hoping Evan knows where she is. I'm worried she might have been arrested.'

The man behind Blake walks around to see his face. 'You're the bloke who got Evan a job aren't you? That bloke who escaped from Baghdad.'

'Maybe.' Blake flinches at the man's face. A jagged scar runs from eye to mouth, pulling his lower lid down his cheek and his mouth askew.

Scarface stares for a moment then says, 'we don't see Ev no more. Not since he got a job.'

The first man says, 'hey dude can you get us jobs also?'

'I don't know. I can try, but the hard part is getting I.D. Do you have I.D?'

'Nup,' he shakes his head.

Scarface says, 'think we'd be here if we had I.D?'

'Ah fuck it,' says the first man. 'I don't want to work for the lying thieving turds anyway and big deal, you escaped Baghdad. Whoop tee doo. We shouldn't even be over there. Let them drown in their own shit. Fucking oil that's what. I'm not going to be party to perpetuating the lowlife ambitions of this mob of corrupt arseholes we call a government, stooges for big business more like.'

Blake's surprised. He thought he was alone in thinking this stuff. If other people are thinking it why isn't there more of a protest about what this government is doing? He says, 'why don't you vote them out then.'

'You're kidding right?' The man hawks and spits at the ground.

'No I'm not kidding. I mean it. Why do we put up with this shit?'

Speculatively, the man scans his face then turns to Scarface. 'Dude's a dick.'

Scarface says, 'you know we can't vote, don't you?'

'No, I don't. Why can't you? There's an election next year.'

'Have you been hiding under a log?' The first man's eyebrows knit in incredulity.

'None of my business,' Blake says, 'but it seems to me that someone needs to stop what they are doing. Unless we vote them out, it's not going to happen.'

'Look dude, I don't know what your game is, but you must realise if you want to vote you need I.D.—no I.D, no vote.'

'You're kidding.' But Blake knows they're not and wonders how many people have lost the right to vote because they can't get I.D.

The first man shrugs. 'Come on Aubrey. Let's get out of here. He's no different from the rest.'

'Wait, hey guys I need your help.' Blake's desperate.

Aubrey turns back and says, 'what—you paying?'

Christ, he still doesn't have any money on him. 'I've got no cash on me, but I can get you some tomorrow.'

The first man says, 'give us your watch then.'

Blake looks at his watch. He can't give it to them. It was his twenty first-birthday gift from his parents, and without his watch his e-cript won't work. 'Forget it.' He'll find Evan himself. 'Will you tell Evan I'm looking for him?'

'Maybe.'

Aubrey stops, feeling sorry for the bloke. 'Try the city library. He sometimes hangs around there.'

'Okay thanks.' Blake watches the two men walk away, hugging the shadows and bushes either side of the now deserted road. He contemplates driving to the club, decides it's not worth the risk, and heads off in a long lope to conserve his energy. He's already lost so much time, and he wants to get there while she's still on stage. A glance at his watch, tells him it's close to one a.m., and his stomach constricts with anticipation. He wants to hear her sing again.

It takes Blake less than twenty minutes to run the distance, avoiding streets with potential cameras, or private security. Aside from night roamers like the two outside Ava's apartment block, he sees no one else.

As he approaches the alley down which the club is located, he's cautious not knowing what he'll find. At the top of the stairwell, he waits for his eyes to adjust to the gloom, feeling as if he's walking into an underground crypt. It smells like mouldering death.

There is no blue light tonight, but he pulls out Rory's key ring and flicks on a penlight. The steel door is sealed with police tape. Blake pushes against it in the remote hope it might open to his touch, but it's locked. Now he's sure Charlotte's been arrested. But how long ago and where will they be holding her?

Once he's back in the overgrown yard, he looks around as if there are answers in the rubble. Perhaps Evan lives in the squat that rises above the club. He hunts for an entrance, but finds nothing more in the yard and goes back to the street. Around the block, a short lane leads to the back of the building. Its cordoned off by more police tape and he ducks under it, looking around to make sure he's alone.

At the building, fire doors gape open, showing the dark maw of a passageway leading into the club's interior. Blake takes a tentative step inside, wondering if he's risking his luck. In the small pool of penlight, he sees signs of a hasty retreat.

In each room overturned chairs, boxes, and crates lie abandoned along with personal belongings. The bar trestle table lies on its side with broken glass strewn across the floor. It's odd. If the police came in the back entrance why didn't people leave by the front?

Blake goes back through the club, and stands by the fire exit looking out, trying to piece together what happened. A gleam of reflected light catches his eye. It's an aluminium tear gas canister. Now he knows why they left by the back door, or he can guess anyway. Above his head he sees an air vent and knows how the police tricked them. Angry and in despair he turns back the way he came. There's a dark lump in the gutter, and he bends to pick it up. It's a red beret, and his jaw tightens.

23.

The landscape changes from woodland savannah to layered sandstone outcrops on the hard face of endless red dirt, dotted with dry grass, clumps of Spinifex, Boab trees and the occasional spindly Eucalypt. Charlotte sways in the back of the truck, her body twisted to peer through a rip in the canvass. The countryside gives her hope they are still in Australia.

She turns back to her companions with whom she has spent the days since their arrest, mostly travelling. They are exhausted from lack of sleep, from little food and the ceaseless heat. It's hot here, hotter than Brisbane in January and its only August. Under the tarpaulin covering, it feels airless. Exhaust fumes filter in through the gaps making the air difficult to breathe, and they are caked in the ubiquitous red dust. More trucks follow, although how many, she doesn't know. She's just grateful to be in the lead avoiding the worst of the dust kicked up by other trucks.

There's grit on her face and her fingers touch hair that would make a Masai warrior proud. If only she hadn't lost her beret, but she's tied her hair in a braid, binding it with a bit of string she found lying on the ground at one of their many stops along the road. Even if she had kept her beret, they would have taken it, like they took her bag and her clothes before they put them in the holding cell.

Charlotte has lost all sense of time, but at least they are out of the cells in that last place. It was awful. A small bathroom with a shower and toilet adjoined the room, but no door. There are seven of them, the same seven as in the paddy wagon when they were arrested. The four men are from the band playing at the time of the raid, and the women with them.

It seems if you are arrested together, you stay like that, regardless of sex. They haven't bothered separating men and women. Across from her, Nina cries. She hasn't stopped since the raid, and it's getting on Charlotte's nerves. Lucas puts his arm around her.

The woman on the other side of Nina is Esmeralda. 'Just call me Mallory,' she insists, saying she hates her mother for calling her Esmeralda. Now she stares vacantly into the space opposite, her green eyes shining in luminous contrast with their surrounding dust rings and sunburnt skin.

Every time they stop Mallory ducks for shade to keep her pale skin from blistering. Several times the radio shackle prevented her, and she was forced to stand in the sun with the others as her skin glow deepened and her freckles darkened. Charlotte's convinced the guards did it out of spite.

Oscar sits next to Mallory. At the start of their journey he tried to lift their spirits by cracking jokes, but the last few days he's become resigned. The night of the raid was Mallory's first date with Oscar. Charlotte can't believe such bad luck, but Mallory said, 'story of my life. I always choose men who get me into trouble.'

'Hey,' Oscar said, 'give me a break. Look at us. Our first fucking gig since our discharge and we're going straight back. No one said it was a hot venue or believe me, I wouldn't have been there either.'

'The battalion must miss us,' Lucas said that first day in the Brisbane Watch House when he still retained a sense of humour and hope. 'Can't do without us heroes, but you girls shouldn't worry, I'll explain you are not part of the deal.' He paused, 'if I can get some bastard to listen.'

Charlotte sits between Dylan and Riley. Dylan's the sensible one, and Riley is quiet, not shy but thoughtful and considerate. She turns to peer through the tear in the tarpaulin again and says, 'where do you suppose we are going?' No one answers and she doesn't really expect them to, the effort is too much. If you don't know, why waste precious effort to say so.

She lapses into silence, swaying with the rhythm of the truck, elbows resting on her knees as she tries to work out the date. Is Blake back in Brisbane yet? It must be soon. Will he look for her, wonder where she is? She pushes the image away for it brings about an intense yearning. Life is so unfair. Her thoughts return to dwell on the elusive question; what will become of them? Fear flares in her gut and she tries to suppress it.

For the umpteenth time the truck stops, and she peers out the tarpaulin gap. At first, swirling dust mists her view, but as it settles, she can make out a razor-wire fence behind which is a guardhouse. On the horizon behind the complex, an escarpment glows golden in the sinking sun.

A guard unlocks and opens a gate while two more stand watch, rifles cradled in their arms. The vehicles bump across an empty car park to a large rectangular building, behind which she can see roofs and towers, their iron reflecting the lancing light. When they stop, a guard unzips the canvas and orders them out of the vehicle.

In front of them a corrugated iron building looms, grey and featureless with one heavy iron double entry door that opens as they wait. They are marshalled into lines and march inside where they are handed over to new guards.

These guards wear a different uniform, grey instead of blue. On their breast pockets they each have an embroidered badge with looping gold letters spelling Circe on a black background underscored by a red ellipse. Charlotte gazes around the hall, taking in the concrete floor, and iron-grey walls without windows. The place is cheerless and forbidding.

The guards order them to make two lines, one for men, one for women

'Now they separate us,' Charlotte mutters to Mallory.

Nina clings to Lucas until two guards force them apart. Charlotte looks away. She can't bear to watch as Nina breaks down sobbing on the concrete floor. Lucas joins the men's line. His eyes squint with worry for Nina.

Charlotte doesn't know where they spent the last couple of weeks. Dylan said it was Darwin, Riley argued it was Perth. From her perspective, it might have been a foreign land. No one explained, and if they asked, the guards ignored them.

A Circe officer saunters over to stand above Nina, his legs spread, his rubber truncheon slapping against the palm of his hand. Mallory glances at Charlotte, and together they haul Nina to her feet. Mallory comforts her, trying to stop the hiccoughing sobs. Charlotte wants to slap her.

So far, there has been no overt physical cruelty from their guards, but no one wants to take the chance. They have no idea what will happen next. Charlotte looks along the men's line, searching for her own band members. When she sees them, she lifts her chin in acknowledgement. It's the first time she has seen them since the plane trip from Brisbane.

They remain cautious, returning her greeting with small nods. No one is sure of anything. Letting on whom you know might be incriminating. Charlotte doesn't know why they are being so cautious. There are cameras recording every gesture from a dozen different angles.

She wonders where Flynn is. He's the only one of the band she can't see. She breathes an envious sigh, maybe he escaped. Lucky old Flynn. Evan isn't there either. He must have left before the raid. Lucky Evan.

While they wait, she occupies herself with tying to work out what she knows about the law, wishing she'd paid more attention to the news. The changes over the past years are a haze of gossip and rumour, so full of propaganda you never knew what was true and what wasn't. She gave up taking an interest years ago.

They haven't been charged yet, and she wonders when they will go before a magistrate. Will she get a phone call or a lawyer? Not that a phone call will do her any good. No one she knows has a phone, except the Fullers and Blake. She should have memorised their numbers.

The paper she wrote them on is languishing in her bag, taken by the police to some unknown place. She looks down at her filthy prison uniform, covered in red dust. She's been in the same clothes for weeks, and she's thirsty. Her tongue feels too big, stuck to the roof of her mouth.

A guard gives an order. The line she's in moves towards a door on the left of the room. Charlotte glances back to the men's line and lifts her hand in farewell before she goes through the door. They walk along a corridor that leads to a large communal shower.

Four female guards stand at a row of slatted benches and the women prisoners line up facing them. Four more guards line up behind them. Charlotte estimates there are fifteen prisoners. A ratio of more than two to one. How dangerous do they think they are?

When they are in place one of the guard's, a stout woman with a large mole on her forehead, steps forward. She orders the prisoners to strip. They take off their clothes and leave them on the benches. Naked and embarrassed, they try to hide their exposed genitals with their hands.

At first, Charlotte can't believe what is happening. The guards walk along the length of naked women, looking each of them up and down, sometimes circling a person in crude examination. They mock, commenting on any imperfection or weakness they spot in the target.

A guard with lank greasy hair, picks up a pair of knickers. She calls to her colleague. 'Hey Sal, what the fuck do you think this stinking piece of tat is?'

Sal laughs, 'looks like tank camo that's overdue for replacement.'

When they get to Charlotte, she remains still, staring at the ground in front of her while the guards circle.

A third guard with short black tightly sprung curls says, 'thought we only housed humans in this facility, looks like we're getting all sorts in here now. This one looks like a horse for Christ sake. Look at the fucking mane on it. That'll have to come off, full of lice, check it out.' She yanks Charlotte's braid, pulling her head towards the other two guards for inspection.

The first guard says, 'yup, I can see the buggers. It's heaving.'

Sal shudders and pantomimes avoidance. 'Jesus, she's alive, keep her away from me.'

The prisoners either side shuffle away, fearful of catching something, but Charlotte knows she doesn't have lice. It's just an excuse to humiliate her. Mallory is next. They mock her pale skin, calling her an albino. One of them runs her nails across the sunburn on her arms. Mallory flinches but keeps her eyes downcast. The ritual degradation takes twenty minutes, and every woman in the room wears the shame. A snivel to the left causes Charlotte to glance along the line. It's Nina, and the guards swoop.

Charlotte tries to block out their taunts, wondering if the same thing is happening to the men. Did Blake suffer this humiliation when they arrested him? The thought comforts her. If he could take it, so can she and her spine stiffens. She doesn't know it's just the beginning, and it will become much worse.

After the ritual degradation, they shower and still wet, move to another room. Two trestle tables are piled with lines of clothes, orange jumpsuits, sturdy boots, underwear, and plastic footwear, their sizes in frames in front of them. Charlotte is near the back of the line and misses her size for the jumpsuit.

They give her a uniform that is a size too small and plastic thongs too big. It's pointless complaining, but at least the boots are the right size. She struggles into the ill-fitting orange jumpsuit and pulls up the zip. It flattens her breasts uncomfortably, but she'll survive. Then she follows the others to yet another room. It's a rectangular tiled room, with a row of six steel chairs bolted to the floor.

They line up, waiting to take a seat. Mallory is in front of Charlotte and takes the last of the vacant seats. The guard puts up her hand to tell Charlotte to wait. Mallory turns her head. There's fear in her eyes. Charlotte lowers her eyes in acknowledgement, but otherwise remains deadpan. She's won't give the guards any excuses.

The guards pick up electric sheers and take up their positions behind the row of women. At first, there is stunned silence then a woman with long blonde hair screams. 'No you can't!'

The guard stops cutting and says, 'do that again and you'll cause me to lose concentration. These sheers are sharp so if you so much as breathe heavily, I'll have Ida over there hold you down.' She nods towards a woman standing near the door.

Ida is six foot two inches in her stocking soles and built like a strong man, with roping muscles and thick tendons. Her heavy jaw is held at an angle above a short neck. Her hair is so short it looks as if she uses sheers on herself. Livid acne scars blotch her exposed face and arms, along with freshly encrusted eruptions.

Ida doesn't miss anything. Don't the stupid bitches know they'll be grateful in the coming days. They'll have one less thing to worry them. You can't have hair flying all over the place when you're on exercises. She hates her job, despises the other prison guards, and actively loathes the female prisoners, but they wouldn't take her in the army, which was her lifelong dream.

Her employment record says, mentally unfit for deployment. They said she has a sadistic personality disorder. Bullshit, she is fitter than most men, and she has the perfect warrior mentality, gets things done. She's just pragmatic. Some things are required to achieve the mission, and sometimes people get in the way. It's their own fault. Usually they bring it on themselves.

There is another agenda behind the reason they won't take her in the military, she is convinced of that, but she'll bide her time until she finds out what. Then they'll pay. She doesn't trust any one of the bastards. They brainwash new recruits into becoming warriors, yet in her they have a natural. Ida can't understand it.

She thought this job might be the next best thing, training conscripts for battle, but when she got here, they put her in charge of this mob of princesses. The closest thing she gets to war is target practice on the range once a month. It's not enough. Sometimes she even considers committing a crime so she'll be conscripted. But she reckons the contrary bastards would give her an alternative punishment, given they won't consider her as a volunteer. It's not worth the risk, and many in here would relish her loss of power.

Charlotte is still in the queue waiting for her turn in the cutting chairs. She's resigned to losing her hair. What does it matter? In the months ahead she may lose her life. Hair is a small consideration in comparison.

There's a cry behind her. Nina's fallen to the floor at the end of the queue. The guard kicks her, but Nina doesn't respond. Charlotte says, 'can't you see she's fainted? There's no point kicking her.'

'Shut your mouth slag. If I want your opinion, I'll ask for it.'

When it's Charlotte's turn for the haircut, the guard who kicked Nina says to the guard standing behind Charlotte's chair. 'This one's got lice, and it all needs to come off Deidre.'

Deidre nods and sets to work. She's rough and pulls at long strands of Charlotte's hair, pushing her head around as if she is angry with it. Charlotte's learned her lesson, biting back cries of pain. She won't give the bitch the satisfaction.

When she gets up, blood dribbles down her head and neck. She runs her hand over her sticky pate, and it comes away red, but it's superficial. Her hair will grow again. As she leaves the room, she hears someone scream. It's a woman who Charlotte will later learn is called Jenny. She fights her guard, struggling to get away. Another guard runs over to help restrain the desperate woman. Jenny manages to evade the two guards, and bolts for the door.

Ida steps forward and seizes her by her long hair, dragging her back to the chair. Jenny struggles, but flailing arms and legs are no match for Ida's brawn. The enormous guard presses her great hands on each of Jenny's shoulders. Charlotte doesn't see more before she is pushed from the room, but Jenny's shrieks follow her along the corridor.

24.

The mid-morning sun shafts through a window in Rory's office, lighting dust particles that swirl in the vented air. Along one wall a bookcase, filled with old legal books, revels the source of dust. Blake, Rory, Evan, and Flynn sit in silence around a conference table.

Evan and Flynn stare out the window. Flynn's fingers tap a muted drum solo on the tabletop until Evan leans over and flicks the back of one hand. Flynn scowls but stops drumming.

Blake stews with impatience and leans forward, elbows on knees, head in hands. The inaction is killing him, but he knows now is the time to be smart not forceful. All he wants is to move into battle, but instead he reviews what he knows and looks for flaws in their plans.

They wait while Rory scans a large leather-bound legal textbook, his finger running down columns of tiny writing. Across the table, dirty coffee cups, and the last crumbs of Danish pastries lie abandoned

Earlier that morning Blake found the company accounts supervisor at the head office in Turbot Street, explaining that Evan would join his personal staff. The supervisor looked a little confused but nodded. He recognised Blake even though they hadn't met, and he wasn't going to contradict the company's largest shareholder, even if it was the first time he'd shown himself in the building.

The supervisor led Blake to a large open plan room and pointed at Evan's desk. 'Will you be all right if I leave you with Chandler, Mr Lincoln?'

Blake nodded, and the supervisor returned to his office, relieved to get away. He had heard strange stories about Blake Lincoln, and this experience hadn't altered his preconception.

'Hey Blake, good to see you again,' Evan held out his hand. 'Glad you're out mate.'

'Where's Charlotte?'

Evan saw the strain in Blake's face and glanced around the office. No one appeared to be in earshot so he said, 'she was arrested.'

Blake said dryly, 'yeah I got that part, now fill in the details.'

'Can we go somewhere more private? It's better we don't do it here.'

They went down the lift to the street and sat in Rory's car. Evan told him what he knew about Charlotte's arrest.

Blake stared out the window as he listened. 'How come you got away, and she didn't?' Rage at his helplessness simmered below the surface.

'I wasn't there mate.' Evan felt for the bloke, understanding his distress, but there's nothing he can do to change things.

'How the fuck do you know all this then?' Blake tried to rein in his scepticism, knowing he needed Evan.

'Flynn was there and got away.'

'Who the fuck's Flynn?' Blake's hands clenched the steering wheel until his knuckles showed like ivory welts.

'The drummer of Charlie's band.'

Blake remembered the stocky blonde bloke he saw at the club. 'Where is he? I want to speak to him.'

'He's at work Blake. He works at the dockyards.'

'What does he do?'

'Operates cranes.'

'Can he do anything else?'

'Yeah he can play drums.' Evan doesn't really know if Flynn can do anything else, but he tries to ease his irritation at Blake's tone.

'Fuck.' Blake smacks the steering wheel.

Sympathy eases Evan's annoyance. 'He knocks off at five. I'll take you to see him then.'

'I can't wait till five.' Blake turns his intense gaze on Evan. 'Every minute we delay, the chances of me getting Charlotte out before they send her to the Middle East diminish.'

'You don't know they'll send her. Not everyone goes. They say you have to agree to go.'

'That's bullshit. No one in their right mind would agree to that, but they make the alternative so bad, and your life such hell, you just sign to get them off your case. I'm not taking the chance. Will Flynn come and work for me?'

'Doing what?'

'I don't know and I don't care, anything so long as I have access to him.'

'Geez that's a bit radical.'

'Will you ask him? He can hand in his notice, and if he has to pay a penalty, I'll pay it.'

'You have to say what the job is. He can't just walk out. It gets loaded onto the government database. It's going to look odd.' They sat in silence and then Evan looked at Blake with a small ray of hope. 'Hey, I know, he can be a forklift operator in the warehouse.'

'Will he do it?'

'I don't know, we can ask. Up his pay. That'll help. He thinks his boss is a dick so I know he's not happy there.'

Blake typed something into the GPS and pushed the button to let off the handbrake. The car eased out into the traffic. 'When we get to the docks I'll take over driving, but you'll have to direct me. There's limited data for Pinkenba in the sat nav. Bloody security.'

While the car negotiates the streets and light traffic, Blake called Rory on the car e-cript. 'I need to see you. Are you free?'

'Can be... yes, what's it about?' Rory guards his tone. He hasn't seen Blake since he took Ava home last night and Blake still has his car. He's not sure if he believes Blake dropped Ava off and stayed in a hotel, and can't suppress rising jealousy.

'I'll tell you when we get there, in about half an hour.'

'We?' A surge of anger flowed through Rory.

'Yeah, Evan and me?'

'Evan?' For a second, he's relieved it's not Ava, but what's Blake doing with Evan. It must be to do with Charlotte. 'What?'

Blake interrupted. 'I'll explain everything when I get there okay, but I need you to do something for me in the meantime.'

'What?'

'Can you arrange to put a bloke on the payroll?'

'Jesus Blake. What the fuck...'

'I know—sorry, but Rory I'm desperate man.'

There's a drawn out sigh through the phone and Rory says, 'is this something to do with Charlotte?'

'Yes.'

'Okay, what's his name, and what position?'

'Flynn, ah hang on...' Blake turned to Evan. 'What's his surname?'

'Majors.'

Blake said, 'you got that? Flynn Majors and he'll operate a fork lift.'

'Does he have I.D?'

'Yes, he's working as a crane operator at the docks.'

'Okay what about a forklift licence?'

'Shit I don't know, does it matter?'

'Of course it matters.'

'Then he'll be my bloody butler okay.'

'You are kidding now, aren't you? Please say you're kidding.'

'Rory I don't care what you put in the register. I just need you to do it, all right.'

'All right, keep your shirt on. Hey this time I'm sending a bill, and I actually expect you to pay it.'

'Sure. Text me the position you give him.' Blake flicked a switch on the steering to end the conversation and grinned at Evan. Perhaps there was hope, and at least he was doing something.

Five minutes later a peep on his wrist alerted Blake to the text and an electronic voice said, 'personal assistant.'

Evan grinned. 'Another personal assistant. You're a demanding boss.'

Blake shook his head, but said nothing.

Ten minutes later, they pulled up outside a fenced yard. Evan went into the guardhouse, and came out a moment later, a plastic card hung around his neck on an orange lanyard, and a hard hat perched on his head. He walked towards a building across a dusty yard. It was full of old machinery, and a dozen or more containers.

Blake waited until impatience won, and he got out the car. A security guard spotted him walking towards the gate, and hand on the pistol at his hip, he waited to challenge. At that moment, Evan and the drummer came into view, and Blake turned away. The guard watched with suspicion.

Thirty minutes later, they were sitting in Rory's office. Now waiting for Rory to finish reading, Flynn looks bemused by his sudden transition from crane operator to personal assistant for a nutty bloke who is prepared to pay him twice what he earned on the cranes.

Evan says. 'Ah Blake I have to tell you, I bribed Flynn with a legitimate club gig. Sorry, but I knew you wanted him, and I figured if I asked, you would agree.'

Flynn looks from one to the other worried now. He thought Evan was joking about that. What the hell has he got himself into? If it wasn't Evan who asked he wouldn't have gone near it, but he trusts Ev. Anyway, his boss is an arsehole, always on his case about him being late or tired, so it wasn't hard to persuade him to take up something to help rescue Charlotte, even if he doesn't know Blake.

His fingers scissor-fork the blond fringe flopping into his eyes. It flops back again. Charlotte's sensible, she wouldn't take up with a dick. Screw it, the money's good and it must be legit or the offer wouldn't have been on the database.

Rory stops reading and looks at Evan in exasperation. 'That's a little beyond my scope I'm afraid. The company doesn't have gigs to offer.'

Blake says, 'no matter, I can buy a club.'

'Jesus,' Rory says. 'Have you gone round the bend? It's not that easy to just buy a club or a licence.'

'Yeah but you can do it because you never let little things like, it can't be done, get in your way do you Rory?'

Rory looks away. Blake knows him well. At least he could pretend some gratitude, like he knows how much work it'll take. Everything to Blake is a matter of will. If he wills it, it will be done. Rory knows that if he refuses to do it, Blake will do it himself or find someone who will, and they'll cut corners or stuff it up somehow. Rory sighs and turns his attention back to Evan and Flynn. Between them, they fill in the details of Charlotte's arrest.

At the end of their story, he leans back in his chair, his mouth pursed. 'We'll need a criminal lawyer. I'll give Lachlan Bowery a call. This is beyond me. How long since she was arrested?' He takes his CellTab from his pocket.

Flynn says, 'a month maybe.'

Rory looks at Blake. 'How long did it take before they shipped you out?'

Blake frowns. 'I don't know—longer than that, about three months I think. But remember Rory, I was one of the first, and since then their operations will be slicker. Really, what we have to hope is that she hasn't yet gone to trial. If she doesn't have a lawyer, they will provide her with one and it'll be a farce. We need to get to her before they manage to get her before the magistrate. The whole thing is rigged unless you have a proper barrister attending the court. Only then will it be done right, but that's not all I worry about.'

'What else is there?' Rory looks at Blake in disbelief. 'Look, I know you've been there, but this is Australia and we don't do things like that. Rigging evidence is criminal conduct, and our institutions wouldn't be party to it.'

'Don't kid yourself. Remember, I've been there and seen it.'

'Okay.' Rory doesn't want to argue in front of the other men so he says, 'what's your other concern.'

'It's the treatment to which they subject people.'

'What treatment?'

'Bastardisation.'

'What?'

Blake pulls his hand across his mouth and rubs his jaw, feeling the day old bristles. 'I understand it's based on military training. The first thing they do is subject inmates to humiliation and fear. They find fault with everything you do, with your demeanour, the way you look, your physical shape, your personality and once they find the chinks in your armour they exploit it.'

Evan laughs. 'Sounds like boarding school.'

'Yeah.' Blake pauses. 'It doesn't sound so bad just talking about it, but it's pretty brutal. I saw men wet themselves in fear by the end of it, ending in a blubbering mess which brought more scorn, more derision, and more punishment.'

Rory tucks in his chin and his brow furrows in incredulity. 'You're exaggerating Blake old mate. We live in a civilised world. The kind of treatment you're talking about is tantamount to torture. Actually, according to the United Nations definition, I would argue it is torture.'

'It's true. I saw one bloke woken every hour with them shouting in his ear. Every time he had to drop and do twenty push-ups. After about three days he started to hallucinate. It was only then they let him sleep. They thought it was funny. His crime was his weight. He was unfit and couldn't do push-ups to begin with so they punished him—correcting his behaviour they said. You have to understand that they think that the better they break you, the better they can mould you into a perfect machine.'

'What do you mean, what machine?'

Blake sighs. 'If you are signed on to fight they want an unquestioning warrior who will die if ordered-or if you aren't sent to fight, to mould you into whatever thing they want—the powerless prisoner perhaps. I don't know. For me, I knew the psychology, so it was interesting to watch, but for the other poor bastards it was a nightmare; not that I came out unscathed. It's brainwashing in its purest form and I don't want Charlotte to go through it.'

'No.' Rory shakes his head. 'No one should be subjected to that, but I don't get the point. Surely, they do it for a good purpose. They wouldn't do it otherwise.'

'There is good purpose from their point of view.' Blake begins to reel off the conscript creed. His voice takes on a liturgical quality that scares Rory.

'The conscripted warrior, supreme among men, is pure power, vigour, and control. His commitment and loyalty to his code is unswerving. He spurns personal comfort and safety in the pursuit of the mission. Master of mind and body, he can detach from life, withstanding pain and scoffing at death in pursuit of duty. He is a master tactician, aware of his limitations, but skilled to act with force in pursuit of his mission, which is always the destruction of evil... There's more but you get the picture.'

'Jesus,' Evan says and glances at Flynn, who stares at Blake in disbelief.

Rory says again, 'but why—what's the point to brainwashing?'

'They do it because they need conscripts to respond immediately and unquestioningly to commands. They don't want them thinking for themselves. The perfect warrior's mind-set is to win at any costs. That's what an army needs. I understand why they do it, but I can also think of better ways. It's traditional in the English military system, and we Australian's adopted it. But I don't think it's right. The early stage of adulthood is when a person's identity is set—late teens to early twenties. It's not only useful to the military to mould that identity into whatever they want it to be, but if you catch men in their early adulthood, it's fairly easy to do. The earlier, the better that's why they want eighteen-year-olds to enlist. The problem is, that at the end of their time in the military, that's all a person has left—the identity of a warrior. I was lucky because I was that much older, many conscripts are, and they struggle to brainwash them. That's why so many abscond. When they tried to mould me, I was already on the way to having my own sense of self as a man, but even so they managed to craft me into a warrior to a certain extent, and it served me well. But once you leave the military, it's no use being a warrior. For me, they created a sense of self for which I have no further use. Now I must construct a new identity. It's hard enough when you understand it, imagine what it's like for the poor bastards who have no idea what's happening to them. They lose their way, become anxious and depressed, and often kill themselves.'

Evan shakes his head. 'Surely when you leave they help you to readjust or something.'

'No, they don't. It's the one thing they let you take away. You get to keep your identity.' Blake's smile is bleak and doesn't reach his eyes. 'You don't keep your weapon, your uniform, your sense of belonging and purpose, or your mates, but you do get to keep your sense of self. That bit causes most of the problems. It's hard to adapt because out of the military, a warrior is a highly skilled and competent square peg in a round hole, and it's unsettling. Or it was for me—still is. For some blokes, well they can't take it, and sign on again just to stay where they are familiar and relevant. They call it institutionalisation. It doesn't really explain anything, but it has a fancy name.'

'Jesus, I had no idea.' Rory looks at Blake with new understanding.

'No. I don't think people do unless they experience it. They do other shit as well. They call it developing trust, but it's not really. What they really create is a kind of helplessness where you do nothing for yourself. Then they create a sense of blind loyalty and obedience. They do some pretty horrible things to your psyche to get that out of a bloke as well, but I won't bore you with it. It works while you are doing the job. It's just that it's not an adaptable set of characteristics outside of that job.' Blake's silent for a moment then he looks at Rory, holding his gaze. 'You see that's why I have to get Charlotte out now.'

'Yes. I can see that. We need to talk but...' Rory's eyes signal to Blake.

Blake takes the hint and says to Evan and Flynn. 'Look fellas, take the rest of the day off.'

Evan stands. Thank Christ Blake saved him from that. He doesn't think he's strong enough to have withstood it. He owes the man, and he's prepared to pay whatever it takes. 'Is there something we can do for you today boss?'

Blake shakes his head. 'How do I contact you if I need to?' He needed them when he had questions, but now he has no idea what to do with them. Then he remembers the club. It's a good idea because when he finds Charlotte she can sing in a legitimate club. She won't have to go back to the bar. 'Can you find a club I can buy, something nice, not sleazy. Somewhere Charlotte will be happy to sing.' He casts an apologetic look at Rory.

Flynn glances at Evan who says grinning, 'sure boss. How much can we spend?'

'Nothing, just bring the information back to Rory.'

Rory rolls his eyes and says to Evan, 'how do we get hold of you? Have you got a Cell number I can have?'

Flynn sniggers in disbelief at Rory's ignorance, but Evan remains expressionless and says, 'no sorry. No phones. I'll leave our address and call in here at prearranged times if it suits you.'

'Why no phones?' Rory looks mystified.

Ignoring him Blake says, 'go and buy CellTabs, make sure they are e-cript, and text your numbers to us. Here,' he reaches behind him to the desk, and takes Rory's business card from the holder. He pulls a pen from his pocket and writes his number on the card. 'Now you have our numbers.' He hands the card to Evan. Then turning to Rory he says, 'sorry mate I still haven't arranged any cash. I haven't had time to go to the bank. Can you sub me again? I'll go after this.'

Sighing Rory leans back and pulls his wallet from his pocket. 'I won't have any left either at this rate.' He pulls out a few notes and hands them to Evan. 'I want receipts okay. Make sure I get receipts or it'll be docked from your pay.'

Evan and Flynn leave the room and Rory and Blake watch them go, silent until they leave. Then Blake looks expectantly at Rory wondering what's on his mind.

'I know you don't like it, but if we want Charlotte's release expedited there is someone who has the ability and contacts to manage it.'

'No! Ah shit, I don't know, isn't there another way?' Blake puts his head in his hands again. He had almost forgotten what he saw last night, but Rory's right. The one person who has any chance of getting Charlotte out is Jeremy. Can he do it? Can he not do it—for Charlotte? He'll do anything for her, but Jeremy! It's supping with the devil and then he's in moral hock even further. Can he tell Rory about Jeremy and Ava? If he tells, then Rory will be honour bound to tell Emmy. If Emmy finds out, she'll cancel the wedding. Isn't that what Blake wants, but if the wedding's off, what reason does Jeremy have to help Blake at Rory's request. 'Shit,' he says again, struggling with his conscience.

Rory's brow lowers as he watches Blake struggle. 'Look I know you're too bloody proud to accept Jeremy's help, but seriously you need to consider it...'

Blake looks up, holding Rory's puzzled gaze for long seconds before he makes up his mind. He can't screw his friends for the sake of Charlotte, but he has to save her. Maybe there's another way. 'Last night when I dropped Ava off I didn't go to a hotel like I said...'

'I fucking knew it. I thought you loved Charlotte, but you can't resist can you? You had to screw her again.'

'What? Shit no. Just backup Rory, listen okay.' He waits for Rory to calm down and says, 'last night when I dropped Ava off, and I did drop her off I promise, I didn't go to a hotel as I said because I wanted to go to the club and find Charlotte.'

Rory looks alarmed. 'What—after curfew? You have to be more careful. They'll send you back and I won't be able to help.'

Blake sighs, wishing Rory would stop interrupting, but he knows it's because he's concerned, so he waits until Rory's finished before he says, 'I climbed up Ava's building and onto her balcony.'

'What? Why? What for? Mate that's not cool.'

'Rory just shut up and listen will you.' He sees Rory's chin tuck back in offence and curses his impatience, but he doesn't have time for egos. There is too much at stake. 'I climbed up because I thought something was wrong. She behaved strangely when I dropped her off as if afraid, so I wanted to see if she was okay.'

'Why couldn't you just ask?'

'She lied, and I could tell she was frightened, so I took a look.'

'And...?' Rory realises he is holding his breath.

'And I saw her in there with Jeremy.'

'Bullshit.' His breath whooshes out behind the word.

'No bullshit.' Blake shakes his head. 'Jeremy's shagging her, and that's not all. I think he hit her. They went to her room, she naked and willing. When they came out, they were all friendly again. Jesus. I didn't want to tell you, sorry.' Blake watches his friend's face as his expression changes from horror to grief and pain, and back again to disbelief. He looks down at the table to give Rory a moment to digest the truth. All he wants is to get Charlotte out. Anything else is a distraction, and the waste of time is making him edgy.

Rory gets up and walks to the window, taking out a hanky to blow his nose. Blake wouldn't lie about a thing like that, and he knows Ava would probably never look at him, but he could dream. While he didn't know, there was hope. Now it's gone. His eyes smart.

Slowly, it occurs to him that it's not just about him. His little sister will be heartbroken, but she'll have to know. It's lucky Blake begged her to wait until he was home, or she'd be married already.

Dawning realisation makes him turn back to Blake, and he sees a man beside himself with worry, head in hands, knuckles bloodless as he clutches his head in focused ferocity.

His mind clears as he sees Blake's fear and feels his sense of helplessness. Railing against the system won't do any good. This needs clear thinking and a steady hand if they are to rescue Charlotte.

Much of Blake's odd behaviour begins to make sense, and a rush of compassion swamps Rory's own misery. He pulls his emotions together to focus on the things that threaten the two people in the world most dear to him.

'Okay as I see it we have two problems.'

Blake looks up surprised at Rory's firm voice. 'What?'

'Emmy can't marry the bastard, and Charlotte must be released.'

'Yes.' Blake waits.

'Question is how?' Rory punches the palm of his hand. 'I don't know how to do either of these things. I don't know how to tell Em, and I don't know how to get to Charlotte quickly enough without going through Jeremy.' He walks back and sits down opposite Blake. 'Can we bring Dad into it Blake? Three heads and all that. We can trust Dad and he may come up with something sensible.'

25.

'We were at school together, the three of us, Fuller, Lincoln, and me. Fuller's a bit of a plodder but Lincoln was the teachers' blue-eyed boy, the slimy cunt.' Bart Priestly leans his head back on the couch, his silver mane luxuriant against the red mahogany of its leather, remembering his years of frustration at school. Jenna sits next to him sipping her drink, bored by the familiar lament, but saying nothing.

'He fooled the teachers; they thought he was wonderful. Idiots, but it gave me the shits I can tell you.' He sits forward agitated. 'It should have been me. I should have been Head Boy. Lincoln stole my birthright. I was the best athlete, good academic grades, and an all-round achiever. It was mine by rights, just like father and grandfather before me. I deserved it— they owed me, especially given the amount of money Dad donated. And it would have been mine, if that arsehole Fuller hadn't dobbed me in, saying he saw me cheat on an exam.'

'And did you?' Jenna can't help the sarcasm in her voice.

'It was a stinking lie.' Bart checks his temper. 'Arnie stood up for me, saying it wasn't me who was cheating, instead he pointed his finger squarely at Fuller and Lincoln. That was the beginning of our partnership. Prior to that the poor bastard copped flak from the other boys.'

'Surely the school investigated?' Jenna stifles a yawn, knowing how the story must progress.

The Principal did investigate, but the moron couldn't inspect his own toenails. He wouldn't budge. Lincoln was a lying toad, but it knocked me out of the race. I reckon there was something unsavoury going on between the two of them.'

'Poofters?'

Bart glances at Jenna, detecting insincerity in her tone. She sits forward and lifts her drink to her mouth. She will have to be more careful. They lapse into silence. The only sound is the brush of leaves on the window outside, stirring in the breeze.

Bart's mind drifts into the past, remembering. He hadn't noticed Arnie before the boy stood up for him. He owed him and becoming friends was easy. Arnie made him feel good about himself. It wasn't long before they were inseparable. Even his parents thought Arnie a good influence and encouraged their friendship. At the time, the shock of the school choosing a scholarship pupil as Head Prefect left him numb for weeks, until Arnie coaxed him out of it.

Later, cold rage took over, and with Arnie's help, he plotted revenge. When he heard Lincoln was trying for a scholarship to the University of Sydney, Bart convinced his father to intervene. He later heard Lincoln had won a scholarship to Cambridge University in the U.K.

In his final undergraduate year, Bart won the Rhodes scholarship to enter postgraduate studies at Oxford. At Bart's request, his father paid for Arnie to go with him. His mother organised a send-off that rivalled any social event over the past twenty years. The newspapers were full of photos and praise for the only son of Australia's richest mining tycoon, and Bart had almost forgotten Lincoln existed.

When he arrived at Oxford, he couldn't believe Lincoln was already there, courtesy of another scholarship. That, as far as

Bart was concerned, sealed Lincoln's fate. Together he and Arnie set out to destroy him.

Then Helena Macri arrived, and he forgot about Lincoln. Bart was in love. He chased the beautiful Italian student for weeks, but she resisted which only fuelled the fire in Bart's loins. She toyed with him, tantalising as she held herself out of reach. But she would succumb. He had time and played her game, sending her roses, which she sent back. Sending her fluffy toys, which she returned. Sending her pastries flown over especially from Paris, but she left them on his doorstep with a note for him to stop. She didn't want his gifts. It was all part of the game. She was playing hard, but he could play harder for someone so worthy of his passion.

Then his happiness crashed. Arnie said he saw her and Lincoln in a café, holding hands. Bart went to pieces, but none of that mattered now. He had his revenge although he didn't want Lincoln and Helena dead but... Ah who is he kidding he couldn't hide his delight when he heard the Embassy in Riyadh was bombed. He imagined the two of them maimed and disfigured, never to be Mr. and Mrs. Perfect ever again, but dead was better. Pity their son wasn't with them.

He really believed the Lincoln boy would die in the war. The push to take back the Middle East was bloody, which was why he sent him. Then the usual cock-up occurred. Never give someone else a job and expect them to do it properly. The idiots killed the boy's unit, but still just like his fucking father, he comes up trumps. When he heard about Lincoln's capture, Bart raised his glass to Arnie. The gods were on their side, but the man has more lives than a cat.

Now it's not just revenge, Bart's moved on from that. Like his father, Lincoln's son can't interfere in his plans if he's dead. Just like his father, he's becoming a pain in the arse with all that hero bullshit. Bart's not going to tolerate Lincoln's son derailing the blueprint for Australia, but he also knows how to control his temper for longer-term goals.

His father-in-law taught him hatred is a wasted emotion. Plans are everything, emotions nothing. Learn to control your own emotions, he cautioned Bart when he lost his temper yet again at some perceived slight. Find self-control or you're out.

For a while, Bart lived in dread of the mogul. It forced him to learn control. Despite Elspeth's demands that Daddy allow their engagement, Bart wouldn't continue to live with the little he had learned about the Table of Twelve, or the role for which he was being groomed, unless he did as he was told.

He leans forward and lifts his drink, swilling golden malt around his mouth, savouring its peaty flavour, tasting the pure mountain spring water bubbling over virgin highland sod, remembering where he got his taste for fine whisky.

He was just up at Oxford when his mother told him to contact an old friend who was interested in his career. It was the start of many weekends at the Highlands castle, which his mentor, in his Grand Old Party way, called his hunting lodge.

That was where Bart learned about transcendent power, which enables the decisions of one man to bring a nation crashing to its knees. That was before the terrorists made gold less relevant than oil. It was also where he realised that James Lincoln and Helena Macri were nothing, merely by-products of the main game. It was where his mentor said something that stuck in his mind. 'Every leader knows the easiest way to govern is scare the shit out of people.'

Now Bart's a member of the Protogenia League. The international group was set up by his wife's grandfather and his associates in the 1970s. In part it was established to counterbalance the Bilderberg Group's growing power. But after the economic shocks of 2008, it became more focussed on amalgamating political affiliates who wanted to limit business tax, and reduce government interference in the market.

Since Bart's induction, he has risen through the ranks and his star is on the ascendant. Last year they allowed Marabaux, as aid-de-camp, to join Bart at the annual meeting, but even Arnie doesn't know about the inner sanctum of Twelve. That is where the real decisions are made.

Bart plans to take the Table Chair as soon as his father-in-law departs this world. He has the charisma and connections they need, and they trained him well. Now whom else do the masses adore. Whom else will they believe when people like Jonathon Castile shout foul? Whom else, but God's anointed Mr Silver tongue himself. In the battle for Australia, he is winning and his reward will be the Chair. They promised him that.

He's so nearly there he can taste it and he can't fail now. None of his Cabinet has what it takes to take the Australian leadership from him and they don't have his backing. The opposition is all but dead in the water. They are more interested in the pig-trough he fills for them weekly, rather than any altruistic care for the rest of the country, although the new bloke Valentine, is a bit of a worry. He hasn't behaved according to type. Who knew he had scruples, but with every conscience there is a flaw, a way in. It's just a matter of finding it, and Arnie will have that in hand.

Over the years Bart has cultivated the press, restricting their freedom increment by increment, all the while feeding them information through press releases. Now they are too comfortable to change their model to survive outside his patronage. The burgeoning underground is a worry, but Arnie says he has a plan to rid them of pirate set-ups once and for all. Bart can taste success.

He leans back on the sofa and Jenna rises. 'Top up Bart?'

'Please.' He watches her walk to the cabinet. She is an attractive woman, thirty-one, shorter and thinner than Helena, but Helena had something else. He shakes his head. No, Jenna's still up there. She has a mind like a rapier without a shred of sentimentality. He isn't sure if she is completely within his control, but they have a common goal, and the uncertainty of her is exciting.

She hands him his glass. 'I've been thinking about how to control the Lincoln boy.'

'Yes,' he's interested.

'What sweet revenge on the father if you could bring his son into the fold as your surrogate son.'

Bart raises his eyebrow. 'The boy is a man, and a little long in the tooth for adoption.'

'Yes I know. I'm speaking metaphorically. The fallen angel scenario. Create some disgrace, then raise the young hero from the mire, forgiving him publicly. She chants, the young man might be morally weak, but he was the Nation's hero and we should not forget the sacrifices he's made for his country... Or words to that effect.'

Bart purses his lips. It's true; he needs to get Lincoln's son on side. The Military won't forget what he did to save his fellow soldiers, and neither will the Americans or the British. The man is a protected species. If it weren't for them, he would have had him arrested for wondering the streets after curfew and shipped back to the Middle East. He wouldn't survive another deployment.

The threats of his father-in-law ring in his ears and he shudders at the memory. Mentor! He's more ogre, but there's no way out. Perhaps the replacement gene therapy will fail and the old man will die soon. There's always hope, but Bart hasn't yet sown up his succession to the Table Chair. Perhaps if he achieves the Australian conclusion...

He shakes his head, remembering his mother's maxim. You catch more flies with honey than with vinegar. He pats the seat next to him, forcing a smile. 'You have the sexiest mind my dear. Come here.'

'Bart what have you done with the Lincoln boy's memoirs?' She would like to get her hands on them, judging by what Marabaux said the contents contained.

Bart covers his mouth with the palm of his hand and wipes his lips. Blake Lincoln has killed a lot of people, not only with the weapons shoved at him by his government, but also with his bare hands. Publish that and see how much the public admire him. Of course, the identities of the murdered will be sanitised: innocents not enemy, he'll make sure of it, but all he says is, 'Marabaux has it safe.'

Jenna sits again on the sofa. This is Bart's Achilles heel, this unrequited dream that can never change, no matter how high he climbs, no matter what he achieves, it will always be what he can't have that he hankers for, to re-invent his youth. It gives her the advantage, and she plans to hold on to it. One day it will come in handy. She can play this game. While he tells her the rest of the story, she'll pretend fascination and empathy, although she knows what's coming.

'You know, I thought Lincoln and Helena had survived the Riyadh bombing. Imagine if he had succeeded and managed to persuade the Saudi's not to join the Caliphate. If the Houthis hadn't bombed the Embassy, our plan might have taken years longer to achieve.' He smiles. His luck has held him in good stead.

'Was it the Houthis? They denied responsibility didn't they?' Jenna says.

'They claimed the bombing was done by an international drug syndicate, but really, is that likely? What motive could a drug syndicate possibly have for bombing an embassy for Christ's sake?'

He turns to gaze at Jenna. She's so gullible despite her brilliance. Doesn't she know she'll never see her dream materialise. He'll have to be careful she doesn't find out. Alienating Elspeth is not an option, and Jenna will run tattletale to Elspeth of that he's sure.

His father-in-law will not tolerate his princess being hurt, but once he pops his clogs, well... once the new laws regarding a husband's rights come into effect, she won't own anything, regardless of her inheritance. And if he's dead, her father won't be able to help her.

Idly he wonders if Arnie can speed up the old man's demise, but he knows it's too dangerous. No, if it comes to a choice between Jenna and his wife, he knows who will win. It's a pity, but then Jenna knows the score, and she knows the plans. Hell, she devised most of them.

'So m'dear what's the plan in that pretty head of yours. How do we get the boy into our care? He hasn't come running yet although I thought I made the offer quite clear.'

'Hem, what about the memoirs. Is there something in that we can use?'

'I don't think so, although I haven't read it myself,' Bart lies, his hand sliding up Jenna's skirt. 'Come here my lovely.'

'Wait up Bart. We need to deal with this first. There's not enough time before they arrive.' She pushes him away, trying to hide her irritation behind a girlish giggle. 'It'll be sweeter for the wait darling.'

Bart sighs and sits back with his drink.

Jenna straightens her hemline. 'What does Arnie say? Has he heard from his son?'

'Yes.' He takes a sip of the whisky. 'Apparently Lincoln knows the girl has been arrested. He's employed a barrister, but he hasn't yet approached Marabaux's son.'

'It's just a matter of time. Can we get to the barrister? Who is he? Or perhaps we can leak something to the media to raise the urgency of Blake's activities. Are you sure there's nothing we can use in the memoirs?'

Bart picks up her hand, kissing her wrist. 'Your mind is so sexy darling, always scheming, always on the lookout. I love it when you are inspired like this, but if I want to concentrate, I need another. Can I top up your glass?'

'No Bart, I haven't touched the last one, and you should take it easy. We can't work sozzled. Perhaps we should wait until Arnie arrives with Admiral Bowan.'

'He's not bringing that ass Ken Bowan, is he? What's Arnie thinking? I can't stand the man. Pompous clown. It's bad enough I have to see him at the Cabinet meeting in a few days. Tell me, why he insists on a military title when he resigned twenty years ago. It beats me. He's been a politician longer than he was ever in the Navy, yet he behaves as if he's running this war. Arnie knows I want to talk in private. Why bring Ken?'

'He is running the war darling. Well, his generals are. You made him Minister for Defence, against my advice I might add.

Never put an expert in charge of their portfolio, especially such a moralistic buffoon. You know that rule Bart.' She realises she's said too much and mitigates the criticism with flattery. 'Anyway like everyone else, he's devoted to you, and he wants to talk about the Chinese.'

He smiles at her, seeing the unsubtle attempt to mollify, but inside he's struggling. How dare she lecture him? Sometimes he'd like to strike her. He dreams about it, what it might feel like to lift his hand and bring it back across her mouth, to watch the blood spurt from those glossy lips. Instead, he wipes his hand across his mouth. 'The Chinese. What about the Chinese? They're fine, on our side so long as we let them farm our crops, and mine our resources. Anyway, Ken's hardly what I would call an expert, but I agree with the buffoon part, so easily manipulated through his ridiculous ego. I needed someone I could control. You know that darling otherwise I would have taken your advice. You know how I value your opinion.'

Jenna is oblivious to Bart's anger. 'But he doesn't have the respect of the forces he commands. We need someone whom they respect.'

'Good heavens, no,' Bart snaps. He modifies his voice. 'That's the last thing we need.' Jenna looks piqued. He hastens to add, 'I know your rule is a good one darling. Normally I would take heed, but we need Bowan.' He pauses watching her. 'Besides he's smitten with you and is putty in your hands. You can get him to do anything, you divine temptress you.' He pulls her towards him.

She leans against him for a moment. 'They'll be here any second Bart and he won't be putty in my hands if he sees me in your arms. You know how devout he is.' She smiles up at him and he kisses her nose.

'No my dear. I'll behave, Cyril won't let them barge in here. He knows when to be discrete.' Bart gets up, picking up his whisky glass as he makes his way over to the cabinet and takes out a new bottle. There is a knock at the door and Bart calls for Cyril to enter.

Cyril pushes open the door, and stands aside for Admiral Bowan and Arnie. Bart waves the bottle at the two men. The Admiral nods, his ruddy face beaming as he sees Jenna, but Arnie shakes his head.

'Miss Martin, what a delight to see you again.'

Jenna stands up, and walks towards him, ignoring Arnie as she kisses the Admiral on the cheek feeling the loose leathery folds, dry against her lips. 'Admiral how well you look.' She takes his arm and walks back to the couch saying, 'sit here beside me, and I'll get your drink.'

She watches him settle, then joins Bart at the cabinet. He holds the glass and bottle poised as he watches her at work. A smile of pleasure animates his face as he watches her cloak herself in flirtatious feminine submissiveness, beguiling the old duffer who thinks he knows who this clever woman really is.

Yes, despite the occasional annoying habit of thinking she is more important than she is, he admires her. It will be a pity when it comes time for her to go. He drags himself from his daydreaming to pour the drinks, handing two glasses to Jenna. Then he pours two more and walks over saying, 'well Admiral how goes the war?'

The Admiral takes the glass of whisky from Jenna, his large hand with their parchment dry sausage fingers holding and squeezing hers. He once asked her to marry him, despite the age difference because he knows she's attracted to him. Some women are attracted to power more than looks or youth, but she turned him down, saying regretfully that she wanted to concentrate on her duty to Australia. Only when Australia was free and prospering could she contemplate looking for her own pleasure. What a woman, but he could wait. After all, he is only sixty-four. He has time left up his sleeve, and he is still a virile man.

She sits next to him as Bart hands Arnie a drink. Arnie hides his scowl as he takes the glass. It doesn't matter what he says to Bart the man never listens. He said no to the whisky yet here he is with one. It could be worse, the man might not have any flaws, and how can a flawless man be managed.

Once seated, they watch the Admiral smooth his moustache aside to take a delicate sip of the drink before he says, 'things look good in the Middle East. The British seem to have the Mediterranean section under control, with help from the Israelis. The Europeans' focus is on Egypt and Greece, so we are not surprised from the west, and our job is to help the U.S. keep the Gulf under control. The final push inland is still in the planning stages, but we have to hope the Iranians and Pakistanis will keep their word not to interfere. They're under siege from dissidents internally. It's in their interests to help the west, or they'll be next to fall. Your envoy is over there already PM, talking to the Indians in case Pakistan reneges, but overall, it's going as well as can be expected. I have another briefing tomorrow and will give you more details in the National Security Cabinet briefing.'

He says the last part primly in reprimand to the PM who, in his opinion should understand these things better than he does. 'My worry is China, Prime Minister. That's what I wanted to discuss. There's an awful lot of activity going on in the Yellow Sea, and all I have at the moment is speculation.'

'We don't need to worry about the Chinese, but if it makes you feel any better, another international business conference regarding trade might be in order. What do you think Ken? That last one went well, and they are not in the slightest bit interested in our war with the terrorists. They have their own worries with Russia playing their usual games with gas, and Japan rattling its sabre on their doorstep.'

'It's China and Japan that worry me. We cannot stretch our resources to take on another front, but Japan will expect us to uphold our treaty. They are becoming increasingly belligerent.'

26.

Charlotte shrugs at Mallory, watching her flap her hands at the tiny persistent flies determined to settle on her tear ducts. The sun beats on her skull broiling her head inside her hat, and she doesn't have the energy to answer. The question is probably rhetorical anyway. Who here isn't crazy?

She glances out across the shimmering mirage taking in the endless plains, the outcrops of sand and limestone, and the eroded ridges of the escarpment rising above the dry savannah. Twenty metres away, a clump of trees cast wasted shade, and she looks away. The membranes in her nose are so dry, they bleed if she so much as sneezes.

They get crackpot random orders all the time, and if they don't obey promptly without question, they are all punished. This order is no different.

Corporal Anstey said, 'on the double to the top of that hill. At the summit fire at will.'.

One of the regular soldiers in their platoon was brave enough to ask, 'what are we firing at Corp.' Anstey didn't reply.

Charlotte didn't think he knew, and wasn't about to ask for clarity. The last bloke who asked the lieutenant, had his corporal stripes ripped off right there in the field. That's how Anstey was promoted, and he's not about to make the same mistake as his predecessor.

So now they run. It's more rocky crag than a hill and covered with loose stones that slip under Charlotte's feet making her stumble. She avoids grasping the Spinifex. Last time the grass shredded her hand, and it stung. The razor thin scabs still haven't healed properly.

As she puffs her way up the incline she lags behind. Corporal Anstey turns back and shouts at her. 'You know what you and a corpse have in common Miller? You're both dead!'

Charlotte ignores his insults, focussing on her flagging energy. She never knew she had so many muscles in her body, and all of them hurt all the time. Her orange jumpsuit flaps baggily, chaffing as she runs. The lack of decent food and intensive exercise in this hellhole has morphed soft curves into hard angles and bony protrusions. The once too small jump suit is now too big.

She makes an effort, but she hasn't done any real exercise since she was a kid. Even as a child, she hardly walked anywhere. There were always horses or quad bikes to ride. Walking to and from the bar just doesn't cut it as a fitness regime. Although she has resigned herself to the inevitable, she still dreams that by some miracle she will escape conscription. Even if they don't deploy her to fight, she doesn't want to end up as slave labour for industry for the duration of her sentence.

She has discovered that the childhood games with Evan's air rifle has made her a crack shot. She shoots better than all the others. Even the lieutenant looked impressed when he watched her at the range last week. He said they were going to send her for sniper training. To her surprise, she felt an upwelling pride.

The platoon has almost reached the top of the outcrop and she is still eight metres behind them. They stop and fire, the automatic rounds deafening. The breeze blows the propellant from their rifles towards her. She inhales the oily metallic tang, comforted by it, smiling at the memory of Mallory's expression of disgust when she said she loved the smell.

The shooting stops and the others stand at the top of the ridge, frozen in time, their rifles, pointing accusing but silent as they stare over the hill. It's like something sucked out their energy, Charlotte thinks as she puffs up to join them.

At the summit she stares down at a scene of grizzly horror. On the other side, just below the ridge, carcasses of tethered sheep and goats lie in their own blood and gore. A goat struggles to rise, and the lieutenant takes out his pistol and shoots it in the head. It flops over and is still. None of the animals survives.

As Charlotte gazes at the tangled massacre, she notices other things in among the dead animals. Ragged remains of mannequins, dummy babies, and dummy children, with a few bullet-riddled adult female forms, the kind you see in store windows, lie amidst the gore. The adult models wear black abaya and hijab. Scattered among them lie broken everyday toys in pools of animal blood, along with little plastic baby limbs and splintered plastic babies' heads.

The sergeant shouts at them. 'Suck it up kiddies, this is war.'

Anstey pulls himself together and orders the platoon to continue. They follow him down the slope and through the massacre, the metallic reek of fresh blood in their noses. Flies swarm, arriving in their masses to drink at the feast. A Private runs to one side and vomits, setting off others and the lieutenant laughs.

'What's the point,' Charlotte mutters? No one in their right mind would give such an order for real. She has seen dead animals before on the farm, but this is pointless. Why did they do it, to traumatise or desensitise? Perhaps it was just to show who's boss. Surely, it would never happen in any real life circumstance; at least not one she can imagine. Then she's never been in a war.

She hadn't even fired her rifle and yet she feels the collective guilt. She lifts her face, eyes closed against the blinding sun. Its rays burn through closed lids. If she could die now it wouldn't be so bad, at least she wouldn't have to go back again, through the horror.

She opens her eyes looking for the corporal. He's standing by himself, his face blotchy. Poor bastard. Charlotte removes her cap and runs her hand over her spiky head. Most of the razor cuts have healed now leaving dried scabs. Fine hairs prick through her scalp in a fuzzy halo. On the odd occasion she catches glimpses of her reflection, she's glad they have no mirrors in their barracks.

She puts her hat back on her head. Having no hair is a blessing in this place. At least it's one less thing to worry her. She can barely manage to get everything done without having to wash and look after long hair. Vanity is the least of her problems although she hopes it grows back before Blake sees her again. If that ever happens.

A sudden longing overwhelms her; remembering his hands on her body, arranging her hair in long strands down her back, her face buried against his chest, the smell of him in her nostrils. She turns her head looking for Mallory.

They have formed a strong bond since being in the same barracks together. No one knows what happened to Nina. She just disappeared and secretly Charlotte is glad. She couldn't bear her crying anymore. Not even threats from the terrifying guards, punishment, or entreaties by the other women could stop the weeping.

She would lie on the floor, on the ground, on the bed, on the shower floor, in the mess, wherever she happened to be, and sob. One morning about five days ago, she didn't go with them to the showers and when they came back, she had gone.

Charlotte tried asking where, but it brought sneers of derision from the guards in their barracks. The good thing about being out on exercises was that the guards didn't go with them.

She didn't much like the non-coms or officers either, but at least they treated the conscripts like they treated the soldiers.

Their orders hadn't seemed malicious, until today. Perhaps it has a point, but she can't work out what it might be.

After Nina vanished, Charlotte managed to speak briefly to Lucas. She regretted saying anything as she saw his face change from its usual calm indifference to a mask of worry. He hadn't known. The lance corporal of his platoon yelled at her, asking what the fuck she thought she was doing, and she didn't get a chance to say more.

Now Anstey orders them back over the hill. As the platoon trudges back to base, Charlotte's shoulders hurt with the weight of the pack. Her tongue feels foreign and furry, like a lizard's tongue stuck to the roof of her mouth. Still, it's not as bad as the first few days when she thought she might die. She was so unfit she couldn't run two hundred metres without gasping for breath.

At least her skin is not red and peeling like poor Mallory, who trudges beside her. Charlotte doesn't know what she would do without her company. It has kept her from going crazy these last weeks. Mallory is clever, funny and can cope with push-ups, a dark art which eludes Charlotte.

Every day she suffers another punishment for it. No matter how hard she tries, she can't do them properly, not like they want. She's on guard duty again. Every night this week, she has had double-shift guard duty inside the prison barracks wire. Another pointless exercise. The wire is to keep prisoners in rather than intruders out, so having a prisoner on guard duty is just insane.

It's not only pointless, but farcical. Mallory, who had once studied psychology before the cost of tuition and living forced her out, said they were suffering a psychogenic fugue. One day they would snap out of it and be back home with their families. Charlotte laughed, 'a psychedelic what?'

Still the guards threaten she'll be on double-shift guard duty until she can do a proper push-up with her arms and legs straight. Now she tries to distract herself from the pain in her shoulders by working out how long they've been there. Fourteen days she thinks.

Surely, her trial must be coming up soon. How long can they keep them locked up without the courts deciding on their fate? They should at least decide they are guilty of something before sending them into combat training. It's as if her fate is a foregone conclusion.

It's dusk as they arrive back at the compound. There are four barracks. One is for the regular male soldiers, and one for the few women regulars. The conscript barracks are on the far side of playing fields, across the parade ground near the river, one for men, and one for women.

For those like her on remand, there is no separation from the convicted. In this place at night you are either a convicted conscript or a regular soldier. The place for innocence or even innocent until proven guilty is long gone. During the day, they are all soldiers and at night, she and Mallory plot their escape.

27.

William leans through the doorway of his son's office, his hands on the doorjambs either side. 'What's this about son? Your summons sounded urgent.'

Rory looks up from his desk and rises to greet his father. 'Thanks for coming... Um, it was a request not a summons, but yes it is fairly urgent.' His father is early, and he's not sure that's a good thing. He'll ask questions and Rory doesn't want to answer them until Blake gets there.

William enters. 'You've done a fair old job here my boy. I didn't realise how well established you've become. Well done. I suppose I should have seen it before now but...'

'Dad it's okay. I'm happy you approve, but that's not why I asked you here. I need your advice.'

'Okay good.' William rubs his hands together. 'How can I help?' Rory never asks for his help or advice. Since the boy studied law, he thinks his old Dad doesn't get where he's coming from, but William studied political history at university, and isn't that the law's birth place?

'Come and sit down Dad. It's not about me, and I would prefer to wait until Blake arrives before launching into explanations. That's if you don't mind waiting a while. He won't be far away.'

William is glad to be able to do something for his son. He's a good boy, works hard, and never gets into scrapes unlike Blake who is always in trouble. He takes after his father. Perhaps both boys took after their fathers.

When he was Rory's age, all he wanted was to be as dashing and exciting as his best friend James Lincoln. Later he learned that dashing and exciting has its ups and downs, a roller coaster of daring and terror in equal quantities.

With hindsight, being the tortoise of the duo was definitely preferable. After all, look who won the race. Not that he wouldn't give it all to have James and Helena back, but Rory should take comfort he's not like Blake.

Look at the furore James created when he married Helena. Her family disowned her but it didn't stop him. What James Lincoln wanted, James Lincoln took regardless of consequences and Blake seems to be following in his father's footsteps. Far better in his opinion, for Rory to be the slow and steady one who wins the race. There's a lot to be said for being the rock—longevity for one thing.

'Is Blake in trouble again? Good lord, he's only just back...' William's brow furrows as he sits in a chair facing the desk.

'No Dad, it's his girlfriend. You remember Charlotte, the one he brought to dinner.'

'Pretty young thing.' His face lifts as his chin juts. 'She's not pregnant is she? Oh dear, oh dear.'

Rory sighs. 'Dad relax, she's not pregnant.' He walks over to the sideboard. 'Have some coffee. Its freshly brewed. Blake's gone to fetch a couple of blokes, and he'll be here soon. In the meantime if you can hold off on the questions it'll be good. How's the new contract?'

A minute later, Blake walks into the room followed by Evan and a moment later Flynn. William looks at the men in surprise.

'Hello Mr Fuller thanks for coming.' Blake throws himself into a chair near the coffee table at the other side of the room.

Evan and Flynn hover inside the doorway. William's gaze slides from one to the other and back to his son.

Rory shakes his head. Blake is really quite obtuse sometimes. 'Dad these men work for Blake. Evan Chandler was working in accounts in head office; you may have seen him in the building, and Flynn Majors, a new acquisition for the company.'

William raises one eyebrow at his son and then looks back at the two young men. The brown haired boy looks familiar. Hardly a boy, he is probably in his late twenties or older, but they all look like boys to him. The other man is fair haired, cheerful, and cheeky with a defiant attitude that would get on Mr Fuller's nerves. It's as well he works for Blake and not him. Although what Blake's up to is a mystery, he's been home less than a week. What sort of work does he have them doing? He shakes his head.

Rory watches his father with a small frown between his eyes. 'I'll explain later Dad. This is not why I asked you here. Come and sit at the table. It's easier than trying to crowd around the desk.'

His father gets up and Rory sees he has that faraway look on his face like he's trying to find the underlying cause of a knotty problem. He hands his father a cup of coffee then turning to the others he says, 'help yourselves fellas.'

Flynn makes a dash for the coffee. Evan follows with more decorum. Blake sits slumped and brooding, barely aware of the others in the room. Rory sits next to his father. Evan and Flynn join them and aside from the spoon knocking against the china as Flynn stirs in sugar, silence settles. William waits for someone to speak.

Rory glances at Blake and says. 'do you want to start Blake?'

Blake looks up, his eyes blank as he struggles upright in his chair. His mouth opens then closes with a heavy exhale of breath, and he leans forward to rest his elbows on his knees and stares at the table.

They wait and William finds he's holding his breath and relaxes his shoulders. Blake has the same trick his father used, to command absolute attention. Neither of them do it consciously.

Blake struggles to form a coherent thought. He clears his voice. 'Charlotte's been arrested.'

William waits, knowing there's more. It's bad, but what do they expect him to do about it? He sure that's not why he's here, but Rory will explain. 'Son, what's this about?'

Rory sits forward. 'Charlotte sang in an underground club. The police raided it a few weeks ago and arrested her along with the other patrons. We are concerned she will be tried, convicted, and conscripted before we can get to her. You know what red tape they throw in your way. Anyway, I thought Jeremy could help cut through the mess so we could get her released sooner, but Blake has reservations about using Jeremy for a number of reasons, not least of them being, he doesn't trust him.'

William's relieved. This is simple after all. He leans forward. 'Son...,' he says.

Blake interrupts. 'He's treacherous Mr Fuller, and he's screwing Ava behind Emmy's back.'

William flinches and sinks back in his chair looking to Rory for confirmation.

Rory nods, his face pinched with worry. 'Thing is Dad, we have two problems and we need your help. How do we tell Em, and how do we get Charlotte out? Jeremy could turn nasty once Emmy dumps him.'

William latches on to the challenge. Having a concrete problem to solve helps his emotional re-balance. It dawns on him that it's a family matter. What are these two employees doing in here? He looks up at them and says, 'what's your role in this?'

Evan shifts. 'It's bigger than just Charlie and your daughter sir.'

'Who is Charlie now?'

'Ah, Charlotte sir. She and I go back a long way, so I'm as concerned as Blake here.'

'And you?' William turns to Flynn.

'Yeah, I know Charlie. She's the singer in my band.'

281

William shakes his head. 'Never mind. What's bigger? What's going on?'

'Dad it's big. The threads go everywhere. Evan's been researching some of the stuff Blake uncovered and it's bad. Jeremy and his father are right in the centre of a web of corruption and they have been telling the public a lot of lies.'

William glares at his son. 'What lies?'

'Sorry Dad, I'm not trying to put you on the spot, but it's hard to know where to begin. Evan's pieced together some information, but there's a lot we don't know, or only suspect.'

Evan gets up and walks across the room. 'With your permission Rory?' Ignoring the interface, he takes an old-fashioned keyboard from a cupboard and picks-up the remote off Rory's desk. He angles a screen on the wall to face the coffee table. 'I think it's easier to understand if you see what's going on.' He taps the keyboard, and the screen goes black. One by one white letters and numbers appear on the US House of Representatives homepage. Evan clicks on the Office of Congressional Ethics icon, and more writing appears, this time blue on black. He opens a file and clicks on a document.

William reads the writing on the screen. Dear Sir, in reference to your protest of the ethical issues relating to the joint U.S. Australian surveillance system in Central Australia I am afraid your complaint is beyond the jurisdictional function of this committee.

There is a lot of other bureaucratic language explaining Australian sovereignty and other legalistic jargon, but the gist of the email is a refusal to investigate a complaint lodged against the Central Intelligence Agency's role at Pine Gap. The email is signed, with the scrawled signature of the Chairman of the Congressional Ethics Committee.

William looks for the addressee. 'My goodness!' He gasps as he reads the name. 'Jonathon Castile.'

'Yep, that's what started my search. He's accusing a small section of the CIA of using satellites and drones to help the Australian Government's surveillance of its own people, but it gets worse. This was why he was arrested and charged. Marabaux wanted him out the way. But this letter was just the thread that began unravelling a bigger ball of barbed wire. At first there were too many missing bits for me to work out what they were doing, but when Blake told me what he knew, the rest was easy to fit together.'

While he's typing, a satellite image fills the screen. He zooms into what looks like a prison compound with high razor wire perimeters. Inside, barrack-like buildings are interspersed with huts, and palm thatched shelters with added on lean-tos. Vegetable gardens fill the space between buildings. As the image clears, he can see people walking around the village. There is an orchard and paddocks with animals grazing.

What is it? William asks baffled.

'Refugee camps, I think.' Blake shifts in his chair. 'They call them Internment Camps or ICs.'

'What?' William is startled. 'Where are they? In Africa.'

'No here, Cape York,' Blake says. 'There are no terrorist infiltrations up there, just Government secrets.'

William shakes his head and opens his mouth to speak, but Evan changes the image on the screen. This time the picture shows a barren wilderness, with red earth, and craggy outcrops. People, some in camouflage some in orange coloured clothing, stand next to a pile of rubbish. William looks closer and sees it's not rubbish, but a slaughter yard of dead animals.

Blake gets up and walks over to the scene. 'That's Charlotte.' His voice catches as he points at an indistinct face held to the sky, eyes closed. 'This was taken three days ago.'

William sees a person dressed in what looks like an orange jumpsuit, holding a rifle. She is completely bald. 'It's not a very clear picture. How do you know?'

'I know Charlotte. I know this scene. They did it to us too.'

'Did what?' William coughs to clear his throat.

Rory intervenes. 'Look it doesn't matter now. What matters is how we get her out of there, and how we deal with Jeremy. If he so much as realises we know any of this, I imagine none of us is safe.'

'How do you know Jeremy's involved?' William's voice is sceptical.

'Because Arnold Marabaux is the conductor of this little corruption orchestra, and Jeremy is his go to man. The lobby group is a front,' Rory says.

William is exasperated by the conspiratorial nature of the conversation. 'Look it's common knowledge that Jeremy is first and foremost the chairman of Reliquum Pharmaceuticals, the lobby group is just a sideline hobby. Reliquum has always been our hospital supplier. My father knew the man who started it; began it on a shoestring in his garage here in Brisbane, in the '70s. When he floated the company, Jeremy managed over time to get a controlling interest. That's just the way business operates. I wasn't happy about the way my father's friend was treated, but it's just business. I don't much like Jeremy, but...'

Evan says, 'yeah but what you may not know is that Jeremy used a high ranking police contact to get information on one of the partners, whom he blackmailed into selling him his shares, so he could take over the company. Now that same police officer has the community policing contract that has a branch of which none of us are aware.'

William glares at Evan as it dawns on him what the man is saying. 'Ah come on now. What you're saying is there is some kind of corrupt secret police force doing his bidding.'

'It's true Dad. Evan's shown us enough for me to believe some very shonky deals are going on here. I'm not a criminal lawyer, but I don't think we have enough evidence for the courts. It will take forever to piece together, and at this moment we have more urgent matters at hand. Showing you this much was for you to understand the urgency and extent of Jeremy and his father's corruption. When we have more time, we can pull it together and expose the bastards to the nation. But before we get to that, we need to save Charlotte and decide how we tell Emmy about Jeremy so she can break-off her engagement.'

A thought suddenly dawns on William. 'Are you saying the contract tendering is rigged because we buy from Jeremy?'

Rory is concerned he might have stepped too far, too fast. He hesitates, wondering what he can say. After all, he has no proof. 'I don't know.'

Blake interjects. 'there's other stuff we haven't tracked down yet. Evan's working on it. In Baghdad, my gaoler told me stuff I didn't believe, about us trading refugees and wheat with the Terrorists for oil. He said they kill the returned men and use the children and younger women as slaves. I took that to mean sex slaves. They take a dim view of Caliphate subjects leaving the country and want them back. Evan's uncovered information that Jeremy might be involved with the capture and ransomed of journalists who they use to trade with the West for captured Caliphate soldiers. Anyway, until Evan gets something we can use, I don't know how much is true or if we can find proof. But, at this moment, I don't give a fuck. I just want Charlotte out of it. Then I'll worry about the rest.'

For a minute William tries to piece together what he's been told. None of it makes sense. The information is so disjointed he can't see what Blake's driving at. 'Let me understand,' he says, his voice heavy. 'You are saying that Marabaux and Jeremy are in cahoots with the Caliphate—our country's enemy.' His inflection rises. 'And they are holding refugees in hidden camps to use as bartering tools!' He's angry now. 'You are telling me that Marabaux is also in league with the CIA. It's nonsense. The two things contradict each other. The CIA wouldn't tolerate trafficking with the Caliphate.'

Rory sighs and looks at Blake. Then he turns to his father. 'No Dad, not quite. We haven't explained things very well, but what we are trying to say is that Marabaux and Jeremy are corrupt and the government is lying to us. We can't trust them and we can't trust the legal system to do the right thing by Charlotte. We can't ask Jeremy to help. Not only because he's corrupt, but also because he's cheating on her. She'll have to dump him.' He stops speaking and scans his father's face. Then he adds, 'we don't yet have enough evidence for any of it, except that Blake saw Jeremy and Ava together. We told you what we know to date, in case you can explain any of it. Dad you know these people, you've known them most of your life. Have we got it wrong?'

William shakes his head. 'I don't really understand any of it. I don't know how I can help. I don't have much time for Arnold Marabaux or the Prime Minister and I must admit I don't understand Jeremy's attraction, but he's Emmy's choice. Now you say he's cheating on her, so you can't ask him to help get Charlotte out. I understand that bit, but how are government secrets relating to refugees and spying linked?'

Flynn stands up, and scissor-forks his fringe away from his face as he says, 'look, I might as well make myself useful. This stuff is beyond me. While you all rack those big educated brains of yours, I'll go arrange lunch. I'm starving and finding food is what I am good at.'

'Thanks Flynn.' Rory pulls his wallet from his trousers. 'Get more of those Mediterranean Panini sandwiches.'

'Okay boss.' He grins pocketing the money.

'Oh and Flynn...'

'Yeah boss I know. You want receipts. Got it.'

To William's consternation, the boy winks at him as he leaves the room. William turns to Rory, his eyebrow raised. Rory shrugs.

Evan sees the exchange and defends his friend. 'He knows everyone and everyone likes him. If you're in a jam, he's the man who can help.'

William says, 'you live in a very different world I'm afraid. It's one I suppose I will need to learn about before I can make a judgment.'

Evan glances at him askance, 'whatever man.'

William frowns. 'Rory what is it you want from me?'

Blake replies. 'We thought your knowledge would be useful, not only in knowing how I tell Emmy about Jeremy, but also in finding a way to get Charlotte out. Is there anyone beside Jeremy who can help?'

'That's difficult. Certainly I can deal with the former. Emmy should know, but I am not sure what I can do with the latter or with the other information you have told me. It all seems so improbable, and you don't seem sure of its authenticity. I know this government has its problems, but... well I can try to find out more, but don't you think we should take your suspicions to the police?'

'No!' Blake says. 'The police are in Marabaux's pocket. If they so much as catch a whiff of what we know, we are all dead.'

William stares at Blake, shocked at his vehemence and wonders if Blake's right. There is something wrong he knows that. It's a feeling more than fact and what Evan's shown them might be the tip of an iceberg, but there could also be another explanation. Not that he likes the establishment much. It's why he avoids political society. He used to love the cut and thrust of it, and at one stage, after he left University, he contemplated running for office.

Priestley's rise to power began the rot in his opinion, abolishing taxes for business, punishing the poor for things beyond their control, reducing the public service to a shadow by contracting out services and moving policy units into Ministerial offices. There is no longer any public scrutiny or accountability and the press have been effectively muzzled. Any dissent is ridiculed. For their own political ends they smear the name of good people opposing their views. They use the police as pawns to charge any opposition with trumped up criminal behaviour or corruption. If you played their game you got rich, but if you got in their way you were finished. He knows that, but what does Blake expect him to do about it. It is a democracy after all. You get the government for whom you vote and he's never voted for Priestly.

William wipes his mouth. 'Blake I don't like these people much, but I think you are over reacting son.'

'Sorry Mr Fuller, but you are wrong. Never mind that now, all I want is to get Charlotte out, but we can't use Jeremy for more than one reason. If you can think of anything we have overlooked that would be great, but you can't repeat any of what we've told you.'

'He turns to Rory. We need to get the process working through legal channels while Evan has time to investigate further. With any luck, one of us may stumble on something that will help, but in the meantime you need to make sure we use the law to protect Charlotte. Who's the bloke you have as barrister?'

'Lachlan Bowery. He's doing it as we speak. We'll tie the bastards up in so much legal red tape they won't be able to move her.'

'Okay, from the satellite photos we know she's in a camp east of the Cockburn Ranges, west of Kununurra in the North West quadrant of the Kimberly Province. The same camp I was in. It's in the middle of the restricted zone. So once we have the date for the trial, we need to find out what the police have up their sleeves. Where are they likely to hold the trial?' Blake looks at Rory.

Rory shrugs. 'Hey if we still had States I would know, but it's different now.'

'With me they held the trial in Darwin, before they shipped us off to the camp for training. We have to hope they haven't done that to Charlotte, but it seems too quick even if they have streamlined the process. I was in a camp in Darwin for three months before they sent us to Cockburn for our final training. Evan that's your job. Find out everything you can.'

'I'm on to it.'

William watches Blake take charge. It is so reminiscent of James that he feels a lump form in his throat. He clears it saying, 'and me, what's my job?'

'You need to look after Em and Mrs Fuller after I tell her what I saw.'

'You'll tell her?'

'Yes. I guess it's best coming from me. I saw it and that's better than hearsay. She'll want to ask questions. I know I would.'

'Hm.' William is not so sure. 'I don't know if she'll be that reasonable. You know Em she can be a stubborn little thing.

Jeremy's slow tortuous death might suit her better than answers to questions.'

Blake grins for the first time since he's been home. 'I can arrange that too.'

28.

Emmy sits in the dining room with William and Blake picking at her thumb cuticle. When her Dad said he wanted to talk to her about something important she knew it must be money. That's what concerns Dad most. Maybe they lost the hospital contract and can't afford the wedding, but where's Rory? She wishes her mother would hurry.

Her round-eyed gaze travels across the table to Blake. He looks so sad hunched in his chair. Her heart goes out to him. She's a selfish girl always thinking about herself when he's heartbroken. She doesn't know what she would do if Jeremy disappeared the way Charlotte has.

At least Ava, for all her other faults, had the courtesy to write breaking it off, but this girl just disappears into thin air. She didn't even have the decency to say goodbye. No wonder he looks so worried. If only he would get back together with Ava. Things would be perfect although she couldn't have a double wedding, not with her looking like a frump.

She smiles. When they were kids she would tease Ava, saying 'skinny daddy-longlegs, flat banana feet.' It made her wild but look at her now. She's a top model and gorgeous. A sharp sting brings her back to the moment. She sucks the ripped cuticle.

Her Dad says, 'a penny for them.'

Puzzled, she says, 'what?'

'I said a penny for them. You were smiling, now you are frowning.'

'It's nothing.'

He gets up. 'I'll just see what's holding up your mother.'

Emmy concentrates on smoothing the jagged cuticle and returns to her daydream. She swears as she gets plumper Ava gets skinnier. Even the diet she's on doesn't seem to help. Jeremy said he likes her curves, but she would like to be thin. Her wedding dress would look much nicer on a slender figure.

An exasperated William stomps into the dining room. Mrs Fuller follows, saying, 'I don't know what the hurry is. I was in the middle of a video link with the florist.'

Emmy drops her hand from her mouth. 'I want to choose the flowers.'

'Well she probably won't speak to me again. She had just brought out a bucket of Lily of the Valley when your father cut us off. Why can't this wait? What's it about anyway?' She can never read William's expression, but a glance at Blake's scowl makes her realise there is something amiss. 'What's so important it can't wait five minutes?'

William walks back to the head of the table and grips the chair, his knuckles pale with tension. Blake is on his left, Emmy on his right, and both look up at him. He clears his throat. 'Blake has something rather upsetting to tell us Margery. I thought you should hear it.' He looks at Emmy, 'it's about Jeremy my girl.' He pulls back his chair and sits at the table.

Mrs Fuller sinks down next to her daughter, her gaze flicking from William to Blake.

Emmy also turns her gaze on Blake, who shifts in his chair. It was all very well saying he should be the one to tell her, but now confronted by it he wishes he let Mr Fuller. Poor Emmy, she's looks so much like Rory, but Em lacks her brother's confidence. She doesn't deserve this, but better the heartbreak than marrying the bastard.

He clears his throat. 'Em, there is no easy way to say this. I'm sorry, but Jeremy is a treacherous bastard, and you have to dump him.'

'Huh!' Emmy's eyes narrow. 'I knew you were against me marrying him. I knew it. That's why you wanted me to wait, isn't it?' The inflection in her voice rises. 'Just because all your girlfriends dump you.' Her eyes fill with tears, and Blake wants to put his arms around her. If only he could shield her from this.

William says, 'let the man finish what he's trying to tell you Emmy.'

Mrs Fuller looks from one to the other, her forehead creased. She folds her hands in her lap and bites her bottom lip.

Blake sighs and runs his hand over his head. He's not doing a very good job of this. 'He's cheating on you Em.'

She leaps up, and her chair tips back, hitting the parquet floor with a crash. Tears run down her cheeks, and her face flushes. 'You're a liar.'

Her mother grasps her arm, 'sit down Emmy. Hear the man out. He wouldn't say that unless he knew something.' Surely to God, he must know something. 'Oh dear,' she glances at William.

Mr Fuller gets up to pick up the chair, putting it back and pushing on Emmy's stiff shoulders until she relents and sits. She glares at Blake for a moment before slumping onto the table, and sobbing into folded arms. He wouldn't say that if it weren't true.

A tiny part of her knew it couldn't last. Why would Australia's most eligible bachelor love her? But if Blake hadn't made her wait until he came home, she would be married now. She sniffs as she realises how unjust that is and uses her tee shirt hem to wipe her face and nose.

'Emmy!' Margery says horrified. 'Here I'll get a tissue.'

Before she can get up William pulls his hankie from his pocket and passes it to Emmy. Margery places her hand on her daughters back, rubbing circles. She's going to have to cancel the wedding. What will people say? They'll think Jeremy dumped Emmy. She stops, chastising herself for caring what others think when her daughter's heartbroken. She'll just make sure the guests know what a lying cheating dog he is. Just as well she didn't manage to order the flowers.

Margery's gaze falls on Blake. His worried eyes are so like his father's. She had such a crush on James throughout high school, but she never acted on it, just fantasised from afar. It's why she first dated William, hoping to get closer to James. For years, it was just the three of them and a string of girls who she knew would never last.

That was until he met Helena. At first she hated the woman, called her that green-eyed Italian tart much to William's dismay. Gradually, Margery came to realise she loved William, not James. He was just a fantasy. When she and William married and their first child miscarried Helena was so kind to her. Margery was full of remorse and tried to make up for it.

She felt awful when Helena told her how strange she found living in Australia knowing she had probably contributed. Poor Helena estranged from her family in Italy, and living in a foreign country with no friends and no family, with only a jealous witch for a friend. Guiltily, she turns her attention back to her daughter.

Emmy blows her nose and a sense of fate settles over her as she says, 'who is he seeing?' But she already knows.

Blake struggles. Conflicting expressions run across his face as he searches for words. She lets him off the hook and says, 'it's Ava isn't it?'

Blake nods and she sees the pain in his eyes. She feels awful about her accusations and walks around the table. He stands as she arrives, and she hugs him. 'I'm sorry I was mean.'

Blake holds her, amazed that she always thinks of everyone before herself. She doesn't deserve this, and anger wells inside him. He looks into her face, tucking her hair behind her ears and says, 'I want to kill the bastard for doing this to you Emmy.'

'Me too.' She rests her cheek against his chest, 'but vengeance is best served cold, don't you think?'

'Pardon?' He steps back.

She looks up and says, 'I want serious revenge Blake, and I want you to help me get it. Death is too easy. I want something lasting; and agonising; and horrible; and tormenting; and I want Ava to suffer with him. Can you make that happen, or shall I do it myself?'

29.

Raindrops splatter against the dining room window as clouds mask the sun, making the room feel colder than the freezing outside temperature. Hester shivers and looks at her empty cereal bowl wondering if she should have a piece of toast. She looks up to see if her husband will notice.

He's frowning at Jeremy. 'You're an imbecile!'

'Arnie...'

'Stay out of this Hester. This has nothing to do with you although it's your indulgence that has created this worthless lump of shit you call your son.'

There is one slice left in the rack and Arnie and Jeremy seem to have eaten their fill. But yesterday when she took a slice, Arnie sneered at her saying she was getting fat. Perhaps she is, but she's fifty-five so a little middle-aged spread is normal, isn't it? She lifts her hand from her lap. A bit of toast with marmalade and coffee goes so well together. It rounds off breakfast nicely.

Perhaps Arnie will be too busy being cross with Jeremy to notice. Her hand steals across the white tablecloth towards the toast rack. The phone rings startling her, and she jerks knocking it over. The last remaining slice tips out onto the table leaving a trail of crumbs in its wake.

'Look what you've done now you clumsy woman.' Arnold Marabaux gets up to answer the phone. It's a conventional phone because he won't have an image transmitter in the house, other than the ones he has in his office where Hester is forbidden entry.

Jeremy stretches across the table to pick up the toast and puts it on his plate. Hester watches him slather on butter, followed by marmalade. The knife leaves a glob of crumb-laced butter in the jar. He picks up the whole slice uncut and takes a bite with a satisfying crunch. With his mouth full he says, 'pass the coffee mother.'

Hester swallows a spurt of saliva and gets up to walk over to the sideboard where a glass pot sits on its heating pad. Then she walks around the table to her son and pours the last of the coffee into his cup. She replaces the pot, switches off the warmer, and goes back to her seat as her husband says, 'I'll ring you back.'

Marabaux replaces the phone in its cradle and turns to see Hester lowering her bottom to her seat. 'I am going to my study and don't want to be disturbed. You,' he points at Jeremy, 'return to Brisbane and make it up with that woman. If you fail, don't bother coming home again. You,' he points at his wife. 'Clean up this mess. The place is a pigsty.' He points at the crumbs on the table where the toast tumbled.

Before Hester's bottom plumps onto her seat, Arnie has left the room. She hovers bent at the waist, wondering if she should sit while Jeremy finishes his breakfast, or if she should clear the table as her husband instructed. Gravity decides, and she plops onto the chair. Life is so much less complicated when Jeremy isn't home.

Jeremy gazes out the window, but once his father leaves the room he says, 'how anyone can live in this place, beggars belief.' He nods to the portrait of Saint Francis of Paola above the sideboard. 'Why must you display such barbaric imagery?' His gaze rests on Hester, his nostrils flared and upper lip curled. 'You'll have to drive me to the airport Mother, so stay off the pills until after I've gone. I don't want you driving me into a ditch again.'

Hester clutches her hands together on her lap, head bowed. Spite, borne of decades long hurt, curdles in her stomach, but she remains silent, thinking, the son should listen to his parents. Her mother said that, but Hester knows that washing the head of the donkey is a waste of soap. Her son will never hear her words. Even if he did, he couldn't change. He let the devil take his soul, now he has none. If her father were still alive, this would not be allowed.

She should muster the energy, perhaps the courage to chastise the boy for his blasphemy, but he will scoff. He cares little for the oath he made at St Francis's shrine all those years ago. All he cares for, is himself and his own comfort. Perhaps if she has one more tablet later, she will have the courage to talk to Arnie about him.

Jeremy pushes back his chair and stands up, throwing his napkin onto his plate. It falls over the partly eaten toast and untouched coffee in his cup. A brown stain grows in the white linen as a corner of the napkin sinks. He stretches his jaw as if his collar is irksome, and leaves Hester staring at the mess.

In his study, Arnold sits at his desk. He straightens his suit jacket, tugging the sleeves to cover his white linen shirt cuffs and pats his pale blue tie. He left a message earlier that he would call Bart about Jeremy's break-up with the Fuller girl, and he dreads the conversation.

Bart will say he's weak. It is true that his son is the only part of his life where his control is tenuous. How can a childless man understand, there is a limit to controlling one's own children? Perhaps he can turn the situation to his advantage. It used to be so easy to make Bart lose his temper, but as he ages, it becomes increasingly difficult. At least, he can distract him. He leans over to press the e-cript speed dial.

'What the fuck's going on Arnie?' Bart says as soon as he sees the image on the screen in front of him. He's alone in his study, his second glass of whisky full in his hand. A drop of the golden liquid falls onto his immaculate trousers and he curses, rubbing the stain with his palm.

Arnold waits until Bart settles, and in an even voice says, 'these things happen, but Jeremy is on his way to woo her back.'

'We need Fuller tied up. He knows too many people to...'

'Yes Bart I know.' Arnie sighs as if dealing with an exasperating child.

'The G-G for one,' Bart adds.

'It'll be okay. Jeremy's on his way to persuade her to take him back. The marriage will take place immediately.' He pauses. 'There is good news.'

'What?'

'I've arranged for the illicit club crew to be tried as one group rather than individually. It'll make it difficult for Lincoln to get the girl off the charge. We'll make it public and begin a media campaign about rampaging drug addled street gangs. There are a number of ethnics among the crew so it will be easy to convince people. The public have little sympathy for lawbreakers, given the escalating crime, and now they fear there's a serial killer on the loose.'

'What if Lincoln sides with them instead of following her to the Middle East...'

Arnie interrupts. 'If she goes, he will go after her, of that I am certain. Of course if he follows her he will be in breach of the anti-terrorism laws for entering a prohibited zone. This will be public evidence of his radicalisation, and we will withdraw his citizenship. If he returns to Australia we will have good cause to lock him up and there can be no outcry.'

'What if he doesn't follow her?'

'Lincoln's already been arrested and released on suspicion of murdering one woman based on blood samples on his shirt. We leak that, and they'll bay for his blood. The footage of him roaming the streets after curfew will show him as an outlaw. If I release the footage of his fight with my men the public will believe it.'

'You can't let on they were your men Arnie.'

'Bart, give me a little credit will you. They will be off duty soldiers arriving back from war for a well-earned rest. Besides we have plenty of evidence from his diary of his ruthlessness.'

Bart drinks his whisky in silent contemplation before leaning forward to slam his empty glass on the table. He looks at the screen saying, 'Arnie we are so close. I can't afford for Lincoln and Fuller to fuck with my plans.'

'They won't.'

'You better make sure they don't, or it won't be me answering questions.'

He depresses the button in the arm of the Chesterfield to end the call. The image disappears and Bart leans his head back against the sofa, closing his eyes, seeing the image of James Lincoln's face. He sits forward cursing and picks up his glass to walk over to the liquor cabinet.

30.

Margery Fuller stands looking at the growing flower arrangements festooning their entrance hall. 'That's enough—no more Mrs Clarke.' She puts her hands on her hips. 'The next delivery that arrives—you must turn away. I am getting hay fever from the blasted things. Tell the florist no more,' her mouth purses.

The front door opens and her husband walks in, his face registering surprise at the plethora of plant life filling his home. 'Good grief, what's this now?'

'William, you're home! It's ridiculous, but he's obviously keen to win her back.' She pauses seeing the flowers for what they represent. 'It's quite touching really.'

'Are all these from Jeremy?' William's hand sweeps an arc in front of him before covering his mouth. He tugs his lips as he stares at the floral forest, and a kernel of an idea forms. 'What does Emmy say?'

'She hasn't seen them yet, but I'm expecting her at any moment. I imagine they will infuriate her. They made me angry when the first ones arrived, but now I'm just fed up with the silly man. I've had to take an antihistamine tablet.'

William hugs her to his side. 'Poor Margery, but this could be just the thing.'

'What do you mean?' Margery pulls from his embrace looking up at his face, her brow furrowed.

'I'm not sure yet but I have an idea. Can you let me know when Emmy's home. I'll be in my study. I have research to do.'

'Don't be long dear, dinner's almost ready.'

'I forgot,' William stops and looks back at his wife. 'Can you tell Mrs Clarke we'll be rather more than just the family for dinner? Blake's bringing two of his staff.'

'Tch,' Mrs Fuller clicks her tongue in irritation. 'She made cottage pie but there won't be enough.'

'Sorry dear, I should have phoned ahead. Perhaps she will defrost steaks to barbeque.'

Rory arrives with Lachlan Bowery, Blake, Evan, and Flynn.

'Jesus what's with the flowers?'

'Rory watch your language. They are from Jeremy.'

Rory laughs. 'Sorry Mum, but you have to admit it's a bit over the top, even for Jeremy.' He introduces her to Lachlan, Evan and Flynn then they go out to the terrace with Mr Fuller to discuss Charlotte's impending trial.

Margery goes to speak with Mrs Clarke.

Half an hour later, Emmy arrives home from Pilates, and Margery rushes to intercept her before she sees the flowers, but she's too late. Her daughter stands in the hallway, her face flushed.

'Darling, are you all right? You are so late I was beginning to worry about you.'

Emmy looks at her mother as if she is not sure who she is. 'I'm fine. I went for a drive.'

A card from the nearest bouquet flutters to the floor. Emmy picks it up. It reads please forgive me darling. She lets it drop to the floor and selects another. You are the only one I love. The next one says, let me prove how I've changed.

Scrunching the last card into a ball in her fist, she says under her breath, 'Then why are you at Ava's right now, you bastard.'

Margery says, 'What was that dear? I didn't hear you?'

'It's nothing Mum.' Emmy forces down her resentment and kisses her mother's cheek. 'What's for dinner? I'm starving.'

'We're having a barbeque on the terrace. There are rather a lot of us, and Daddy's cooking steaks.'

'Who's here?'

'I don't know, people discussing Blake's girl's trial. I've never seen the poor boy look so bleak. The longer this takes the more I worry. I feel so sorry for him.' She looks at her daughter, 'and you of course. It's so sad to lose someone you love.'

'Don't worry about me Mum. I certainly don't love Jeremy any longer. I can't believe I was sucked in by the arsehole.'

'Emmy.'

'Sorry Mum, but he is you know. I've just seen his car parked outside Ava's apartment block. She's a prise bitch, but never mind me, let's get Charlotte back.'

'I nearly forgot. Daddy wants to talk to you about something.'

'All right. Tell him I'll be out in a sec. I'm all sweaty. I'll have a shower and make myself respectable for our guests.'

Emmy goes into her bathroom and turns on the shower taps then walks over to the weighing scales. 'Still five kilos too heavy,' she mutters. No matter how much she starves herself she'll never lose it all. The Pilates instructor tells her to stop worrying, but maybe that's why Jeremy preferred Ava. The bitch is skin and bone.

Perhaps he prefers thin women. She sighs taking off her clothes. Obsessing over his infidelity is not healthy and really, did she love him? Perhaps she was just flattered that Australia's most eligible bachelor wanted her. Her mouth turns down in a grimace. But he clearly didn't.

She stares at her face in the mirror. All he did, was criticise, saying she looked frumpy in her favourite dress. He insisted on buying her a new one to replace it. Then there was the time she wrote an article on fashion, and he told her the copy was amateurish. When she asked him if he could talk to the Randolph's about getting a position, he refused saying he'd prefer her not to work unless it was unpaid charity. After all, they didn't need the money and she should leave paying jobs to those who needed them. Why did she go along with him, feeling selfish about stealing some poor person's paid position? She feels used.

Steam from hot water obscures her reflection, and she swipes her hand across the mirror as if obliterating her thoughts. In the shower she considers how nervous and insecure she was in Jeremy's presence. It's almost a relief he's not around any longer.

Ten minutes later, Emmy, dressed in cut off pants and tee shirt, walks out to the terrace. Her wet hair spreads a damp stain across her back. There are several men sitting with Rory and Blake around a low table covered with beer bottles. William stands at the barbeque grill, flipping steaks. She assumes her mother is in the kitchen and wishes she had dressed up a little. To avoid the men, she joins her father who drops a kiss on her head as she slips her arm through his.

'Hello dear. How was Pilates?' He asks.

Blake looks up at the sound of William's voice, and pushes back his chair saying, 'hey Em can I get you a drink? He walks over and hugs her. How're you travelling—okay?'

'Yeah Blake, what about you? Have you had any news of Charlotte since you wrote to her?'

'No, but it's not easy for her to get a message out. I don't expect one. Anyway I hope to see her soon. The trial starts in eight days in Darwin. We are talking tactics with Lachlan.' He sees the blank look on her face. 'You haven't met the Barrister. Christ, where is my head. I guess you know none of them. Come on, let me introduce you and then I'll get you a drink.'

He takes her hand, worried that she is still fragile from Jeremy and Ava's betrayal. It's been nearly a month since she found out, and he hasn't got over his anger at them.

'Blake I heard on the news that there's a cyclone up in the Kimberley area. Will Charlotte be okay?'

'She'll be fine. The buildings are built to withstand category five. We had a cyclone when I was there. Nothing happened except wind and rain.' He smiles to reassure her.

As they reach the men, Lachlan stands and Evan follows. Flynn looks at Evan surprised. Evan jerks his head. Flynn gets the hint and stands too. Rory remains seated. He doesn't see why he should stand for his sister.

'Hello Em, are you keen on flowers then?' He laughs at the flash of annoyance across her face.

'Shut up Rory.' She looks at the others, blushing and wishing she could control her tongue. She should learn to ignore her brother's teasing, but he always seems to catch her off guard.

As Blake introduces her, Flynn grins saying, 'hi Emmy,' and slumps into his seat. Evan nods and shakes her hand, then hovers behind his chair, embarrassed by Flynn's lack of manners. Lachlan stares at Emmy, stepping closer and interrupting Blake.

'I'm Lachlan, a friend of your brother's. It's good to meet you.' He takes her hand, holding it with both of his until he realises he's gawking, and averts his hot gaze.

Emmy's pulse beats in her throat and her cheeks warm as she lets her damp hair fall forward to hide her face.

Blake watches the exchange and holds out a chair. 'What can I get you to drink Em?'

'Um, um, did Mum open champagne?'

'I'll find out,' he says and goes indoors.

Emmy sits in her chair, eyes cast downwards, picking at the ragged skin around her thumbnail as Rory resumes the discussion on the impending trial.

'I don't know how we handle it. If they persist with the charge of conspiracy as a cartel, to pervert the natural pursuit of law and order, we're in trouble. Wasn't that one of the charges levelled at Jonathon Castile and his fellow protestors a couple of years back?'

'In addition to the corruption charges–that's right.' Lachlan says.

'So, it means one in, all in. If anyone of them is convicted, and they prove an alliance, then they will all be guilty by association.'

Emmy fidgets wanting to join the conversation, but afraid she'll look foolish. She gathers her courage, thinking too bad. If she doesn't, and it affects Charlotte, she'll never forgive herself. 'Rory...'

Lachlan turns to her immediately attentive, but her brother ignores her saying, 'how many of them are alleged to be a part of the cartel?'

'Steaks are ready,' William calls. 'Em, see where your mother is with the salad, will you?'

At that moment, Mrs Clarke wheels out a trolley of crockery, cutlery, and bowls of food. She sets a long outdoor dining table. Margery comes out the house holding a tray of glasses followed by Blake with the champagne and ice bucket.

'Let the steaks rest a minute William,' Margery says. 'We'll have a glass of bubbly before eating.'

Lachlan sees Emmy's agitation and leans towards her. 'You wanted to say something Emmy?'

She glances at him in surprise, and then looks at her brother who is rising to help his father. As soon as Lachlan speaks, Rory sits back on his chair.

Emmy says, 'um it's probably nothing, but I overheard Jeremy saying something about the law being unconstitutional.'

Blake walks over with a glass of champagne for Emmy. She takes it, smiling up at him. He squeezes her shoulder.

Lachlan says, 'are you sure?' He sees doubt creep across Emmy's face and wishes he could bite out his tongue. 'I mean, what isn't constitutional about it?'

'He didn't tell me.' She picks at a loose thread on her tee shirt, her head bowed. 'He was talking to someone on his CellTab and I overheard. He thought it was funny that no one, not the Chief Justice nor any of the Silks defending him noticed. He said there is obscure wording in the revised constitution, but I can't remember what it was. I only paid attention because it was the second time I heard poor Jonathon Castile's name mentioned that week.'

'You're brilliant. I could hug you,' he smiles at her. 'You have given me the first ray of hope in this whole miserable affair. Thank you.'

She blushes as he takes her hand, shaking it in congratulations, holding it longer than necessary, his palm warm as his strong fingers dwarf hers. A surge in her stomach causes her breath to catch under his searching gaze.

Evan pushes back his chair. 'I'll do some research, see what I can find. How long ago Emmy?'

Rory says, 'wait until we've eaten. There's plenty of time.'

'If it's within the last two years we can subpoena the transcripts of his Cell conversations.' Lachlan is still gazing at Emmy.

'You'll never get that through the system. Anyway, I can do it quicker.'

Lachlan drags his gaze from Emmy to Evan, his eyebrow raised in question.

Blake shakes his head. 'You don't want to know Lachlan.'

Emmy crinkles her nose, trying to remember. 'I think it was when Blake came home the first time, about five or six months ago.'

'Brilliant.' Evan says.

A warm glow suffuses Emmy. She doesn't know if it's the champagne or so much approval, but she's buoyant.

'Come on everyone, dinner's ready,' Margery calls. There's an almost empty glass of champagne in her hand.

Over dinner Emmy turns to William, 'Mum said you wanted to talk to me about something Dad?'

William chews a piece of steak before answering. 'Mm, yes. It's about Jeremy and the flowers, but it can wait,' he glances at their guests.

'It's okay Dad, you can say it.'

'Well, I thought if he's so keen to get you back, maybe you should play along, but only if you feel okay about it. Unless, of course, you want him back...' William realises how insensitive he sounds. 'It was only a passing thought my dear. Don't mind me.'

All eyes turn to Emmy and she's aware of Lachlan's scrutiny. 'Why would I do that?'

'Um. He could get Charlotte released.'

'No!' Blake's voice is hoarse. 'Don't do it Emmy. I don't trust the man. I'll get her out, even if it means going up there and... and....' He lapses into silence, unable to voice his growing frustration. He knows he must act legally or they will become fugitives from their own country, and he will be as corrupt as the ones who put her there. All the same, he plans a fallback position in case all else fails, but he's not ready to go there yet or discuss it with the others.

31.

Ava stands at her balcony railing, watching the swirling waters of the river. She wishes she had the courage to jump. It's pointless. Jeremy wouldn't care if she died. Anyway the drop might not be enough to kill her, just hurt a lot especially if she hit the rocks of the retaining wall.

There's no one with whom she can talk, and it's her own fault. She has alienated everyone who ever cared for her, and for what, a mad passion that consumes her. A sob escapes, and she turns to walk inside to find a drink.

On the dining room table, resting between artfully arranged crimson rose petals, are two glasses of wine she poured earlier. They stand sentinel at the head of unused place settings that she laid to the music of Pachelbel's Canon, thrilled with the prospect of having Jeremy unencumbered by the spectre of his fiancée.

The wine's ruby light reflects on her cheek as she drinks. She takes the second glass to the door, staring out into the darkness beyond the balcony. Her image, reflected in the glass, absorbs her until she sees how thin she has become. She was always slender as a model should be, but now she looks scrawny. A light wind could carry her away.

She takes another gulp of wine, rolling it around her mouth, trying to savour the black cherry, blackberry, and liquorice of the 2018 Gevrey-Chambertin, but her senses only reflect the bloody metallic taste of bitterness.

This was to be her special night. When Jeremy phoned from the airport to say he would see her in an hour she was so excited. Finally, with Emmy out of the way he will declare his love. She ordered a special dinner along with the wine, convinced he would propose.

Now she walks over to the occasional table next to the sofa and puts down the glass to pick up and light a cigarette, sucking the smoke deep into her lungs. She should give up, but smoking keeps her from eating and she can't afford to get fat. Unlike Emmy who couldn't care less about her dimpled thighs. She shudders.

How could Jeremy want Emmy back when he told Ava he likes thin women? They used to laugh together at dumpy gullible Emmy. Jeremy loved it when Ava mimicked her Pilates' moves. She felt guilty about that, but love is war isn't it? You use what weapons you have to win.

An overwhelming surge of nostalgia for Emmy's friendship surges through her, and she picks up her wine again. Will Em take Jeremy back, or reject him? All the Fuller's are so righteous it makes her sick, and she knows Emmy will never forgive her, not enough to have her as a friend again anyway. She might forgive her in a good Christian sense, but she won't ever regain that trust or the intimacy of sharing secrets they used to have.

Even Rory, mooning over her all those years, never propositioned her. Not that Ava's complaining. It would have been awkward if he had, but she knows he did it from a sense of duty towards Blake's feelings.

He's a fool, Doesn't he realise that women like bad boys? They marry decent blokes, but only because they are rejected or dumped by the more interesting ones. Is that what her future holds? Rory might marry her out of pity.

Her lip curls at the thought, and she walks out to the balcony again, smoke in one hand, wine in the other. The Fuller's and Blake will never speak to her again. She flicks her half-smoked cigarette over the glass-panelled railing. The wind blows it back onto the balcony below, and Ava leans over to see where it's gone. She hopes it doesn't set light to anything. Christ, that's all she needs. The butt rolls across the floor and disappears from sight.

The apartment below is vacant so there's nothing to catch fire. She shrugs and lifts the wine to her mouth. The glass is empty and surprised at how quickly it disappeared, she goes inside for a refill. She may as well drink the bottle. There's no point letting a liquid kings-ransomed go to waste. The scent of roses fills her nostrils as she leans over the table. Suddenly unable to bear the smell, she scoops up handfuls of petals and rushes to the balcony throwing them out to the river.

They flutter back in the breeze and stick to the glass like droplets of splashed blood. She leans over the rail to brush them off and then returns inside for the rest. Not until the last flower petal is gone from the table is she satisfied. When she finishes, she goes inside to pour more wine.

A little unsteady on her feet she takes the now full glass outside, and lights another cigarette. While she sips the wine, she sees a petal clinging to the aluminium rail separating the glass panes. That won't do. She places her glass on the table, determined to brush the offending blot into the river, and stretches over the railing but can't reach. Her fingers wriggle and stretch towards the recalcitrant bloom.

On her tiptoes, one foot on the cold balcony tiles, the other in a horizontal ballet point, she eases her waist onto the rail. The petal is still beyond reach. She'll have to get the broom.

As she tries to right herself, her foot slips and loses contact with the floor. She lurches forward, her weight shifting towards the void. Her hand pushes against the glass to stop her fall. She screams for help, but no one hears.

Terror gives her strength as she strains to regain her balance. Her right hand presses flat against the panel above the rose petal, her left hand twists under her body as it grips the railing. Every muscle in her body tenses against the pull of gravity. She holds herself board-stiff. The hand, pressing flat against the glass, is all that prevents her plunging to the rocks.

She gets a better grip of the rail with her left hand. Then she jerks her right hand higher up the glass. Her body rocks and she stiffens. With a final push with her right hand against the panel, she lurches backwards to land on the floor of the balcony. Her ribs are bruised, her left wrist burns with pain, and her heart hammers in her chest.

For a moment, she lies panting with fear and exertion, until the cold drives her upright. Then she hobbles to the outdoor setting, collapsing into a chair, smelling the scared sweat of her own armpits.

The aberrant petal still clings to the white railing; a dark gash marring purity. It torments her. Her hands trembles as she picks up the wine glass and gulps. She lights another cigarette. It calms her.

Gradually fear turns to anger as she feels the pain in her wrenched shoulder and twisted wrist. She nearly died, and it's Jeremy's fault. The bastard will not get away with it.

She finishes her wine, and takes a final drag on her cigarette. Then she gets up, stubbing the burning stump in the ashtray, and goes indoors to change. Five minutes later she's dressed in black jeans, long-sleeved tee shirt, and sneakers.

Before she leaves her apartment she picks up her keys, credit card, and CellTab and pushes them into her pockets. In the lift she checks the time. It's gone midnight, and she hopes Bert the doorman is asleep.

When the lift doors open she sees his head resting on the back of his chair, his mouth hanging open. She tiptoes past his desk. Small noises escape his swollen adenoids as she passes.

She's afraid of breaching curfew. It's not something she has ever done. Outside the night is silent and deserted as she peers to her left, and then to her right. With a deep breath, she steps onto the pavement and heads south. She stays close to the shrubbery next to the cyclone fence, walking away from the security guardhouse.

Jeremy's block is about 300 metres from hers so any chance she'll be caught is slim. She'll reason with him. Surely, he will see sense. He must love her or he wouldn't keep coming back. She knows he doesn't love Emmy so why is he trying to win her back. She hiccoughs. At the very least, he owes her an explanation. A cat jumps out in front of her. She gasps and her heart hammers against her rib cage. It's too scary out here alone. What if she's caught, will Jeremy save her?

As she draws close to the entrance of his apartment block, the gate to the underground parking rises, shattering the night with its maniacal screech. She presses her back into a bush and waits. A moment later, his vehicle noses out, and in the light from the basement parking she sees he's not alone. There's a woman with him, gazing from the passenger window, staring at Ava. Surely, she must see her, but she gives no sign.

Quickly Ava snaps a photo with her phone. She doesn't want him denying this latest infidelity. Before Em takes him back, she should see what a bastard he is. The vehicle turns and recedes down the road into darkness. Automatically the basement parking closes.

An angry Ava runs home and falls into bed sobbing. She awakes late, her tongue thick in her mouth, her head hammering, and rolls onto her back, remembering the night. Her eyes are gummed with stale make-up, so she gets out of bed, still fully clothed, and walks unsteadily to the bathroom.

There's a pain in her shoulder and the base of her ribs hurt. She winces as she turns on the shower. Her wrist is tender from the near fall from the balcony and she has a line of bruises forming across her hips and ribs.

An hour later, dressed and looking as glamorous as usual, her hair and make-up flawlessly arranged, she is ready. She sits on the balcony smoking and fretting as she looks at the photo on her phone.

The woman is clearly visible in the foreground, her face is expressionless, staring directly at where Ava stood pressed against the bush. Behind her, Jeremy's profile is unmistakable. He sits in the driving seat, looking straight ahead. What should she do about it? Should she send it to Emmy?

Poor Emmy, she doesn't want to break her heart all over again, but she should know what a snake Jeremy is before she takes him back. Her thumb hovers over the delete button then moves back to send and taps. She leans back closing her eyes.

32.

Charlotte turns from gazing at the pool of still, olive-coloured water, to look at the lieutenant. 'Hey sir, are there crocodiles?'

'Never seen one up here, but no guarantees. Climbing into this gorge would be difficult I imagine. It was tricky even for us.'

'Can we swim then?'

'Why do you think we are here?' He unbuttons his shirt.

The men are already stripping, their rifles stacked against rocks like sentinels, boots lined along their base. The squad is hot after the gruelling march and setting up camp in temperatures in the high forties. Now, as the sun falls towards the western horizon, Lieutenant Brookes has ordered an hour recreation to cool off before they head back to camp.

A man runs naked across the hot rocks and jumps into the water with a splash. He swims with strong over-arm strokes to the waterfall at the other end of the pool. More men follow him, all naked. Charlotte glances at Brookes. He's pulling off his webbing.

There are five women with this platoon, three regulars, and two conscripts, outnumbered and shy as they hang back, unsure about stripping off in front of the men. Mallory walks up to stand next to Charlotte. 'Are you going in Charlie?'

Charlotte gazes at the cool and inviting water. The men don't seem to care about their nakedness. She takes off her hat and rubs the couple of millimetres of golden fuzz, its new growth plastered with sweat to her scalp.

'Yeah but I might keep my undies on although the bloody knickers are so huge I could drown with the wet-weight of them.' She smiles at Mallory. 'Come on Essie, last one in is a squashed frog.'

The others follow Charlotte's lead and soon they are splashing in the water. The cold sucks the heat from her tired body as she floats on her back. The over-large knickers inflate with air, and she squashes them to her sides. Air and water bubble up, embarrassing her, but no one seems to notice.

The water fills her ears and blocks the surrounding sounds as she floats on her back. She watches the pitiless sky drift north. Perhaps there'll be rain soon. The heat is oppressive. The air heavy with humidity. There's a menacing quality to it she hasn't felt before, and it fills her with foreboding.

To distract herself, she flexes her hard muscles, marvelling at how fit she's become after ten weeks in this place. The incessant training means she can even manage press-ups although she still sticks her bottom in the air.

It must be October, but she is still unsure of her trial date. There have been so many rumours and false starts, she can't help thinking she'll be here for the rest of her life.

A head surfaces next to her, causing her to flounder and go under, inhaling water. As she coughs and splutters the man puts a finger to his lips, his shoulder muscles rippling. He beckons for her to follow and she glances around, but no one pays attention.

Groups splash about, or swim, some stand talking, water up to their chests. Mallory swims a bizarre doggy paddle across the other side of the pool, her neck stretched to keep her face from the water.

Charlotte follows nervous, but curious. Conscripts and soldiers don't mix. The bloke's name is Willard, Private Pete Willard, the platoon's forward scout and an expert tracker. The lieutenant once sent her to find something for dinner with Willard and Private Nelson. As they were leaving he called after them. 'If one of you two ladies misses the target, the conscript will show you how it's done.'

Neither of the blokes spoke to her. In fact, they treated her as if she didn't exist. She was glad Nelson shot the kangaroo. On the way back, she lagged behind and got lost. Willard had to return to find her and his face showed his disdain. Now she follows him to a part of the pool sheltered by rocks and vegetation, keeping a wary distance until he speaks.

'Hey, is it true you're Blake Lincoln's girl?' His low voice is friendly.

'Yes,' she says hoping it's still true. 'Who told you?'

'One of your lot, Conscript Baswan—says he's the lead guitarist in your band. He told me you were dating Lincoln.'

'How is Jay? Is Atif with him and Tyler? I haven't seen them for ages—since we got here. Are they all right? Please, please... um can you tell them I'm okay?'

He nods. 'I'll tell them. So if there's anything else I can do for you, you'll let me know.'

'Thanks, but why?'

'Lincoln saved my brother's life. I owe him.'

Her mind whirls with longing. An overwhelming urge to see Blake makes her eyes sting. She scans Willard's face, trying to work out if he's trustworthy and says, 'Can you get a message to him that I am here?'

'I'll try.' Willard ducks under the water, swimming back to the middle of the pool where he surfaces near the other soldiers. He says something and the men glance back at her.

She swims to a rock near where she left her clothes and pulls herself onto the rocks, hoping to dry off in the humid air. As she lies on her stomach, a breeze ruffles the water and sends goose bumps over her wet flesh. Does Blake know what's happened or does he think she just vanished? Perhaps he didn't worry about going to see her when he came home. Maybe he's forgotten her now he's a free man. Sadness swamps her as she thinks it's possible she will never see him again.

Days later, Willard passes her a letter. She is so excited she can barely get through cleaning the barracks. When they have leave to go to the ablution block, she loiters at the back of the queue. Only when she's alone in the cubicle does she open his letter.

'My love,' it begins. Tears spring into her eyes and she holds the letter to her breast trying to get a grip, blinking to stop the spurt of tears.

A guard raps on the door. 'Hurry it up in there.'

'Yes, I'm coming.' She folds the letter and puts it back inside her bra before pulling up her jumpsuit and flushing the toilet. The rest of the letter will have to wait until tonight, but nothing can dent Charlotte's euphoria. As they cross the ground towards the mess, she looks up. The sky is obliterated by a lead coloured sheet of cloud, stretching to the horizon as it moves northeast. The air feels charged with vengeance.

Three hundred and fifty kilometres North West of them, Cyclone Zillie tracks west across the Timor Sea. At lunch, a senior corrections officer called Elizabeth Belfrieze, or Batty as she is known, reads out the latest bulletin. The cyclone is north of the Daly River mouth, travelling at nine kilometres an hour. No one expects it to turn south, but as a precaution they are ordered to stow everything this afternoon, and to tape windows.

Mallory says under her breath, 'another fucking ridiculous waste of time.'

Charlotte smiles at her, undaunted by the extra work as she hordes her secret. She dare not tell anyone about the letter in case it's discovered and confiscated before she gets a chance to read it, but nothing can spoil her mood now.

That evening in the ablution block, Charlotte whispers to Mallory, asking her to keep lookout while she reads the letter. She sits again on the steel toilet pan and takes it from her bra. Its limp with sweat, but the ink is still legible.

Mallory waits outside the cubicles peering at her face in the steel sheets behind the basins, hoping she won't develop skin cancer. When she arrived in this hellhole, her skin was pale and smooth under copper hair. Now there are so many freckles, if they all join up she'll have a tan for the first time in her life.

She once had a white cat called Peggy until she discovered it was a boy. He developed black spots on his nose as if he had been digging in mud, so she changed his name to Piggy. Now her face resembles that of a mud splattered cat rather than a young woman.

She sighs, leaning against the cubicle door, her mouth near the gap at the hinges. 'Hurry Charlie, they'll come looking for us if we are much longer.'

Charlotte's crazy for mooning over a bloke she will never see again. Still, that he wrote is nice, but it'll turn to tears when she realises she can't be with him. Better to stop thinking about men. They are usually trouble, in her experience.

Look at Oscar. The first date and he expects her to watch him playing in an illegal club. She shakes her head, and she didn't even think he was that hot, just persistent, and funny. They went out more as friends than for romantic reasons, but even then look where it got her.

The boys from the other two bands are in different platoons and they hardly see them. When they do meet, it's hard to manage an exchange. It's not a place for casual conversations. If you want to get a message out, you have to craft it in clear sentences that can be passed in a fleeting exchange, as Charlotte did when she asked Lucas about Nina. They still don't know what happened to Nina. Mallory doubts they ever will.

Mallory thinks about her parents. Will they be worried they haven't heard from her? She was never much good at writing letters home. Do they know where she is or what's happened? If the job exchange hadn't sent her to Brisbane, she wouldn't be in this situation. Not that she had a choice. When the company she worked for shut down, they made her move cities. There were no jobs in Adelaide and only that stinking cleaning job available in the chemical factory south of Brisbane. At least she's out of that cancerous cesspit now. There's always a positive spin if you search hard enough. She grimaces.

'Hey Charlie, you nearly finished in there?'

The toilet flushes and Charlotte comes out, her eyes red and her face wan. 'I need to hide it.' She looks around as if a hiding place for the letter will miraculously appear.

'Flush it Charlie.'

'No, not yet. I can't.'

'Here, give it to me. I'll do it.' Mallory looks at the stubborn set of Charlotte's mouth and realises she's lost the argument. 'It's not worth it Charlie.' She sighs, 'come on then, we must hurry.' She turns to leave.

Charlotte follows her out. Mallory walks to the back of the building and steps up to a narrow ledge and grasps the drainpipe. She shakes it to see if its solid. Then she holds out her hand for the letter. When Charlotte hands it to her she puts it between her teeth and hauls herself up to the eaves where she slides it into a space beneath a protruding roof beam.

'Jesus, you're like a monkey. Where did you learn that?'

Mallory ignores her saying, 'it should be okay now. Come on, we have to get our shower kit before they send out a search party.'

Later that night, Cyclone Zillie turns south, increasing speed to eighteen kilometres per hour as it funnels towards the coast. In gathering rage, it travels across the shallow Timor Sea. Then it races across the Joseph Bonaparte Gulf, churning the sediment from the basin. It rips an unmanned oil platform into matchsticks, and slurps it into its voracious maw.

Five mighty rivers, flow from the Kimberley plateau, the Ord, the Pentecost, the Durack, the King, and the Forrest. From time immemorial they have deposited silt in the Cambridge Gulf, spreading it across vast coastal plains. The cyclone's cavernous vortex barrels onwards, hoovering mud into its maelstrom, drawing the already high tide higher than in recorded history.

It rips up mangroves, Boab trees, and Devonian reef fossils, which have survived from the time of Gondwanaland. It whirls its imprisoned captives around the wall of its eye, along with fish, and other creatures sucked from the sea. Trapped sea birds, fly upwards to be slapped against the walls of the funnel. The huge pull syphons waves in a tidal surge that swallows the coastline as far as the abandoned seaport of Wyndham.

As the eye crosses rocky ranges, mini tornadoes break out of its ferocious grip, flinging hostages across the ravaged land. It sandblasts ancient rock paintings, strips, and snaps trees, and decimates the last of the local Gouldian Finch population.

Mallory awakes in the predawn as Zillie's southern edge reaches the coast. In panic, she sits up in her bunk and hisses across the black void between the beds. There is no answer. Fear grips her as she listens to the mysterious howling pressing against her ears, and she throws her pillow to wake Charlotte.

Charlotte's awake listening to the sounds of the approaching storm when the pillow lands on her face and tumbles off the bed. 'What the fuck! Did you throw something at me?'

'Shush,' Mallory says, 'listen. What's that noise?'

'Duh, I am listening or at least I was until you threw something at me.'

'What is it?'

'What's what?'

'That banshee howling.'

'A frigging storm, what d'you think? I reckon the cyclone's turned south and is on its way.'

'Christ, we'll be killed.'

'Tch,' Charlotte sucks her tongue from the roof of her mouth in scorn. 'No we won't. The barracks are built to withstand cyclones. They happen often up here.'

'Did you ever see one?'

'Yeah plenty. When I was a kid, there'd be at least a couple a year along the coast, but mostly small ones. This one is huge. The last one this size I saw scared me shitless. That one caused havoc, especially along the low-lying areas of the coast. We were fifty kays inland, up in the mountains, but still it was bad. It took my Dad months to set the farm back to rights. Not a lot of damage to the buildings, but lots of fallen trees and broken fences. I thought our roof would come loose. That was scary, but the worst thing that happened was the trees knocked fences down and all our cattle escaped.'

There is a moment of silence while Mallory absorbs what Charlotte says. Her experience helps, and Mallory feels calmer as if the storm is a known beast she can manage. A sudden intake of breath across the void between the two beds makes her jump again. 'What? You scared the bejesus out of me.'

Charlotte swings her legs out of bed. 'We have to rescue my letter. It'll get lost if I leave it there. It won't be safe from the cyclone.'

'Charlie you can't. It's too dangerous.'

'We'll be fine. It's just a bit of wind and rain now.'

'We'll get caught.'

'Okay, I'll do it myself. Stay here Mal. I'll only be a tick.'

'How are you going to climb the pipe? You can barely push yourself up on those skinny arms.' Mallory swings her legs out of bed, resigned to her fate. 'Charlie wait.'

'It'll be okay. Those bitches, Sal and Deidre are on shift tonight, and they always go to sleep as soon as lights-out.'

'But what about the cyclone?'

'It's still far away. We have a few hours before it gets here. This is only the vanguard,' Charlotte says more hopeful than certain.

'But it's nearly muster.'

'We'll be back before muster. Mal I have to go.' She retrieves her boots from next to the bed.

Malory sighs. 'Wait up then.'

Charlotte suddenly feels uncertain. 'No I'll go alone. If we both get caught, we're in for it.'

'Too bad I'm coming, so just wait a sec while I put on my clothes.'

'Wear your boots then.'

33.

Blake crouches on the floor beside his bed, woken by his own shouting. He's in his bedroom at the Fuller's home. The echo reverberates in his head, and it takes a moment to realise where he is. As he sits on the edge of the bed. The dream's imagery still clings to the dark edges of his mind.

He puts his head in his hands. This was not the usual dream. Not the frantic crawling through irrigation ditches. Not the one of him powerless to stop Richard sinking beneath the sucking mud. It didn't have the fruitless, arm wrenching panic as Richard's wrists slip from his grasp. It didn't have the guilt of seeing the scummy water choke off his gurgling scream.

In this dream, he runs silent and crouched through the warren of mud-brick prison buildings, ducking through stone arches into dim corridors. A piece of sharpened steel, that was once a spoon, is strapped to his arm, but he won't use it unless he must.

He knows the positions of each guard, and their habit of sleeping on watch. Tonight he made sure their slumber would be deep with the amount of morphine he emptied into their nightcap of sweet cardamom tea. The crack of each spine is loud in the dark as he feels the final give and slump and lowers the body to the floor before finding the next guard

Tonight is perfect for an escape. All the soldiers from the barracks near the prison are engaged in battle, and only a skeleton crew of prison guards remains. He can hear the fight coming closer, and he knows its American firepower. No one has firepower like the Americans.

He's seen their stupefying barrage of bombs and heavy artillery before when they took back Basra. This run is to the southwest, but it can't be helped. Maybe it's taking out Dora power station and oil refinery. He must change his plans and take the road east of the Tigress via Amarah. It'll take longer, perhaps an hour or two above the six he anticipates, but better that than run into a raging battle.

The prison camp is in darkness, blacked out against the bombing raid. Most of the guards are asleep at their post so it's easy to sneak up on them. It was hard to kill Mohamed Abdullah Al-Jishi. He had become a friend; if you can call your gaoler a friend. But his death was necessary, wasn't it? This is war. Abdullah would never let them go even if he allowed Blake freedoms from confinement in the cesspit they call cells.

At the gatehouse, he kills another guard who slumps over a desk, snoring loud enough to be heard outside the building. Then he lifts the boom in case someone comes. It's unlikely, but better they're suspicious about useless guards sleeping than they come into the guardhouse to find a dead body.

The guard outside the cellblock has the keys, but when Blake rounds the corner, the man is not there. He pauses, his back glued to the mud-brick wall as he tries to reassess his position. There's a noise, and he peers around the corner as a door at the far end of the building opens.

The corridor is cloistered, open to the parade ground on his right, with an alcove at each end. In the alcove at Blake's end is what passes for a kitchen area, stinking of fermenting beans, rotting food, rancid fat and fireplace soot, all of which will make up tomorrow's soup.

At the far end, a door leads to a stark, fly infested ablutions room, its single shower and bucket toilet festering from overuse and neglect. A dozen narrow cells line the left of the corridor, in front of which is positioned a guard's green metal chair.

Outside Blake and Liam's cell is a stretcher which rests against the wall. It's the one he uses to treat the injured and sick that are brought to him from the sick bay across the compound. For the worst cases he can go to the clinic, but mostly they wheel the patients across in the morning and evening. It's just one of the irrational decisions made by the commandant who needs Blake's medical skills. But it is important to remind Blake he is still a prisoner who is a reluctant deal away from death.

A door opens and a dim light spills out, illuminating the guard adjusting his uniform. The bloke couldn't have drunk the tea or he wouldn't be standing. He shuts the door and walks along the corridor.

Blake presses himself against the wall, trying to work out an alternative plan, but nothing comes. The guard is coming closer. He passes the stretcher, pushing it to one side. Then a chair scrapes against the concrete and something clatters to the floor. Blake risks a quick look around the corner in time to see the man bending to retrieve his AK 47, which he props against a pillar. He lowers himself to the chair and folds his arms, staring out into the darkness of the parade ground.

Blake runs on the balls of his feet as the guard settles his bulk on the chair. Although he's unbalanced, the man is an ox and struggles. The chair clatters over, but Blake is quick, and experienced as he takes the man in a blood choke, compressing the carotid and jugular in the crook of his arm, constricting the guard's airway, and denying blood and oxygen to the brain. The guard loses consciousness without a sound. Blake releases his hold while he uses his steel spoon to open the jugular.

He calls to Liam who waits behind the cell door. It's unlocked but Blake said for him to wait until Blake had taken out the guards. Now Liam takes the keys from the man's belt and begins to unlock the other cell doors, freeing their fellow prisoners.

Blake lowers the dying man to the ground. Blood pools on the concrete and Blake rescues the rifle. He points to the alcove and Liam leads the emaciated men into its shadows where they wait. Then he returns to help, and while Blake drags the dead guard to the cell, Liam closes all the gaping cell doors and runs back to join the men.

Blake drops the body and turns to leave the cell just as headlights brush the compound walls. A truck pulls into the bare dirt parade ground outside the cellblock. Two soldiers leap from the tailgate, calling out for the doctor to help with the wounded. The soldiers don't see the men hiding in the alcove.

Blake opens the cell door and shouts to the soldiers, calling out to some unknown person for medicine and bandages. He slips the AK under the plastic coated mattress of the stretcher and pushes it towards them.

As he nears the truck, he pulls out the rifle and fires from his hip. The bullets rake from rear to cab as he takes out the two men and the driver. He crouches, waiting for retaliation, and prays these are the only able-bodied soldiers.

The only sound is the distant bombing raid, and wounded men groaning in the back of the truck. When nothing happens, he peers into the dark recess under the canopy. It's difficult to see in the gloom, but he counts nine bodies lying on the floor of the truck. Beneath them is a shiny black substance, and he knows at least one person has bled out, possibly more.

In Arabic he tells them to wait while people come to help, and runs back to the alcove where the freed prisoners crouch.

'The truck's full of wounded we'll have to unload them. Come on, hurry.'

Jason Willard is first at the truck and grabs one of the rifles from a dead soldier before peering past Blake into the truck. 'Fuck,' he says, 'they look just about dead.'

Liam picks up the other rifle and joins him. 'There's no time, we'll take them with us.'

Blake opens his mouth to argue, the men are wounded and need treatment. If they take them they'll die, but in the end he says nothing. He's a doctor, and he doesn't help, doesn't even object. It weighs on his conscience, but they'll have to wait until they reach Basra, then he'll try to help any who survive. His first duty is to his mates.

Noah hauls the dead driver out the cab, and Blake goes to help. He's aware of the irony of worrying about saving the wounded when he's just killed eight other men. His original deal with his prison commandant was a life for a life. He saved a life of one of their soldiers, for a life of one of the prisoners.

Now he's done the opposite, saved eleven prisoners and himself. Perversely, it means twelve Caliphate soldiers must die. He's just killed eight, so four of the nine wounded in the back of the truck must die for him and his mates to live. No, he can't think like that. He'll go mad. He shakes his head to drive out the craziness.

The route from Baghdad is etched in his mind from studying it for months, but they can't go as planned because of the unexpected bombing raid. Mentally he reviews his new direction, certain he can do it. His luck just needs to hold for a few more hours. The truck bursts from the compound, its wheels spinning in gravel as Blake wrenches the steering wheel to the left, turning onto the main road.

That's when the dream took a wrong turn. Instead of the normal flight down dark roads with the electrical storm of detonations above, percussion waves battering his eardrums and making the road tremble, he finds himself alone on the red plains of the Kimberly. The stench of Baghdad sewers is still strong in his nostrils as hot, thirsty, and lost, he runs across an open expanse of red dirt. Bombs rain from the sky, turning the ground from horizon to horizon into an inferno.

He races for cover to a rocky outcrop, in what he thinks is the Cockburn Range, but it's a mirage. Instead, he finds he stands exposed in a featureless wilderness. The beating whump of an attack helicopter moves towards him, its cannon pointing at his chest, and he knows he will die. In despair, he gazes around the vast wasteland. As the gunship opens fire, he lifts his face to the heavens and shouts Charlotte's name.

The grey Monday morning light skulks at the bedroom window, and he drops his hands from his face, feeling his body slick with sweat from the dream. He must do something practical to push the lingering images away, so he goes through to the bathroom and runs the shower. As he stands with his head under the cascading water, he wonders if Charlotte has received his letter.

It's a rare bit of luck in all this disaster that Jason Willard's brother is in the same camp as Charlotte. Not that Blake could say much in the letter. He was too concerned it might fall into the wrong hands so he kept it cryptic. He's sure Charlotte will understand.

It was also a lucky break that Emmy remembered that bit about the law being unconstitutional. Two lucky breaks in the space of weeks, but he won't rely on luck. He's made contingency plans, moving most of his money offshore to Switzerland where the Australian Government can't touch it. If he and Charlotte have to bolt, they'll have somewhere to go although he doesn't know if Charlotte will go with him. It will mean leaving her parents and who knows what will happen to them if she escapes.

Silvia and Liam will help he's certain, but while he's making plans for the worst-case scenario, he doesn't want that. Instead, he wants to get Australia back the way it was. He just doesn't know how or what he can do, but if he's not here, he won't ever be able to influence anything.

The next thing he needs to do is borrow the Fuller's boat and get it up to Darwin. That's tricky too. What reason does he have to get a permit? The camp is not far from the Ord River so if he gets to its mouth, he'll find and rescue her if all else fails and she's convicted. So long as they take her back to that training camp after the trial and not somewhere else.

He towels himself dry and walks back to the bedroom to get dressed. His phone rings and he looks at his watch. It's early.

'Lincoln here.'

'Hey boss. I need to see you. Can I come over, it's not something to discuss on the phone...'

'Evan?'

'Yeah, sorry to ring so early.'

'Do you want me to come to you?'

'No I'm not at home, it's a long story. I'll catch the six-thirty ferry and be there in an hour.'

'Okay.'

Blake terminates the call. He must have found something good. For an economist he made a good lawyer, or hacker or spy. He's a talented man, Blake smiles wryly, for an assistant.

34.

Blake is drinking coffee on the terrace with Rory when Evan arrives. Despite his increased wealth since working for the company, he still doesn't look much better dressed or any fatter than when Blake first met him. The only difference seems to be his new boots, and his improved colour now he can spend time in the sunlight.

'Morning boss and boss,' Evan says.

Rory looks up waiting for Evan to speak, but Blake leans over and pours another cup of coffee pushing it toward Evan. 'Sit and tell us what you have.'

Evan sits down and picks up the cup. Rory fidgets but Blake knows Evan is trying to marshal his thoughts into a coherent sequence and waits, sipping his own coffee and gazing out over the city's shimmering heat haze.

'I found shitloads. Ah excuse me.' He glances at Rory. 'I mean I cracked into Jenna Martin's home computer.'

'I thought you were researching constitutional flaws for the case.' Rory's voice rises in indignation.

Blake holds up his hand. 'Hang on Rory this sounds important. Go on Evan.'

'Well, I guessed her password. It's not hard to see what she's interested in, and I just thought I would have a go. She wants to be First Lady.'

'Yeah never mind the passwords, what did you find?' Blake leans forward.

'Well I don't know how well you know your history, but some governments way back tried to stop people fleeing their countries because of war or famine or persecution or whatever. The refugees arrived here in droves.'

Rory interrupts. 'Get to the point Evan.'

'Yeah okay sorry, well you have to understand the history to understand what I found.'

'Tell us,' Blake says, his eyes fixed on Evan.

'It was a big political issue at the time. Neither side of politics could win. The media coverage was relentless, but their focus was all on boat arrivals although more people came in by plane. That was before the anti-terror laws restricted what the media can and cannot report. Anyway the Government sent people, who arrived by boat, off to camps in other countries. They called them detention centres, but they were pretty grim places. As the Caliphate took hold in the Middle East, other Muslim countries refused to house fellow Muslims on behalf of Australia. Countries like PNG figured they would become a target of terrorism if they helped. Anyway, they sent them back to Australia, but we didn't want them. We were scared by then. Terrorism had reached our shores, and we were just too frightened. The government at the time fell because they couldn't keep them out, despite their promises. That was when Jenna came up with the idea. Find them before they make landfall and house them in secret camps in a remote part of Australia, but don't let the public know. Keep them in what she termed "villages" where they can go about normal daily life with their own kind, but don't let them into our towns and cities. The operational secrecy moved from Operation Sovereign Boarders to Operation Sovereign Shield. At first, it wasn't so

330

bad. The villages had their own churches, schools, health care, markets, and everything. They were practically self-sufficient, but confined to the internment camps.'

'Jesus you're kidding.' Rory breathed.

'But that's not the end, is it Evan?' Blake's focus is intense. What he suspected was almost right.

'No.'

'Fuck what else.' Rory stands. 'I'm not sure I want to hear anymore.'

'Go on Evan,' Blake says ignoring Rory.

Evan glances at Rory and continues, 'well, as the camps grew it became harder to hide the refugees. So, to protect the secret they moved whole communities out of the Cape, but it was expensive. Basically, anywhere north of Townsville is a restricted zone. And that cost the government so to recoup the money they used people in the camps as free labour to offset the costs of housing them.'

'Are you telling me we run slave camps?' Rory puts both hands on the top of his head, and turns away from Blake and Evan, staring out across the river. 'You know it's a breach of international law. Whoever authorised this will be prosecuted.' He's horrified by what he's hearing and doesn't want to believe it.

Evan hesitates then continues. 'They are manufacturing hubs, making Military hardware mostly, but a few years ago they got a case of TB. You know that new strain from PNG. Anyway, it's resistant to all the antibiotics or gene therapy and we haven't found any other way of combating it. Until Reliquum Pharmaceuticals began using a very experimental drug, which has pretty radical side effects. Basically, the drug switches off hormones and no one would volunteer to trial it. So they began using it on the people of the ICs by putting it in their drinking water supply. Now they trial all sorts of drugs on them. I think they are also involved in the manufacture and worldwide distribution of Meth salts. They use the camps to manufacture and experiment with medical interventions and drugs. It was Jenna's idea at first, but Marabaux brought in the drug trials.'

'Christ Blake, the company buys drugs from Reliquum. We have to warn Dad.'

'Hang on we need to think this through.' Blake says. 'It has far-reaching consequences, and if they get wind of what we know, we're dead for sure. I think we should talk to Lachlan and Mr Fuller, but otherwise keep it under wraps until we work out tactics. Evan, it might be a good idea to keep Flynn in the dark for a while.'

Evan nods. 'That's not all I found. I think the Constitution's been altered—secret-like.'

Rory looks at him in disbelief. 'You're kidding!'

Evan presses his lips together and shakes his head.

'What did you find mate?' Blake asks.

'At first I wasn't sure. There were these cryptic emails between Ms Martin and Sir Newel Bramly.'

'The Chief Justice. Bullshit! I don't believe it.' Rory paces back and forth at the edge of the swimming pool.

Evan glances at him and looks back at Blake. 'I checked the Australian Archives, and found traces in the structural metadata that mean the original Constitution might have been replaced, but I can't be sure. The person who did it was either a tech expert or an insider. I thought we'd have to look at the original document, but even then if it were an insider, how would we know. Then I had an idea and trolled through Ms Martin's computer. That's when I found the original text, and the amended version. The changed copy is in all the legal libraries and on-line. The changes aren't much, just the odd word here and there, but they alter the meaning and context in places. I guess that's why Jeremy knew the laws they are holding Charlie under aren't legal, but it doesn't answer why no one else has spotted it.'

Rory throws himself down on his chair. 'They convicted Castile under the same law. If it's true Evan, you've uncovered explosive stuff.'

'What's explosive stuff?' Emmy walks across the terrace towards them. She sits down and holds out her phone. 'That bitch sent me a photo. Jeremy's cheating on her as well.' She grins, showing Rory the photo of a woman staring vacantly out a car window. Jeremy is in the driver's seat in the background. Emmy says, 'it couldn't happen to a nicer person.'

Rory takes the phone, and after a glance, passes it to Blake.

Emmy says, 'why she sent it to me I have no idea, but if she thinks she can wriggle her way back into my affections by showing that the two-timing bastard has done the same thing to her as she did to me, she's nuts.'

'She looks drugged up to the hilt as if she's hardly aware of where she is,' Blake says examining the photo.

Evan leans over to see what Blake's looking at, and sucks in his breath. 'Christ her face was all over the news this morning.'

'What?' Emmy says leaning forward in her chair. Blake and Rory both turn their gaze on Evan.

'Sorry... I could be wrong... but it looks just like the murdered woman they found this morning, dumped under Story Bridge. It looks like her although in the paper her face was a bit battered so I can't be certain. They found her covered in gold wrapping paper. It's the same mode of killing as the other women, although the cops are denying a serial killer is on the loose.'

'When was the photo taken Em?' Blake asks.

'I don't know.' Her forehead creases with concern.

Blake takes the phone again and looks at the time recorded on the photo. 'Just after midnight.'

Rory says, 'Jeremy must have been the last person to see her alive.'

'Or he killed her,' Evan says.

'This is getting out of control. I'm calling Dad and Lachlan to get here now. We need to talk.'

'Hang on Rory. We must tread carefully. I know it's bad, but I will not do anything hastily. I won't jeopardise Charlotte's safety for anything. First, we make sure she's out of harm's way.

If these bastards get a whiff of what we know, not one of us is safe.'

'Blake.' Mrs Clarke comes out of the house, her hand shading her eyes against the bright sunlight.

Blake turns. 'Yes Mrs Clarke.'

'There's a Jason Willard on the phone. He wants to talk to you on the e-cript.'

'Thanks.' Blake stands. 'Wait until I get back okay Rory. Don't do anything until then and don't say anything. We don't know if our conversations are tapped. Cells aren't secure.'

'Okay, I'll just ask them to come over for a meeting about the court case.'

Blake goes inside to Mr Fuller's study and picks up the phone. 'Jason?'

'Yes, Blake. Um, I have bad news. My brother phoned.' He pauses.

Blake waits, his breath held. 'What? Jason speak man.'

'Charlotte's missing. There was a cyclone and somehow she disappeared.'

Blake slumps in the chair at Mr Fuller's desk. 'Disappeared? How? Where? Are you sure?'

'Yes mate. Look my brother's one of the best trackers in the business, and he's looking for them now. He volunteered to lead the search and rescue team.'

'But what trace of her will there be after a cyclone. The wind and rain will have obliterated it. Jesus, how come no one mentioned this on the news? We knew there was a cyclone, but the place should withstand that easily, shouldn't it? It did when I was there.'

'Don't know. Jason rang as soon as he could to ask me to let you know. It seems that she and her friend were outside when it hit.'

'How long has she been missing.'

'Two days.'

'I have to get up there.'

'I'm coming with you. What do you want me to do?'

'Get me into the restricted zone.'

'No problems. How soon can you get up to Broome?'

'I'll ring you back.' Blake hangs up and sits back in the chair staring out the window to the street beyond, trying to control a surge of frustrated fury at his helplessness.

He strides resolutely back onto the terrace, interrupting Rory. 'Okay Evan, gather all the documented detail you can find on the internment camps in the Cape and get it ready for distribution. You said Flynn knows people?'

'Yes boss he knows people, but not the kind who can be called pillars of society.'

'Does he know how we can contact the pirate stations?'

'I can ask.'

'Just collect the evidence and get it into every pirate station and every street paper, even if you have to start your own. Then email it to the British and American papers. Make sure it's copied to Liam and Stella Marais so their papers know we're serious. Set up a social media site and copy the material onto it. Disseminate it far and wide; pay to have it distributed. Rory will arrange the money side. Make sure you make it clear that the Australian Government is breaking international law on refugees. Publish something on the constitutional legality of the law they are holding Charlotte under. Make up the details if you have to, but don't use Charlotte's name. I want to galvanise as much outrage and action as I can. Emmy can you let Evan have the photo of the murdered woman. Maybe you can help Evan to write up the story.'

'Finally. I can nail the two-timing prick. What irony—my journalism training he despised so much will be what brings the bastard to his knees. He said journalism is unladylike, and I will show him how much. Whatever did I see in the man?' She pauses and peers into Blake's face. 'What's happened Blake. What have you heard?'

Blake interrupts. 'Rory did you ring Lachlan and your Dad?'

'Yes I did, they are on their way, but what's going on Blake. One minute you tell me to wait, then you're all over it—getting all the information out there like there's no tomorrow. What's up mate?'

'Charlotte's missing, lost in the cyclone.'

'Shit.'

'Rory you have to get the charge changed or the trial date delayed. Get up to Darwin. If the others are convicted of the charge of conspiracy to pervert the natural progress of law and order then she's done for, even if she's missing and can't attend court.'

Evan says, 'holy shit, that's bad man.'

Rory sees the worry etched in his friends face, and he's at a loss to know what to do. 'Okay. I'll talk to Lachlan and we'll go up there as soon as we can get a flight.'

'No, charter a plane and do it now.'

In a flash of intuition, Emmy knows what Blake needs to do. She walks over to him, sliding her hand in his and says, 'Charlotte will be all right Blake. You leave this to us. Find her and we'll bring these bastards down while you're gone, don't worry.'

'Thanks Em. Tell your Dad to go to the Governor-General with the information before it goes public. He's the only one who can get rid of the government outside an election.' She nods and watches him walk back into the house.

The next afternoon, Blake leaves the charter plane and crosses the tarmac to the Derby airport arrivals building. Heat shimmers in waves and the sun pounds on his head. His eyes screw up against the sunlight as he sees a shadowed figure, his arm raised, standing at the entrance.

'Noah. I wasn't expecting you.'

'G'day Blake.' Grinning Noah says, 'you don't think we're going to let you do this alone, do you? Just wait mate, you're in for a treat. Jason's sorting things out on the boat so he sent me to fetch you.' He looks at Blake's bag. 'Is that all the luggage you have? You travel light—where's your hardware?'

Blake shakes his head. 'I'm through with that shit.'

Noah laughs, 'well you'll need to reacquaint yourself. Come on, vehicle's this way.'

They drive north-west out of the airport. Blake gazes out the window at what appears to be sheets of white paper caught on the top of fencing, but as they approach hundreds of cockatoos take off, their voices raucous and complaining.

Noah turns onto what looks like a main road heading north and points out the window. 'Up here is an old Boab tree that used to house prisoners, but I guess you're not into sightseeing just at the moment.'

'Another time, Jesus is that mud?' Blake takes in the vast expanse of mud flat surrounding the peninsula on which Derby sits.

'Yep the King's Sound, but the tide's out. The Fitzroy River empties here. Good fishing at the right time.' They drive on until they reach the town and drive through to the wharf.

'Do you need to stop for anything?' Noah glances at Blake.

Blake shakes his head, his gaze fixed ahead taking in the wide hot streets and arid sky, its washed out blue dome immense overhead. As they drive out of the town, he notices innocent cloud suds on the horizon as if this part of the world could never allow raging cyclonic anger to sully its sultry calm. A surge of emotion chokes him, and he buries his fear, focusing instead on what Noah is saying.

They pull up at the jetty where two trawlers are moored. A third trawler sits out to sea. To Blake they are just fishing trawlers, but as he boards he sees signs they are more than what he thought at first glance.

Jason greets him, a cloth in hand wiping away grease. He looks at his hands and says, 'I won't shake. I'll cover you with engine oil. This here's my Dad. Nate to his mates, and my Uncle Kurt. Dad, Kurt, Blake Lincoln—the reason I'm standing here.'

Nate walks up to stand in front of Blake, hands on hips, legs spread against the slight swell of deck movement on the rising tide. 'I am not one for words son, but what you did, well... anything we can do for you, name it and it's yours.'

Kurt shakes Blake's hand, but says nothing, looking embarrassed at all the unspoken emotion.

Jason grins at his uncle's discomfort. 'The rest of the crew are due back from town any minute and we'll be underway before sundown. There's two blokes I'd like you to meet. They're forward sorting out their berths. Come on, I'll show you around, and you can put down your bag.'

In the cabin, two men sit on bunks cleaning assault weapons, M4A5s Blake notes.

Jason holds out his hand. 'Volunteers to the cause. Mike and Steve have taken leave to help us. Both are veterans of the war and part of Noah's squad and mine. We go way back, and you can trust them with your life. They've been out fishing with us before so they know the drill.'

Steve gets up and shakes Blake's hand. 'If we don't fight for our mates what do we have?'

Mike nods. 'Blake,' is all he says, concentrating on his weapon.

Blake worries. This is turning into something more than he anticipated.

Jason says, 'we'll talk later once we're under way. As far as anyone knows, we're just on a regular fishing trip. Dad often has crew volunteering for a spot of Barra fishing.' He sees the concern in Blake's eyes, and flicks a glance at the weapons. 'Pirates, sometimes we run into Pirates. We have our own armoury on board, but the boys like their own gear, and with the civilian gun laws, they don't get much practice time. Out here no one looks and no one cares.'

Relieved that they are not about to begin a war Blake relaxes. 'So what's the plan?'

Jason says, 'we'll keep up the pretence of fishing until we're out of sight, then it's full ahead to our rendezvous.' He sees Blake's puzzled expression and says, 'I'll explain the details later, but come with me.'

Jason shows Blake around the high tech bridge and explains, 'we'll call my brother Pete, at 19:00 hours so he can make sure he's out of eaves dropping range. He usually goes to the top of a rock for a signal. Says he can't trust the people with him because they're prison officers not soldiers. When he finds Charlotte and her friend, he'll tell them to go to the Pentecost River Crossing where we'll be heading. After the rain Zillie dumped, the rivers will be high. We'll leave the trawlers at the mouth fishing and take the dinghy up the Pentecost. With any luck, by the time we get there, the girls will be waiting. Then it'll be just a question of us getting them on board and smuggling them out of the joint. Pete will try to convince the guards the escapees are dead so they'll stop looking.'

'Sounds like you've thought of everything, so long as we find her.'

'If she can be found Pete will find her, don't worry Blake. I've never seen him fail to track something to ground. Can't sail... chunders at every wave, but across country no one can beat him. Learned it from an old Aborigine who worked for Dad when we were kids. He was a natural.'

'How long will it take to get there?'

'We should be at the Crossing Thursday, Friday at the latest. Can't do it faster sorry, but it's the only way in. Dad has a permit to fish those waters, otherwise the whole area is off limits, and they monitor air traffic.'

'I'm grateful. It's a way in, and three days is better than never. She can survive out there for a few days, so long as she's not hurt or doesn't do something stupid. After a cyclone there'll be plenty of water and Charlotte's sensible.'

An image comes to Blake's mind of her running after him as he walked to the ferry. Christ, she was so unfit, she choked running a few hundred meters. How the hell will she survive, but he keeps the thoughts to himself. After all, the training camp is no picnic although when he was there, there were no women. It might have changed, but he can't imagine it will have changed much.

As the sun drops to the horizon, Blake sits with the four soldiers around the mess table in the forward cabin; a map spread out on the table.

Jason says, 'okay, here's what we know. Your girl, and her mate Esmeralda Mallory, got out of the prison camp through a downed fence. At first the guards thought they were caught out in the storm, but Pete doesn't think that happened although he's keeping stum over it.'

'What does he think happened?' Every nerve in Blake's body is stretched to snapping point.

Jason glances at Blake feeling sorry for the poor bastard. If this happened to his wife, he doesn't know what he'd do. 'Pete thinks it was planned.'

Blake shakes his head, 'planned?'

Jason holds up his hand. 'Let me tell it okay, you can ask questions later.' Blake nods and Jason says, 'right, it seems they found the armoury was broken into and a sniper rifle missing.'

'Jesus.' Steve breathes out.

Jason grins. 'I don't think she's going to waste anyone. It's the one she usually uses. Apparently, your girl is a crack shot.'

A pulse of pride mixed with disbelief runs through Blake, but he suppresses it to focus. 'Keep going.'

'Okay, well Pete had a snoop around and found evidence they hid out the storm in the gate house ceiling.' He's grinning with admiration for the women. 'While everyone was running around like Looney tunes, they were up there keeping quiet until the furore died down.'

'It must have been hot as Hades in that roof space,' Mike says.

'Yeah maybe. It bucketed down for three days after the cyclone so it wouldn't have been too bad. Anyway, after the storm passed, they vacated the place while the barracks was asleep. The guards didn't hear or see anything although Pete reckons the dipsticks were probably asleep. Who are they guarding against in that wilderness, right? Anyway, Pete said nothing just waited his moment, and then when there was no trace of them he offered to lead a small recce of Prison Guards out to see if they could find the bodies. He told the brass he didn't think it likely they were still alive because dingos, pigs, or salties, if they were near a river, would be the first on the scene, but he said it was worth a try. Yesterday he found their trail although he has told no one. It was difficult at first because when they ran, it was still raining. Once he found their trail, he said it was easy to follow them. They didn't cover their tracks although when they moved into rocky country it was trickier. They seem fine. They were running for nearly an hour, heading North-West before they slowed, so it seems they made good time, getting away from base before dawn broke. He'll probably have more news for us when we ring today.'

Blake's stunned. Running for an hour! Are we talking about the same woman. Aloud he says, 'why North West, what's up there? They are not heading for Wyndham surely.'

In Brisbane later that same night, after the dinner dishes are cleared, and the brandy decanter is passed around, Lachlan Bowery looks around the white damask covered dining room table at the family who a few weeks ago he knew only by casual acquaintance.

Soft lamp light casts a rosy glow across Emmy's face as she tipples a centimetre of brandy into her glass. She passes the decanter to Rory and looks across the table to catch him staring. He looks away, his breathing faltering, as he leans forward to take a sip of his drink, glad of Mrs Fuller's clackity departure to the kitchen.

He clears his throat and replies to Rory. 'I don't think we should try to delay the trial. The stuff Evan uncovered about the unauthorised wording of the Constitution is gold.'

Mr Fuller nods, tugging at his lip in concentrated concern. 'It beggars belief this can happen in Australia, but I guess that's why they got away with it for so long. No one expects corruption here.'

Rory re-corks the decanter with a small thwack of his palm. 'Thank goodness for Evan's hacking ability or we still wouldn't know. I am not sure how he does it, but Blake seems to inspire loyalty and genius from everyone around him.'

'Including you,' Emmy's eyes sparkle in the lamp light. She feels wonderful in her new dress. She knows Lachlan thinks so too, just by the way he keeps looking at her.

William looks unconvinced. 'Surely lawyers would check the original constitutional document if they were looking for something like this.'

'I'm not sure about constitution lawyers Mr Fuller,' Lachlan glances at Rory, 'but criminal lawyers are more concerned with criminal law. We assume the National Court has tested the law of the land prior to us using it. All we try to do, other than win our cases, is to try to create a legal precedent, if one is not already established.'

Rory says, 'if Evan hadn't trolled through Ms Martin's computer files we would never have found the forgery.'

William looks up from his musing, his face creased with worry, his lip red from tugging. He sighs and says, 'in hind sight none of its surprising, look who they have as Chief Justice. He is the PM's stooge. That's why they locked up Castile, to get him out the way. I blame myself for my complacency, but I have to stop this.'

'What are you thinking Dad?'

William glances at his daughter. 'I will do what Blake asked me to do and take this to Arthur. The Governor-General is the only one who can stop it, and he must act, but I'll need indisputable proof that the PM and Marabaux are involved in illegal activity, otherwise all he'll do is hand it over to the National Homeland Security Police.'

Emmy says, 'I know Blake said for you to take this to Uncle Arthur, but we should think through the order of events before we act.'

William ignores her. Slapping his hands against his knees he says, 'what documented evidence do we have Rory?'

Lachlan again clears his throat. 'I think we should hear what Emmy has to say.'

William looks surprised but says, 'of course. Sorry my dear I thought you had finished.'

Emmy's cheeks glow. 'It doesn't matter'.

Lachlan frowns. 'Yes it does. We need to consider all angles, and your views might alert us to any possible risk.'

He speaks with more force than intended and glances at William. 'Excuse me sir, but it won't take long to explore all angles, and Emmy's right. Let's take a minute to look at this.' He pauses, his brow clearing to smile at her. 'What were you going to say Emmy?'

Her gaze drops as she twists her fingers, feeling the tip of her nose glowing. She wants to cry with gratitude at the way he defends her, but she straightens her shoulders and clears her voice.

'Well if you take the evidence to Uncle Arthur, what happens to Charlotte in the meantime? I mean if you go to Canberra, you will alert Jeremy and his father you're on to them. Everyone knows how averse you are to the place Daddy. Just by going there, you will create a stir. Anyway, the court proceedings are underway, and if we are not careful, they'll ship Charlotte overseas before we can save her. But if you hang on while Evan collates the information, and I write up the articles we can do it in a coordinated way so they can't escape.'

She pauses, glancing at Lachlan who nods for her to continue. 'Flynn is talking to his contacts in the underground press, and when we have all the evidence we can run a simultaneous publicity campaign, releasing the stuff to the press worldwide. That's when you should talk to Uncle Arthur. Then he will have to act and not hand it to the NHS Police. The whole thing should come together at the same moment.'

Lachlan nods. 'Yes, and there will be no possibility of cover up or interference from Marabaux in the investigation. In the meantime, the Governor-General can appoint a new government while they investigate. Brilliant, well done Emmy.'

She smiles, self-conscious at his overt support for her. She peeks from beneath lowered lashes and says, 'but first you have to save Charlotte or its all for nothing, at least as far as Blake is concerned.'

He holds her gaze and says, 'if we can show the law is constitutionally invalid, we can save not only Charlotte, but all the other poor bastards convicted under it, many over there, or on their way.'

Mrs Fuller comes back into the room. 'If you stop conscription through this, what will happen to the soldiers fighting over there. We can't leave them shorthanded.'

'Hm,' William says. 'That's not our concern at this point. That's for the Chief of Defence to decide. I imagine he'll be relieved. Volunteers are always a more committed and skilled force, and they are in the majority. Besides, we won't have to worry about the increasing numbers of deserters.'

Lachlan stands. 'Perhaps a new government could change our commitment to involving us in foreign wars. In the interim, I need to go home and pack. The flight for Darwin leaves in the morning. Thank you for dinner Mrs Fuller, Mr Fuller.' He glances at Emmy. 'Thank you again Emmy for all your insights.'

She blushes and looks at her lap.

William looks at her and then at Lachlan and it dawns on him that something is brewing, but he says nothing. He's glad Emmy's no longer hurting over Jeremy's betrayal. Then he remembers something else. 'Hang on, what about Jeremy and his involvement with the murdered woman. What are we doing about that?'

Rory rises with the others. 'I reckon we tie it all into our campaign. If we accuse him now they will just cover it up. We need to do it when they have lost authority over both the NHS police, and the contracted police force. Dad, can I leave you to coordinate stuff with Evan and Flynn while we are in Darwin?'

'I'll do it,' Emmy says, expecting Rory and William to ignore her.

To her surprise her father says, 'that's a much better idea. Em seems on top of what's going on, better than I, so I'll leave it to her. We'll call you son, if anything happens while you are gone.'

Emmy pushes back her chair and stands. 'Dad can I use your study? I want to use the e-cript to call Evan so we can start work.'

35.

In the Cockburn Range in far north-west Australia, Charlotte lies on her stomach. The rock is warm against her denim-clad belly. She adjusts the sights on the Blaser tactical 338, holding the rifle steady on its bipod.

The familiar feel and weight of the weapon reassures her as she takes a fix on the curious face of a rock wallaby 150 metres away. It sits on its haunches watching the two women in the distance, trying to gauge the danger. They are too far away, and the wind blows from its back.

'Do it Charlie. Don't think, just do it.'

Charlotte regulates her breathing, and concentrates on the biofeedback of her heart beat, pulsing in her throat. She slows it, ignoring the tiny persistent flies on her face, and steadies her hand. The next thud of her pulse beats, and she fires before it beats again. The wallaby's head shatters.

She's starving, but she hates killing the poor little thing. Her head droops. All they have eaten for days are two Boab nuts they found on the ground. Firing the rifle isn't a good idea, but Mallory has been whining at her for days.

She scrambles up from her position and picks up the rifle to walk back to the shade under a rocky overhang. Mallory bolts across the rocks to retrieve the dead wallaby. She promised that if Charlotte killed it, she would prepare and cook it.

Charlotte squats in the shade, raising her riflescope to scan the surrounding countryside. The sound of a rifle firing carries a long way in this wilderness. She's terrified they'll be caught although they are already on the other side of the range from the camp.

Shafting light from the late afternoon sun slants across the landscape, creating colours that make her wish she could paint. Pulsating reds, oranges, and greens of the ragged escarpment vie for attention under the sapphire sky. New grass sprouts across the plains, looking like a wash of emerald watercolour brushed across stony orange dirt.

She can't believe the savagery of the storm that passed through here only days ago. Its left devastation in its wake. Twisted, leafless and splintered trees dot the land. Water finds its way through what were dry gullies, turning them to raging torrents. But the air is clear, washed clean under a cloudless sky.

When she and Mallory went out to retrieve Blake's letter, the last thing on her mind was running away. Opportunity, and a rush of certainty in their action overtook her, as the tree keeled over in the wind, knocking the fence flat. She thought of her parent's farm, and all the cattle escaping.

They can't take any chances. If they head south to the lower end of the Cockburn Ranges and strike out east, they can follow the track that was once the Gibb River road. This will lead to the old Northern highway. If they follow the highway they'll find Kununurra. It's a long shot, but it's all she has.

Mallory argued to go directly east towards Kununurra, but she insisted on this route around the Eastern Cockburn Range. Logic told her that their gaolers would first look to the east. Her idea was to give them time to get away by heading north then backtracking south, before going east, but its cost so much time, she's not sure she was right.

The journey was terrible. Mallory complained all the way and the Cockburn Creek, in full flood, made the journey dangerous. Mal was probably right. No one is looking for them. They haven't seen another human for days. What does she know about these things, but anything is better than the camp—even tromping around lost in the Kimberly with only flies for company. She's not taking any chances they'll be found.

She pulls a tatty piece of paper from her jumpsuit and leans against a rock to reread Blake's letter. Flies seek out the moisture in her eyes and she waves her hand to stop them settling. The ink is blurred on the grubby page, but every word is engraved in her mind.

She smiles at his caution, realising he was trying not to implicate anyone if the letter fell into the wrong hands, but it makes reading difficult. Rory and some barrister are looking for legal means to get her out. He said he would be in Darwin for her trial.

Charlotte looks up, thinking she's grateful but pessimistic. She's guilty of breaking the law, even if the law is daft and unfair, it's still the law, and she broke it. They'll find them guilty regardless. They'll be shipped off to fight and die like the others who went before them. Unlike Blake, she won't survive.

She's not brave like he is, but if she can get back and see him just once more it'll be worth it. All she wants is to make it as far as Darwin to see him. After that she doesn't care what happens to her, but she has to make sure Mal is safe. She can't be caught.

Mallory suggested they steal a car in Kununurra. She said she knows how to start them without the bio print if they can find one unlocked.

'Screw it, I'll break the window for you if you can start the thing,' Charlotte said raising the rifle. She looks down at her filthy jumpsuit. They'll have to steal clothes.

A smudge of what looks like smoke rises in the distance, and Charlotte stiffens, and raises the scope to her eye. A vehicle heads towards them from the south, kicking up dust in its wake.

Shit where is Mallory? Charlotte leaps up and runs crouched towards the shelter of a rocky outcrop, making her way down the slope under cover.

She yells, 'Mal, get down,' but the wind whips her voice away. She scrambles over rocks, dodging, and weaving for cover, desperate to get Mallory out of sight without giving her own position away.

Mallory squats on the edge of a small steam that trickles down the side of the escarpment. She is oblivious to the danger and hums as she cleans the wallaby. Charlotte should have taken a different rifle with a smaller calibre round. Half the wallaby is lost, vaporised by the impact, and there was no sign of the poor creatures head.

She hums an old gospel tune from her Pentecostal childhood church, and mutters to herself. 'I wonder what old Pastor Dowmer would say if he saw me now?'

He always warned her that demons waited at her shoulder. She smiles, splashing water to wash away the blood as she pulls out the Wallaby's gut. Her stomach rumbles in anticipation and she's tempted to eat the bloody thing raw.

The matches they took from camp are laid out on a rock, almost dry in the sun. They should light. If not she'll rub sticks together. One way or another she will cook and eat this baby until her belly bursts.

Something cannons into her, and she falls forward, stretching out her arms to stop herself hitting her face. She loses her grip on the wallaby. It bumps and tumbles its way down stream. She fights Charlotte, who tries to keep her on the ground.

'What the fuck...You bitch?'

'Mal—the truck... they'll see you.'

'What frigging truck?' Mallory scrambles up and slides down the slope to pick up the bloody carcass. It dangles from her grip as she turns to look in the direction Charlie's pointing. Watery pink blood dribbles down her leg as her gaze sweeps the plains.

'Holy Jesus,' she says ducking down, 'do you think they saw me?'

'Don't know. I reckon we should gap it. Come on.'

'Wait, the matches.'

'Fuck the matches.' Charlotte is already running crouched over, dodging from rocky outcrop to rocky outcrop, moving uphill and away from the truck.

Mallory snatches up her knife and grabs the matches. She drops most of them in her haste. As she runs after Charlotte, the skinless carcass swings wildly, leaving an erratic abstract design of pink dots on the rocks.

In the truck driving along the road, Pete's keen eyes spot the movement on the lower edges of the escarpment. He glances across at his fellow travellers. Ida looks out the passenger window in the opposite direction. The men in the back are asleep. Smithy's chin rests on his chest, and Mason's head rolls against the back seat, his mouth open.

Pete clears his throat. 'I reckon we pull up over in that canyon.' He points to a spot that has an obscured line of sight to where he saw the movement. 'We'll set up camp. I'll scout around, but I don't think they would make it this far. I reckon they went east if they are alive at all. I reckon you got it wrong Ida.'

'With any luck, they're dead.' Ida glances at him. Her acne scars are livid in the harsh light. 'Still, as we are here we may as well do things properly. We'll set up camp and you go have a look-see. Come back immediately if you find anything. You can't track them and round them up on your own, so if you see anything, call me.'

Pete nods and says, 'okay Ida, but don't leave okay, no matter how long I take. I don't want to come back and find you bastards fucked off thinking I'm lost.'

'You need help?' Smithy puts his hand on the seat back behind Pete.

Ida says, 'fuck Smithy, you couldn't track down a beer at the bar. Anyway, you have work to do. Set up camp and make sure my bed's made the way I like it. Comprende?' She twists in her seat to look behind her. ' Mason you get tucker on.'

Mason opens his eyes and licks his lips. He looks bewildered as if he isn't quite sure where he is.

Pete feels sorry for them, particularly Smithy. Everyone knows what a bitch Ida is. 'I'll get along faster without you. Better if you do as Ida says.'

He turns off the road and bumps across country, into one of the rocky fiord like arms of the escarpment. They find a sheltered area that still has leaves on the trees and pull up. Once they are unpacked, Pete picks up two ration packs, two water bottles, his rifle, and Sat-Cell, pretending he hasn't seen the look of wistfulness in Smithy's face.

Thirty minutes later, he reaches the place where he saw the movement. The scattered matches, ragged skin and entrails piled on a rock, tells him all he needs to know. Scuff marks and a bloody trail, shows which way they went. The question is how far.

He's vigilant because he knows the women are desperate. They have a rifle and he doesn't want Charlotte plugging holes in his hide. He knows she'll hit her target, even if he's running. He's seen her in action before and he's seldom seen a more accurate marksman.

Pete stands and scans the escarpment slopes, trying to place himself in her position, to think like her. She's trying to gain height, but why, what's up there? Is she just running blindly or does she know something he doesn't know? Is it likely that they will come back to this spot to collect their matches?

A glint of light catches his eye and a quick scrutiny of a rocky outcrop four hundred metres away, tells him it's the most likely hiding place. If the trees still had leaves, he wouldn't have seen the reflection. If they run from there, they will be exposed on bare slope. So, they are not running.

They are hiding and watching, her rifle sights aimed at his chest, but he's sure she won't shoot unless she has no other alternative. From the little he knows about her he's surprised she shot the wallaby, but hunger and desperation make people do things they wouldn't do otherwise.

He bends down again and picks up the scattered matches. They'll need them. He piles them on a rock, then stands up and cups his hands around his mouth.

'Charlotte,' he shouts, but the wind whips the sound away. He sits down on a rock and pulls a notebook from his pocket. On the first page he draws a rudimentary map of the area, showing where his camp is, where she is hiding, and how it's located in relation to the Pentecost River Crossing, roughly twenty kilometres from where he sits.

On the following page, he writes, Charlotte, base thinks you're dead. I won't disillusion them, but Blake's on his way to the Pentecost River Crossing with my brother, Jason. Make your way to the Crossing marked on the map as quickly as possible. I reckon you have two days max before they arrive and twenty kays to cover as the crow flies. It's rough terrain and you aren't a crow. I'll leave a water bottle and ration packs. It's not much for two people but it's all I can take without arousing suspicion. I'll camp overnight on the spot marked on the map then head on towards the Crossing tomorrow before heading back to base. We should pass back along this track by late morning. Keep out of sight. Please destroy this note.

The two women crouch behind rocks. Leafless trees, struggling to survive in the thin soil, dot the landscape between them and the soldier. Mallory waves her hand back and forward over the skinned wallaby to keep the flies at bay. She whispers, 'what's he doing Charlie?'

'Hang on Mal, I don't know. It's weird, but he's writing in a book. It's definitely Pete. I reckon he saw us from the truck and is tracking us. Shit, I thought he was on my side.'

'No one's on our side. You can't trust any of the bastards. Let me have a go. I want to see what he's doing.'

Charlotte hands the rifle to Mallory and says, 'don't shoot him Mal.'

Mallory gives her a withering look and puts down the wallaby. She takes the rifle, lowering her head to squint through the scope.

Pete takes out the ration packs, spare water bottle, and his compass. He'll say he lost them, fake an incident somehow, but he'll worry about that later. He piles the articles on the rock along with the matches, hoping she will come back to this spot. Then he tears the pages from the notebook, and wedges them between the ration packs and stands up, lifting his rifle and pack. It's all he can do. Now it's up to her and Blake.

'He's standing up.'

'I can see that,' Charlotte says.

'It looks like he's leaving, and he's left a pile of stuff on the rock," Mallory says.

Pete raises his hand to where he thinks they are hiding and waves, then turns and makes his way back to his camp.

'Christ, he's waving.'

'Let me see.' Charlotte squints, but he's too far.

'He's going back the way he came.'

'Let me see. Mal, give me my bloody weapon back.'

Later that night, Pete leaves camp again telling the prison officers he will find a satellite signal to report to base. He makes his way up the escarpment until he finds a suitable place that overlooks the camp. Below the two corrections officers sit by the fire, but he can't see Ida. She might be in the tent. He scouts for a convenient place to wait for his brother's call while he keeps an eye on camp.

The rock he leans against is still warm and he relaxes. It's peaceful up here, the breeze cooler now the blistering sun is gone. Its dying glow on the horizon streaks red and yellow fingers across the fading green sky. Jason, his Dad, and Uncle Kurt will be nearing Cape Talbot, about two thirds of the way. His SatCell buzzes in his pocket and he takes it out. 'Bro,' he says.

Jason is on the bridge. Blake hovers nearby watching. 'Hey Pete, what news?'

'Found them. They are resourceful, but scared as rabbits, not that I blame them. I couldn't get anywhere near, at least not without risking one or two holes in my hide. I left a note with instructions as well as food and water. They should be at the

Crossing tomorrow. If not I'll text you their last known coordinates, and you can search for them. I have prison officers with me so I can't do more.'

'Okay Bro. It's good news they are okay anyway. We should be in position in about thirty odd hours.'

'I'll talk to you again tomorrow night, same time.' Pete hangs up as a rock rattles down the hillside. He stiffens. 'Anyone there?' Shadows leap and shimmer, but Pete knows the tricks darkness can play on human eyes. He steps lightly to where the sound originated. There is nothing but gloom. A wallaby crashes away and with relief he turns away to phone base.

On the trawler, Jason puts his own SatCell into his pocket, and grins at Blake. The poor bloke looks grey with worry. 'She's fine mate. We'll meet them at the Crossing. Pete's left them directions and food.'

The air leaves Blake's chest in a rush. 'Did he speak with her?'

'No. Apparently, she's a bit on the scary side. He left them a note.'

'Christ.' Blake rubs his hand over his head. He feels like he doesn't know Charlotte at all. Scary is not something he associates with the woman he left at the railway platform.

An image fills his mind of her jumping up and down, waving as the train pulled out from the station taking him to Canberra. Her long golden hair blew about in the wind, tears ran unchecked down her face, but she ignored the curious looks of others, keeping her gaze fixed on him. He turns away so Jason doesn't see his face.

High on the escarpment behind a rocky ledge, Charlotte looks with distaste at the charred wallaby leg Mallory hands her. 'Why can't I eat a ration pack?'

'No I told you we need to hang on to them in case. It's the only food we have.'

'But Blake will find us before then.'

'You can't trust that man Charlie.'

'Who Blake? I'd trust him with my life.'

'No, Willard.'

'Pete? But he left us the food and water and the note... how can we not trust him?'

'It might be a trap.'

'Ha! Esmeralda Mallory you are so bloody suspicious. It's not a trap. Pete told me before, he will do anything to help me because Blake saved his brother. He owes him.'

'Yes but he's still a soldier and under orders. He won't stick his neck out for you Charlotte. Not even for Blake. No one ever does.'

'You would.'

'Huh, don't kid yourself.'

'You would though. I reckon I know you Mal, but I would for you too okay.'

'Eat and stop talking crap. I still reckon this rendezvous point at the Crossing might be a trap. What's he going there for tomorrow if it's not?'

'I don't know.' Charlotte feels deflated. She was so sure that Blake was coming to rescue her.

'Yeah well he will probably set it up so when we get there he'll just have to give a signal and whoosca, we're back inside. I'm not taking the chance.'

Charlotte tears a small piece of meat off the wallaby leg and chews. It's like chewing a boot, but she says nothing to Mallory. 'You know Mal. It makes little sense. Why set such an elaborate trap? If Pete wanted he could have called in reinforcements, but he didn't. I don't think he's alone in that camp down there, so if he wanted us captured he could have called his men. I think you're wrong. Anyway, it's our best shot. If Blake's heading for the Crossing, that's where I'm going.'

'All I'm saying is we have to be careful.'

'Got it, and we will.'

Charlotte takes another piece of flesh between her teeth and rips it off the bone. Now she is eating something, she's ravenous. With each bite, her mouth floods with saliva. She chews trying not to think about the furry little wallaby she killed.

You'd think for a farm girl she would be more used to killing beasts. She's got soft.

The night sky is brilliant with stars and Charlotte feels dwarfed by the sheer scale of it. 'I wonder how he's getting here.'

'Who?'

'Blake of course. I wonder how he'll get to the Crossing.'

'Good point and more evidence of a trap don't you think? I mean he's not likely to magic himself here, and this is a restricted zone so how's he going to get in?'

'He can go across country maybe, like we were planning.'

'Okay then, if he's driving, he'll come past us on the road down there, so why do we have to meet at the Crossing?' Mallory wipes her greasy fingers on the front of her jumpsuit and leans forward to pick more meat off the decimated carcass. 'Unless Sir Galahad is arriving via helicopter.'

'Sarcasm doesn't suit you.'

'Fuck off Charlie. It's all I've got.'

Charlotte grins. 'Look at the sky. It's amazing don't you think, like a sea of stars. Oh, the Crossing—duh, of course, he's coming by sea.'

'Now I know you're losing it Charlie. The sea is fucking miles away.'

'Yes but they can travel up river to the Crossing. Come on, Mal let's start walking. We can walk for a few hours and then sleep when it gets hot tomorrow.'

'It's dangerous walking at night.' Mallory looks dubious. 'One of us might fall into a ravine, or slip on the rocks and what about snakes?'

'It'll be okay. The stars make it bright enough to see and anyway if we walk in daytime you'll be burnt to smithereens.'

'That's true.' Mal groans and gets up. 'I think I ate too much, my belly hurts.'

Charlotte smiles, 'serves you right, but make room for water.' She picks up the water bottle and takes a long drink. 'You can bring the wallaby remains with you Mal, just drink lots of water and I'll fill the bottle again just in case.'

36.

Blake sits in a six-metre, rigid-hulled inflatable boat watching the waves run up to lap at a sandy beach on Lacrosse Island. The boat's black rubber looks like the ones used by Special Ops in the Gulf of Oman. This one doesn't have a canopy, otherwise he could almost be back there.

It's been 76 hours since leaving Brisbane to enter the restricted zone, and he has slept little. Now he sits in the prow, bobbing on the incoming tide at the entrance to the Joseph Bonaparte Gulf. An F90 assault rifle rests across his knees. His eyes are red and sore from lack of sleep and squinting against the brilliant light.

Opposite him, on the seat in front of the wheel housing, Noah busies himself stowing his kit. Steve and Mike relax on the seat aft. Blake still thinks the weapons are a little over the top, but the familiar feel and shape pressing into his thighs, comforts him.

Jason fiddles with something in the wheel housing, and answers questions that Steve fires at him. 'How long till we get there?'

Jason straightens his back and stretches. 'I reckon it's a hundred and fifty kays, so it's quite a hike. Then there's the tide. When it's running against us, we'll battle, but if we catch it heading in the right direction we'll shoot along. That's what I'm hoping, to save fuel. There are extra fuel tanks fitted, but still it's going to be tight. We won't have any fuel for sightseeing along the way. The extra fuel tanks, along with you lot, makes us heavy.' He grins at Steve and says, 'shove over I need to get at the engine.'

Beyond the island, as the Gulf channels in towards the narrow Cambridge Gulf, extensive mudflats flank the land. The air is saturated with the fetid stench of mangrove mud. Above the boat, hills rise to the centre of the island. On their slopes, bare poles, that were once trees before the cyclone, point splintered shards to the sky.

'At least five major Kimberly rivers drain into this Gulf so the fishing is good out there.' Jason points to their trawlers anchored in deeper waters.

As they wait for the tide to turn, Blake feels his head nodding. The rocking of the boat, the intense humidity and lack of sleep makes him drowsy, but it doesn't last long. A movement on the mud flat catches his eye, and a squirt of adrenalin has him instantly alert. Through binoculars, he sees a six-metre crocodile slide from the mud into the water. He grips his weapon tighter.

Jason says, 'hey Blake you heard how the trial's going?'

Blake drags his gaze from the crocodile to look at Jason. 'No, but Rory tells me it could go on for weeks. The barrister was trying to have it chucked-out, but somehow I don't like his chances.'

'What will you do if she's found guilty?' Steve asks, masking his concern by staring past Blake, at the open sea.

'I'll get her out of the country.'

Jason turns away from the engine. 'Do you know how?'

'Across the ditch to New Zealand.' Blake says referring to the Tasman Sea.

Mike says. 'No mate, it's not possible. Contractors patrol that now. My cousin's in the Navy. He told me it's almost impossible to get across with all the surveillance drones in operation. They use autonomous weapons systems. Cuts down on manpower costs. If you are an unidentified craft, the AWS fires. No questions. The bastards shoot now and ask questions later. My cousin said the pricks blew a whale out the water because there was no identifying signal.'

Jason looks at Mike, his face crinkled in disbelief. 'For what? Are we targeting our own people now?'

Mike shrugs. 'Since when haven't we? I'm just telling you what my cousin said. It's not supposed to be aimed at our citizens, but to keep terrorist infiltration at bay. Any legitimate boat would have a permit, or that's the story.'

Blake rubs the back of his head. 'Shit that's all I have. The Fuller's have an ocean cruiser, and I was planning to take that.'

The men have sympathy in their eyes.

'They're all scumbags,' Steve says.

'Who, the contractors?' Jason asks.

'Nope, cake eating mind fuckers,' Steve says. 'You can't trust a pollie. Look at the sandbog; what they got us over there for? Hundreds of our own KIA for a war that's got fuck-all to do with us.' He shakes his head. 'But still they send over more clueless conscripts as meat shields.' He looks at Blake. 'Sorry, I don't mean you, but they shouldn't send girls over there. Volunteer girls are different. They're well trained and good as us, some of them, but not conscripts. It's not right. I have a sister and I would waste any bastard who tried to send her there.'

'Jesus Steve!' Jason says grinning.

Steve looks down at his weapon, embarrassed by his outburst.

Mike shakes his head. Then he looks back at Blake. 'Anything I can do mate... well you know...'

Blake nods. 'Thanks Mike.'

'Yeah, same for all of us. Goes without saying,' Steve says.

Jason puts his tongue in his cheek and makes a circle with his thumb and fingers, moving it back and forth past his mouth.

'This love-in's getting a bit tense for me. I reckon we head on out. It's still light, but the tides turning. Daylight makes us sitting ducks, but I have seen no sign of life about the place for years.' He starts the outboard engine. 'As far as I know, no one lives in these parts anymore. Dad and I come this way often, so if we're caught on satellite we'll just say we're fishing.'

Blake points at another crocodile in the near distance. 'Better to go by daylight anyway, I don't fancy getting bogged on a sandbank.'

Jason pretends shock. 'You have no faith in my navigation skills. Me and Dad have never been bogged on a sandbank. Capsized yes, but never bogged.' He laughs at the worry on Blake's face. 'You can swim can't you?'

'You better be joking Willard...' Blake sees the laughter in Jason's eyes.

'This rig is small, but it's equipped with state of the art navigation aids, even in the dark. You couldn't be safer.' Jason says. 'Hell, I'll even ferry you and your girl across to Timor in it. We've got permits for these parts, so we should be safe from any stray AW systems, at least.' He pauses. 'Hopefully it'll never happen, and she'll get off.'

'I might take you up on that,' Blake says. 'Can a crocodile puncture this thing?'

Jason shrugs. 'It's bullet resistant polyurethane. Just don't fall in the water. There's an abandoned town further inland. We'll camp there tonight.'

Blake falls silent, scanning the distant banks and hills of the narrowing Gulf. Grey meandering water and mudflats stretch from horizon to horizon with low hills at their edge to break up the monotony. They pass the occasional islands, cyclone thrashed but still green oases in the mass of dreary water and mud. The incoming tide moves the boat at speeds greater than the motor would otherwise achieve, and Jason eases off on the throttle to conserve fuel.

On every mud bank, crocodiles bake in the sun, sliding into deep water as they hear the boat approach. The fathomless blue dome above collects white puffballs at its edges as the sun sinks in the west. It makes the earth seem vast, but Blake barely notices. He's on edge, watching for danger and worrying about how he will get Charlotte away.

Anger slides in unnoticed, curling in his stomach, rising to his chest, and pulses in his throat. He wants action, blood in payment; he wants to hurt someone. Shaking his head, he pulls himself up remembering where he is, and tries focusing on solving the problem. First things first, and first they have to find her.

The narrowing Gulf changes from mudflats to mangled mangrove-lined banks. Unruffled waters mirror the broken overhanging trees until the boats wake ripples the reflections.

Forty minutes later, Jason points to an island, and shouts above the noise of the motor, 'Adolphus Island—mouth of the Ord River.'

They pass Fairfax and Russel Islands, and then the Forest River mouth and the Canal Creek outlet. At the base of a hill, Blake spots a small town in the distance. As they get nearer, he can see it's in ruins. Neglect and Cyclone Zillie are to blame in equal measures.

Noah and Steve tie the boat to a relatively stable part of the wharf, and Jason kills the motor saying, 'welcome to Wyndham. We'll camp here tonight and move out in the morning. It'll take a couple of hours to reach the Crossing. If we leave at 06:00, we'll have plenty of daylight to find the girls.'

That night Blake dreams about Charlotte. He's back in the club listening to her sing, watching her long hair cascading around her shoulders. Her face is a pale oval, her eyes closed, and her mouth obscured by the microphone. He wants to stay there forever with her song soothing his soul.

Someone is shouting. Blake is angry at the interruption, and scans the room, but everyone in the smoky club is watching Charlotte sing. Through the dream's fog, he registers that the shouting is coming from elsewhere. The dream fragments. He clutches at its images, trying to ignore the noise to focus on Charlotte, but she's gone.

He opens his eyes, and he's back in the world. Across the cold coals of the campfire, Jason is in the throes of his own demons. Confined by his swag, he thrashes and yells. Blake rolls over to get up, but Noah beats him to it.

'Jason mate, it's a dream, wake up.' Jason opens his eyes and stares blankly at Noah. The compassion in Noah's voice tells Blake this man suffers too.

Mike wakes and gets out from his swag. He stretches his back and wanders away to pee off the wharf. When he returns he picks up the battered kettle and shakes it to see if enough water is left. Then he squats to stoke the fire.

Blake gets up and rolls up his swag. He uses the roll as a seat and stares across the lightening Gulf. Steve opens his eyes, but remains in his swag. The sky above the hill on their east glows with predawn light.

Jason sits up and rubs his haggard face. He turns to Noah. 'Sorry mate.'

Noah grins, 'hey we had to get up anyway. You make a good alarm clock.'

Blake listens to birds squabbling as day begins to break, wishing he could rid them all of reliving their trauma. Perhaps he'll specialise in Psychiatry when things settle and he and Charlotte are free. That way he'll at least know how to deal with it.

The sun pops above the low hills as the men board the dingy and cast off. Blake says, 'how far now Jason?'

'Maybe sixty kays. If we average twenty knots, we should be there in under two hours. The tide is high, and if we get to the river before it turns, we should make good time. Once in the river we will battle the current with all the rain dumped by Cyclone Zillie.'

As they travel inland, the sun rises higher and Blake can feel its promise as he sits hunched in the prow, but he's experienced worse. He shuts his mind to discomfort as he concentrates on scanning the banks and river ahead. None of them speak, conserving their energy. At least with the dinghy's movement, there's a breeze.

They pass the King River outlet, and the Gulf narrows further to a channel bordered by ravaged mangroves. After travelling about ten minutes, the channel opens out again to the upper reaches of the Gulf. Mangroves line its banks and ahead Blake sees several islands, also covered with ragged, cyclone damaged mangroves.

As they pass the last island, Jason's satellite phone rings. He gives Noah the controls while he takes the phone from his pocket. He shouts at Noah. The current's a bitch mate. Keep it steady.'

Noah nods and takes over, while Jason presses the SatCell against his ear.

'What? I can't hear you bro—too much noise.' He squats down out of the wind. 'What, can't hear, shit! I'll find somewhere to pull up and call you back.'

He hangs up and takes the controls back from Noah, shouting, 'that was Pete, but I couldn't hear what he was saying. We need to get into the river and find a quiet spot where we can pull up, so I can call him back.'

They head into the mouth of the Pentecost River, battling against the raging floodwaters. Ahead on their left is a small island of mangroves with a side channel of calmer water. Jason steers into it, cruising close to the mangroves. Noah leans over the side of the boat to secure the painter to a nearby mangrove. With the boat secure, Jason turns off the engine.

The dingy rocks in the shade. The men are glad of the relief from the sun, but it's fleeting. Without air movement, they swelter and mossies swarm around them. Blake slaps his neck. Sweat trickles down his flanks and runs down from the crease behind his knees, into his socks. He searches the mud flats and water, worrying about the delay, preoccupied with trying to spot danger, scanning for crocodiles. Sweat stings his eyes, and he wipes it away with the heel of his palm.

A splash to his left causes him to jerk his head, staring at the rippling water's muddy surface. There is nothing, but the swirling opaque eddy of the river backwater. He pulls up the neck of his tee shirt to wipe his eyes.

Jason's SatCell pings as a message comes through. He angles the screen away, leaning to shade the screen from light. The boat lurches.

'Shit!' Jason's SatCell flies from his hand, over the edge of the dingy and plops into the river. The boat shudders and Jason grabs the wheelhouse to steady himself. The phone sinks from view. 'Fuck, what was that?'

They all hang on, peering at the river to see what might be below the water. Eyes and a snout surface, then disappear and Blake fires, loosing-off a volley of rounds into the water. Noah moves closer to Blake and they both stare at the point where the snout disappeared, but they can see nothing.

Noah says, 'I reckon the bastard hit the fixed hull. Let's get out of here Jason.'

'Hey what about Pete? That bastard croc made me drop the phone. It might have been important. We should try to find it. I can use the net to scoop around. It might not be that deep here. It's waterproof so it'll still work.'

'Bugger that.' Blake takes out his CellTab. 'No signal.'

'Na you need a SatCell in these parts.'

Noah says, 'It's not worth it Jason.' The boat shudders again. 'Let's get out of here. Blake, keep me covered while I unhitch the painter.'

Noah crosses to the other side of the boat to retrieve the rope from the mangrove branch. Jason glances once more at where the phone sank and reluctantly starts the motor. He noses the prow closer to the mangroves as Noah leans over the side.

Blake kneels on the seat at Noah's elbow, rifle pointing at the water. Steve covers the spot on the port bow where Blake fired at the crocodile, and Mike covers aft. The men are tense, knees bent to cushion against further attacks on the boat.

As Noah reaches out to unhook the painter from the mangrove, the crocodile lunges from under the boat. Noah jerks backwards, as Blake fires.

A line of holes runs from between the beast's eyes into its primitive brain and down its spine. The crocodile rears back, and tumbles thrashing in the water, churning mud and blood as it sinks from sight.

The boat rocks wildly and the men grab at the wheelhouse to save themselves. Noah reaches back to unhook the painter and shouts, 'get the fuck out of here before more come!'

37.

Emmy sits at the head of the Fuller's dining table. Evan sits slumped on her left. On her right Flynn leans with his elbows on the table, nodding as he listens to a laconic voice coming from the e-cript conference phone. The smell of vanilla biscuits baking in the nearby kitchen, drifts into the room and Emmy's stomach rumbles.

Flynn says, 'Thanks Muzza. So everyone, are we good to go?' No one speaks, and he leans closer to the phone. 'Shorty what about you?'

A disembodied voice, tinged with feigned boredom, comes from the phone speakers. 'Yeah, we're all good, so are the others. Stop panicking Flynn. It'll be fine. We all know the gig. Papers printed, and tonight we distribute, then we melt into the shadows. Who's the journalist who wrote these pieces? They're good.'

Emmy blushes and shakes her head at Flynn.

'I'll tell her.' Flynn grins at Emmy. 'Okay, what about radio... Hilda?'

Hilda clears her throat and says, 'it's set for broadcast from six-thirty to nine. By the time they find the equipment, the whole fucking country will be in an uproar. Don't worry. Where d'you find the equipment Flynn. Its state of the art. Wish I could hang on to it.'

'Maybe they won't find it Hil.'

'Yeah they will Lizzy.' Hilda addresses another pirate operator involved in the conference call. 'It'll take them less time than the broadcast's set for, but can't be helped, no time to take it offshore.'

'If they don't find it Flynn,' Lizzy says, 'can we keep it?'

Flynn glances at Emmy who smiles and nods, but doesn't speak. He says, 'yeah if they don't find it you can keep it, but it won't matter anymore. With any luck, the bastards will be finished, and all you guys can go legit.'

'Jesus, that'd be one for the books.' Hilda says.

Flynn says, 'okay, so we're set. See you on the other side. Good luck or break a leg or something.' He ends the call and looks at Emmy. 'What now.'

'That's it. We sit back and wait. Dad should be in Canberra soon. His sister expects him, but they haven't told my Uncle because he might get worried about the cloak and dagger stuff. Until Dad can tell him what's going on face-to-face he doesn't want him panicked. We don't want him blowing the whole thing open by getting advice from the wrong person, or something equally stupid. It's hard to know who to trust. Anyway, Dad will be okay, he knows what to do.'

Evan straightens his back. 'Have you heard from Rory? How's the trial going?'

'Court is adjourned until the Judge considers the evidence that Lachlan provided. Rory said that Lachlan doesn't think he's seen anything like this come before him before. The poor bloke was nonplussed by the whole thing, especially when Lachlan said it was constitutionally unlawful. He's retired to review the evidence and probably take advice. The phones to Canberra will run hot tonight.' She smiles, her cheeks turning pink. 'Lachlan's brilliant. Rory said he was so convincing in court today and had the prosecution tied in knots.'

Flynn forks his fringe from his eyes. 'Won't they use the substitute Constitution anyway. Who's to say it's a substitute if no one can find the evidence on what's her name's computer.'

'Jenna Martin,' Emmy says.

'But as soon as they hear about Lachlan's constitutional argument they'll cover their tracks.'

'Evan's fixed that.' Emmy gazes at him in admiration.

He glances at her and back to Flynn. 'We have a copy of her hard drive, but otherwise they'll be hard pressed to find a fake copy of the Constitution to point at. I replaced all the fakes with the original. So, even if they cover their tracks, any search on the Constitution will bring up the real one, at least in the court libraries and government departments. I can't be sure a fake copy doesn't still exist, but the Judge will search the court database, I imagine.'

Flynn looks up at the ceiling, silent for a moment, trying to think of any other loophole he can imagine. 'Okay, but can't Marabaux order the Judge to do it.'

Emmy says, 'no, the courts are constitutionally independent from the government. Marabaux has no jurisdiction over him.'

'Ha! Supposedly,' Evan says, 'but most of the Judges are appointed by Marabaux so they understand where their survival lies. Let's hope this bloke isn't one of Marabaux's appointees.'

The next morning William flies back to Brisbane, his mission complete. As he embarks at the Canberra airport, Australia wakes to a barrage of illegal broadcasts, and underground broadsheets. By the time he is in the air, Sir Arthur Scott has ordered the Prime Minister to attend Government House.

The police are quick to act and trace the pirate stations broadcasting the messages. They shut them down and seized the equipment, but not before half the population has awoken to the news.

On buses, on trains, and on ferries, people sit silent and watchful, wondering if it's true, but unsure who they can trust to ask. The whole story seems preposterous. Corruption, slave labour, serial killers and conspiracies. It's like all their woes can be laid at the feet of their elected government. But who voted for them? Is it possible to rig elections in Australia? That happens in Africa not here. Is any of it credible?

Friday continues as it always does. People's thoughts jumble in turmoil as they try to make sense of events. Is this a terrible hoax?

Mr. Con Del Garcia, at the Southgate coffee shop counter just off Princes Highway in Sydney, asks his customers, 'is it so bad to keep refugees in camps? We don't want them over here.'

Many of his customers agree. Mrs Bellville arrives for her morning coffee. Con hands her the usual latte and says, 'and conscription is not so bad. If there was more conscription there would be less crime—isn't it?'

Mrs Helen Bellville agrees. 'What better way of repenting crime than serving one's country, right? If there wasn't a law like that before why can't they make one now? Where's the problem?'

The homeless community's grapevine kicks into action. For the first time in years, hope shines in Scarface's mutilated face as he looks at his friend Aubrey. 'Do you reckon it's true mate?'

Word filters through the Melbourne prison population as a corrections officer asks Jonathan Castile to explain what the broadcasts mean. Castile, in disbelief, wonders how he never uncovered the forgery. Perhaps he didn't deserved to be the Chief Justice after all—wasn't up to the job.

Jarrod von Wilkins watches the scenes around the country from his Canberra office, via various public closed circuit cameras and eavesdropping devices. He scans the airwaves, and drops in clandestinely to listen to random conversations on buses, trains and in the street, as well as in certain homes, offices and hotel bedrooms as he tries to gauge the mood of the population. Occasionally, he flicks the remote to give a direction to one of his men, stationed around the country, to make an arrest.

The underground broadcast material and equipment was quickly found and disabled, but he wonders where they got it. The state of the art equipment is expensive. Someone's backing them, but who? He has a sinus headache and its affecting his thinking.

He needs to call his wife. Should they get out, leave Australia? Where would they go? The whole thing is becoming untenable, but it's probably safer to wait for Minister Marabaux's signal. He said to hold their nerve, or all is lost.

How Jeremy expects him to clean up the evidence in the photo is beyond him. He's already told the Press, Jeremy found her drugged and unconscious in the street outside his apartment, and took her to hospital. The difficulty will be getting a hospital admission record.

Money works miracles for enhancing memories, but it's dangerous playing in Fuller's domain. The man is no one's fool. Perhaps one of the private clinics in Brisbane, somewhere that isn't under Fuller's contract, will do. He presses the remote and speaks to his head of operations in Brisbane.

Over at Government House, the Governor-General paces back and forth in his office. It's already 10 am and the Prime Minister is an hour late. Arthur leaves his office to speak to his secretary, Sir Robert Leighton. He stands at Rob's door with his hands held palms out, eyebrows raised. He looks quizzical, but remains mute.

Rob looks up, his gaunt face is worried, and his narrow shoulders hunch. 'I just got off the e-cript. The PM's Chief of Staff says he's on his way. Apparently, there was some crisis. He will fill you in when he gets here.'

The PM's audacity amazes Arthur. 'No! I don't want him to bring me another problem. He is the problem. The place is in an uproar. I won't stand for it. The gutter Press has taken over. It's an embarrassment.' Arthur checks the rising inflection in his voice and says, 'call Picardy to arrange tea please Rob. When the

Prime Minister arrives, have him wait. I shall take tea with my wife. Ring the opposition leader, Valentine, and delay his arrival by an hour.'

Arthur stalks along the corridors to his private quarters, head down, and hands behind his back, cursing his brother-in-law. He didn't take this job on, to sack Prime Ministers. Look at what happened to the last G-G who did that. He became a pariah; lived in self-imposed exile for the rest of his life. Although the circumstances are a tad different this time, and this bloke appears psychopathic in the depth of his corruption. It's just as well they found out now, or he might have taken the country into a dictatorship, as it seems he is hell bent on doing. William acted correctly, but why couldn't it wait until he retired next year?

The phone rings as he opens the living room door. The butler picks it up and turns to Arthur. 'Sir, the Prime Minister has arrived and is waiting for you.'

'Tell him to wait. No Picardy, don't. Say I will be along directly.' Arthur leaves Picardy speaking into the phone and goes to the sitting room to find his wife.

'Hello dear, did Rob organise tea.' He kisses his wife's cheek.

It surprises her but she doesn't show it. 'Yes, Picardy says it's on its way. How did the interview go?'

'It didn't.' Arthur sighs and rubs his forehead.

'I beg your pardon.'

'The blasted man is an hour late. Now he can wait while I drink my tea.' Arthur goes to the door and calls, 'Picardy where's that tea?' Then he turns back to his wife.

She sees the strain in his face. 'Sit down Arthur. Bad temper won't help.' She leads him to a chair and massages his shoulders. 'Relax dear. He's the one in the wrong. You are doing the right thing. After all, you are merely dissolving the government, and calling for new elections. It'll be up to the people to judge him, not you. If it's corruption, then the police will investigate.'

'But is this new fellow Valentine, up to running a caretaker government? I should warn the Crown.'

'No. That is exactly what you shouldn't do.' She checks the vehemence in her voice and moderates her tone. 'You have the constitutional authority to act. You can inform the King after its done, not before.'

'Yes dear, I'm familiar with my role, but it's a courtesy, isn't it.'

Exasperated, she says, 'no, it's sovereignty.' The butler comes in followed by a woman bearing a tea tray. Miranda waves her hand. 'Ah Picardy, leave it on the sideboard will you.'

Picardy directs the maid to lay the tea on the buffet, and turns to Arthur. 'Sir?'

'Yes Picardy.' Arthur looks at his butler.

'Sir Robert says the Prime Minister has the Chief Justice and the head of Intelligence with him.'

'What?'

'And there's a crew of National Homeland Security Police outside, along with the Press.'

Lady Scott interjects, 'thank you Picardy, that will be all.'

Arthur rises. 'I'd better go.'

'Drink your tea first. Really the man kept you waiting this long. Let him wait.'

'Yes, but what's the crisis and why is the Chief Justice here?'

This time it's Lady Scott who sighs. 'Very well; go if you must.' She watches him walk to the door and calls, 'Arthur, stay strong my dear. Crisis or no crisis, from what it appears he's done, the man deserves a great deal more than merely having his government sacked.'

In a room downstairs from Arthur and Miranda Scott, Prime Minister Priestly takes the whisky from the cabinet and holds it up to Sir Newel Bramly. 'Dram of Dutch courage?' He's enjoying himself, and Bramly's pinched face annoys him.

They are in the same room in which he entertained Blake at the Award ceremony. It's the one Jenna ensures has a stock of his own brand of single malt.

'It's really not so bad Bramly, and it'll be over soon. Perhaps we'll make you the next G-G.'

Bramly shakes his head at the whisky, and the reference to becoming G-G. This is going too far. The man's a maniac, but he says nothing. He will play this out just as Marabaux instructed, but he wishes it were over already. He's terrified it will all go wrong. Even more terrifying, it might go right. What a mess. What's that saying in Marmion, the poem by Walter Scott. Oh, what a tangled web we weave, when first we practise to deceive!

The door swings open and Arthur stands in its frame. His face is flushed with fury. He gave instruction that the PM was to wait in the formal reception room, not make a beeline for this one.

Bart looks at his watch and says 'ah Arthur, good of you to make the time.' Bart sits down and leans back in his chair. It's as if the Governor-General is late and not him. 'You know Bramly of course.' He waves his hand in the Chief Justice's direction.

Arthur stalks into the room. 'Bart this is beyond the pale.'

'Indeed, indeed, but then good things can't go on forever can they Arthur?' He lifts his whisky glass in salute and downs its contents. 'Bramly, get the door will you.'

'I'm glad you see it like that.' Arthur's relieved. Perhaps this will be easier than he thought.

'Quite. Whisky old chap.'

'Yes, thank you. That is rather civilised of you.'

Bart gets up and pours another whisky for both Arthur and himself, while Bramly shuts the door. 'Take a seat old man.'

Arthur sits down and takes the glass from Bart. He takes a sip while Bart lounges in his chair, examining him in the curious way of someone taking in an exotic animal in a zoo for the first time.

Bart holds up a finger. 'It's unfortunate, this sudden resignation, but better than a scandal, don't you think?'

'What?' Arthur pauses confused.

Bart continues as if Arthur hasn't spoken. 'Bramly is here to act as temporary representative for the King in your absence, so the disruption will be minimised.'

'My absence!' Tiny droplets of spittle shoot from Arthur's lips with his words. Bewildered, he wipes his mouth.

'Yes. I would like to make this as low key as possible given the scandalous, but bumbling nature, of your attempt at damaging the good name of the legitimately elected government. Of course, we will ensure your good lady wife is not inconvenienced or embarrassed, but it might be advisable that she take an extended holiday. It's bound to be embarrassing for her.'

'Miranda?' Arthur stares at Bart unable to comprehend what is happening.

'Yes dear Arthur; Miranda is your wife. That vision of feminine loveliness whom none of us believe will pine for you. But come now, Mulholland is waiting outside with an NHS police escort. It's most unfortunate, but it seems the Press have wind of what's going on... Well, can't be helped. The people should have the truth.' He laughs. 'Bramly will take over here, in a temporary capacity, and Mulholland will ensure you are aware of your rights.'

'Rights! A magistrate. Are you out of your mind.' He sees Bramly's set face, and it dawns on him he's in serious trouble. 'You have no authority.'

'Au contraire, my dear fellow. No one is above the law, not even the King's representative. I spoke to Westminster less than an hour ago. A signed copy of your resignation is on its way. The Royal House will not interfere in Australian decisions, especially in the case of criminal conduct. The fact that you regret and repent your actions will play well for you. Without the evidence, I should not have believed your treachery myself. I weep with the great Australian public at such betrayal, but we will endure.'

Arthur feels groggy and his vision narrows. He tries to stand but his leg is too weak and he stumbles. As he falls he hits his head on the edge of the glass table.

38.

Charlotte and Mallory walk most of the night. The terrain is difficult because they have to avoid Pete's camp. If they could go down to the plains and walk along the road it would take a fraction of the time. Instead, they take the long way around, climbing up and along the sheer edges of jutting cliffs, heading north, then east, then west, going with the tortuous terrain, but always with the rendezvous to the west in mind.

Charlotte checks their compass bearings with an obsession borne of fear, worrying they will go wildly off track with all the meandering. As dawn breaks, they find themselves high above Willard's camp.

They hide in a cyclone-ravaged grove of leafless trees, the spindly trunks barely enough for cover. Charlotte squints down her scope looking for Willard. Two men in guard uniforms pack up camp. Pete walks out from behind a Boab tree, adjusting his fly. Another person comes into view from behind the vehicle.

Charlotte gasps. 'Ida's with him!'

Mal says, 'I would recognise the bitch from a thousand paces—more reason not to trust the bloke Charlie.'

Pete walks over to the fire, now a heap of hot ash. He kicks up dirt to smother it. When the fire is covered, he climbs into the driver's seat. They reverse, bumping across tussock grass, then turn back onto the rutted gravel track, heading towards the Crossing. Dust billows in their wake.

Charlotte says, 'I reckon we have less than an hour before they return. Let's go now. On the flat we'll make good time, and their dust will be visible for kilometres. We'll see when they return and have time to get off the road.'

'Can't we rest, I'm tired?' Mallory says, waving flies from her eyes. 'Anyway, what if someone comes from the other direction and we don't see them? You said, walk at night and rest in the day.'

'Soon, but we need a better possie to hide. If you're worried, walk backwards and keep an eye on the rear. I'll watch the road ahead.' Charlotte grins, then sees her friend's face is drawn and pale, under days of Kimberly dust, and charred wallaby grease. She puts her arm around her and says, 'come on Mal. It'll be okay. We'll be careful, and we'll keep an eye out for a handy spot to hide. If anyone comes, we'll duck for cover, quick smart. We can't stay here. If we can find water, and somewhere to hide out for the day, then we can eat our rations and sleep. How does that sound?'

'Like bliss, pure joy, but my feet still hurt.' Mallory stands and stretches. 'Come on, what are you waiting for?'

After about half an hour of trudging across undulating plains at the base of the escarpment slope, they come across a small sickle-shaped cliff face. The position must have protected it from the cyclone because it's thickly wooded with leaves still covering the trees. The crescent shape of the small cliff acts as a natural drain. At its base, water seeps from the earth to form shallow pools in the uneven rocks. The water seepage is strong, overflowing the rock depressions to meander through the trees in a small stream.

'It's perfect.' Charlotte is enchanted, but Mallory looks at the pools dubiously.

'What about crocodiles?'

'This pool wouldn't have been here a week ago. It's just rain from the cyclone seeping out. Any crocodile will have to be quick to beat me to a bath.'

'Charlie you can't get in. It might be dangerous.'

'Mal it's shallow. You can see the bottom. I'm going to have a bath and wash my clothes. Blake can't see me like this, I stink.'

Mallory rolls her eyes and walks closer to the water. She's a city girl. What does she know about things like crocodiles? It looks inviting and she can imagine soaking her sore feet in the cold water. She squats and scoops up a handful, taking a cautious sip. 'At least its fresh.' The pool can't be more than a dozen centimetres deep. 'I guess it looks okay.'

Charlotte is already naked and leans the rifle against a tree next to her clothes before paddling into the pool. 'It's shallower than I thought, never mind. Lie in the next one Mal, and I'll lie in this one.'

The water soothes her weary body, and she lies back to soak her head. Her hair is like the pelt of the wallaby she thinks scrubbing the new growth. She wonders what Blake will think of her now, bone thin, brown with sun, and dirt, and almost bald. At least she doesn't have to smell bad.

Water fills her ears as she lies on her back, and gazes up at the branches. The last time she saw Blake was when he left for Canberra. She went with him to the station. It was the day after dinner with the Fuller's.

The dinner was okay, better than she expected. She liked Emmy and Mrs Fuller was funny. Rory is a snob, but he's a decent sort. Mr Fuller treated her with old-fashioned courtesy that was almost embarrassing, but he was the genuine article. She found herself relaxing, and much to her own surprise, she enjoyed the evening.

Afterwards they took the last ferry back. She went with Blake to the hotel. It was after eleven and she worried Patterson would see her. To her relief there was no one around to see her go into Blake's room.

As they walked in, there was an ice bucket, with white wine chilling in it. She looked at him questioningly.

'I hoped,' was all he said.

The wine was delicious. She took a sip and looked at him with her face screwed in concentration.

'What, don't you like it?' He looked worried.

'I love it. It reminds me of something. I'm trying to work out what.' She took another sip. 'It tastes like something, but I don't know what.' She shrugged and took another mouthful, searching for a word to describe the cold crispness flavouring her mouth.

He bent to kiss her, his lips warm on her cold ones, and she forgot the wine. Later, they sat in bed and drank the rest of the bottle. She took another sip, searching for a way to describe the flavour.

Then she had it. 'I know... it tastes of grapes.'

He laughed, and she realised how naïve she must have sounded. The blood rushed to her face and even now, she still cringes with embarrassment.

A scream penetrates through the water in her ears. She leaps up, her blood racing, and looks for her weapon. Foolishly, she left the rifle metres away.

Mallory stands naked next to the other pond, staring at a goanna disappearing into tussock grass at the edge of the trees.

'Fuck Mal, you scared the daylights out of me.'

'The baby crocodile stole my wallaby.'

'That was a bloody goanna, you moron.'

'It was huge.'

'Shhh, what's that noise?'

Mallory crouches. Charlotte scrambles out of the water and runs to her rifle. She wedges herself behind a tree and looks out across the rocky plain between them and the road. A cloud of dust signals a vehicle travelling at speed.

Mallory calls softly, 'what is it Charlie?'

'It's only Pete and co. on their way back. Come on, let's get some shuteye.'

Six hours later a fly crawls across Charlotte's face. She wrinkles her nose at the tickle, but doesn't open her eyes. She's comfortable and resents being woken. Her back is wedged against a rock, her rifle cradled in her arms. Remnants of her dream cling as the persistent fly drags her from slumber.

She gets up, slick with sweat, and leans her rifle against the rock where water oozes into the small spring. She plans the day ahead as she scoops water to her mouth. First, she'll have another bathe in the pool and then they need to eat. Thank God, for Pete's rat packs. If they share one meal between them, there'll be one left for tomorrow.

Charlotte strips off again and lies in the puddle. Once she has soaked enough she walks over to Mallory and kicks the sole of her boot. 'Wake up sleepy head, it's time to go.'

Mallory stretches. 'I ache all over. Jesus, Charlie another bath. You'll stink again after the walk tonight so I'm not sure why you bother.'

'Thanks for that. It's really reassuring.' Charlotte waves away a mozzie buzzing around her face. That's the trouble with a bit of rain, the flies and mossies come out in their hordes, flies in the day and mozzies in the evening. She picks up one of the ration packs. 'Come, let's eat some of this muck and go. Ah shit, the gomper's liquid,' she says looking with disappointment at the chocolate bar. 'You'd think they would think up something decent to put in these things.'

'Don't care what's in it. I'm starving. I would eat my boot if I didn't need it to walk—that thieving goanna.' Mallory stands with a groan. 'Do you think we can risk walking down the road tonight?'

'It's tempting. I can't imagine anyone other than Pete and co. using this track. It doesn't look used at all, it's in such bad shape.'

'If we take the direct route, we can be there in a couple of hours. It'll give us time to find a good position to cover the rendezvous zone.'

They make good time, but it's dusk when they arrive at the Crossing. To the east, five kilometres behind them, the escarpment rises. Its summit is golden, lit by the sun's dying rays, that bounce off clouds on the opposite horizon. As they watch a full moon crests its peak.

Mallory stands on the banks of the swollen river, staring at the road which disappears into raging waters. 'Where's the Crossing? All I can see is water.'

'Don't know. This is where Pete has marked it on the map. Come away from the edge Mal, there might be crocodiles.'

'Shit!' Mallory walks backwards. 'Where will we camp? I don't fancy a visit by a croc tonight.'

'No, we should do a recce, maybe check out that hillock over there.' Charlotte points to raised ground about a kilometre to their north. 'That'll give us a reasonable three sixty vantage point for when Blake arrives.'

'Can crocodiles get up there?'

'Jesus Mal. Crocs can get to most parts of this region where it's flat anyway.' Charlotte sees the fear on Mallory's face and says, 'we'll make a barrier from rocks, but why would they climb up there when they have all the fish they need in the river. Come on, let's get out of here, it's too exposed.'

In the early hours of the next morning Charlotte wakes, certain she heard something, but already the sound fades in her memory. She sits up looking towards the rock wall, fearing it's not sturdy enough to keep out a crocodile. Maybe the noise was a dingo or wild boar snuffling after their scent. Either way it's dangerous. Rifle in hand, she wiggles on her belly to peer over the circular pile of rocks.

Last night Mal kept asking, 'is it high enough.'

Charlotte humoured her. 'Any crocodile scrabbling to get over, will wake us.'

There was nothing else to do all evening and having slept all afternoon Charlotte wasn't tired. By the time they finished collecting and piling rocks she was filthy again and longed for the pool they bathed in earlier.

Now lying flat on her belly, she has a view of the plains. A hunter's moon sinks low in the west casting its luminosity across the land. The light is so bright she can make out colour, but there are no animals to threaten them.

As she turns away, her eye catches a vehicle taillight disappearing into the brush on the far side of the road, next to the Crossing. She raises her riflescope, but it's hard to make anything out. The trees and bushes next to the river are taller and leafier than the rest of those on the plains.

'Shit, shit, shit,' she says under her breath shaking Mal's shoulder. 'Wake up Mal. I think they're on to us.'

As the sun rises, Mal and Charlotte lie side-by-side taking turns with the sniper scope, trying to work out who lurks in the trees and what they are doing. Someone comes out with a tree branch and brushes tyre tracks from the road.

'Isn't that the bloke who was with Pete?' Mal asks peering through the scope.

'Give me the scope.' Charlotte takes it from Mallory and adjusts the settings. 'I think you're right. It's that gawky warden. He's unmistakable. Christ, there's Ida. She's carrying a gun. Fuck Mal, it's an ambush. They set us up.'

Ida points at the road, giving instructions to Mason. When she goes back into the bush, Charlotte follows the line in which she walks, hoping to catch another glimpse of her through a gap in the trees. A few metres further on she sees a glint of light from something, binoculars perhaps.

'I told you Pete couldn't be trusted,' Mallory says holding her hand out for the scope.

Charlotte doesn't believe Pete betrayed her. Is that wishful thinking? 'How do you know it's Pete's doing? Perhaps they smelled a rat when he drove to check out the Crossing. I don't think he dobbed us in.' She peers into the scope. 'I reckon I could take Ida out from this distance. I have someone's position in scope, but I am not certain it's her—maybe one of her team.'

'I wish you would, the woman's a sadist. Remember poor Jenny when she complained about having her hair cut, and Ida held her down. Pus-face enjoyed it and Jenny had bruises for weeks. Come on, give us a go at the scope. You know you won't shoot anyone. You can't even hunt when you're starving.'

'Hang on Mal,' Charlotte says as Mallory tries to take the scope. 'Let me just check this out a bit. What about Blake? What happens if he comes here while they're in there?'

'Do you reckon they're waiting for Blake?'

'No ways, they're looking for us—must be. How would they know Blake is coming here?'

'I told you. Pete's dobbed us in. I said you can't trust the bastard.' Mallory watches a log move across the riverbank and realises it's a crocodile. The huge beast lumbers into the water and disappears.

Charlotte says, 'I don't believe it. They must know we're heading for the Crossing, and are waiting for us, but obviously they don't know where we are or they wouldn't be hiding.'

'Pete never said why he was coming here. I bet it was to check out a good ambush spot.'

'Mallory you are so mistrustful of everyone. Pete's a good bloke. What would be the point of pretending to be our friend and then ambushing us? He could have just trapped us with the others when he found us. He's a scout. You don't think we could have hidden from him do you.'

Mal takes the scope and Charlotte lapses into silence, worrying about what she doesn't know. If Blake is coming up river, they can head downstream and warn him, but the possibility that Ida will spot them, makes it too risky. Once they stand up above their rock wall, they are exposed, and someone down there has binoculars.

'Hang on old bluey's gone back into the trees now too. He's not very stealthy. He's stopped. Yes, I can see him,' Mallory says.

'I think we should try to get further downstream,' Charlotte looks around for cover. 'They might know Blake's planning to come by boat.'

'They'll catch us Charlie.'

'Maybe, but what other choice do we have. If we stay here, and Blake comes up river, he's a sitting duck.'

'What about I go, and you take out anyone who pops up their head to take a pot shot at me?' Mallory grins.

'Would you do that for me?' Charlotte takes back the scope.

'Sure, so long as you don't chicken out when it comes time to pull the trigger.'

'No it won't work. They'll come after you in the vehicle and I might not get them all.'

'Jesus Charlie, one minute you can't shoot a wallaby, next you sound like Jet Jade from Fearless Warriors,' she says referencing a cult classic.

Charlotte bites her lip. How can she stop Blake coming up river and keep them both safe? The ground is too exposed along the riverbank; they won't get away with it, but she can't let Blake sail into the trap.

'Come on, help me rub dirt into my overalls so I won't stand out as much. I will chance it. If I don't make it Mal, you will have to shoot the bastards before they get Blake.' Charlotte lies on her back rubbing dust into her overalls already covered in red dirt. 'I shouldn't have washed them yesterday. Fuck I'm a fool; I'll stand out like a cliché.'

Mallory picks up the scope, checks out the Crossing, then swings it down river, sucking in her breath. 'Too late Charlie. He's here.'

Charlotte rolls over and takes the scope. She can make out the boat as it rounds a bend in the river a few kilometres away. She turns to look upstream. The boat is still hidden from Ida's line of sight.

'If we run now Blake will spot us and maybe we can stop them.' Charlotte is already scrambling to her feet, but Mallory pulls her below the rock wall.

'Don't be daft Charlie. Concentrate on using your brain. If you can shoot anyone who shoots at them, you might just save us. It's no good leaving me to do it at this distance. I'd miss but you can do it.'

Charlotte nods, horrified at the thought of killing a human, but even more horrified at the risk of them killing Blake. She fixes the scope to the rifle saying, 'keep me posted on the boat's movements Mal, every second okay. I want a running commentary. When you think they are coming into Ida's line of sight, tell me.' She tries to convince herself that it's just target practice.

A binocular glass flares at the Crossing, and through the high-powered scope, she sees the barrel of a rifle poking out from the bushes aimed up river. So they know Blake's coming. How? She sets a bead on the rifle barrel in the trees. If she can knock that out, she doesn't have to kill anyone. Although they might have more rifles and it's a tiny target. Perhaps she'll aim hoping for just an arm wounding.

'Okay,' she mutters to herself, 'take a breath.'

The range between her and Ida is 1,272 metres. It's too far for her, but she knows of snipers who have killed at twice that distance and more. The wind has died down, and the magazine has three rounds left. After doing quick calculations she thinks it might be possible to hit the target, so long as they don't move.

In the brush next to the river, Ida organises the prison officers. 'Okay boys, Willard's phone conversation said the escapees would be at the Crossing this morning so look lively. We don't want them spotting us and fucking off.'

'We should let the boss know Ida,' Smithy says.

'Screw that, it's our mission, and I'm not giving that arsehole the glory of nabbing the bitches. It's a piece of cake. They come to the Crossing, try to cross and we leap out at them. Perfect ambush. They'll wet their panties.'

'But they have a rifle.'

'So do we. If we surprise them, they won't be able to get the thing raised before we'll be on to them. Where's the radio Mason?'

'On the backseat of the truck.'

'Okay. When we have them, we'll radio base to let them know.'

Mason says, 'check out the size of that flat dog. Do you reckon we're too close to the water Ida?'

'No, she'll be right. Look sharp boys. Smithy, you get on the binocs and scan the plains north for any sign. Mason, you keep watch to the south and be ready to radio base when we catch them. Do you have the restraints? Good,' Ida says as Mason pats his pocket. 'Right I'll take the rifle and watch the road.'

'Shit, what's that down river? Fuck, it's a boat. Ida, check this out. There's a boat coming at speed, about three clicks away.' Smithy hands her the binoculars.

'Bugger. To your stations boys, we have a fight on our hands.'

'I don't think that's a good idea Ida, we only have one rifle between us,' Smithy says looking worried.

'Well we're even then. The prisoners have one, but a sniper's rifle is no good in close combat. What you need is rapid fire and lots of it. The people on the boat are probably just fishermen, but we won't take any chances. Surprise always counts more than firepower. We'll wait until they pull up, and get out of the boat, then arrest them.'

'What if they piss off. You can't shoot them. You don't know who they are,' Smithy says.

The hesitation in his eyes makes Ida more determined. 'I'll shoot the boat. It looks like an inflatable. They'll sink, and then we can leave the crocs to take care of them. To your stations—no talk.'

Ida leans against the tree where the rifle rests in a forked branch. She adjusts the sights, and tries to get a fix on the boat, but it's too far away and moving too fast. The road to the east is still clear, and she refocusses her attention on the river. Her blood thrums with exhilaration. This is what she's always longed for, a real fight, real action, the next best thing to going to war, none of this babysitting pathetic girl prisoners bullshit.

'Jesus, that croc is close Ida.' Mason says.

'Shudup jerk-off.' Ida says automatically, concentrating on scanning the plains for movement and positioning the rifle.

Charlotte sees the barrel move, its dull surface catching the light, and she recalculates, finding the body's location in relation to the weapon. 'Where's the boat Mal?'

Mallory says, 'wait, wait, five, four, three, two, one—now Charlie!'

Charlotte squeezes the trigger, and leaps up shouting, 'come on Mal.'

Behind her, Mallory is surprised at this change of plan, but she scrambles up and follows Charlotte. Adrenalin races through her, but in the back of her mind a voice shrieks, no, it's madness. The voice doesn't stop as she runs after Charlotte, skidding and bounding over lose rocky ground, down toward the river bend, expecting a bullet to knock her off her feet any second.

The sniper's bullet Charlotte fired is a .338 lupua magnum, travelling at over 900 metres per second. It misses its target by centimetres and punches through the tailgate of the truck. It continues through the back seat, barrelling through the radio before blowing a hole in the radiator and exiting the steel bonnet.

A moment later, the sonic report alerts Ida to the danger. She leaps backwards and slips down the bank. Her arm shoots around the branch of a tree to stop her fall. Her feet scramble to regain a foothold. She hangs in mid-air and moves her hands to get a better grip. Slowly she raises her legs to hook over the branch.

Below her, the crocodile waiting in ambush, gauges the distance to Ida's form swinging from the branch. Its muscular legs and tail propel it from the water as its powerful jaws open and snap shut.

The jolt races through Ida's body as its tooth snags the back pocket of her heavy cotton trousers. With adrenalin-fuelled strength, she clings to the tree. The pocket rips and the crocodile sinks back to the river to recoup for another attack. Smithy rushes to her aid and pulls her to safety.

Without hesitating further Ida yells, 'get in the truck, we have to go after them. They're not getting away.' She slips as she runs for the truck, and her left buttock protrudes from her ripped trousers.

Down river in the speeding boat, Blake is unaware of Ida's drama in the bushes two kilometres ahead. He scans the plains either side of the river. A movement to his left catches his eye. Two people run across the sloping land. They must be eight hundred metres away, and he can't make out if they're male or female. One holds what looks like a rifle above its head. He tenses, and lifts the binoculars, shouting above the noise of the engine to warn the others. Jason sees where he's pointing and throttles back.

'It's them,' Blake says uncertainly. Could it be so easy? 'It's Charlotte.'

She runs ahead of the other woman, leaping over clumps of grass, and boulders, and dodging between the saplings.

Jason pulls into the bank, and Blake leaps out into ankle deep water followed by Noah, Steve, and Mike. They take up defensive positions, eyes searching the surrounding plains for any foreign movements.

Blake moves towards the two women, his eyes scanning the landscape. He's still uncertain, but he can't think who else would run around these parts. Hope flares, but he quashes it. He doesn't need distractions. Focus on the mission.

The truck with the prison officers bursts from the trees at the Crossing.

Mike shouts, 'Blake, get Charlotte, we'll take care of the truck.'

Blake runs towards the women, slowing as he gets closer, turning to scan the ground, making sure no further surprises await them. The other men stand in a semi-circle waiting. Charlotte reaches him and stops. Mallory skids up behind her.

Blake stares at the women and says hesitantly, 'Charlotte?'

Her face is brown from the sun under a short fuzz of hair that makes a pale halo around her head. She's stick thin, her face gaunt and covered with dirt. He barely recognises her and his throat closes. For a moment, he forgets where he is and the danger looming behind him.

Suddenly nervous, Charlotte doesn't know what to do. She stands helplessly, staring back at him, the rifle hanging at her side.

Mallory pushes her forward. 'Charlie there's no time to stop. Get to the boat.'

Blake looks in surprise at the wild woman behind Charlotte. Her face is burned into a mass of dark splotches, with defiant green eyes staring out of the rings of red Kimberly grime, her short copper hair is matted and filthy. She's even dirtier than Charlotte.

He says, 'she's right Charlotte, keep running.' He turns to see the truck bounce across the road a kilometre away.

In the vehicle, Smithy has his foot pressed flat to the floor as the truck leaps across the road next to their ambush position. Its spinning wheels send small rocks flying. They bump over the gravel shoulder, and down a short bank to a plain covered with tussock grass, shrubs and spindly trees.

In their haste, none of them has fastened the rudimentary seat belts. The stripped down old rust bucket they borrowed from the laundry, was intended for running back and forth across the prison compound. It was never intended for cross-country chases and doesn't have the suspension or any other modern protection. As it bounces over the rough terrain, they occasionally become air borne, and the engine revs at high throttle before landing with spine crushing thuds.

Smithy grips the bucking steering, trying to ride out the jolts with thigh and buttock muscles clenched. Mason bashes his head on the door rim and clutches the back of Ida's seat to avoid falling out the door-less cab. Ida hangs on to a bar on the dashboard.

Trees obscure her view, but she can make out several men crouched in a semi-circle guarding the boat. She is too far away to make out detail and doesn't notice their weapons. She dismisses them and searches for the fugitives, shouting directions at Smithy and ordering him to go faster.

A flashing red light on the dashboard catches Smithy's eye. 'Shit the motor's overheating.' He eases his foot off the accelerator and brakes.

Ida shouts, hitting the back of his head. 'Why are you slowing down you moron? We'll lose them.'

He jerks away from the blows and turns to look at her in disbelief. He tries to keep his voice reasonable, not quite believing Ida hit him. 'The engine's overheating, and we still have to get back to base.' The vehicle bumps to a halt. 'We'll blow a gasket.' He turns off the motor. 'We'll chase them on foot. They're about five hundred metres away and you can shoot a hole in the boat so they can't use it.'

Ida's face is a mass of pulsating fury. She shouts, 'fuck that. Put your foot down or I'll make sure you're charged.'

Smithy stares at her.

She glares, her eyes a fanatical silver. With some awkwardness, she manoeuvres the rifle to point it at him. 'You have an order soldier.'

'Jesus Ida, you've got to be joking.' He glances back at Mason who looks frightened.

Mason's voice is a squeak as he says, 'Ida we aren't soldiers.'

Ida ignores Mason and says, 'do as you are ordered now or...' She jabs the muzzle against his flank.

Smithy is seriously worried now and leans forward to reach the ignition. The engine catches, and he puts his foot back on the accelerator. The vehicle leaps forward, and with a loud bang, a piston blows. Ducking in reflex from the noise, he loses control of the vehicle. White smoke pours from the bonnet, but his foot is still pressing the accelerator to the floor. The truck, in its dying leap, plunges headlong into a tree, its trunk too big to bend or give way.

Mason is taken unawares and flies forward, his face hitting the headrest. Ida bangs her forehead on the windscreen. It's not enough to knock her out, but she's dazed. Fury and adrenalin turn her wrath onto Smithy whose nose runs with blood from his own lurch into the steering wheel. She strikes her fist at his head, but misses and her knuckles punch air.

The vehicle stalls with a low hiss as it settles on its axles.

'Out, out now,' Ida yells, falling from the cab.

She picks herself up and runs towards the boat, hoping to cut off the women. Ida still has the rifle. Smithy stands next to the truck gazing after her, his chin is covered with blood from his dripping nose. Mason runs after her, his arms and legs flapping in an uncoordinated stagger. Smithy sighs and follows.

Ida breaks out of the scattered trees onto a bare plain and stops. Mason and Smithy reach her and wait. The boat is about 300 metres away, and they can see the women clambering onboard. Ida lifts the rifle to her shoulder, and fires off half a magazine.

Noah says, 'Bloody hell!' Bullets zing wildly about them, but none hit the target. 'Mike lay down cover, 250 metres, but no injuries.'

Mike fires off a magazine his rounds kicking up dust and dirt. Bark splinters fly off saplings. Smithy and Mason turn to flee to the cover of the trees behind them, but Ida holds her ground, aiming her next shot. Mike glances at the dingy and sees Mallory boarding. He changes magazines.

Noah sees Ida lifting the rifle again. 'Steve your turn mate.'

Steve fires, aiming short, hoping to frighten her. No one wants to kill the prison officer, but she is undaunted and aims more carefully.

The bullets create mini splashes in the water and Jason yells, 'She's aiming for the boat. Time to high tail it out of here fellas.' He starts the engine.

Charlotte is just about to follow Mallory into the boat when the bullets splash short of where she stands ankle deep in water. She turns around and raises her rifle. Before Ida has time to squeeze off another round, Charlotte fires. The bullet grazes a fleshy part of Ida's left arm, just where Charlotte intended. She turns back to clamber on board.

Blake follows in astonishment, and sees a secret smile of satisfaction playing on her mouth. Noah, and Steve back towards the boat and board. Mike keeps an eye on Ida and waits until the others have boarded before he runs after them. Blake hauls him in as Jason opens the throttle. A sweeping turn sends

Gillian Long

a wash running up the banks as they head north, back the way they came.

Smithy runs to Ida who clutches her arm. Blood seeps from the shocked flesh where the bullet seared her skin. She's deaf in her left ear from the close quarter sonic boom.

'Jesus Ida you were bloody lucky she missed.' Smithy says looking at the wound in awe. 'You'll need a tourniquet.'

'She fucking didn't miss you moron.' Ida shouts to compensate for her limited hearing. 'None of them wanted to kill me, or any of us. That would make them in real trouble.'

'Aren't they already in real trouble?' Smithy says. Despite his loathing of Ida, he's impressed by her courage. 'There's a first aid box in the truck. We can patch you up and radio for help.'

'They're not out of sight yet,' Ida raises her rifle with her right hand and fires off several rounds, but the boat is too far away, and the bullets fall short. 'Fuck,' she says lowering the weapon. 'You think they're in trouble? We'll be in worse shyte when base finds out we let them go.'

Smithy shakes his head. He's worried. 'Ida we should keep quiet about this. We were acting outside orders, and we will be in deep shit.'

Mason comes out from the trees. His freckled face pales as he takes in Ida's wound, averting his eyes from the sight of her large white protruding buttocks to focus on the blood running down her arm.

'What you gawping at moron?' she says.

'Nothing, sorry Ida,' he hesitates. 'The radio's got a hole and doesn't work.'

Ida turns to Smithy. 'How do you propose we explain that then, clever dick?'

Smithy shrugs.

Mason says, 'you can say you fired at the crocodile and missed and hit the truck.'

'Did I speak to you dip shit.' She glares at Mason. 'I don't miss my targets.'

Smithy says nothing at the inconsistency, trying instead to reason with her. 'Come on Ida, Mason's right. We can say it happened because of the croc. If we clean your wound and bandage it, we can say it was done by a tree branch. If they find out what we've done without back up, they'll blame us for the escape. Let's just say we didn't find any sign of them and blame the croc for everything else.'

Smithy gazes down river wishing they had never set eyes on the two women. He wonders if he should apply for a transfer. It will be less money than he earns in this remote posting, but Ida's a maniac and he wants to be as far from her as possible.

Around the bend of the river the dingy travels at high speed, the floodwaters pushing it along. They pass Five Mile Creek before Blake relaxes enough to turn to Charlotte. She huddles on the floor with Mallory in front of the wheel housing. He looks down at her and she looks away, self-conscious and ashamed of her appearance.

He leaves his position aft and makes his way towards her, unsteady in the speeding dingy. She pulls her knees to her chest as he squats down and takes her hand, feeling the rough palm in his.

He's aware of the intense scrutiny from the green-eyed woman, and an image of two trapped animals comes to mind. He's overcome with emotion and pulls the stiff, resisting Charlotte into his arms, holding her until she slumps. Her shoulders shudder and heave.

'Charlotte?' He lifts her chin. 'You're crying.'

She buries her face in his chest. He strokes the pelt of hair on her head, feeling sweat soaked tufts under his palms. She's skin and bones and feels fragile in his arms. He talks in a low voice, his mouth against her ear, telling her how he's missed her, how worried he's been, how he knows what she's been through, how he loves her, and how it's going to be all right.

Eventually she looks up at him, her eyes red rimmed, but resilient. Only then does he let her go and turns to her friend. 'Hi I'm Blake.'

Mallory looks at him with disbelief. 'No kidding Einstein, I thought maybe you were Santa Claus.'

Blake laughs and turns to nod at the other blokes. 'That's Jason at the helm, Noah, with the big hooter, Steve, with the blond hair and the short arse is Mike.' He turns back to Mallory. 'And you are Esmeralda.'

Charlotte says, 'her name is Mallory, Mal for short.'

Blake recognises the protective fury in Charlotte's eyes. He glances at Mallory. 'Okay Mal, nice to meet you. Here's what's happening next.'

39.

In Canberra, Bart Priestly walks back into his office in the Parliament building, running his fingers along the wood panelling as he walks over to the window. Under the window is a drinks cabinet that pops up when he presses a panel. The whisky glass is Moser crystal, and he holds it up to the light, admiring the delicate wattle and waratah patterns designed especially for him. He's feeling on top of the world as he savours the peaty warmth of the single malt.

At lunch earlier, Sir Miriam Randolph was gratifying in his praise. Randolph never liked Arthur Scott or his wife and is glad to see the back of them. There'll be no issues with the press releases. Randolph's advice to put out that Scott suffered from extreme depression, rather than treachery, was good. It will be more palatable to think the man lost the plot, rather than think he might be a danger to them.

Who knew Scott would have a stoke. Well, he's been sent to the best private medical facility available—no expenses spared. Marabaux and he had argued. Arnie said no one would believe the G-G was a traitor. At the time Bart was furious, but in hindsight, perhaps he was right.

He walks over to his desk. The surface of Huon pine gleams in the filtered light, and he runs his hand over it. Still, just because Randolph agreed, it doesn't excuse Arnie's behaviour, calling his PM an idiot. The man is getting above his station. The ping of his CellTab alerts Bart to a message.

He swears when he sees it's from Jenna. Her text says, 'urgent Party room meeting called—purportedly by you???'

He hits Jenna's number, and when she answers he says, 'what's going on?'

'There's a party room meeting called. Did you call it?'

'No, of course I didn't. Well, I did for Monday. We don't meet on Friday's. It's a mistake.'

'It's from your cell, Bart.'

'I didn't call it. Fuck!'

'You better get down here pronto.'

Bart drains his whisky and hurries out of his office. His mind whirls in confusion, bordering on panic. This is a monumental surprise, and he doesn't like it. He pulls himself together and slows his stride. It wouldn't do for anyone to see he's worried. He feigns nonchalance, moving as fast as he can without appearing in a hurry.

'Always assume cock-up not conspiracy,' he hears his father-in-law saying. The old man's right. After all, he is the most powerful man in Australia. He's just proved that by sacking the Governor-General. He'll see what's going on in the party room, then send them all about their business. Why they haven't flown back to their electorates for the weekend is beyond him. If he tried to get any of the lazy fuck-knuckles to stay and do a bit of work, there would be a mutiny.

It has to be a cock-up. Bart's anxiety dissipates. Marabaux will handle it. This is probably a wasted trip. By the time he gets there, they'll be gone. Really, Jenna is a panic merchant. How did she let this happen?

Jenna hovers outside of the closed party room doors. She is talking with a dark haired reporter who towers above her. Bart recognises him as one of Randolph's star journalists, and frowns. How did he know about the meeting? There are no other reporters, which tells Bart, this is either a very big coincidence or someone's playing a game.

Peter Cassey glances up, as Bart approaches. Without hesitation, he leaves Jenna and dashes up the corridor, micro recorder in hand. 'Prime Minister is it true you called a meeting to quash a leadership challenge?'

Bart keeps the shock from his expression and produces one of his famously charming smiles. Inside his heart hammers. 'You blokes will believe anything.' He chuckles as he turns to open the door of the party room.

Every seat is taken, in a room silent with expectation. Bart looks for Marabaux who appears engrossed in his phone and doesn't look up. The Chief Whip and his deputy sit at a table alongside the lectern.

The Chief Whip, wipes his face with a large handkerchief and reaches for a heavy, silver, water jug. As he pours water into a glass, he angles his head at the deputy slouched in the chair next to him. The deputy shakes his head, and watches Bart walk down the central isle to the raised platform.

Bart grips the edge of a lectern his arms held straight as he appraises each of the members in turn. People shuffle in the seats and look away. Then he clears his voice to speak. 'You've been misled...'

Admiral Bowan stands up. Bart is astonished by the interruption.

Unperturbed, Bowan continues. 'With permission Prime Minister, prior to this meeting, I submitted, to the Chief Government Whip, a motion to spill the leadership position of the Party. The spill motion should be considered via a secret ballot as the first item of business in our Party Room meeting. This motion is seconded by Treasurer Barry Searston who shares my views.'

He sits down and Searston a dumpy, shabbily dressed man with a gravelly voice stands up to speak.

But Bart interrupts. 'This is a farce. None of it is permissible. I did not call a party room meeting. You are all here under false pretences. The leadership challenge is preposterous. I will not accept it.' Bart glares at Marabaux, 'what's going on? Who called this meeting?'

Marabaux refuses to meet his gaze, but he lumbers to his feet. 'Prime Minister you know very well you called the meeting. Yesterday we discussed it. You said you wanted the spill over and done with because it was destabilising, and now the G-G's stroke makes a stable government vital.'

'Liar!' The word explodes from Bart before he can contain it. It's like he's entered a parallel universe. Fear coils in his gut as adrenalin fuels his anger.

Marabaux ignores him and addresses the party room. 'I have been a loyal party member for fifteen years and a member of Cabinet since we first snatched victory for which I give you full credit Prime Minister. I have been your stalwart supporter for years and your closest friend and ally, but recently we have lost our way. The people are suffering and they begin to doubt our path is the right one. The pre-emptive strike at the Governor-General this morning has created a constitutional crisis not seen since '75. The poor man is ill and should be hospitalised not arrested. Frankly, I am shocked. We should not treat the vulnerable so harshly.' The room breaks into a hum of supportive murmuring.

Bart stares in disbelief at his old friend. How does the party know about what really happened with the G-G this morning unless Arnie told them? They agreed, at lunch that only the stroke wouldn't be mentioned. Unless it was the Chief Justice, but no. This is Arnie's treachery.

This is the man he nurtured and protected against the bullying of the other boys at school. The man whose childhood secrets he kept. The man who he raised up to become a Minister of the land, a criminal's son, a pariah of society. This is the man whom he helped change his identity and hide his lunatic wife. Who he protected despite his bigamy and his degenerate offspring. This is the man who Bart thought was always his closest ally, his brother in arms; the man who rode Bart's tail coat to the top. This is how he is repaid. Rage curls from his stomach, rising into the kind of volcanic eruption not seen since his youth. It swamps reason, and he loses the battle for control.

'Traitor!' Bart shrieks and his voice cracks. He flings the lectern out of his way and rushes at Marabaux. He is past caring, his whole attention focused on the man who betrays him.

Marabaux's throat feels pudgy under his large hands as he squeezes. All he wants is to watch the look of surprise in those black eyes, turn to fear. This is something he's longed to do for years. Why did he leave it so long. His thumbs press against the blood vessels either side of Arnie's Adam's apple.

Bart begins to giggle as his friend's eyes bulge. Then a sickening shock of pain jerks through his neck and down his shoulders. His vision narrows as darkness coalesces and he crumples to the floor.

Marabaux coughs and rubs his throat. A ringing sound fills his ears as he acknowledges his rescuer, who stands beside him. Both men look down at the prostrate form of the Prime Minister, lying spread-eagled on the green and gold carpet.

Admiral Bowan breaks the silence. 'Extraordinary!' In his gnarled hands, he holds the silver water jug, taken from the Chief Whip's table, and used to render the Prime Minister unconscious.

The room erupts, but Marabaux holds up his hand for clam. 'Call an ambulance,' he croaks.

After the ambulance has taken the Prime Minister to hospital and calm is restored Marabaux calls for proceedings to continue.

An hour later Prime Minister Marabaux calls his son. 'Find Lincoln and the girl.' He stops while Jeremy speaks, then interrupts. 'I don't care if they arrest you. Sort out your own mess in your own time. It's your self-indulgence that's brought you to it. My concerns are more pressing. We need Lincoln. He needs to believe it's all over and they are safe. Make a grand gesture. Who is presiding over the court case? Tell the man to throw it out.'

Marabaux listens once more as his son speaks and then says, 'he's the judge, tell him to use the not enough evidence.' He stops again. 'Yes I am aware it will let all the others off the hook—can't be helped. They'll slip up again. We need Lincoln in Australia under our control. Apologise to the Fuller girl and make friends with her, if she won't take you back.'

Jeremy interrupts his father. 'why are you so keen to look after Lincoln. He's not worth the effort. Let me fix the problem once and for all.'

'I'm warning you Jeremy. This is not your call. You will do as your oath requires. We have a lot of sanitising to do to get back on track. I want it sorted before Monday and I haven't time to worry about you getting it right. Don't cock it up this time.' Marabaux hangs up.

He dials another number and speaks to von Wilkins. 'Arrest Jeremy and hold him for a month or two. I want citizens to know no one is above the law, not even my son. Then release him saying you have another suspect for the murders.' He waits patiently while Jarrod speaks then says, 'there will be no retribution. My son needs a lesson.' He hangs up and dials Lady Priestly.

When Marabaux has finished commiserating with Bart's wife over her husband's sudden illness, which required hospitalisation and an immediate resignation from politics, he calls the Departmental Secretary. To him, he explains that Jenna is no longer required and needs to vacate her office and the apartment near Kirribilli immediately. He hangs up and looks around his home office.

Even as PM he won't work anywhere else. In fact he doesn't even need to move into the Lodge although he might spend the odd night there for appearances. Perhaps he should move Hester into the Lodge or even Kirribilli in Sydney. That way he won't have to put up with her every day. He wonders why he married her. Except for the influence her father held prior to his death, she's not much use to him. Perhaps it's time for a change.

He pushes back his chair to rise, and walks over to lock the office door. He unplugs the e-cript and switches off his Celltab. Then he unlocks his desk drawer to pull out a device not seen by anyone since it arrived two months ago.

The iridescent black box simmers in a haze on the desk. It reflects its surroundings, making it seem to disappear in space. Marabaux flicks up a latch and lowers the sides. A squat, star-shaped dome sits in the centre of four smaller bronze cylinders. He takes each of the cylinders and lodges them in a square around his desk. Then he sits down and straightens his jacket sleeves, tugging them to cover his cuffs. He pats his tie, and smooths his hair, before leaning forward to touch the star.

It pulses. An aura grows to fill the square between the cylinders enclosing Marabaux in its midst. Seconds later he is connected with the Castello di San Luca in the Aspromonte Mountains in southern Italy.

A viewer from outside the star's sphere, would see that Marabaux sits alone at his desk. From inside, Marabaux appears to sit opposite an old man hunched in an armchair, plaid rug across his lap, hair sparse and wispy grey, his irises pale in rheumy sclera. The men sit in a warm shaft of sunlight pouring through a large window. Beyond the window, the mountains rise to snow-capped peaks, stark against the sapphire sky.

The old man speaks a dialect of southern Italy as he says, 'it's done?'

'Yes Capo.'

'Good. Cumpidenza è patruna da malacrijanza—He who gets too familiar will finally become disrespectful.'

'There is much punishment warranted.' Marabaux nods his head slowly.

'How is Helena Macri's boy?'

'Blake Lincoln?' He glances at the old man. 'We are trying to find him. I have given instructions he is not to be harmed.' Marabaux hesitates. 'Papa Macri, indulge me for a moment.'

'What is it my son? Speak; you have done much to deserve special favours.'

'I don't understand your interest. His father was not 'ndrine—one of the family.'

'Ah, but his mother was, God rest her soul. She paid dearly for her rebellion, but her son is innocent of her betrayal. Now he is my only surviving descendant, my great grandson, and he will keep my family's dynasty alive. Who knows how his children will turn out, but they are my hope for our future. You have done well and will be rewarded. We will be in contact.'

40.

Two months later, Charlotte stands at the window looking out across the river. In the background, music plays. The sustained Vincerò, Vincerò, echoes in the room as tenor Daniel March ends Puccini's Nessun dorma. Her gaze travels to the western sky, smudged with pollution in the dying evening light.

Have they really won like Emmy said? She can barely believe it. The new government has a big job ahead. There is so much to fix, not just pollution, but unjust laws to rescind and a never ending war from which to extract Australia.

Last week at dinner Lachlan said, 'it can't be done quickly, because it must be done properly, so what happened can never happen again.'

Blake had grunted in disbelief, 'any government run by Marabaux can't be trusted. I don't think we have changed anything getting rid of Priestly. Marabaux is worse.'

Rory laughed. 'Same old Blake? Suspicious to the end. He still thinks there are shonky dealings going on under every bed.'

The door opens behind her and she smiles, knowing who it is without turning.

'What are you doing loitering in here, Mrs Lincoln?' Blake slides his arms around her waist and rubs his check against her short, soft curls.

She turns around to face him, her dress twisting as the ample satin catches the carpet, bunching behind her. 'What's Dad been saying to you?'

Blake laughs. 'Were you spying on us?'

She points out the window to her father, standing in the garden below where Blake left him a few minutes ago.

'He threatened me with dire consequences if I ever let you come to any harm again.' He grins, 'but he also agreed to help me find a suitable property, somewhere high in the mountains, with lots of rainforest and pools and tumbling waterfalls. We can turn it into a clinic and respite centre for returning soldiers and conscripts. And your Dad says, if we are near them, he can keep an eye on me, make sure I don't get you into any more trouble.'

The door crashes open and bounces off the wall. Charlotte smiles up at Blake's raised eyebrows. They both know who it is.

Without turning around, he says, 'Hello Mallory.'

'Blake! I didn't know you were in here.' Mallory looks at Charlotte. 'Come on Charlie, everyone's waiting for you and you haven't even changed yet.'

'Where's my Mum?' Charlotte says moving out of Blake's arms. 'I was waiting for her. She said she wanted to be here when I changed into my going away outfit.'

'I doubt very much she's coming Charlie. Mrs Fuller's been feeding her Champagne and the two of them are giggling like school girls out on the terrace.'

'Mum?'

'Yup.'

'But she doesn't drink.'

'She does now,' Mallory says grinning. The ravages of sun exposure on her delicate skin are fading now, but they still make Charlotte think of the camp. Her hair falls around her face in a bright copper cloud. Darkly mascaraed eyelashes fringe her green eyes.

Charlotte smiles and thinks, Mal is so beautiful, but she'll never be accused of being dainty. She looks up at Blake who watches Mallory, his face alight with amusement.

He says, 'I'll let you two get on with doing whatever it is you do. Don't take too long my love,' he squeezes Charlotte's hand.

As he reaches the landing, he sees Emmy in Lachlan's arms. She turns guiltily when she hears the door close, and turns to the stairs.

'I have to go and help Charlotte,' she whispers.

Lachlan smiles, watching her climb the stairs, holding her skirt above her ankles with one hands so as she won't trip. In her other hand is a bottle of champagne with three glasses, their stems clutched between her fingers.

She looks up as Blake comes down. 'Hi Blake, I'm just going up to help Charlotte get ready.'

'Get ready?' Blake wonders why when women get married they are suddenly incapable of dressing themselves. They seem to need an army of women around to help. 'And the champagne will help?'

Emmy grins. 'It won't hurt.'

Blake walks across the entrance hall with Lachlan. Both men's leather soled heels click on the parquet as they return to the reception marquee in the garden.

The bell at the front door chimes. Surprised, Blake stops. 'If they're guests for the wedding they've left it a bit late.'

Lachlan waits as Blake opens the door.

Peter Cassey stands with micro recorder in hand. 'Hello Blake.'

'Fuck off Cassey.' He grins, 'or come inside and join the party, but take off your Walkley winning hat and leave it outside.'

'Okay fair call. It is your wedding day. But before I do I just wanted to let you know that Jeremy Marabaux has been released. Do you have a comment?'

Blake frowns. 'No. But I am surprised.'

'Apparently, Jeremy was telling the truth. The police have arrested the bloke who did it—Seems he's responsible for several of the women murdered over the last few years.'

'Still surprised, and don't believe a word of it. But that's all I am saying now Cassey. Are you coming in?'

'Okay, I will thanks. How is Arthur?'

'On the record?'

'Na. I'm off duty now.'

'Okay. He's not good. The stroke left him very frail.'

'That's a shame. He's a good man. What about Miranda?'

'Come and ask her yourself. She's outside taking to Jonathon Castile.'

'Interesting guest list. Wish I hadn't clocked off.'

'You wouldn't be allowed in, if you hadn't.'

'It's quite a story Blake. Perhaps you will give some thought to telling your side of it.' He sees Blake's frown, and adds hastily, 'when you come back from honeymoon of course.'

'One thing I will say Cassey, and you should take note, but I'll deny I ever said it.'

'Okay, I'm buying—what is it?'

'Marabaux's not to be trusted. Watch him.'

'Cassey's eyebrows rise.'

'Do you know something?'

'No, but believe me. Watch him and his son.'

'Okay.' He shrugs. 'But what about you Blake? What are your plans?'

Blake grins and says, 'Lachlan have you met Peter Cassey, Walkley award winner and royal pain in the ass.'

The three men walk out to the garden. Blake leaves them and walks over to Jason who stands with Pete, Noah, Mike and Steve and a group of other men.

'How are you guys doing?'

'Good party mate.' Jason raises his beer.

'I'm off in a minute, but make yourselves at home. Rory will look after you.'

A tall man in his mid-thirties breaks away from the group. 'Blake after the honeymoon, you'll come on over to the States won't you. My family really want to meet you. They want to show their gratitude in true southern style.'

'Thanks Liam. That'll be great.' A commotion distracts him and he turns to see what it is.

Charlotte steps out through the glass doors and walks towards him in jeans, tee-shirt and sneakers. She drops her backpack on the veranda before descending the stairs to the lawn. Mallory follows her with Emmy close on her heels. Charlotte stops to kiss her parents and to hug Evan.

Her mother looks at her jeans with distaste. In a mild voice she says, 'Is that your going away outfit dear?'

Charlotte smiles. She knows that tone. Her mother disapproves. 'Are you squiffy Mum?'

Her mother looks indignant, then glances slyly at Mrs Fuller and giggles. She leans against her husband, who looks at her indulgently.

'That's it!' He says, 'all the farm profits will be lost to champagne.'

'No dear, I want to grow grapes and make this delicious juice.'

'You can't grow grapes where we are,' he says.

'Well we'll just have to move then.' She giggles again and looks at Charlotte. 'But seriously Lotte dear, I'll come and help you get into your going away dress now.' She hands her empty champagne glass to her husband.

'Mum, this is my going away outfit. We are going camping.'

Her mother looks bemused. Charlotte turns to speak with Evan. The two of them walk over to join the band members who stand nearby. They are subdued, and she hugs them one by one. 'What's up Tyler, cat got your tongue?'

Blake watches her, pride welling in his chest, and he knows what a lucky man he is.

Emmy moves away from Charlotte's Mum, to stand beside Lachlan.

Mallory moves closer to Rory and slips her hand through his arm.

Rory looks at her with surprise. She stretches on her toes and kisses his cheek. He looks stunned and looks self-consciously around the gathering. Blake is grinning at him and blood surges up his neck.

Mrs Fuller raises her glass, 'to a wonderful couple, Blake and Charlotte.' The guests echo, 'Blake and Charlotte.'

Blake walks over and takes Charlotte's hand. 'Come on, Mrs Lincoln. The mountains await.'

About the Author

Gillian Long has a PhD in Literature and creative writing, and a background in publishing, psychology, politics and executive leadership in both civil service and the not-for-profit sector. Gillian has lived and worked in Africa, and Europe but now lives on a farm in the Australian wet tropics of Far North Queensland.

Her previous novels, short stories, forthcoming titles, and other writing can be seen at https://gillianlong.wordpress.com

ABOUT THE AUTHOR

www.ingramcontent.com/pod-product-compliance
Lightning Source LLC
Chambersburg PA
CBHW030246270626
47156CB00020B/118